Advance praise for Don
The Road to Bittersweet

"You will fall in love with Wallis Ann Stamper as she meets the bitter challenges of her hardscrabble life, inspired by her sweet love for her family Her grit and unfailing faith in herself will melt your heart, as it did mine."
—Sandra Dallas, *New York Times* bestselling author

"Donna Everhart has created a heroine with real girl power. The teenaged Wallis Anne is persistent and tough and above all competent in the face of catastrophe, steering her bedraggled family through a series of crises. In the end, the biggest challenge she has to contend with is her own human weakness and her willingness to forgive herself. Donna Everhart has written such an engagingly fast-paced story that the pilot pulled me in from the first pages."
—Julia Franks, author of *Over the Plain Houses*

Books by Donna Everhart

THE EDUCATION OF DIXIE DUPREE
THE ROAD TO BITTERSWEET
THE FORGIVING KIND
THE MOONSHINER'S DAUGHTER
THE SAINTS OF SWALLOW HILL

Published by Kensington Publishing Corp.

The
ROAD TO
*B*ITTERSWEET

DONNA EVERHART

KENSINGTON BOOKS
www.kensingtonbooks.com

KENSINGTON BOOKS are published by

Kensington Publishing Corp.
119 West 40th Street
New York, NY 10018

All Kensington titles, imprints, and distributed lines are available at special quantity discounts for bulk purchases for sales promotion, premiums, fund-raising, educational, or institutional use.

Special book excerpts or customized printings can also be created to fit specific needs. For details, write or phone the office of the Kensington Sales Manager: Kensington Publishing Corp., 119 West 40th Street, New York, NY 10018. Attn. Sales Department. Phone: 1-800-221-2647.

Kensington and the K logo Reg. U.S. Pat. & TM Off.

eISBN-13: 978-1-4967-0950-9
eISBN-10: 1-4967-0950-0
First Kensington Electronic Edition: January 2018

ISBN-13: 978-1-4967-0949-3
ISBN-10: 1-4967-0949-7
First Kensington Trade Paperback Printing: January 2018

10 9 8 7 6 5 4

Printed in the United States of America

For my children,
Justin and Brooke

Chapter 1

Stampers Creek, North Carolina, 1940

Whenever I hear the birth stories Momma repeats on our special day, I can't help but think of Laci, how she ended up. Her name alone conjures a frail and delicate being, someone who don't fit in with the harsh way of life here. With arms and legs as slender as the limbs of the willow trees growing alongside the Tuckasegee River, their movement as fine as the lines of Momma's bone china teacups, Laci seems out of place. Momma says Laci's looks come from her side, from our great-grandma Devon Wallis. Her hair shines like an Appalachian sunset, shot through all gold and red, while a sprinkle of freckles rides the bridge of her nose. Deep green eyes swallow any thoughts she might have, except we don't rightly know what she thinks since she don't talk.

Laci's birth story is dramatic. When she got born, Momma said the cord was in a true knot. Pulled tight during labor, Laci come out the color of a ripened blueberry. She was quiet, limp, no hollering, no having a little hissy fit like me on my own birthing day, none of the flailing, strong movements of a normal baby. The granny woman who come to deliver her smacked her hard on the behind, and silent she stayed. That granny woman flipped her around butt first, then head, and finally, Momma said, poor Laci squeaked out a little breathless cry at the rudeness of it all, and promptly fell silent again. Breathing, eyes blinking, flushed a bright healthy pink, yet silent. Momma said the one squeak was the only sound she'd ever heard Laci make.

The granny woman exclaimed, "Law, this child ought to be squalling after all a that."

I've often wondered if Momma regretted the name she'd give her, considering her ways. I relinquished my own stronghold from her womb fourteen years ago this very day, dropping into the capable hands of the same granny woman.

She'd asked Momma, "What's this one's name gonna be?"

"Wallis Ann."

The granny woman was said to have give a look what conveyed her thoughts about the choice.

Momma explained. "Wallis, my family name, and Ann, my given first name."

The granny woman grunted, then questioned her. "Like a boy's? Like W-a-l-l-a-c-e. It's a right odd name for a girl, ain't it?"

Momma shrugged, and replied, "Girl needs a strong name in these parts."

Upon learning it, Papa said, "It suits her. She looks more Wallis than Stamper anyway, that's for sure."

Momma said, "Well, thank you sweet Jesus for that."

They was only fooling. They're always saying that sort of thing to each other.

Whereas I'd kicked and pushed, rearranging Momma's insides to suit myself, Momma said Laci had barely moved, a prelude to her actual nature. As an infant, I'd shoved against her hands as she tended me, latched on to her at feeding time, and when she removed me from her breast, I'd screamed like I'd been stung by a thousand bees. Laci never whimpered. To this day, she exists like a whisper you barely hear, or a shadow on a partly cloudy day, appearing to fade, then unexpectedly bursting forth like a hot ray of sun. She's two years older, yet she'll never know the things I know. She'll never read. Or write. Or solve problems. I've tried to teach her, only to see if I could, and, sometimes, I believe she's listening, so I keep on telling her what I know, keep on reading to her what I'm reading, keep on talking to her like she's going to answer me back. In truth, I've spent a lot of time wondering what she's thinking.

Momma took her to Doc Stuart years ago and to that thought, he'd said, "Not much. Not unless it involves music. Then her brain does what it does with astounding proficiency. An idiot savant, Mrs. Stamper. I'm sorry, she'll never lead a normal life. Only the music truly speaks to her."

Momma's lips pressed together at the word "idiot."

On the way out of his office, she whispered to me, "He's the idiot. Well. She'll have her music, won't she?"

She was right. Laci's never talked, yet she can play any instrument handed to her. Fiddle. Banjo. Mountain dulcimer. She's not had one lesson neither. This come as a revelation when she was six. Back when Momma and Papa was only sparking, they sung together for churches, fish fries, tent revivals, weddings, funerals, county fairs, wherever anyone wanted them, they'd go. One day they stood in a church singing for Homecoming and they sat me and Laci on the front pew so they could keep an eye on us. I pressed against Laci and seen how she watched the lady playing the piano, eyes fastened on the woman's fingers. She never moved, not once, but I felt her breath quicken.

After Momma and Papa finished, everyone went into the church yard to eat. While plates was being piled high with fried chicken, tater salad, biscuits and pie, nobody missed Laci. Momma and Papa got preoccupied with the preacher, and that's when I heard piano music coming from inside the church. I was the one who found her banging away on the keys. She won't strong enough to pull the heavy wooden bench close, so she stood playing "When the Saints Go Marching In," the very last song the lady played. Mesmerized, I stood beside her, watching her small, dainty fingers fly. That's how Momma and Papa found us and when they realized she was special.

It was known as The Piano Incident, and after that, Laci learned a bunch of songs fast. Sometimes Papa would play his banjo, or fiddle, and Laci watched until he'd hand it off to her and she'd turn right around and play the song. Momma and Papa got to where they let her join when they went singing, cueing her by starting the song off so she'd know what to play. I was left to sit by myself, and I remembered not liking it one bit. Laci didn't like the separation either. She would stop in the middle of a song and stare at me. Just stopped playing whatever instrument they'd given her, and there we'd be looking at each other. After a time or two of this happening, Momma stood me beside Laci.

She whispered, "Stand here beside your sister. You know some of the words, so you can sing too, okay?"

I was petrified looking at them faces seeming to expect something out of me. One day my words got unlocked and I started singing. Folks pointed and smiled, and feeling encouraged, I become a little more animated each time, swinging my feed sack dress side to side, bouncing on my knees along with the tune. Soon we was going lots of places, and after a while, Papa decided we ought to have a name. He started referring to us as The Stamper Family. He was lucky enough to also work for Evergreen Sawmill Company in Cullowhee, and he saved up to buy an old truck, a Ford 67 model with wide footboards, and we left our holler, and headed into Cashiers, Sylva or East LaPorte, just about any place to sing and entertain folks.

I reckon that's how we got to be sort of famous throughout Jackson County, plus the fact folks was always curious about Laci. I was of a mind they only invited us because they'd heard about her, and considered she'd been blessed by the Holy Spirit. Her ways are as natural to me as breathing and eating, and I don't like it when people want to touch her, or want her to touch them. She don't understand the attention, and it scares her. Sometimes I want to drag her out of sight, away from the poking hands and curious stares. After little brother Seph got born three years ago, Momma has come to depend even more on me to watch over Laci. Her needs come first, even afore mine because she can't help the way she is.

Heavy gray clouds resembling a pot of boiling water rolled overhead while thunder shook the floor beneath my bare feet. A hard rain beat on the roof, sounding like a distant train rumbling along the tracks, as an odd milky vapor swirled through the woods, covering everything the way a good mountain fog settling in tends to do. Two weeks ago, a similar downpour made Stampers Creek rise over the embankment while strong winds uprooted massive trees, felling them like weakened saplings. Still cleaning up from that, I could picture all the hard work for naught.

Laci sat in a corner chair with the dulcimer on her lap playing "Sally in the Garden" nonstop. Seph was patting my arm to get my attention and I picked him up, before walking to the window to look at the churning brown waters of Stampers Creek. The creek had risen quite a bit, and was close to the trunks of the wispy willow trees Momma planted years ago along the embankment.

I squinted, studying the barn, chicken coop and hog pens, noting where the outbuildings sat compared to the creek. I dropped my gaze and tickled Seph's belly and he struggled to get down, his cheeks flushing pink while his robin's-egg-blue eyes got watery from giggling. The sound of Papa's boots stomping outside on the front porch signaled he was home early. I let Seph go as Papa come through the door looking like he'd been dunked in the river. He pulled his cap off his head and hung it on the peg. Water dripped off his beard, making the front of his shirt wet.

He glanced at me and said, "No cutting trees in this weather."

He tousled Seph's hair and looked over at Momma, who was pulling my birthday cake out of the oven. He set his lunch pail on the kitchen table, and I opened it to find most of the food we'd sent uneaten. There was still slices of fried side meat, and one of two cathead biscuits with pear preserves untouched. I handed Seph the biscuit, and he immediately crammed it in his mouth.

"Too much rain," Papa said to Momma, and she handed him a rag to wipe his face.

She replied, "Nothing anyone can do about it. Lord willing, it'll stop. Might as well go on about our business."

Papa said, "The Tuckasegee is still running high from that other storm. River's worse than anyone's seen in a long time. Some say another hurricane's on the way."

Momma walked to the kitchen window and looked out at a yard filled with geraniums, black-eyed Susan and hydrangea. She loved walking the edge of the woods where mountain laurel flourished along with her favorite, fringe trees, or "Old Man's Beard." She tended her flowers like everything else, though she said being prideful was a sin because anything of beauty was truly God's work. We was only here to cultivate it, help care for it. She couldn't hide some of her pleasure though when visitors come and admired what she'd done. Her face would flush red as a plum when complimented. She could coax near about any plant or flower to life and make it thrive.

Momma remained composed as Papa went on with dire flood predictions, listening as if he was discussing painting the bedrooms, a recent pursuit and desire of hers, a way to rid the walls of being tacked with newspaper and magazine coverings.

She swiped a hand over the wood grain of her worktable, considering the words he spoke, and maybe she was calm because she'd been in a flood before, the one in 1916 when over eighty people was killed.

Papa walked over to the same window I'd been at earlier, and Momma turned to me and said, "Wallis Ann, go on and let's get supper started. Have Laci chop the greens."

I said, "Yes, ma'am," and retrieved the mustard greens in the bright yellow bowl Momma had cooked earlier. The music had gone silent from the other room. A floorboard creaked when Laci come to stand beside me, her warm, gentle fingers seeking to hold mine. I thought of all the timber Papa had planed, the bark he'd stripped off the logs, all the notches he'd wrested out of the hardwood for tongue-and-groove joints. He'd laid his hands on every part of the cabin, down to the dovetail joints along with each and every nail holding the walls together.

I said, "Here," and give Laci the bowl.

She went to sit at the kitchen table, and picked up the metal chopper. I turned to my own task, stoking the fire in the stove first, then I sliced some side meat and put a pot of beans on to boil. Momma took over frying while I scooped out flour for more biscuits, my fingers working the lard and flour together by feel. I'd made enough in my fourteen years such that I could near bought do it blindfolded. Supper was ready an hour later and we went on and ate. No one mentioned how early it was, or how Momma kept putting more and more onto our plates.

"Eat good now," she urged.

After supper, she placed my birthday cake in the middle of the table. It had chocolate icing, a rare treat, and for a brief moment I had uninterrupted attention from my parents. I studied their faces while they sang "Happy Birthday," Papa's ruddy from working outside, his beard already sprinkled with gray, while Momma's delicate-featured face remained young and fresh appearing. When the song was over, she cut each of us a huge slice. We ate cake, and drank glasses of cool milk poured from the clay jug brought up from spring house earlier.

After we finished the dishes, Momma took off her apron, smoothed her hands down the front of her dress and said, "Well. We best get some sleep."

Papa said, "Wallis Ann, put your shoes by your bed, and get you and Laci some extra clothes together."

We don't never wear shoes till it comes a frost, and Papa's instructions said more about his thinking than a long explanation. I didn't ask questions. Laci and I climbed the steps to the sleeping attic. Once there, I put our shoes by my bed, and put each of us a pair of socks in them. Next, I got our extra dresses off the individual hooks, one each, and folded them neatly. I retrieved a piece of string from the bedside table, and tied it all together into a tight bundle. I believed what I'd been told to do was in preparation for some unexpected event, though no one said so.

Chapter 2

Laci fell asleep immediately while I listened to the rain hit the hand-split oak shingles over our heads. The wind blowed hard over the gabled roof, and the howling sound filled our tiny room. The light cast from a lantern stretched my shadowy form against the wall like a gray ghost as I tried to read the forbidden *True Love and Romance* magazine I'd found in the trash behind a store in Cullowhee one day. I'd hidden it under my coat, my curiosity stronger than my worry over Momma finding me out. The cover was torn and slick from repeated handling, and the pages fell open to the parts where lots of kissing happened. Despite the noise from the storm, and a strong sense of something about to happen, I eventually got tired. I leaned over the edge of the bed to tuck the magazine under a loose floorboard, then blowed out the lantern and closed my eyes.

A loud, splintering sound followed by a heavy thud close to the cabin woke me. I scrambled out from under the thin muslin sheet, breathing heavy like I sometimes do when we're about to sing. The spot where Laci's arm had pressed against my side left a moist imprint on my nightgown, the humid night air sitting heavy inside our small room because we couldn't open the window with all the rain. I pinched a section of my nightgown to free it from my sticky skin. My newly cropped bob allowed some air to reach my neck, and hot as it was, it was an odd but welcome sensation I hadn't growed used to yet.

I could hear the creek. It didn't sound right, not the soft whoosh over the rocks, more like an angry churning, which meant it was running swift and fast. The downstairs clock chimed four times. The heart pine floor under my feet vibrated with every boom of thunder, and the wind's force made the cabin creak with every gust. Lightning flashed constantly, and the odd flickers illuminated the room. As I made my way to the window, I glanced over my shoulder at the spindle bed, but Laci had her face turned towards the wall, her form a slender twist of long arms and legs under the sheet.

I stared out, waiting for lightning to flash again, and when it did, I seen the creek foaming like the mouth of a rabid dog, the edges sloshing into the garden in rivulets. It was much wider than what it had been earlier. I recognized that kind of fast rise would only keep on, and I backed away from the window, my mouth gone cotton dry, my chest tightening like somebody was squeezing me. I rushed over to the bed and shook Laci. She rose on her elbows, looking at me like she always does, without expression, without alarm.

I said, "Get up, Laci!"

She swung her legs over the side of the bed, and without waiting, I run from the room, my feet finding the stairs in the dark. Momma stood at the bottom, her face tense, pale, and she whispered because Seph was still asleep on her shoulder.

"Wallis Ann, you know what to do and be quick about it. Help your sister, understand?"

Papa was tucking his shirt into his coveralls.

I asked him, "We going to try to get up to Salt Rock?"

He nodded, facial features fixed and tight, like his skin was too snug, removing the usual soft crinkles and curves. He got the lantern off the worktable, striking a match to light it. He carried it to the door and slapped his hat on his head. I hurried to open the door, and he went out. I heard Liberty, our horse, and Pete, our mule, down in the barn, their hooves delivering a sporadic pounding to the stall doors. They was animals we sure couldn't afford to lose.

Papa run across the yard, the rain quickly obscuring his shape so he looked flat and gray, while the spark from the lantern was so weak, it didn't give any more light than what a firefly might provide. It vanished seconds later as he entered the barn. Another boom of thunder and a flash of lightning wrapped around everything. The wind turned into this enormous force, pushing on the door as I struggled to close it. I finally slammed it shut, and hurried to the kitchen window, where I could see the creek water was now well past the weeping willows. The stormy sky pulsed with continuous flickers of light.

Momma cried, "Wallis Ann, why are you staring out the window? Get dressed! When you're done, be sure to get the basket in the kitchen I've packed. Hurry now!"

I hurried back up the stairs and seen Laci sitting on her bed, dress in her lap, fingering the material. The dresses made me think of Momma working late at night sewing them from feed sacks, attaching Peter Pan collars, stitching extra cloth at the bottom of Laci's since she was so tall, just to make it respectable. Laci made like she wanted to lie down in the bed again.

I said, "Nooooo," while pulling off my nightgown, putting on my underthings, and stepping into my dress in less than a minute.

Everything I did was like a ritual, because that was how I got Laci to do what I needed. Thunder clapped overhead, and there come the familiar press of Laci's fingers on my arm.

I told her, "It's only a thunderstorm."

I motioned again for her to get her dress on and she pulled it over her head, then turned around for me to button it. I lifted her hair out of the way, did her up, and then we sat on the edge of the bed to pull on socks and shoes.

I stood up and said, "Laci, come on!"

Her chin went forward, and her mouth turned down in one of a handful of expressions we sometimes witnessed. Of all times for Laci's stubborn streak to show up. I grabbed her hand. She refused to budge, her arm gone stiff and resistant as a board.

"What? What is it?"

Her eyes went to the corner of our room, past the old wooden washstand, beyond the cane-back chair by the window where I'd often sit, chin in hand, daydreaming about what the world looked like beyond Stampers Creek, beyond the hills and hollers I called home. Laci's intense gaze fell on the dimmest part of the room to the one thing she had to have. Her fiddle. I retrieved a blanket from the chest at the foot of the bed, wrapped the instrument in it and handed it to her. She hugged it tight, like you would a baby, and only then did her chin square into its rightful place. I grabbed the extra clothes I'd tied into a bundle only hours ago.

I clattered down the stairs, Laci on my heels, and rushed into the kitchen. I grabbed the basket from the table as Momma had directed and set it by the front door. I took the bundled instrument from Laci, set it on the table and handed her the burlap sack I'd retrieved from a hook by the wash pan. I motioned to the pantry. She went for the fiddle again, and I put my hand on her arm.

"Leave it there, for now, and help me."

I sighed with relief when she obliged, my attention drawn to the window. The creek was even closer. My sense of urgency increased as I put beans, a small poke of flour, coffee and sugar into the bigger one Laci held open. I wrapped slices of cured bacon in cheesecloth, grabbed a loaf of bread, and added all of it to the basket by the door. Another clap of thunder shook the cabin as Momma come into the kitchen, dressed and leading Seph, who stumbled along, not understanding, and seeming determined to outdo the noise from the storm. Her hand shook as she brushed a strand of hair back. Momma's own papa was swept away along with their house after twenty-two inches of rain fell in a twenty-four-hour period over near Altapass and Grandfather Mountain. She'd been Laci's age then. Her demeanor was still calm, but with the squall right over us, a hint of fear had entered her voice.

Her tone elevated, she asked, "Did you get everything?"

"Yes, ma'am."

"You sure, Wallis Ann?"

"I did, see?"

I pointed at the basket by the door, and took the poke from Laci and held it for her to see. She nodded distractedly and give the kitchen one last look. She went to Granny Wallis's pie safe, opened it, looked in at the birthday cake she'd baked, only to close the small door again. It was a family keepsake, given to her and Papa on their wedding day along with Grandma Wallis's chifforobe. She went to her prized possession last, a green and cream-colored Glenwood C stove. She traced a hand along the burners, and turned to distractedly brush cake crumbs from the worktable. It was as if by doing these little things, she was reassuring herself all would be well. She turned to me, the look on her face causing my heart to race, like Papa revving the engine on his truck.

I whispered, "It's going to be fine, Momma."

Sometimes saying words helped me believe what I wanted

others to believe. We went to the front door and Momma tugged on Seph's small jacket. I put a scarf on my head, nervously twisting and tying it tight as I could stand, and Laci did the same. We pulled on our coats, and stood there for a few seconds preparing to make our way out into the storm. Momma bent down and got Seph, holding him tight in her arms. I lifted the basket, and the poke filled with food, and Laci had her fiddle. Momma give me another one of them looks and opened the door, exposing us to a blast of wind. It actually pushed her back a step or two. The fiddle dug into my backbone as Laci's forehead pressed between my shoulder blades.

We heard Papa yell, "Git on! Shoo!" to the animals in the barn.

We moved as one, stepping into a violent wind what drove the rain at a slant, and soaked us in seconds. Hunching our bodies, we made a run for the truck, our shoes slapping the puddles of dirty water and soaking through our socks. The rain actually hurt, and stung my exposed skin like millions of needles. It reminded me of the time I'd stood under Dismal Falls, only there I could control how the spray hit me, my toes digging into slick rocks as I stepped in and out of it. This almost took my breath away. Laci stayed pressed against me, and it's a wonder one of us didn't trip over the other's foot and fall flat-faced into the mud.

Reaching for the door handle, I paused as Liberty and Pete went galloping by full speed, taking to the hill behind the barn. Their instincts told them what to do, and they faded into the gray, heading away from the rising creek, which was looking more like a river by the minute.

"Wallis Ann! Hurry up! Open the door!" Momma hollered at me while Seph screamed in her ear.

I yanked the door open and stood aside as she scrambled in, setting Seph on her lap. Even above the storm, I could hear the Tuckasegee. The usual soothing flow of water we could only

hear on the quietest of days had intensified to a loud and constant rush, like the sound of a locomotive. I couldn't see how it
was possible for rain to come down any harder, or for wind
gusts to get any stronger. Momma reached for the basket and
slid it under the seat, and then Laci crawled in. She was still
trying to get her legs in good when I come in right on top of
her, onto her lap, holding our food tight against my chest.

Typically, Laci and I would ride in the truck bed, not
crammed into the cab. I slammed the door shut, and looked to
Momma. The whiteness of her face and her shadowed eyes was
almost spooky. With our wet clothes pasted to our skin, flattened scarves on our heads, not one inch of us was dry to
speak of. I shivered, and felt Laci doing the same. Papa come
running from the side of the cabin where we had the chicken
coops and hog pens. He'd opened the doors, giving hens, the
rooster and the pigs an opportunity to fend for themselves
however they could. When he got in we was packed tight as
ticks. He had trouble cranking the truck, but, after he adjusted
the throttle and the advance, it caught. He hammered his fist
on the dashboard as if to encourage the vehicle, and we started
driving away from Stampers Creek.

The tail end slid in the mud once or twice, and Papa turned
the wheel to compensate. I had the urge to look at our cabin,
only I couldn't move. We headed down the dirt trail before
turning onto the dirt road running alongside the Tuckasegee.
It was hard to see anything, and it looked like we was driving
in the middle of the river where the water already started
washing over the lower areas causing deep ruts. It was nerve-
rattling, and Papa gripped the steering wheel tight with both
hands, spinning it one direction and the other to avoid what
he could, when he could. Still, we heard a lot of thumping, and
banging underneath. Every now and then, curious scraping
sounds come from all sides, like some creature might be trying
to claw its way in.

The continuous rushing water had created huge holes and ruts and even with the headlights, we couldn't see to avoid them. At times we'd hit a pothole and bounce around inside the cab like peas in a can. Papa said a few choice words when that happened. Momma stayed silent, concentrating on keeping Seph from hitting his head on the dashboard. The further we went, the worse it got. Out the front window the waterlogged road continued to look as if it had merged with the river, like there'd never been any separation of road or an embankment. The truck abruptly went horizontal, then jerked straight.

Momma said, "William."

Papa said, "We got to go quicker, if we can."

And then, it went sideways again, losing purchase, and this time it didn't regain traction. Almost immediately it was like we was in a boat. As we went to floating, we picked up speed.

Papa cursed, "Lord, damn it!"

Momma would usually say something about all them curse words coming out of his mouth except the truck going along of its own accord had put a fear into her and struck her silent. Her hand patted Seph a little quicker and the truck jerked violently as it found its purchase with the road once more. Papa steered erratically to straighten us out, and we kept on till we finally turned onto Highway 107, where Papa become a little more confident. He mashed on the gas pedal and the needle went from fifteen mph to twenty-five mph.

Of course, when things go really, really wrong, you tend to think back on what you did or didn't do. You wonder if staying put might have been a better choice. The tires lost their grip again and then we went sideways once more, floating. My feet felt wetter than they'd already been, and curious, I leaned forward to touch the floorboard. Water sloshed about, touching my hand. No one else seemed to have noticed. Papa was fixated on getting the truck to go right, but when I raised up quick, he glanced my way. I nodded towards the floorboard. Momma closed her eyes and went to praying. Papa leaned forward to see out the windshield better, yet with no control anyway, he might as well have taken his hands off the wheel and been blindfolded.

Maybe what was about to happen should have been expected, yet, when the engine sputtered, then knocked off, Momma bowed her head, silent again. I stared out at the storm-whipped trees and the blackness beyond the dim headlights that seemed to bounce one way and the other. Water swirled all around and I wished we could somehow find a way to maneuver away from the flood, as it took us where it wanted, faster and faster. I drew up, realizing there won't anything we could do about it.

"William." Momma said Papa's name again, real quiet, yet her voice held a special level of fear and alarm what set my heart to jumping the way an earthworm does if caught out in the hot sun.

The water started coming up faster inside and I now felt it on my ankles. The truck jerked hard and went dead still again, like a giant hand had been placed on the front end. The water rose steady, inside and out, and there we sat. Seph whined, and Momma jiggled her leg while shushing him. The slow rise and fall of Laci's front against me showed me she won't afraid—not yet. The only noise she produced come from a finger occasionally trying to pluck an exposed string. Our predicament created a bizarre lull in me too, as my throat felt closed off, my voice gone. I become as mute as Laci, waiting for Papa to tell us what to do. He studied what lay ahead, which, best as we could all tell, was water and more water. It kept rising inside and now reached my calves.

Finally, after what felt like hours, he said, "I think the water's broke over the dam. We got to get out, get in the back where we can get on the roof if necessary. Roll your window down, Wallis Ann, quick now."

The rigid sound to his voice burned my belly, and I tasted a bitterness in my mouth. That's what fear tastes like. It's bitter, and nasty, and makes you feel like you're going to throw up.

I managed to say, "Yes, sir."

I cranked the window down. I got it only halfway when the rain blowed in and made Laci lean towards Momma in an attempt to shy away from it. Papa had his down too and it was like each side tried to be in contention with the other as the wind created a cross draft through the cab.

Papa yelled to be heard above the storm's noise. "Sit on the window's edge. Be sure you can stand on the runner without getting knocked down. Be quick as you can, and get in the back. Understand?"

No speaking my nickname, Wally Girl, no wink, no smile to ease my worry. This situation we was in scared me worse than anything I'd ever been scared about. Worse than the stories Papa told about them haunted rooms over at the Balsam Inn in Sylva. Worse than the time Momma got real sick and we won't certain she was going to make it. Worse than when the mean boy Harlan Tillis from my class threatened to push me down the long, slippery rock at Jawbone Falls, knowing I'd get hurt bad—or worse.

Papa continued, "Grab hold tight wherever you can, and then help Laci. I'll help your momma and Seph. Understand?"

I replied, "Yes, sir," only it come out more like, "y-y-yes, s-s-sir."

It was awkward as I tried to maneuver myself off Laci's lap so my rear was on the window's edge. Somehow I managed. Where the runner should be won't nothing but swift running water. I ducked my head to look inside the cab, only Papa was already out, standing by his window. I looked over the cab of the truck and he was barely visible through the driving rain.

His hands rested on the top of the roof and he motioned at me, yelling above the noise, "Wait!"

He stuck his right leg into the truck bed and hurried to pull his self in. Holding on best as he could, he come over to my side and reached out for one of my hands. He'd probably realized I was too short to do as he'd said. I shot my arm out and he grabbed it. I let go with my other hand and when he had both my wrists, he'd hauled me into the back and I found myself standing beside him.

He hollered into my ear, "Help Laci while I get your momma and Seph! Hold on to her hands tight!"

Petrified, I could only nod.

He carefully eased his way over to the driver's side, and leaned down to the window. I could see through the back glass Momma was behind the steering wheel, and Seph's mouth was wide open, crying at fever pitch. I couldn't watch no more. I had to get Laci.

I smacked the glass right behind her head and yelled, "Laci!"

She sat with her fiddle clamped to her chest. I stuck my hand through the open window for her to give it to me, pleased when she shoved it into my hands. I took it, and turned to the old box Papa used for carrying tools and other things when he went into town. I lifted the lid open, set the instrument inside, hoping it would be protected. By now Laci had noticed how we'd all bailed out on her and she sat on the window's ledge like I had.

"Laci! Wait!" I yelled at her.

Without waiting at all, she clambered out onto the running board. Them long legs a hers did what mine couldn't, because with little help from me other than the fact I'd grabbed hold of one of her hands, she was suddenly standing beside me. She turned and sat on the box where her beloved fiddle had gone. With Laci out, I took Seph from Papa. He'd managed to get him and now needed to help Momma. She sat like we had, and it made me nervous seeing her perched there, because she was too focused on Seph screaming in my arms and not paying attention. She found her footing on the runner, and her hands gripped the opened window's edge while the water was only inches from breaching the truck bed. She thrust her hand out to Papa, but an unexpected surge moved the truck and took her feet right out from under her, and she was forced to grab the window ledge again. She let out a tiny scream as the drag of the water stretched her body horizontal. I almost couldn't look. I was afraid the water would rip her hands loose.

Papa leaned over, holding both her wrists and yelling at her to "let go!" and every time he did, Momma screamed at him, "No!"

He bellowed, "Ann! Listen! On the count of three! One! Two!"

Momma's expression become set with a determined look, lips thinned out like when she was mad at something.

When Papa said, "Three!" she let go.

It had to have required tremendous effort to pull her over the side and into the back, considering it appeared impossible, but he did it. Momma lay flat in the truck bed for a few seconds and then she pushed herself into a sitting position. Papa gripped the side, and after he got his breath, he reached down to grasp her hands and helped her sit on the box beside Laci. He kissed each of her hands and brushed her hair off her face. He placed his hands on her cheeks for a few seconds, and she covered them with her own. She wanted to cry and wouldn't. She stared up at him, and times like this, I seen their love so clearly, it was like somebody had placed me in front of a dirty window and then wiped it sparkling clean. Love like theirs was what I wanted, the kind what held on and never let go. The lasting kind, equal in measure for each person.

The moment passed and Papa released Momma's face, motioning for me to hand him Seph. Above the wind, and the pounding rain, Seph's crying was barely audible. Spreading my legs to gain some balance, I passed him off carefully.

I bent toward Momma's ear, "Rest, Momma, catch your breath!"

She leaned against Laci while Papa set his feet wide, and held on to Seph, facing her. I stood on Laci's other side, hanging on to the top of the truck. It shifted, going sideways until something large and solid slammed into it, throwing us all off balance. Momma almost lost her seat, and I fell to my knees. Laci looked like she wanted to crawl into the box she sat on. Thing was, Papa couldn't grab nothing since he held the squirming, crying Seph. It happened so fast and yet so slow as he stumbled backwards, a look of stunned surprise on his face. One second, he and Seph was right there, and next, the back a Papa's legs connected to the side of the truck bed and he flipped over and into the water.

It was odd how it got quiet for the length of a breath, with me and Momma staring dumbstruck at where they'd been standing only seconds ago. It was like hearing the big sawmill at Evergreen going for hours on end until it was cut off. The silence what followed always seemed louder than when it was on, an eerie hush what lasted until me and Momma broke it with shrieks of disbelief. We crawled to the side where he went over, as if it would be possible to see him and Seph. There was only the whitish froth of the water.

Gripping the slick, wet metal sides, our frantic screams blended together. "Papa! William!"

Lightning flashed, and I seen them about thirty feet away. I pointed, gripping Momma's shoulder with one hand while my other trembled and shook. Papa held his arms rigid and above the water as he fought to keep Seph out of harm's way. He was moving away from us fast, and seconds later with another flash of lightning, he was barely visible, his head a tiny, dark knot in the current, and beyond hearing our shouts. What shook us to the point of absolute panic was seeing how hard it had been for him as he tried to save Seph.

Momma said, "He'll do it, he'll keep Seph safe, no matter what, he'll keep him safe."

She kept repeating it over and over. I said nothing, my breaths short and hard, like I'd been running hours on end. I thought it impossible. Papa's resolve was something I'd seen in the past, but how long could he last? We leaned out far as we dared, even long after they'd disappeared around a bend. We kept screaming till our throats was raw, our hopes relying on fickle weather, and a capricious river. More objects hit the truck, like the storm would beat it to expel its anger. Water started seeping in where we were, yet all we could do was splash from one side to the other while continuing to holler for Papa. After a few minutes, I fell into a shocked silence. Then, Momma did too. The Tuckasegee had them now. It would do as it seen fit.

She sank onto the box beside Laci, mouth open, crying without noise. Laci sat hunched, rocking back and forth, back and forth. Right then, I wished I could be like her.

Unmindful of what I'd seen.

Chapter 3

The truck shifted like it might start moving again and we clambered onto the small, cramped roof, driven by the relentless rise of water in the back. Momma faced forwards, legs hanging down the windshield, her body slumped as if she'd already give up on everything. I kept hold of her, linked at the elbow, while I sat with Laci facing the other direction. My back rested against Momma's, only there was no warmth to share. Our backbones knocked together, and only later would I notice a bruised soreness.

Thing was, if we'd thought the worst had happened we was wrong. So wrong. Above the storm's fury, I somehow discerned another noise I couldn't rightly place at first. It reminded me of walking through the woods when off in the distance comes a sound, a constant, deep rumbling what turns into an unrelenting roar. That's how you know you're coming to a waterfall. You can hear all them millions of gallons of water rushing over the edges, and crashing onto rocks below, and when a noise like that come from the front of the truck, I turned my head to look over my left shoulder. It was like the monstrous storm *wanted* me to see what it had planned for us, because right at that moment, the heaven's own lantern lit the sky. A muddy wall of water was coming straight for us, a churning, swirling mass, and I barely had time to grasp its enormity.

I yelled, "Momma!"

Linking my arm tighter with hers, I grabbed Laci's hand as it slammed into us with all the power of a charging, angry bull. The truck rose and bucked. I slid off the top, pulling Momma and Laci with me into the bed of the truck again, and for a few seconds we went into a sodden, crazy spin. Despite the fact I was petrified, I was strangely aware of Laci's silence. It was like she existed somewhere else other than here in this moment with us. The truck jerked violently, knocking me sideways, and like Papa I was flipped, without warning, over the side. The last thing I seen as I hit the water was the horrified look on Momma's face, her mouth a black hole where no sound come out.

I went under and then I was rolling around, topsy-turvy, and didn't know which end was up. Hard, sharp objects hit my legs and body as I was spun about. The water tossed me like I weighed no more than a twig. I fought hard, panicking when my arms and legs made no progress, and my lungs began to burn, feeling full to bursting. I kicked and kicked till my head broke the surface. I gulped in as much air as I could, and then I was dragged under again. I let the current carry me, sensing the flows and swells as I struggled to the surface. When my head broke, a large object banged into my lower back. It hurt something fierce, but I ignored the pain, quickly turning around, letting my hands explore and finding the rough, uneven bark of a tree. My fingertips dug into grooves, and I hung on for dear life, clinging to it like I would have clung to Momma, had she been there. I felt I might cry, only there won't time for it.

I tried to see what was ahead, worried about being crushed or caught between other trees and large rocks. I took a beating as other objects thumped against my back and legs. A cow bellowed as it went flying by. If it had been Angus, I'd have never seen it, except dawn was near upon us and it was light enough to know it was a breed called Charolaise. I made out the creamy pale head barely above water, and the disturbed and desperate lowing of a creature nearly spent. More farm animals went by, most already dead, and if not dead, close to it. Pigs floundered, trying to swim, and the ones already gone spun and twirled like bloated pinwheels.

There was lots of chickens bobbing by, and it was hard looking at their wings and legs all bent and broken, their dingy white feathers chaotic and in disarray. I felt something soft brush against into my side. I twisted and jerked away from someone's head, full of gray hair. The current changed and whoever it was floated facedown by me. I almost let go of the log so I could go after this person, lift his head and see who it was, except he remained facedown, and that told me what I needed to know. The water took him quick downstream and I was glad it won't one of my family, and then immediately felt guilty for thinking in such a way. Afterwards, I prayed I wouldn't see nobody else, at least not like that. I felt sick to my stomach when I thought of Momma, Papa, Laci, and Seph. Was someone else letting one of them slip by, while looking the other way and thanking their lucky stars it won't someone they recognized? Was it selfish to think about protecting my own life?

My arms began to really ache. The awkwardness and instability of the log meant it wanted to roll so I was constantly struggling to keep my head and shoulders from being dragged under again. Cold set into my bones, like when a fever comes over you. My teeth chattered and clacked, and I shivered and shook, muscles burning. Enough time had passed since we'd left the cabin for the sky to lose some of the night dark, and I kept my eyes peeled for a standing tree. If the opportunity presented itself, I would swim hard as I could for it. Despite the rain hindering my vision, I finally made out a huge one with limbs hanging low, and I prepared to let go of the one thing what had kept me safe.

I moved towards the rear of the log so I could be free and clear when ready. I was moving fast and had to time it just right. About a hundred or so feet away, I took my hands off the trunk, and began swimming. I got close enough to reach a narrow bough and when it hit my palm, I closed my fingers tight around it. It won't thick as I wanted, but what was odd was how sluggish my arms felt when I lifted them, like they weighed hundreds of pounds. I could tell the limb won't going to hold me anyway, and I let go.

As soon as I did, the water closed over my head, and my mouth instantly filled with a brackish, foul taste. I had no choice but to fight being dragged under all over again. I kicked hard, and resurfaced, coughing and sputtering. I passed line after line of trees, frantic to get to them, but I was swept by much too fast. I was growing weaker, my efforts hampered by my coat, expending energy with each chance. I was about to go under again when a massive tree come into view. As I was swept beneath it, I reached up and snagged a branch. I willed my fingers to hold on, my weakened arms straining and trembling with effort. I learned right then what it felt like to try and go against the current. It twisted me about like clothes hung on a line in a stiff wind. My arms felt like they might get wrenched clear out of their sockets, and yet I got to going in a hand-over-hand climb, like going up a rope. The higher I went, the more determined I got, and slowly, gradually, the river let go its sucking hold. Finally, I was free of the pull of the water, dangling above it.

I rested a few seconds and when I thought I could lift a leg up and put it around the limb, I did. There come a sharp, stinging pain seared into the center of my hands as my weight pulled at the skin, yet I only had this one chance. I closed my eyes, panted and grunted with frustrated resolve. I used every ounce of muscle I had to lift my leg and hook it around the branch. I lifted the other, and now I hung upside down, like a slaughtered pig. I gritted my teeth and wiggled my way around until I was on top. Unbelievably, I was at last straddling the branch and completely out of the water. I felt momentarily victorious, and I bent forward so I could lie there, exhausted, my cheek resting against the damp bark, my arms and legs still shaking.

After a while, I sat up. I felt spent as a nickel in a dime store. I stared down at the roaring mass below me and seen the water yet rising. My hands throbbed and I touched my palms where puffy, soft blisters had formed. I traced fingers over the scratches and scrapes of my shins, and everything I touched burned or felt badly bruised. I found raised lumps here and there, and realized I'd also lost a shoe. I was lucky. I hadn't been killed, and I didn't have any broken bones. I looked up, trying to determine how tall the tree was. With the rain coming down and the wind acting like a huge hand determined to shove me off, it was impossible to make out what was above me. No matter, my instincts said climb higher and that I should be on the side of the tree where I wouldn't have to fight against the wind so much.

I carefully inched backwards towards the trunk. Once there, I stood up, and maneuvered around to the other side. I put my foot on a higher limb, and tested. It held, and seemed strong. I climbed until I sensed I shouldn't go any further, certain the water wouldn't come this high. Holding tight to the trunk, I lowered myself to the limb and sat, tucking my face into the crook of my right arm, away from the force of the rain. I closed my eyes, thinking I would rest a little, best as I could. I refused to cry over what I didn't know, but the raindrops made up for it, as I sat shivering among the branches, waiting on the day to come and a new hell to begin.

* * *

I moved one more time for reasons I can only describe as panic that come more from the noises below me than anything I'd seen. The wind remained relentless, and I was in a precarious position, with the tree swaying like it was. As much as I kept my head buried, I was actually more exposed than ever and after such a long time in the elements I was wearing down, consumed with an aching chill, and hands so wrinkled and pruned, they'd gone to the point of hardness. I kept shifting, from sitting to standing and back to sitting to keep my feet from going numb, while watching the churning, muddy river beneath me. Eventually, I quit looking down. Wouldn't do no good no ways.

Midmorning the rain and wind let up and like some distant, long lost relative, the sun found a hole in the fast-moving clouds and peeked through. With better weather, I could see the extent of my dilemma. I first gazed down the length of the trunk. It was amazing in of itself, how the tree had held its ground with the water rising halfway to where I stood. Papa would've said I'd picked a "good'un." I pushed the memory away and looked out beyond the dripping branches, first one way and then the other. I had no idea where I was. Off to the west was a clearing, and I thought it could've been the road we'd been on, except now it looked like the rest of the river, as if it had grown in width by hundreds of feet. What else was alarming was the destruction, everything had been taken, like swiping a dishrag across a dirty table.

Seeing the devastation took the air straight out of my lungs and I gripped the trunk hard, feeling a blister break. My hands, truly, was only a minor hindrance. What was more disturbing was wondering where all this water would go, and how long it would take. I dropped my gaze from the destruction of the land and instead I anxiously waited to see what the river brought. It was a never-ending line of dead farm animals, blow flies already buzzing above their poor, swollen carcasses. Various parts of property, even a bicycle, drifted by. My mind stayed with Papa, Momma, Laci, and Seph, worrying about what had become of them. Soon, I couldn't look no more, and I studied my palms. Two large, red-looking blisters sat in the center of each, looking like bull's-eyes. I carefully reached for the hem of my dress. With apologies to Momma and all her hard work, I worked at the stitching until it come loose and tore a strip off. I tied a piece around my right hand. Then I tore another section, and fashioned a similar bandage for my left.

It was a long and strangely hot afternoon. My dress dried out, and I hung my damaged coat on the end of a branch. I was actually warm for a change, but that soon turned to a damp sweat, and my mouth felt sticky and tasted like old rags. With twilight, I thought I would welcome the shade and cooler air. I should have known better. With it come different afflictions, different levels of what a body could conceive as worse than what it had already been through. Without regard for my misery, a variety of bugs swarmed, bit, and tormented any part of my exposed skin. I swatted at them, and did my best to slap at my legs without falling. Bats appeared and flew, swooping in and out of the trees to eat the bugs, close enough to my head they brung a wisp of cool air as they went by. Night fell, and screech owls shrieked.

An unidentifiable huffing sort of noise rose somewhere off to my left. It sounded as if it come from a tree about a hundred feet from me. Wildcat, I thought. Something making that noise had to have teeth. Did it know I was sitting here, almost beside it? Could it scent me? Once the water was gone, would it skulk about, waiting for me to leave? I detected a faint stink on the night air, a distinct smell of rot wafting up, reaching me even this high. And with the odor of the dead, another memory of a man I'd heard about from time to time crept its way into my weary mind, dislodging concerns about a wildcat and anything else in that moment.

I realized what would be worse than anything in that moment would be dying like Coy Skinner.

Chapter 4

Coy Skinner's ghost sat with me through the night like a heckling haint. Trying not to think about him was like being able to ignore the facts of where I was and why. I kept telling myself he'd been really old, and I was young. He'd been weak, whereas I was sturdy. His death, one of many in that 1916 flood, was legend round Jackson County only because it had been so peculiar. Momma had talked about it, and her account had worked its way right into my head the way a worm works into a tomato or an apple. Lemuel Dodd, a neighbor of his, found him dangling amongst the branches of a sourwood tree he'd climbed to get out of the water, five miles from his shack on Pistol Creek. He'd waited and waited, growing too weak and feeble to get back down. Remembering Coy Skinner's demise only made my unease about my own circumstances worse.

I got thirstier and thirstier. I was hungry, and my empty stomach made my head pound like I was banging it against the tree trunk. The second day come, and the sun now shone bright and hard, and again I welcomed it. About midmorning it irritated me when I went right back to sweating. I was in the shade for the most part, but the temperatures climbed, and with the unseasonable heat come humidity from all the water. The bugs arrived and stayed. Gnats, skeeters, biting flies, the lot of them swarmed like I'd been put out as a feast. No amount of swatting or slapping kept them away. I went to swinging my head like I was saying "no," whipping my hair back and forth in an attempt to keep them off my face. Sort a like a horse's tail, only that made me dizzy. That was when I discovered I'd lost my coat. I was so busy fighting the bugs, I'd not realized it was no longer where I'd hung it. Staring down the length of the tree, I seen nothing. I felt nothing. I felt empty.

By the third day, I seen snakes, or thought I did. When I closed my eyes and opened them again, it was only a couple broken limbs waving around. If I tried to concentrate looking at something too long, funny spots danced about in front of my eyes and I swatted at them, thinking they was gnats. I spent a lot of time transferring my weight from one foot to the other, relying on the foot with the shoe most of the time. When that leg felt weak, and began to shake, I switched off a little while.

I thought I heard somebody hollering for me, "Wallis Ann! Wallis Ann!"

I got so excited I waved my hand around, thinking to bring attention to my location.

I yelled, "Here! I'm here! In this tree!"

I suspected it was only my mind fooling me again, for the voices never replied and nobody ever come. In the late afternoon, I again studied what was below, and seeing the water much lower than before, my agitation intensified. I scratched at my dirty head, pondering my decision. Should I take a chance? I stepped down onto the next branch, and then I went a little lower and once I got going, I couldn't stop. I wanted out of this tree. Down I went, limb by limb, like a spider, like the spirit of Coy Skinner was chasing me. I made it to where I'd climbed the first morning remembering the relief I'd felt as I went up instead of down. I stopped, and lay on my belly again, considering my choices, the fear of staying or for what I might encounter once down on the ground.

From the branch I rested on, I gazed about, noticing how the muddy water hadn't yet receded enough to follow the road. I'd have to cut my own path through unknown areas. I might get lost. Rain might come again and maybe I'd end up stuck in another tree, no better off than now. Likely worse. I rationalized on the other hand I could pick berries or wild grapes to eat, whereas if I stayed, there was no way to find food or water. No way to lie down and truly rest. Besides, eventually I might find other people, even if I didn't find my own family right off. I concluded my chances to survive increased on the ground, not in a tree.

I braced myself to hang by my hands, which had been throbbing for the past day. I planted them and prepared to swing down, the pain shooting across my palms as my body committed itself ahead of my brain. Gritting my teeth, I hung for a second, and then let go. I almost laughed after I landed, only up to my calves in water and mud. I pulled my feet free and took the one shoe I had off. I tied the shoelaces together and stuffed my muddy socks inside. Though one shoe won't going to do me much good, I hung on to it, unable to bring myself to leave it behind. It was all I had and I aimed to keep it. Without thinking about where I was going, I started walking, stretching my legs as far as they could go. The ground squelched, and the beginning started off as more sinking and slipping.

Everything was coated under a layer of dark muck, while a musty stench rose, making me think, *Swamp water must smell like this*. I tried to stay on dry ground, only there won't much of it. I sloshed and slurped along, realizing walking won't so bad because the ground in a lot of areas was soft beneath my feet. There was parts where it got difficult, requiring that I crawl over tree trunks, and times when I had to step on sticks and brushwood the river had collected and dumped along the way. Broken white pines, red spruce and hemlocks littered the path, and sedge grasses, once tall and green, lay flat like a giant hand had mashed them down. The river had sliced through the land like a scythe through hay.

The sun shimmered overhead, and soon I was sweating again. I kept hoping I'd see someone. I went up a hill, and seen a split rail fence with a pasture beyond, and unbelievably a couple cows grazing near a collapsed tobacco barn. I stopped to watch them for a bit, feeling better at seeing something so normal. I went on after a while, and soon come to a tiny cabin set against a hill, leaning so far over, I couldn't picture how it still stood. In the yard littered with rubble and fragments of what I perceived to be her things was a woman with frizzy, gray hair, knotted in a loose bun. The hem of her housedress was tinged with mud, and like me, she was soaked through with sweat. She was bent at the waist, studying on a black lump of something.

I hurried over and when I got within ten feet, I stopped. She still hadn't seen me, so intent was she on the object in front of her. She was talking to it, or herself, while brushing a hand back and forth across the dark thing. I stood quiet until she looked over and seen me standing there.

She pointed behind me and said, "You alone?"

"Yes, ma'am, my family had an accident 'bout three days ago. We was piled up in my papa's truck and everybody got throwed into the river. I climbed a tree and stayed till it was safe to come down, and now I'm looking for the rest of 'em."

"I hate to say it, I ain't seen a soul go by here in days."

Disappointed, my voice rose in distress. "You ain't seen no-body?"

She stared down at the ground. "I'm sorry. No."

I closed my eyes. I shouldn't have got my hopes so high.

I said, "I've not looked too long yet. I'm bound to find them if I keep on."

She said, "Yes, it would seem the thing to do. It's bad all over, I reckon."

She'd went back to petting at the dark thing on the ground, talking to me in a sad voice. "This here's only family I had left. My husband, Silas, he went on to the Lord 'bout two years ago. Some folks would say it's crazy to call this cat family. 'Cept, Silas got her for me when she won't but a bitty thing. Had her going on twelve years, and now she's gone too."

I would a never known it was a black cat by looking at it. I shivered in the heat, and rubbed at my neck.

I said, "I'm real sorry for your loss, ma'am."

She gazed at me, the crinkles around her eyes filling in and overflowing not unlike the waterways round here.

She said, "Ah. Well. She *was* old. Getting on up there. Like me." She pointed her cane at the stone foundation, and said, "That's what's left a my cabin. Water come down off a the hill-side, looked like a river too. I told Silas we should a moved to higher ground after last time. I had to crawl into my attic and pray it didn't come no higher."

I brushed the hair off my forehead, and said, "Was you in the '16 flood?"

"Sure was. Same thing happened then too. Lost part of our home. I had Silas then, and so we was able to rebuild. Don't know what I'll do now. Reckon I'll have to move in with my son and his wife down to Asheville. Can't hardly stand city life, but I got no choice this time around."

She spit out a stream of brown tobacco juice and moved away from the cat. She got to poking around, moving aside items, peering underneath trash, and I looked back the way I'd

come, about to tell her good-bye when she drew in a breath
and took notice of my distressed state.

She leaned forward, eyes scrunched, and said, "Child, you
look like you 'bout to pass out. Come on here with me."

She led me to a circular stone well in her backyard.

She grabbed the handle and began cranking it. "I reckon
it's safe. Water come up over and into it, so it could've gone
bad, 'cept I been drinking it for a few days and I ain't took up
sick yet."

After a few more turns a dented bucket appeared with a tin
dipper hung off the side. She plunged it into the bucket, then
waved me closer. I stared at dingy water, then closed my eyes and
drank. It won't the sweet water I was used to. Like our own well,
I was sure this one was spring fed and normally crystal clear, yet
despite the murkiness, it was the best water I'd drunk my entire
life. I handed the dipper to her and she filled it again and I
drank that one too. I wiped the back of my hand over my
mouth, and immediately began to feel better.

I said, "Thank you kindly. I've not had nothing to drink in
days."

She waved her hand and said, "Hope you ain't the sickly
sort."

I shook my head. "I ain't hardly ever took sick in my life.
Momma says us Stampers are a tough lot. I was so thirsty, I've
gone and forgot my manners. I'm Wallis Ann Stamper."

She said, "I'm Edna Stout, pleased to meet ya. You're part a
that singing family?"

"Yes, ma'am. That's right. Me, Momma, Papa, and my sister,
Laci. Seph's too young, but when he's older, I'm sure Papa'll
have him picking on a banjo, or something."

My voice faltered as I thought of them, and I went quiet.
Mrs. Stout turned her head away from me to spit another
stream of tobacco juice into the dirt.

She wiped her mouth and said, "It's going to be all right, child. Wait and see. They's likely looking for you like you're looking for them. Funny, I believe I seen you all last year at homecoming for Mount Pleasant. Enjoyed it immensely."

I appreciated her conversation, yet felt the need to get a move on. I smiled politely, nodded, then turned in the direction I'd come.

I said, "Thank you kindly. I best be getting on. Guess I'll keep my hopes up and keep looking. I don't know what else to do."

Mrs. Stout said, "Here. Take this walking stick since I got me another somewhere. And wait, I got some crackers I saved too. They's in a tin what was laying right over there, airtight, and all."

"I don't want to put you out none. You might need them for yourself."

"Aw, child, you're not putting me out a'tall. I'll make do. I got more, and I got water. I'm gonna sit tight. Someone in my family is liable to come by, and we'll start getting all this cleaned up, and it'll all be good as new, don't you know it."

"Well. I sure do appreciate it."

"Don't even think about it."

She offered me the small tin of crackers. She filled a jar she found in the grass with some of the murky well water. I wished I had something to give her in return, except she'd already turned her back on me after handing me the jar. I tucked the tin of crackers into the front of my dress, and when she didn't look at me again, I kept going. I glanced over my shoulder a little ways down the hill to see her standing over the dead cat again, her lips moving as she stroked the matted fur.

Chapter 5

After I left Mrs. Stout, I walked fast to make up time, only stopping long enough to eat a couple crackers. I worked the lid off, and inside was flat, uneven wafers, and I had the notion I ought to eat sparingly, and conserve. They was the kind you bought in them big barrels, like at Dewey's store, thin, still crispy and near bought as good as anything I'd ever had. I thought about how Momma would sometimes purchase a wedge of wax hoop cheese and a pound of rag bologna to go with crackers like this for Papa's lunch. The thought made my stomach growl. I opened the jar of water, swallowed more to feel fuller, then capped it and kept going.

I followed a soggy, litter-filled Highway 107, and as time went on, a smell I'd noticed got worse as the heat of the day took hold. It was hard to breathe when the fusty, rank odor of rotting weeds, souring wood, and distended, bloated animals filled your nose. I maneuvered around the mounds of uprooted trees, the roots exposed like huge, twisted snakes. I prodded at chickens and pigs, more than I could count, and what all else I couldn't tell you. I finally did see a few other folks along the way, their look of disbelief matching my own perfectly. I stopped and asked each and every one of them, Had they seen a man with a beard and blue eyes toting a small boy? Had they seen a woman with brown hair, brown eyes? Maybe with a girl who had red hair?

No.

No.

No.

This one man stood alone with his coonhound by his side. The dog's big old sad eyes stared at me as I come closer. Then he ignored me and looked to his master as if to ask, *Now what?* The man never acknowledged me at all, and so I went on by. He was too distraught by the site of his broken little cabin what looked like the least of winds could send it toppling. The dog paced, tail curved under his belly, sensing his owner's distress.

By the way the sun looked, I suspected a couple hours had gone by since I'd talked to Edna Stout. I come to a remote area with only the sound of a few birds here and there. I climbed and climbed, and then I'd stop and rest. After a particularly strenuous effort, I stopped, not to rest but because I heard the swishing of weeds. I looked behind me, and nothing was there. It had to have been my imagination, or my mind playing tricks on me. I started walking, using Mrs. Stout's stick to knock things out of my way. There. There it was again. I was certain I'd heard the distinct sound of someone following me.

I picked up my pace, moving along with a purposeful stride. After a ways, I made it look like I was searching for something on the ground. I poked at nothing with the walking stick and then sudden like, I turned and sure enough. A man stood only about twenty feet away. He had on nasty-looking coveralls, with no shirt. On his head sat a sweaty, leathery hat, and from the knees down, his legs was covered in mud like he'd been slogging through the same muck for some time. His hands was in his pockets. One eye tended to wander off.

I narrowed mine, and pointed at him with the stick. "You following me?"

He give me the same look I'd given him, squinting his eyes tight in suspicion and working what looked like a small twig to the corner of his mouth. He grinned suddenly, revealing a set of black, rotten teeth. His appearance was ragged, but that won't saying much considering how I must look to him. He didn't answer my question.

He ignored it and said, "I seen you come out of the tree back a ways. Wondered when you would come on down. I beat you by a day."

Maybe the noises I'd heard, the curious breathing I'd taken to be something wild, the huffing sound, had been him nearby. The thought run goose bumps down my spine.

I waved the stick at him again. "Stop following me."

He inched closer.

"I'm only trying to be friendly. From the looks of it, you might need you some help. I'm thinking we ought to pair up. Help each other out."

I moved away, and said, "Thank you kindly. I don't need help."

"How old is you?"

"Ain't none a your business."

"You look like you about, what . . . sixteen?"

I didn't answer. He inched his way closer while I moved backwards.

He made a cooing sound, like a dove. "You got you a boyfriend? Hey, whyn't you let me see what all you got. Ain't nobody around, jes me and you. Come on, sugar britches, let's see what all you got under yer dress. You look like you got some titties. Hooey! I bet you ain't even sullied. You let me see, and I'll give you somethin' that's real good. Deal?"

The urge to look behind me, to see where I was going, was strong, only I was nervous about taking my eyes off of him. My stomach tightened as this went on another few seconds, him advancing, me retreating, clutching my water jar and Edna Stout's walking stick like it was a sword. Eventually, I had to give a quick glance over my shoulder. There was only the woods. I felt a stab of fear when I faced forward again to see he'd moved even closer, stepping light as a bird, silent as a snake. I jabbed the stick at him and he stepped back. He scowled and got bold, regaining the step.

He spit off to the side, and said, "Hey, girly. Look'ee here. Look'ee what I got fer ya. All yours if'n you want it. Jest a little peek is all I'm a wantin'."

He'd dropped his hands down in front of his coveralls. I kept my eyes on his face, troubled by what he might have in his hands. I knowed what male parts looked like, and though I'd never seen a growed man's, I preferred to choose when I would. He made sucking noises like he was calling a cat.

I yelled, "Stop! You stay right there or you'll wish you had!"

My arm was strong cause I'd cut many a cord of wood, and I sliced the air in front of him with the walking stick, and the movement made my dress ride up my legs. His eyes widened like he was imagining things he ought to not be thinking about. The whistling noise of the stick give him cause to draw back. His lips pursed like he was about to set off whistling. He hesitated, and muttered something under his breath while I watched him carefully. He opened his hands and the motion pulled my eyes down, and I caught my breath.

He held two chicken eggs.

My mouth dropped open. I'd been so scared, him talking nasty like he was, and he only held eggs? This was surely the most puzzling encounter I'd ever had in my entire life.

Unexpectedly, a new voice called out, "Hey? Hey you, miss! You all right?"

I turned to see a younger man, hand shading his eyes, and the other holding a shovel over his shoulder. This was getting a might complicated. Two men and me. What now? Was they in cahoots? The younger man didn't move, waiting on me to answer.

Holding his gaze, I gestured and said, "This man here was . . ."

I looked over my shoulder meaning to confront the stranger again, only he was gone, vanished as if he'd never been. I stared right and left. The young man made his way down the hill to stand by my side, and I was sure my face conveyed my confusion.

I spoke, doubt in my voice. "He was right here. I seen him. He acted odd, said things. He had a couple eggs. I reckon he was going to give them to me."

The younger man said, "Yeah, you don't want to mess with him or his eggs."

"You know him?"

He said, "That was Leland Tew. He ain't right, a little tetched in the head. You could blame it on him being drunk most of the time off a moonshine, except most anyone knows him knows he gets these crazy spells. Good days. Bad days. He lives in an old hunting shack over that a way."

I shivered and looked over my shoulder again.

While I continued to survey the woods, expecting Leland Tew to pop out again, the new acquaintance said, "My name's Joe Calhoun."

I quit looking for Tew and replied, "Nice to meet you. I'm Wallis Ann Stamper."

There was an awkward few seconds of quiet, and in that short bit of time I picked up an air of misery, his shoulders rounded under the weight of a sorrow so tangible, I thought if

I touched him I would feel his pain shooting into me, merging his grief with my own.

He said, "Pleased to meet you. Like I said, I heard yelling and come to see what was going on. If it's all right, I got to get on back to my place," and he pointed at a hill. "It's that a way, not too far."

I was certain that was the source of his unhappiness because his hand shook when he pointed. He lowered it quick, as if it had embarrassed him.

He said, "You're welcome to follow me and refill your water jar. I got cleaner water than that."

He gestured at the half-empty jar I held. I hesitated. I was a bit uneasy after what just took place, but the idea of fresh water was tempting. He didn't wait for me to make up my mind, heading off in the direction he'd pointed out, and after a few seconds I followed. We took a crooked trail and there won't any more talking. A log cabin come into view within a few minutes, and like many others I'd seen, it was damaged badly. In this case, a huge pine tree lay over one end, and a mule, with a length of chain hitched to the animal's harness, stood waiting. Nearby squatted a small boy by the pine tree lying partially on the cabin. He stood when he seen us, dropping the other end of the chain he'd held, his face red from crying. They'd been working on moving the tree, and considering the pile of limbs and logs they'd cut off it and gathered, they'd been at it steady.

Joe Calhoun wiped sweat from his brow while the boy pushed his straw hat up on his head, staring at me like he couldn't put together where I'd come from. I set the walking stick and jar down. The boy looked as if he was thinking about running to hide. He was barefoot too, wearing only a ragged pair of coveralls that looked like they was about to fall off him. Streaks of wet cleared two rows down his dirt-covered cheeks.

Joe Calhoun hesitated, then said, "Where's your family?"

"I'm from over to Stampers Creek. We got separated during the flood. My papa is William Stamper, and Momma is Ann Wallis Stamper."

Joe Calhoun watched me as I took the end of the chain the boy had been holding in my hands and started towards the broken end of the pine.

"What're you doing?"

"Helping out."

"It ain't necessary."

"I aim to work for that water you're gonna give me."

Joe cocked his head and looked surprised, then said, "Suit yourself. Think I heard a y'all. You're part of that singing family what goes around the county, The Stampers, ain't you?"

"Yes. That's my family. I'm looking for 'em."

He scratched at his arm, and said, "I'm sorry."

Anything else I might have offered sat in my throat heavy as the biggest stones in the river, and thankfully he motioned towards the section of cabin under the tree and stated the obvious.

"When the storm come, that old tree come down."

He looked like he didn't know exactly what had happened or how things got the way they was now.

I said, "Is it only you and your boy?"

He shrugged uncomfortably, his words choked off like mine. I looked at what appeared to be a jumbled pile of cut and scraped logs under the tree, just a heap of rubble really. Some fluttery kind of material like curtains, maybe a tablecloth rippled and danced between the mangled wood. I was about to turn to him when I noted something what didn't belong. When it clicked what I was looking at, it felt like somebody had all of the sudden dropped me from a great height. My stomach bottomed out as I stared at the foot, turned all blue and purplish, like a beet. The fluttering material was a dress. I stumbled backwards, my mouth opening and closing only no words coming out. They was crammed so far down into my throat, I couldn't bring them up. I stared at Joe Calhoun, disbelief and alarm apparent on my face. He wore a rather stoic look while I processed what I seen while the boy made a noise, gulping in sobs. Joe Calhoun pulled a handkerchief from a pocket and give it to the boy.

He motioned towards the foot, his words tumbled one over the other in a hushed tone. "We tried to git her out all day yesterday. Her and the little one she'd held. That's my wife, Sally, and our little Josie, who won't but two years old."

I found my voice, and I said, "How horrible. I'm so sorry."

He moved closer to the distorted, swollen foot and stared at the flapping material. I was half nervous he was going to touch it. Flies landed all around and on it too. He flapped his hand to shoo them off.

He said in a voice flat, broken sounding with disbelief, "Course, it come on us so quick. And when it was all said and done, I realized she was gone. I tried with my bare hands, at first, and of course, nothing won't budge. I finally found our mule upstream just today, and I was hoping maybe with him we can get her out." He looked my way and said, "No need for you to stay and see this. Let me get your water, and you can be on your way."

"No. I mean, I'd like some water, but what do you need me to do?"

Joe Calhoun stared at my hands, and I clenched them to hide the blisters. He seemed to assess the potential strength of my arms.

I guess I didn't look as puny as I felt, because he said, "If you don't mind, go and give young Lyle a hand there."

I walked over to the boy, a miniature of his papa. He refused to meet my gaze.

He was too young to be wearing the look he had, and I whispered, "I'm real, real sorry."

He didn't respond. He only wiped at his eyes quick, and then he and I worked together to wrap the chain around and around the end, while he hooked his end to the mule's harness. Soon, it was all set, and he took the reins in his hands and stood directly behind the mule like he was going to plow.

He said, "Heeya!" and slapped them. The mule leaned into his harness willingly. I didn't want to see what might be happening behind me, so I focused on him and so did Lyle. Joe Calhoun guided the mule to the right, then to the left, and with some momentum, the mule got his feet under him good and after a few more seconds of steady pulling, we heard a heavy thump.

He yelled, "Whoa!"

I still didn't turn around. He patted the mule on the shoulder, and from that vantage point he slowly glanced where the section of the tree had rested. When he crumpled to his knees, I didn't know what all to do. I was scared of this kind of a death. I didn't want to look. I'd never seen such awful things, and won't sure I wanted to now. Compared to this, Coy Skinner's story was like listening to a radio. Same thing with the awful tragedies Papa talked about at his job. Trees not going where the workers intended; equipment malfunctions; people losing digits, limbs, or lives. Seeing it right in front of you is different altogether. Joe Calhoun motioned to Lyle to come to him. I stared intently at my dirty, mosquito-bitten arms and the scratches on my legs. The boy thundered past me into his papa's arms. I looked away as the two of them hugged, the boy starting to sob again. I give the sky my attention, and wondered why such hardships was delivered to such good people. Momma always said, *The Lord works in mysterious ways.*

I didn't want to think about if they'd suffered something long and enduring. I dropped my gaze from the sky to stare at the undamaged side of the cabin, and then slowly let my eyes slide towards the crushed end, skimming over Mrs. Calhoun's foot, then, going a little higher still. She had her hands clasped together and held off to her side and around a clump of different material altogether. It weighed heavy on my heart when I seen them tiny arms and legs, and I had to blink, and then I leaned forward. I thought I'd seen movement. I squinted. Lordy, them little legs *was* moving. I drew in a sharp breath and started running towards Mrs. Calhoun and the little girl named Josie.

Joe Calhoun shouted, "Ain't no use! They's gone!"

I kept running, seeing how the small, curly blond head turned this way and that, while her small arms pushed until suddenly she was sitting up, moving away from the protection of her momma's side. The little girl, her hair a wild array of spun gold, started to wail. Footsteps thudded behind me. Mrs. Calhoun was surely gone, the nasty blow to her head visible, yet her face remained beautiful, and so was the child's cry. I clambered over crushed wood to reach her, and lifted her out and away from the ruin. She clung to my dress, shaking, covered in dirt, leaves, and dried blood. She stunk to high heaven, having soiled herself time and again.

Holding her carefully, I stepped over the twisted pile of logs, slipping a little from the mud on them. Joe Calhoun reached for her, and Josie for him. Lyle, hypnotized by the sight of his little sister, stood several feet from us, his red-rimmed eyes wide and blinking. Recovering after a few seconds, he approached and stared at his baby sister, a dusty hand rubbing her bruised leg. It was startling how the child had survived, protected by her momma's body, tucked in a little divot, out of the way of the weight that could have crushed her. Such a miraculous thing, yet sad at the same time.

"I can't hardly believe it," I said.

Joe Calhoun buried his face in the tangle of his daughter's hair. She was quiet now, her head lying on his shoulder.

He spoke with a shaky voice. "A blessed miracle."

My thoughts only moments before retrieved a similar word. "It sure is."

I felt a great need, a tremendous wanting for an outcome like this for my own self and my family.

I said, "I'm happy I stayed, but I best be on my way now." I gestured at the mangled wreckage of his home, the distressing view of his wife's body, "I'm real sorry about Mrs. Calhoun, and your home."

Joe Calhoun asked me, "What will you do?"

Staring back the way I'd come, I replied, "I'll keep looking," my hand gesturing in the direction I'd walked. "They may be waiting on me at our place, that is, if it's still there. Either way, I'll wait for'em if they ain't."

Joe Calhoun said, "You happen to know the Powells, who live just beyond Stampers Creek?"

His question startled me, but I said, "Yes, that's them folks over to the next holler."

Joe Calhoun said, "You see'em, tell'em, all's well except for Sally. And if anybody comes by here lookin', I'll be sure to tell'em I seen you, and where you was headed."

"Thank you kindly."

I waved at them and began to retrace my earlier steps, looking over my shoulder only once before I got out of sight. Joe Calhoun watched with little Josie's head on his shoulder and Lyle beside him. The last I seen of them, they was going towards Mrs. Calhoun. I faced forward and trudged on. It took me only a short while to get where I'd stopped to address the problem of Leland Tew, and as I walked along, I ruminated on Joe Calhoun. I couldn't quit thinking about what happened, and what a stunning turn of events it had been to find his little girl alive. The idea he was familiar with the Powells won't all that surprising, but I couldn't help but wonder how come we'd never met before.

Within the hour, I was wishing I'd remembered to get the

water he'd offered. Passing the grossly swollen Mill Creek, I come to the stretch that would take me home to Stampers Creek, and knowing I was so close set me to singing to cut through the quiet, and to keep myself company. The afternoon sun sat plump and full, and I was glad I'd get there before dark. I stopped to rest, preparing for the final push. I sat down on part of an uprooted oak tree and finished what was left of the water, yet still felt parched. I pulled the tin from my dress and ate two more crackers, hoping to stave off the light-headed dizziness I kept having, like I'd been spinning in circles. I shook the can lightly, peered into it and counted only six more crackers.

Sliding the lid in place, I stared at the broken, littered trail ahead and noticed how the ruts made from years of use was gone, smoothed over from the passing current and filled in with sediment and mud. To the west, in the hazy, bluish distance, Cullowhee Mountain met Cherry Gap as they had for maybe millions of years. The distant hills opposite cut a familiar jagged line across the blue sky, offering a view of deep valleys and crests that shifted from rich greens to black shadows, an ever-changing display created by the sun as the peaks punctured the clouds. I never tired of the view. I breathed in and out slowly, taking it in, and bracing myself for the rest of the walk home, and what I might find. I didn't sing no more the rest of the way.

Chapter 6

The dirt path to the cabin was blocked by a gigantic fallen oak. I recollected Papa telling me once it had been a sapling when my great-grandpa Stamper was a boy, and seeing it lying over on its side felt like part of our history had been taken. Momma had spoke of seeing coffins floating by in the flood of '16, and after seeing this huge tree torn up from its roots, I thought about our family graveyards, and wondered if anything had happened to them. Momma and Papa's people was buried only a short distance away, set apart in different areas as if the idea of burying Scottish and English together won't a consideration, even though Momma was Scottish, and had married Papa, who was English.

During winter when trees was barren, I could see both graveyards. They was set in right pretty places, each having old wrought-iron fences circling them. All but two of Papa's brothers was buried there. My uncle Seph, who little Seph was named for, and who died in WWI, was buried in Arlington National Cemetery, and Uncle Hardy, Papa's oldest brother who lived in Pine Mountain, South Carolina. I seen Uncle

Hardy all of twice in my lifetime, and Papa hardly ever talked about him. All of Momma's family was buried about a half mile away from Papa's family. There we set flowers on graves holding my grandparents, Momma's little sister who died as a baby, and a great-aunt and uncle.

I went on by the tree and turned my ear to the alder fly-catchers, sapsuckers, and various other birds crying out, chirping along the way as if telling me about their lives interrupted by the storm. I got to walking faster, my concern growing by the minute as I realized Stampers Creek had risen to the highest point ever. Seconds later I come to where our cabin should have been. I immediately dropped everything I carried on the ground. I stopped and stared at the stone foundation laid by Papa almost twenty years ago, the only thing left. My breath pumped in and out of me as I moved about the edges of the property. I thought of Momma and those last moments seeing her touching this and that as we was about to leave.

The barn still stood, although it won't going to last long from the look of it. I'd hoped maybe the chickens might be roosting in some of the trees, but there won't a squawk or the grunt of a hog to be heard. I whistled for Liberty and Pete. I got nothing from either of them, not a whicker or a bray. I went and sat on the foundation, realizing the day was near bout gone. With a wary eye towards the setting sun, my immediate necd was on having something to eat. Maybe the garden would have a remnant of a vegetable, a tomato, some beans, or maybe a melon.

I walked to the backside of where our cabin had been, to where the rows of vegetables once thrived, and found not even a spare shucky bean. The garden existed of a few stripped stalks what had somehow withstood the surge of water. Melons, once abundant, with vines growing as long as fifteen feet, had only two of the fruit left behind, but they'd split open and the pale, carroty flesh had gone yellow with rot, while a swarm of fruit flies fizzed about happily. The root cellar had been exposed to the flood, and a nasty-looking slurry reached the top step. I had the feeling the jars of the vegetables we'd canned had been broken, or was buried under it.

I swore to myself I'd find something. It was better to think like this, optimistically is what Papa would say. I continued exploring, looking for some part of our lives what had existed only days ago. While hunting for food I also looked for other possessions, like the wooden benches used at our kitchen table Papa made. The worktable. Momma's lovely bone china from Granny Wallis. It was eerie not finding even a fragment from our home intact, like it had all been imagined. It made me feel like I had when Leland Tew did his disappearing act, making it seem like he won't real. Other than the rock foundation, and the barn, all other traces of our presence here was gone.

I was pretty thirsty after all the rummaging around. I went back to the foundation wall again, my hands hanging between my knees, throbbing in time with my head. I shut my eyes, not wanting to see any more. I sat that way for I don't know how long, wondering should I leave. Only, there was something about being in this spot where I'd been born what made me want to stay, even though I had nothing to hold on to, nothing to gather and save. I thought of Joe Calhoun and his boy, and it come to me he'd likely rather have his wife alive than any of the possessions they'd salvaged. I straightened my back at that thought. Papa always said if you go round with your head down, it's hard to be mindful of what you got, and you might overlook something important.

It was growing cooler as the sun dropped behind the ridges. It would be nighttime soon. I started looking around again, and having had a bit of time for things to sink in, I regarded the scenery with a degree of calm. I went to a different area I hadn't searched and spotted something after a few minutes of poking around near the woods. There was some shapes what didn't match the natural lay of the land. I hurried over, and found, of all things, Momma's stove, covered in mud, setting on one end, and banged up, an unbelievable find. I yanked the door open and inside was the small kettle and skillet. Behind them was the familiar coffeepot what usually sat on a burner in the mornings. I retrieved these and took them over to the foundation. I was almost giddy with a happiness I couldn't explain.

The other shape was an even more remarkable find. It was Granny Wallis's pie safe, caught between two tree trunks, and still, somehow, held in an upright position. I nudged the small latch and opened it. Unbelievably, inside was what was left of the birthday cake Momma had baked the day of the storm. My stomach rumbled, and I took it out and inspected it. It was flattened and soggy, yet still it smelled all right. Hunger won out. I swiped a finger through the frosting and tasted it. It tasted off, but more like chocolate than anything. Using the tips of my dirty fingers to scoop mouthful after mouthful, I crammed the wet, pasty cake into my mouth. I closed my eyes and thought about nothing else except eating. I finally come to my senses and stopped, took a deep breath and let it out slow.

Already I felt better, more clearheaded and even had some energy. I set the remains of the cake back inside and nudged the little door closed again. The gnawing hole of hunger filled, I looked at the property with fresh eyes. I tried to feature what Momma would do since nothing hardly ever ruffled her. While sitting in the tree, I'd felt sort of protected, uncomfortable, but protected. Here, on the ground, and surrounded by woods, the unusual quiet filled me with apprehension. The shift from day to night would leave me exposed to whatever might ramble by, be it two-legged or four-legged. There could be bear, or bobcat, or wolf as desperate as me for food. The last thing I wanted to do was sit up all night, my back to a tree and vulnerable.

I was going to need some sort of shelter. There was enough branches, limbs, and other foliage on the ground I could use, some of it dry even. I grabbed the walking stick and began looking more carefully for what I could use. I spotted one particular clump set higher than others. I poked at it with the stick, and it made a hollow sound. I bent over and dug through all the wet leaves and branches and uncovered the bucket from our well, rope still attached. Encouraged, I kept on, all too aware the faster I went, the faster it seemed the sun went down.

As I continued gathering what I needed, I looked east, towards the Powell farm. Maybe once I'd done what I could around here, I'd go over there, check to see if anyone was about. I recollected there was a few pecan trees between here and there, and it was time for wild grapes to be in season too. I dragged armful after armful of loose limbs close to the foundation, then paused to catch my breath, noticing how heavy the air was around me. Sweating profusely, I wiped my forehead and pushed on. Back and forth I went, into the woods again and again, a little further each time. After a couple more trips, I was surprised to find what looked like a section of one of the inside walls to our cabin, the fragments of newspapers and magazines still tacked onto the wood, the way we'd kept heat or coolness in. All this gathering had led me to exactly what I needed. I grabbed one edge, and winced as pain shot through my hands, but after gripping it tight for a few seconds I was able to haul it into the yard. I placed one end against the foundation and peered underneath. This would do and saved time. I sifted through the pile I'd collected, feeling like I could be choosy selecting branches with the most pine needles, or leaves.

I proceeded to fashion myself a bed under the lean-to, piling it thick, and then I wished for a fire. Papa had told stories about living out in these woods when he was a boy, using what he had on hand. I was glad I'd paid attention. He gone into the woods one time for three days when he won't but eleven, with only a slingshot, the clothes he wore, and nothing else. He'd made a fire out of the rotted inside of a tree from what is called punk wood. There was always downed trees in the woods, the ones what fell over from decay. And along Stampers Creek there might be some quartz rocks, what he'd said was best for creating a spark. I decided I would search for those things tomorrow.

I surveyed my makeshift camp, and felt as ready for the night as I could be. I brung everything I'd found, along with the tin of crackers, the walking stick, the jar and my one sorry shoe, setting it all nearby where I could keep an eye on things. I opened the tin and, with apologies to my family, I ate the last of the crackers. While I munched, I let my eyes get used to the gloomy surroundings. The dark don't never seem as bad once you get acclimated. With my bones heavy as the waterlogged timber I'd moved, I finally crawled under my lean-to like a cur dog slinking under a porch. I swatted at the mosquitoes, and listened to a few frogs croak. They was likely the only ones happy.

I let the images of Momma's and Papa's faces come to mind, then I did the same for Laci and Seph, featuring them like pictures in a frame. I wondered what Joe Calhoun, Lyle, and Josie was doing. Was they sleeping under the stars too? I studied the night sky, watching the moon slink across it. Some buried fear within allowed me only a brief nod of dozing here and there, until I eventually gave up on sleep. I turned onto my belly and propped my chin on my arms while staring out into the still night, feet pressed against the stones, which somehow still felt warm from the sun.

I said, "Go to sleep, Wallis Ann."

It sounded peculiar, the sound of my voice speaking my name and no one to hear. It was a little unnerving. I remained on my belly for a long time, half asleep, half awake. As was bound to happen, the urge to use the privy come on me. Since our outhouse was gone along with everything else, I was going to have to do my business like I'd been doing on my walk home. Out in the open. Even with the yard lit by the moon, and nothing around best as I could tell, I had the oddest sense of being watched. Crazy Leland Tew and his egg offering come to mind. That won't helpful. What if he'd somehow followed me here? What if he was right there in them dusky woods, watching me?

The very idea made me stay put until I could no longer hold it. When it got to be a must, I crawled out carefully, and stood in the moonlight, still as a night owl. I moved away from the lean-to, but not so far I couldn't see it. I dug myself a little hole in the dirt. I looked over my shoulder. My belly burned with urgency. Hesitant, I reached under my dress and pulled down my drawers. I waited again, then, with the notion it was now or never, I went on and got myself situated above my little dip in the ground.

I was in the middle of it all, and starting to feel some relief, when a huffing noise come from directly behind me. If I hadn't already been doing what I was doing, it would have come on like I was a bitty baby with no control. I remained crouched as the huffing come closer, and closer yet. The odor of my pee rose, and I was petrified whatever animal stalked me would smell it and fear too. I had a stench about me, in general after being in the river, along with several days of sweating. Grime covered me from the top of my dirty, greasy head to my filthy feet. Maybe I stunk too badly for whatever it was. And whatever it was, was taking its sweet time. I closed my eyes and tried not to move, which was asking a lot.

My thigh muscles trembled and ached. My ears went to buzzing with the effort to hear and track the movements. I thought it drifted to my left. Or was it to my right? Worst of all, I felt sure no matter what direction it went, left or right, it was closer. Goose pimples speckled my arms and neck. A twig snapped right behind me, and I went to praying.

Lord, dear Jesus, God, don't let me get eat up by whatever this is.

It didn't seem possible after all this time and what I'd been through I was about to be mauled by some wild animal. Another noise, and then I smelled its raunchy breath, so close it brushed over the back of my neck. I wanted to vomit. As hard as I tried to be still, I quivered and shook, and a cold shiver of dread raced up and down my spine at will. I tensed, waiting for a horrific roar, anticipating the first painful bite on my shoulder, neck, or wherever it chose to chomp down on. All I could think was wildcat. Or wolves. They hunted at night. My whole body ached with the need to take a lungful of air, and my mouth opened, prepared to match the scream of whatever was about to attack me and rip my skin to shreds.

On the verge of blacking out from fear, and when I was about to shriek from sheer terror, the softest of touches whispered over my shoulder, and then a velvety nose snuffled my hair. Next come a hard bump against my hip, the stomp of a foot, and I dared look over my shoulder at the long, graying snout of our mule, Pete. Like the brush of a cool breeze on a hot summer's day, relief flooded over me and I almost collapsed on the ground. Meanwhile, that old cantankerous mule moseyed on over to the barn, waiting for somebody to let him into his stall like it was any old ordinary day, even though he couldn't fit through the door as it was leaning too much. If I hadn't already been so exhausted, and recovering from being scared out of my wits, I might have laughed, except I won't in a laughing mood. I stood, fixed my clothes, then I stumbled over to him on legs like jelly. I put my hand on his neck, rubbing down its length.

"Old Pete, you sorry old thing, you sure did give me a bad scare," I said.

Leaning my forehead against him, I scratched his ears and took some deep breaths. I went back over to my lean-to, eased myself underneath and finally fell asleep.

Chapter 7

The change in the air brushed my skin like polished, cool metal against exposed arms and legs. I wished for the old ragged coat of mine once again. My need for the fire escalated. Shivering, I stared down at my feet, noting my toes had a bluish tinge. I wrapped my arms around my waist real tight and considered I ought to move about in order to get my blood stirring, except it was hard to rouse any gumption for doing much when my mouth felt like the inside of an old rag and my belly was so empty it was gnawing at my backbone.

One way or the other, it was morning, and today I'd resolved to do two things. First take care of a fire. Second, work my way over to the Powells and check on them. I walked into the woods, using Mrs. Stout's walking stick to knock against felled trees. It won't long when the unique hollow sound rang out as I poked hard at the sides of a mountain gum. A section collapsed, and come apart, and inside was exactly what I needed. I broke the chalky pieces off, and then searched a bit of rocky area, happy when I come across some moss too. It was another good burning material. I collected as much as I could and then I went and dumped my fire-building material into a pile near a little stack of kindling wood. Next, I gathered pinecones for their resin.

What took me the longest was my search for rocks with quartz. Stampers Creek was still too high, and the rock beds was mostly hidden. I dug around close as I could get near the edges and finally give up, deciding instead to get two plain rocks and try them. I studied what I'd gathered, and strangely, I felt nervous, like I was about to stand in front of my class and read out loud. I was parched, and all I could think was, if I could do this, I'd be able to boil water. And if I could boil water, I could drink and drink and drink without fear of getting sick. And I'd be able to cook—if I could catch or kill something. I fixed the punk wood into a tiny pile. I got the kindling, and built a small teepee of the sticks, laying them this way and that. I had some dead pine needles too, and I fashioned a little bird-nest-looking bundle and added the moss. Finally, I lifted the two stones, and took a breath.

Papa's voice come to me, "Don't smother it. Start small."

I crouched down close to the punk wood and smacked the rocks together at an angle against one another, *click, clack, click!* I kept going in the same direction like Laci strumming the dulcimer. After a minute of knocking them stones together, a tiny spark hit the crumbly wood, and a fragile tendril of smoke curled like a tiny gray worm into the air. Excited, I carefully cupped one hand around the tiny glow and waved my other hand to encourage it along. When the miniature pile went to smoking a bit more, I carefully scooped the tiny smoldering bit and ever so carefully set it into my pine needle and moss nest. I leaned over and nursed the smidgen of a flame by pursing my lips and by blowing delicate puffs of air over it.

I was fearful any minute I'd blow too hard on the itty-bitty flare I had going and snuff it out before it had a chance to take hold. Small as it was, I persisted, and soon most of the pine

bundle was ablaze, and I hurried to set it into the small opening of kindling I'd collected. My tiny blaze caught onto the lit-
tlest of branches, and sputtered. I froze, willing it to life, like a
struggling newborn kitten. I felt the first bit of warmth coming off it soon after, and reached for the bigger sticks, slowly
building it until I was certain the blaze won't going out. My
little flame expanded to the size of a melon.

I'd done it. I had a fire.

I stared at it with pride, my sense of triumph immense. I
hurried to get Momma's kettle, and pulled it close. I added
even more wood, and soon it went from reasonable size to a
roaring blaze. I thought, *It can't get too big and I can't get close
enough, but I still got more to do.* I got the water bucket I'd found
and I headed straight towards Stampers Creek. I was careful to
steer clear of any nearby standing water, and only filled it from
areas where it flowed swiftly. I come back and dumped the
water into the kettle. After it boiled and cooled, I was going to
fill that jar to the rim, and I was going to drink it down, and fill
it again. I felt right proud of myself and I believe I might have
even smiled a little bit right then. I patiently waited, and when
I was sure it had boiled long enough, I poured some into the
jar and set it aside to cool. I stacked more wood onto the fire
and watched it burn a little longer.

Gazing towards the sky, I decided if I was going over to the
Powells, I ought to do it now. It wouldn't take long to get there
and the water needed to cool anyway. I set off at a good pace,
following the trail. I'd only been there a time or two, but after
several minutes, I come to the wood fence that separated our
cow pastures. I took a second to admire the fall colors tipping
the uppermost part of Cullowhee and then I went over the
fence and down into the holler. There I had to climb over
fallen trees until I come to another field of flattened fodder.
There won't no livestock to come eat it, or signs of anyone
who would bundle it for use later. I was on the Powell prop-

erty now, and I kept on, looking over my shoulder now and then to be sure Cullowhee Mountain and Cherry Gap was behind me, which meant I was going in the right direction.

After a few minutes I come to another clearing for their place where I found the circular rocks for their well, some strewed planks of wood, maybe from the cabin's porch, and a tall post, with a bell hanging crooked. That was all.

"Helloooo?"

I walked over to the well, searching the ground for a rock or something to drop into it. I found a small stone and tossed it in. It clattered down and I heard a splash within seconds. I poked my head in and jerked it out, gagging. Something had got in there and died. The Powells had experienced the same fate as us. Their home was gone, their well contaminated, and there was no way to know how they'd fared. I needed some way to signal them to come to our place. I grabbed another rock. I went over to the wood post holding the dinner bell, and I scratched my initials, W.A.S., and the date, September 8, 1940. It was all I could do. I headed back, sad about what I'd seen and discovered.

When I got home, I rushed over to check on the fire and the water. The blaze was still going strong, and the water in the jar had cooled. I grabbed the hem of my dress to wrap around the handle and dragged the kettle from the flame. Pete come moseying along from where he'd been feeding on some nearby timothy grass and red fescue. I was glad he could forage for his self, and I eyeballed him, filled with a new confidence about what all I could potentially do. I started planning a few things to keep myself busy, so I wouldn't think so hard on being alone. I lifted the jar and drank the water I'd boiled, filled with the sense I was going to be okay.

On my fourth morning I woke to overcast skies. Each day I'd began with a sense of anticipation. I was always convinced for the first few hours something good would happen, but, as morning passed into afternoon, and afternoon into nighttime, those expectations evaporated along with my hope. It helped to stick to a routine. Stoke the fire, add wood, boil water, plan the day. Today I was going to hunt through the barn. I'd waited for fear it would fall on me, but now I was tired of waiting. I entered it and familiar smells hit me right away, like the leather from harnesses, and the saddle we used to ride Liberty. The dry, sweet odor of hay, sawdust, and damp wood. After searching in the corners and behind a stall, I located Pete's work harness crumpled up into a corner, with a bit of mildew already growing on it. I picked it up and began to pull and stretch the damp leather. I walked outside where he was nipping daintily with his hairy mule lips at bits of timothy grass. Old Pete could be tricky, and I wondered if I ought to hide the harness from his sight. He lifted his head and his ears twitched at my approach, only it won't me or the harness he seemed interested in. He was looking towards the path, and then I heard what he did, a distant, soft singing.

I went still, my hand hanging midair, the straps of leather dangling. The wind what had whistled through the tops of the trees this morning had calmed, and it was so quiet, I wondered if my ears was doing that funny thing again, filling my head with noises that won't there. I tilted it to hear better. Maybe I was getting feverish. Could be hunger was causing my ears to ring. There it come again, louder this time, a recognizable song, and a singular voice, combined with the deeper one, as familiar as the ground beneath my feet. Us Baptist got this way of singing with a definitive expression of our words, like an insistence we be heard. We sing and chop our hands up and down and really get our insides into feeling the music. This was the singing I'd heard all my life. Momma's clear soprano, peppered with Papa's striking alto, their voices soaring as they drew closer.

I dropped the harness and sprinted towards the sound, paying no heed to the rocks jabbing my bruised, sore feet. I don't
reckon I really know who seen who first. It was like we all
seen each other at the same time, yet my mind wouldn't let me
believe what was in front of my very eyes. I stopped, my hand
over my mouth, and everything went blurry. There was
Momma. I couldn't move towards her, though I wanted to, and
behind her was Papa. And behind him was Laci, arms hanging
by her side, wide-eyed and silent. Momma and Papa, they
come running towards me and I still couldn't budge. I couldn't
trust my legs.

Momma hollered, "Wallis Ann! Wallis Ann!" and Papa, his
eyes steady on me like if he looked away, I'd be gone. I didn't
see what Laci done after that, cause my view of her was covered by Momma and Papa's bodies as they squished me into
the middle of them like a piece a meat between two slices of
bread. I felt their hands pressing down on me, from my shoulders to my head and to my shoulders as if they couldn't believe
I was for real. I was gripping hard onto them, breathing deep
the scent of their clothes, like rainwater and dirt, like trees and
wood smoke, like all the love and comfort I'd ever known, and
none of it, not none of it seemed real in them first few seconds.

Momma went from hollering to simply whispering my
name with a question in it like she was finding it hard to believe I was standing there in the flesh. "Wallis Ann? Wallis Ann?
Thank God, oh, sweet Jesus, praise the Lord." And then an as-
tounded, "You're alive?"

I couldn't say nothing, I was too choked up. I couldn't do a
thing except stand there stupefied, my head on Momma's
shoulder first, and then leaning into Papa's chest. Papa had hold
a both me and Momma, cinching us so tight with his muscu-
lar arms I thought my ribs might crack. After a minute or so,

we let go of each other and took a step back to look at dirty faces, scratched, tired and most of all happy. I felt a familiar, soft touch, my sister's hand burrowing into my tender palm like a small mouse come home to nest. I closed my fingers around the familiar, dainty bones, noting how her hand was clenched in a tight little fist. It was almost more than my heart could bear, this happiness, this relief to know they was here, and they won't dead, and we was all together again.

Except, where was Seph?

I hardly dared look, or ask for the one small person not present. I was fearful to speak his name, to ask the question I had in my head. Please. Not our little feller. A vision of his face come to mine as I searched Momma's for answers. The whites of hers was red and wet with tears, but untroubled. She and Papa had bluish circles underneath, like they hadn't slept in days, otherwise, what worry had been in them had been cleared away, like clouds burned off by the sun. Momma's expression was clear, giving me courage to ask about my little brother.

"And Seph?"

Her eyes spilled over, and she smiled slightly and shook her head no, like she wanted to rid herself of a painful memory. Her differing reactions provided me no answer.

My heart fluttered with fear, as fragile as a butterfly in late summer. "Momma?"

She heard the alarm in my voice.

She said, "Oh, honey, he's fine, he's with Mrs. Barnes over to Sugar Creek Holler." The rest of her words come out fast, all tangled together like a patch of briars.

"Your papa said after they fell out, he never let go of Seph. And poor Seph. He probably thought Papa was trying to drown him. He went under time and again, and Papa told me how he had to fight the river *and* Seph. He kept their heads clear for the most part, though Seph didn't make it easy. Papa said he screamed, and fought him like a little wildcat. Don't that sound like him? Your papa said he was fearless."

I wanted to know everyone's story, what they had done, and how they'd found one another.

"What about you and Laci?"

"It took some doing to get out of the water. I still can't explain how we both landed on a section of the embankment only about a hundred yards apart. That had to be God's hand. We walked about a half a day, and we found your Papa coming along with Seph riding high on his shoulders like he likes to do. I tell you it was a sight I never thought I'd see. Mrs. Barnes was on her front porch, and she offered to keep him while we searched for you. Finding you here, it's the answer to our final prayers."

Momma squeezed me again and rubbed my arms with her hands like she'd do when we was chilled to the bone. She shivered like me, and I noted their clothes was torn. Momma at least had her shoes, as did Papa. Laci's, like mine, was gone. The condition of her feet looked bad as my own. Red-toed, scratched, and bruised. And nobody had coats anymore. Papa waited for me and Momma to finish.

His eyes watching me carefully, he asked, "Wally Girl, how did you fare on your own?"

I didn't want to think about it, or have to live it all over again. I spoke quickly.

"The water carried me a ways too. I don't know how far. I was getting beat up and I figured I had to get out of the river. I somehow managed to snag hold of a branch and climb into a tree."

Papa give me a hard look, and he asked, "You climbed a tree?"

"Yes, sir."

"How long did you stay there?"

"Going on three days."

"Three days."

"Yes, sir."

"I bet you thought of old Coy Skinner too, didn't you?"

"I sure did, that's why I didn't stay in it any longer."

Papa laughed, though not with his usual easy-sounding chuckle, more like relieved.

He said, "And once you was able to come down, you made your way here by yourself."

"Yes, sir, once I figured out where I was."

Momma said, "See? I told you she was strong."

Papa said, "Did you see anyone you recognized?"

"You mean alive?"

He frowned and said, "You seen some not?"

"Yes, sir."

"Do you know who it was?"

"I can't be sure . . . I couldn't tell since I couldn't see his face. He went by me in the river. Facedown."

Momma said, "Oh, dear God."

I kept on because now I'd started, I wanted to tell them and be done. I told them about Edna Stout, and about the Calhouns, how I helped them, and how Mrs. Calhoun hadn't made it.

Papa's eyes squinted. "Calhoun?"

He frowned at me again, like the name Calhoun bothered him somehow, but all he said was, "Why, that's got to be at least twenty miles away."

I'd already figured it was pretty far since I'd walked it and it took me over a day, and it felt like it had been a good ways. I told them I'd gone to the Powells and things over there looked no better than here. No sign of anyone been home.

"I scratched my initials on the dinner bell post and dated it."

"You done good, Wally Girl. Real good. Look a here. You got a fire. Got boiling water. I'm proud of you."

Papa spun on his heels and looked at Momma, who was toasting her backside.

He said, "How about it, Ann? Our girl here'd, she'd put any man to shame, wouldn't she?"

Momma said, "Of course. She's a Wallis, after all."

It did me good to hear their old banter. Even better, it was good to hear Papa say the things he said. There won't ever any praise for what was expected, only when you done something startling. I decided to say nothing about Leland Tew. What would be the point? I had to tell them about Pete scaring me bad as he did, so I launched into that story. Right about then, here come Pete to check things out.

Papa was pleased, and he patted Pete from one end to the other while saying over and over, "This is good. We got ole Pete."

Papa got to walking around the property with Momma. I went along too, with Laci trailing behind me. Papa shot questions at me about what else I'd found, and I showed him and Momma both the stove and pie safe. I said nothing about the cake and nobody asked. I pointed to the skillet, and of course the water bucket back at the camp. They'd already seen the kettle with the water boiling, and the coffeepot. I explained I'd been about to harness Pete to start cleaning up some of the heavier stuff from the storm. Papa commended me again, and I felt a bright glowing heat warming my insides. Papa peeked into my little old lean-to, and he didn't say nothing, but his chest kind of expanded and it won't hard to tell he was proud of me all over again about how I'd done for myself and all. Momma give the property a once-over.

She said, "Everything we've worked so hard for."

Papa said, "We'll put things right, don't worry none."

I watched as she considered what was left, her face transforming from relief and happiness to an odd, flat expression, as if to hide her doubt.

She straightened, and said, "I reckon we'll have to start over from the beginning."

Papa walked back to the path, picked up a sackcloth I'd not seen, and handed it to Momma. He searched the edge of the woods and selected a flat piece of wood and set it on the foundation. Momma took items out of the sack and set them on the wood. There was a poke of grits, and a small container of coffee, a wedge of hoop cheese, some cornmeal, and last, she pulled out a box of matches. I smiled. No reason to knock stones together again, not for a while anyway.

Papa said, "Wallis Ann, I take it you didn't find nothing in the cellar?"

Without taking my eyes off what Momma had laid out, I replied, "No, sir. It's filled with mud and water. There's no way to tell what's in there, if it's busted, or what."

He looked across the way, towards the garden, and said, "I can see from here the garden is gone."

My eyes still on the food, I answered, "Yes, sir."

I pointed to the kettle, and said, "I'm pretty sure the well water's tainted. It looks like the water went high enough to go right over it."

Papa frowned, and said, "Damn. I's afraid of that."

Momma scolded. "William."

Papa give her a flabbergasted look.

With a raised eyebrow, and a sweep of his arm to include where our home once stood, he said, "Could say a lot worse, considering, Ann."

Momma said nothing further and only held out her hand, palm up. Papa handed her his pocket knife. He'd always kept it in an inside coverall pocket, so it too had survived the flood. In my eyes, having these few things meant a difference in how we'd survive. I watched every move Momma made, my mouth watering.

She said, "We'll have to be careful, not eat too much. We

need to conserve best as we can, cause this is what it'll be till it runs out, unless we find some things around here."

I asked Papa, "Will you be able to go back to work?"

He shook his head and looked away. I wish I could have said something else, something to make him smile instead of scowl.

He said, "Lumberyard's gone. The outbuildings got carried off bout like everything else, and that means there won't be no job, no money 'cept what I got left in my pockets, no way to buy things for some time. We'll have to do the best we can. For now, we'll be thankful we found one another. It could a been a lot worse than this."

Papa said all this in a matter-of-fact way, and after all I'd seen and been through, I agreed, it could a been a lot worse. There'd certainly be no expectations from me. Momma stood near the foundation, staring at what she'd laid out. We had some food, we had each other, and when Seph come home, I'd have him to hold on to as well. I felt grateful. After our separation, and going so long unaware of how things had stood for days, I couldn't imagine things could be any more unpleasant than they'd been. Yes. I was certain we'd seen the worst.

Chapter 8

The next day Papa was unusually quiet after he and Momma had a spit fight over whether he ought to bring Seph home.

Momma's voice was harder than usual, "He ought to stay put for now. Considering there's no roof over our heads, that would be best, don't you think? Can't we get things situated first before he comes? He's so young, William."

Papa said, "How long you think it's going to take to get 'situated'? I can only work so fast. It could take weeks."

Bothered by the unusual discord, I interrupted. "I'll help you, Papa."

He shifted his look from Momma to me, eyebrows knitted together into one deep line across his forehead. I picked at the soiled rags around my hands, worriedly pressing into the still-tender sores stamped in the center.

After a second, he continued on slow and insistent, like he was tired of explaining things. "This is how it's going to be for a while. We'd better get used to it. Wallis Ann, you won't be able to go to school for some time. It's going to be some weeks to do all this work. Ann, you know the longer he stays with the

Barneses, the more obligated I'll feel. I want to get on with what needs doing here, the quicker, the better. Once I get started, I don't plan to stop."

Momma said nothing. When she gets real aggravated, she'll simply go quiet, and while Papa sometimes gives in when he knows she's not pleased, this time neither one did. I stood near Laci, who rocked, detached from the discussion, detached from our predicament. The dank smell of wet pine and balsam filled the air, and my dress lay tight to my skin, like clothes tend to do in summer, except I felt cold. Papa motioned for me to come with him, and we worked like we always did, hard and fast, putting our backs into gathering wood for the fire. He had gone inside his self, and I didn't talk none either. I collected what I could find, all different sizes of limbs, branches, or chunks of wood, wet or dry.

Papa finally held up a hand and said, "That ought to hold y'all for the time I'm gone."

That meant he'd made a decision, whether Momma liked it or not. I took the last bit I had and dumped it on the pile close to the fire, and then I got close to the flames. Laci stood by my side, and when I turned to toast my backside, she turned too. Too quick, my front was cold. I couldn't get close enough to the heat. My clothes smelled sour with sweat and dirt, and now wood smoke, which actually helped with the other odors. I wished for the extra dress. I wished for our big tin tub and enough warm water to soak in, and one of them bars of Ivory soap Momma would get at Christmas from Papa. I wished for all that food we'd packed.

I sure wished for a lot.

Papa got to walking around the foundation again, looking it over, pushing on one side and then the other, studying it for stability. My attention went from watching Papa to Momma and what she'd put into the skillet. She stood over the boiling water and tossed in a handful of grits. She searched the ground for a stick and stripped the bark off it at one end. She squatted by the fire and used it to stir. I watched carefully as the grits turned creamy and thick. After a few more minutes, she pulled the skillet away from the fire and reached for the hoop cheese. She broke off a hunk and crumbled it into the pan on top of the grits, letting it melt. My mouth watered as I thought of how it would all taste. Momma took the jar and put more of the boiled water in it and added it to the coffeepot. She scooped in grounds, closed the lid, and set the pot close to the fire.

I finally quit turning myself around like a piece of meat on a spit. I sat cross-legged on the ground, and Laci placed herself beside me. Smelling the coffee, I closed my eyes, reminding myself of early mornings in the cabin and waking to the same odor. A few minutes later, with the scanty meal laid out, Papa stopped his inspection and come over to bless the food. He spoke in a hushed tone, thanking God for our safety and each other. After we raised our heads, waiting for him to gesture to Momma as he always would so we could start eating, he spoke again. Really, it won't part of the blessing. It was more after-thought to what he'd already said.

He said, "It ain't like we're empty-handed altogether. We got us these few things here what Wallis Ann found. And there's something else we got money can't buy aside from finding one another." He swept his hands in front of his self, passing by each of us, and said, "We got each other and our good name."

Momma remained silent while the skillet had all my atten-tion. I stared at the grits and melted cheese, like a thick, golden gravy, and my mouth watered. Momma gripped the edge of the jar as she poured the hot coffee into it and set it aside to cool a bit. She motioned for us to start eating. We knelt in a tight little circle around the skillet, each of us using a small piece of bark to scoop grits and cheese into our mouths. It was rustic, and not easy, but we was too hungry to notice. I never knowed something so simple could taste so good. Who cared about little bits of bark and dirt left behind in one's mouth? I closed my eyes and swallowed the first bite of hot, strength-giving food, letting my tongue work over the sharp taste of cheese. Nobody talked. Everybody ate slow, taking our time so as to not spill one drop between the pan and our mouths.

We then passed the jar of coffee around, sipping the hot liquid till it was gone. I couldn't believe I was full from so little. I also couldn't believe how much better I felt.

Papa sighed, stood up, brushed off the front of his coveralls, said, "I'm going to get Seph. I ought to be back in a day."

Momma's head dropped, and her eyes closed. I thought there could be words, but she held her tongue. Papa hesitated, then he went off down the path, his stride long and sure.

I said, "Momma, I'll clean up, and I'll get the water, and boil more so we have enough, if you want to rest awhile."

Momma walked away like she hurt, limping a little as she went over to the stone foundation. I watched her gather the ragged hem of her dress, her long hair falling out of the bun to hang down her back. I swear, Momma had aged about ten years. I told myself it was only fatigue, that them circles sitting below her eyes was only temporary. I give Laci an appraising glance. She had a smudge of dirt sitting on her cheek, and her hair was in a wild tangle. Her dress was dirty as mine, and her feet too. Still, none of this took a thing away from her. If anything, her less-than-perfect look made her even lovelier. I brushed a hand over my hair, then scratched furiously.

Momma plopped down heavily on the stone wall, looking like she was studying everything that happened to our home all over again. I went and got Edna Stout's walking stick.

I give it to her and said, "Here, Momma, use this till you feel stronger."

She took it and set it beside her. She allowed a little half smile at me, and then her eyes drifted over to the Glenwood stove sitting several yards away. She didn't look at me again, so

I went to the fire, and got the skillet, coffeepot, and water bucket. I carried them down to the creek with Laci padding along behind me. The creek was low enough now to reveal the familiar flat rock, the one I called the wishing rock. I would sit on it with Laci and make random wishes like, *Laci wished she could talk. Laci wished she could go to school. Laci wished she could see what was beyond Stampers Creek.* I made them wishes on Laci's behalf, but in reality they were mine too. She drifted over to it, and next time I looked, she sat facing me, hands forming the motions of playing the dulcimer. I wondered what song she heard in her head.

For all that happened, Laci seemed able to take these circumstances in better than the rest of us. I mean, she didn't appear no different, except she'd taken to rocking more than usual. It was like she didn't notice our home was gone, or nothing. I remembered thinking I wanted to be like her the moment after Papa and Seph fell out of the truck, but deep inside, I understood it won't true. I felt sorry for her right now, watching how she picked at invisible strings, hearing some tune in her head. Keeping an eye on her, I found a nice sandy spot and scooped some in the skillet. Using the tips of my fingers to scrub the remnants out of the bottom, I cleaned it, then did the same for the pot. I rinsed them good and would scald them with boiling water from the kettle afterwards. All the little things I had to do, the tediousness of it, I didn't mind. All of this was only temporary.

I rose from cleaning and filled the bucket, and gathered up what I'd washed. Laci didn't see me ready to leave, so absorbed was she in her head and whatever she heard there. Since my hands was full, I walked close enough to brush against her foot dangling off the rock. She stared with the glazed look she got when she was enthralled with a song in her head. She bent her head and went back to fake playing. I bumped her foot with my hip again, indicating with my head to come with me. She remained seated, as if not at all inclined to do as I said. I felt a tiny flicker of anger, like the little flame I'd first conceived days ago.

Frustrated, I half yelled, "Laci!" making my voice sharp

She jumped, startled, then rose quickly and fell in behind me as I stomped my way up the embankment. Within minutes I was rationalizing what she done, why she'd done it. After all, everything was different. Her routine all scrapped and in disarray. All that was expected of her had been so repetitive, and now there won't a thing in place she could use as a way to guide herself. I felt guilty for getting aggravated with her, so quick too, especially after we'd only come together as a family again. After a minute or so, I felt her gripping the back of my dress, all she had to hold on to, since my hands was full. I felt a small smile tug at the corners of my mouth.

Chores done, I decided to remove the wrappings off my hands. They felt some better, so I tugged at the rags, and tossed them into the fire. The center of each hand where the blistered skin had long peeled away showed two reddened slick spots about the size of a quarter. Laci was staring at them, and then she reached out, took one of my hands, and traced her finger over a wound. She blinked. I leaned in towards her looking at her eyelashes and what looked like water on them, what actually looked like tears. But Laci had never cried. Or smiled. Or laughed. I leaned back to consider her expression again, and concluded it was water splashing from the creek where she'd sat close to it. I bent over and cupped some of the leftover water in my hands and rubbed at my face. I splashed to rinse off. It felt good to clean up, if only a little. Momma sat in the same spot where I'd left her.

I called out to her, "You want to wash afore I dump the water out?"

She rose, moving slow, and come over to where I stood waiting.

"Maybe that'll make me feel better."

She did the same as me.

Then she said to Laci, "Come on and wash your face."

Laci didn't move. I touched her arm, and she stuck her hands in but didn't splash her face. She closed her eyes, and I looked at Momma.

She shook her head, and said, "Well, least her hands will be clean."

It was another one of Laci's quirks coming out. After a minute Laci dried her hands, and I turned the kettle over to dump the dirty water. I refilled it from the bucket and then I stoked the fire good, knocking down the ashy logs, and sending a wave of burning flakes into the air. It looked rather peculiar, what I called devil's snow because the tiny pieces glowed red and bright yellow, and floated about like snow. I added more wood, and went to the creek again for more water. I made two more trips. In the meantime Laci had gone to the pie safe, and was busy opening and closing the door time and again. On my last water trip, I seen Momma kneeling at the front of her stove, doors open. I was ready to sit a spell, only it was hard to do with her poking around the insides. She shook her head in despair.

I went over and asked, "What're you doing?"

"I don't know."

"There ain't nothing in there, is there?"

"No."

"Do you want I should help you?"

"No. I just got to keep busy. If I don't do something, I'll sit and think too much."

This didn't sound like Momma.

"Well, we could investigate the barn and see if I missed any tools when I was looking the other day. Maybe there's some what didn't get washed away. I was going to do that again anyway. We might find something, and then, when Papa comes back, we can show him what all we got."

Momma didn't say nothing for a full minute.

Then she sighed, and said it again. "I guess."

"Sure, Momma. There could be some things we can still find, right? I bet so."

Momma squared her shoulders and faced me.

Her voice was too bright when she said, "Sure, we might find something useful. Let's have a look."

We went into the barn and Laci stopped whatever it was she was doing to the pie safe and come too. We stood inside the door and surveyed the dim interior. I went to the left and Momma went off to the right. I looked in the spot where Papa had kept his tools and spotted one lonely tool.

I bent down, grabbing it, and said, "Here's Papa's hammer."

The handle was slick and smooth, worn down from use. I went to searching further for Papa's broad blade axe, his regular axe, the sledgehammer, his hacksaw and anything else he might have had, but I only found that one hammer. Momma found the harnesses used on Liberty and Pete. Last thing we located was Liberty's saddle. Papa had it mounted over the stall Liberty used. We spent most of the day poking about the barn, and the yard, hoping we'd overlooked something useful.

Finally, Momma said, "I doubt we're gonna find anything else."

"No."

She looked sad about our lack of success, while I tried to sound positive.

I said, "Well. If nothing else, we found the hammer."

Momma said, "Wallis Ann, I do believe you are capable of seeing sunshine, even on the rainiest of days."

I won't sure if she meant that was something good or not. It was getting on towards sunset, and I hauled in extra firewood so I wouldn't have to get it in the middle of the night. Momma cooked some corn pone, and we ate and drank only water, saving the coffee for morning. I settled down close to the glow of the fire and let my muscles relax. I hoped Papa's trip to get Seph was going all right. I'd be glad once he got back since I felt safer with him around. Laci tucked her hands under herself, and her head went lower, and lower, and mine was soon bobbing too, until we finally lay down to sleep.

When dawn broke, a cold dew had settled on my clothes overnight, despite the fire. After a breakfast of more corn pone and hot coffee, I suggested to Momma we go dig in the sodden field near to the garden to look for taters, and I was happy she agreed. We got on our hands and knees, pushing wet soil aside and hoping for little spud miracles to surface under our fingers. After only ten minutes, Laci dumped four into a little pile.

She kept digging, apparently liking the feel of mud between her fingers given how she didn't need me to keep telling her, "Dig, Laci, dig!"

Momma found two. I discovered a couple rotten ones and a petrified lump what must have been overlooked last year, hard as a rock and shaped almost like a pinecone. We set the ones with soft rot into another pile far away from us. They smelled something terrible. I told Momma we could burn them in the fire once we got done. All said and done, we had us six taters and that was better than none, and we still had another row to go. We crawled along, scraping, and turning the dirt over, inching forward bit by bit. Every now and then, I'd glance at Momma. She was covered in a layer of grime, coating her skin making it look like she'd rolled about in the remnants of old, chalky firewood.

Momma rose and said, "Have mercy," as she reached around to rub her lower back.

I stopped digging for a minute and done what she done,

rubbing on my own back before I stooped over once again. The sun was out, and a breeze out of the north stole some of the warmth. At higher elevations, I was sure the leaves was turning, and my typical appreciation for the beauty of fall was replaced with a nagging worry about colder weather. As we dug there come a loud hoot from down in the holler, followed by a whistle. It was Papa's signal, and Momma and I jumped to our feet while Laci kept going, slinging dirt over her shoulder like a hound dog digging for a bone. I poked at her shoulder. She stopped, and squinted up at me.

I said, "Come on, Laci, Papa's here!"

Without waiting to see if she followed, I took off half running, anxious to see little Seph. He sat high in Papa's arms, and I stopped running to watch how his face changed when he spotted us. He struggled to get down, and when Papa set him on his little legs, they went to pumping hard as he could get them to go. I ain't never seen a little boy run so fast or smile so big. He screamed and went even faster, if that was possible. Momma knelt down and let him smack right into her.

Seph was so happy he grabbed her face with hands black as pitch, and squealed, "Momma! Momma!"

Momma got busy covering his face with kisses, so she didn't see what else Papa had held, but I sure seen it. A great big old country ham. Papa had a grin on his face, about to split it in two. He waited patient while Momma and Seph filled themselves full of each other. Finally, she put him down and wiped tears from her eyes. Papa went over and hugged on her real tight, squeezing the breath out of her.

He nodded at Seph, who hung on Momma's hem and said, "All the way here, all he did was ask the same questions over and over. 'Is Momma home? Is Wally home? Is Laci home?' Round and round, over and over."

Having Seph back was like putting a bow on a gift, like the final touch of paint to the picture of our family together again.

Papa held up the ham and said, "Grits, redeye gravy and ham sound good?"

Momma gawked at it, and went still, staring like she'd never seen a ham in her entire life.

She said, "William, you *bought* a ham?"

"I did."

Momma stood up and walked off while Papa held the ham awkwardly, a funny look coming over his face. Seph followed after Momma, reaching for her with his arms held in the air. We'd never had us a boughten ham, not once in our lives. We always had us a few hogs for slaughter. The quick burst of happy I'd felt left me like a fox slinking away with a chicken. I was torn between what was right or wrong. Papa dropped the ham on the ground, frustrated. He went over and squatted near the fire, poking at it till it had grown a foot taller. He went and got the ham from where it sat and began sort of hacking at one end of the burlap material it was wrapped in. He cut off a few slices, and tossed them into the skillet. He wrapped the rest up and headed for a tree to hang it so nothing could get into it. When he come back, he raked a few hot coals out of the fire and slid the skillet over them. Soon the ham started sizzling and the smell what rose from the pan made my mouth water. Traitorous ham or not, I couldn't help but inch myself a little closer to it.

There was a noise over my shoulder, and I looked to see Laci holding the hem of her dress up, carrying all them taters we'd found.

I pointed and said, "Look, Papa, at what we found. There's taters in the field by the garden. We still got another row to dig, so maybe we'll find more."

Papa, his mouth still pressed tight with irritation, took out his pocketknife, and said, "Hand me a couple."

I started to pick out two potatoes when Laci handed me two. Exactly two. I give her an odd look before I passed them on to Papa. He rinsed them in the bucket of water, peeled and sliced them into the pan along with the ham. It was hard not to think positive. Long as we had fire, water and food to eat, we'd have the strength to work. And if we could work, we could fix things, just like Papa said. Least that was how I seen it. I sat as close to the fire as I could get without getting burned. Momma continued to walk near the edge of the woods, still out of sorts. Seph won't whining no more. He simply followed behind her like a baby chick tagging along after a hen.

Papa broke his silence and said, "Wally, watch them ham and taters."

He handed me the stick he'd been using to stir. I squatted near the pan and poked at a sliced tater, watching as he walked over to Momma and started talking to her. She crossed her arms over her chest, and listened. In a minute or so, she come back to the fire. She remained quiet as she sat on the small bench Papa had fashioned out of a broken board and two rocks. Everyone was plain tired. It's always hard to manage one's moods when you feel wrung out.

We ate the ham and taters out of the skillet, using our fingers, and at one point Momma conceded, "It does taste good."

Afterwards, I lay down by the fire and Laci lay the opposite way, her feet touching mine. Seph was in Momma's lap, head bobbing in a half sleep. The flames threw long shadows all around us, stretching Momma and Papa's individual silhouettes into exotic, murky phantom-like shapes. I watched them move, until, for the first time in days, I fell into a deep sleep, my mind at ease with all of my family around me.

Chapter 9

A drizzling rain fell in the early morning, and I wondered how Stampers Creek or the Tuckasegee would ever shrink to normal size. I'd never been so uncomfortable or miserable, the moist air causing my fingers to shrivel, while a mildew smell clung to my clothes. My skin felt rough, coarse with salt and filth. I washed my face and arms as often as I could, only when you have to haul water several times a day for boiling, you tend to not want to waste it on ridiculous little niceties.

Silent, we gathered round and ate more hot grits with cheese, and then took turns drinking our share of the hot coffee. As always, I did feel better afterwards. Papa wiped his mouth and made an announcement.

"I'm going to see about rebuilding our cabin today."

Momma's face brightened considerably.

Papa said, "Wally Girl, you ready?"

"Yes, sir!"

I got excited like Momma, though I had no idea how we'd do this without proper tools, and I suspected he didn't neither.

He went to the barn, surveyed the corners, hands on his hips, walking around and kicking at the dirt floor.

"Hm. Hammer and no saws."

"No, sir."

He considered the inside of the barn as if he was studying on one of the fields for crop rotation. He did that until a forceful gust made a wall give a loud creak. We both scooted outside quick, and he stared at the roof.

He said, "Too bad it's leaning like it is. We'd at least have us a roof over our heads till we got the new cabin. I don't trust it, though, looks like it could go any minute."

"Yes, sir."

He headed for the woods and I followed, almost stepping on his heels I was so eager to start.

Laci wanted to follow us, and I said, "Stay here with Momma, Laci."

She stopped and I hesitated, wondering if she should come. Her head was dipped so her hair covered her face. She won't happy at being left behind, I was certain of it.

I left her there and listened as Papa talked. "We'll see if we can find trees already knocked down. With no draw blade, guess we can use the claw end of the hammer and peel the bark that way."

"Yes, sir."

We went to searching for appropriate trees, and at first we had plenty to choose from. Papa prodded at several smaller ones, then scratched his chin.

"Maybe these three," he finally said.

For some reason, I wished I could talk to Joe. See what all he'd do if he was in a spot like this. Papa interrupted those thoughts.

"Well, let's get to work. Won't nothing get done standing around."

I was glad he wanted to get busy. Work was what I needed, and work I did, even though my hands hurt like the dickens.

After an hour or so, Papa said, "Hold up."

He spotted a smear of blood on one end of a tree.

He pointed to it and asked, "That yours? It ain't mine."

I had my hands tucked behind my back. I didn't want to quit on account of a little bit of blood. He reached over and got hold of one arm, tugging it from behind my back. He straightened my clenched fingers and stared at the wound, where the delicate, still-healing skin had been torn away again, leaving a red, gaping raw hole.

I insisted, "I'm fine, it's nothing."

"Wallis Ann, you ain't gonna do me no good if you end up with the blood sickness."

"They was almost healed. I should've kept them wrapped. If I wrap them, they'll be good as new."

Papa said, "Well. Go on and let your momma tend to you."

Soon as Laci spotted me she got up from the fire and followed me over to Momma, who was looking to see what she could do about the mud-filled cellar.

She said, "I was about to bring you all a jar of water. I guess I got sidetracked looking at this mess."

I showed her my hands, and she started making clucking noises, and immediately motioned me to come stand by the fire. She tore off the lower hem on her own dress.

She dipped a section of the strip in the water bucket and said, "This'll hurt a bit."

"Can't hurt no worse than it did a few days ago."

Well, it hurt like the dickens, the wounds all the more tender from repeated exposure to dirt and the constant pressure of the bucket I was always having to fill, and firewood I gathered. I bit my lip while she cleaned, poked and prodded. Finally, she took the rest of the strip, tore it in half and wrapped them again. She shook her head the entire time, and she was likely thinking how we'd had some peroxide, salve and real bandages on a shelf in the old kitchen. I'd thought about it. And all the other things we'd had what made our life seem luxurious, considering.

When she was done, she said, "You're tough as they come, just don't forget yourself out here, Wallis Ann. You're near bout a woman now. There's no harm in working hard, but a woman ought to remain somewhat soft and delicate seeming. A man likes a gal that's not too, too independent."

I had no idea why she said this since she'd never said anything remotely like it afore. My face went hot, and the warmth trailed down from there all the way to my feet.

I replied, "Yes, ma'am."

I started back to where I'd left Papa, motioning for Laci to come along. She was happiest with me, and Momma had enough on her hands with watching Seph. I went right back to work and found I could keep up, even with my bandaged hands. If we wanted to fix things, we'd have to give more than we was used to, even Laci. Papa and I found two more trees, and I directed Laci to peel the bark on a maple we'd found. I give her the hammer and showed her the claw end would work to get things started. She sat down and appeared to like doing it. Anything to do with her hands was liable to keep her happy.

We left her there, and pulled a tree into camp I'd worked on earlier, and dropped it off. Momma give us a little smile. We went back into the woods, and while Papa hunted for another tree, I went to check on Laci, to see how she was coming along. I arrived at a barely peeled maple to discover she won't where I had left her. I looked for several minutes, feeling the same sense of agitation I'd had when she didn't do what she was supposed to. I searched the edges of the woods in a broad circle, and at one point I went to call out, only I didn't want Papa to know. I stayed quiet and started my search again, deciding she couldn't be too far as we hadn't been gone long. I tramped my way in one direction and another, until I'd come full circle. Papa appeared and I dreaded telling him. It was yet another problem, but he was engrossed with Pete's harness and didn't notice her missing.

He mumbled, "I broke this. I got to see if I can fix it."

Relieved, I said, "Okay."

He walked towards camp and I took off running down towards the creek. If Laci went anywhere, it would most likely be there. I rushed along, half irritated and half scared. Sure enough, there she was, sitting on the wishing rock, staring at the rushing water like she was hypnotized. She'd give me enough of a scare there was the initial rush of relief and then come a tinge of anger. I stomped over to her, hands on my hips. She looked straight at me, her face and hair all wet. She might as well have jumped in, and I was sort of shocked how she looked so washed-out, her color gone grayish.

My anger went away quick. Maybe things with Laci won't good as I thought. Maybe the lack of her usual rituals was making her do stuff out of the ordinary. Slipping off like this was totally out of character, yet it was her eyes what struck me, an awareness, or something in them what made me lean in close and take her hand.

"Laci?" I whispered, a question in my tone, like I was knocking on a door and expecting it to open.

We stared into each other's eyes for the briefest of seconds, and I almost quit breathing, waiting to see how long this *knowledge,* or whatever it was, lasted. Almost as soon as I focused in on it, it was over. She blinked, then slid off the rock and when she looked at me again, the something that had been there was gone, like a flash of lightning. I took hold of her cold, wet hand and we started back, me talking to her the whole way.

"Laci, what're you doing? You shouldn't be going off by yourself. It could be dangerous. Don't you know that?"

Laci went to peeling bark again, stripping each piece off, examining it, then letting it flutter to the ground in a pile of shavings we was keeping for the fire. Later that night after me and Laci went to bed, I overheard Momma and Papa talking in hushed voices.

Momma said, "It's harder than I thought, William. We need warm beds, food in our bellies. We've been out here only a matter of days, and I sure can't imagine weeks of it. Especially as it gets colder."

I continued to fake sleep, eyes tightened into slits, yet open enough to see their blurred shapes in the firelight. Papa stared into the fire. I hoped he would discuss a brilliant plan, or at least give some sort of solid answer to Momma's comment, something what could take my own little niggling doubt away. He kept looking into the flames, brooding.

He said, "Winter will be here afore long. Might be we ought to go stay with Hardy."

Now it was Momma's turn to stare at the burning pile, watching as some of the wood collapsed and shot sparks in the air. Papa threw another log on. The fire blazed so hot it turned bluish at the top edge. I was forced to give up on my pretend sleep in order to move back some. Laci did too, then promptly closed her eyes. She was back asleep after a few minutes, deep breathing, ignorant to our new and difficult world. Momma quit talking, her expression saying Papa's idea was one she cared nothing for. In my head Uncle Hardy was a blur of beard, coveralls and a loud voice.

After a while, Papa approached a different topic. "I should go get the truck at some point."

Momma sat straighter, her tone encouraged by Papa's change in conversation. "Where is it?"

"Resting against some trees several miles from here towards Cullowhee. I ain't about to let it sit there. It sure would come in handy. I could check see what plans they got at the sawmill, if any. See if they might have something for workers, a way to make money, buy some food."

"Can you get it running?"

"I don't know."

Having the truck would be nice, only everything planned or worked on so far seemed as fragile as the thin ice we'd soon see forming on the creeks and ponds. I won't going to think on having it, till it was here. Momma and Papa settled down for the night, conversation over for now. At some point during the night I'd unrolled my body out of the tight curl I maintained for warmth. The moon hung low in the sky off to the west, a giant yellow button. The trees looked black against it, except around the edges where they glowed from the moonlight. I stretched my legs, my feet searching for Laci's. I felt nothing. Puzzled, I sat up. She won't there, or anywhere near the fire. Momma and Papa slept like they always did, Papa behind Momma, with his arm around her. And Seph cuddled tight against Momma's front, her arms around him. Judging by their breathing, they slept deep, and hard. I stared beyond the fire to-wards the edge of the woods where we went to take care of our privy needs. Maybe she'd needed to go. I stood and walked to that spot behind the leaning barn. She won't there either.

Papa stirred, snorted, and then coughed. I waited until he settled down, knowing I was going to have to go looking again. Away from the fire, the cooler air hugged me like a heavy, wet coat. I wrapped my arms about my waist to keep from shaking. With every chilly step I took, dread swelled and filled my belly like I'd eaten rocks. In my mind, I realized something was going on with Laci for her to keep disappearing. I crept about quiet as possible, feeling an unlikely urge to whisper her name, as if she would answer. Again, I went towards the creek, and the idea of her out there by herself made me walk faster, the sharp rocks on my feet making me bite down on my lip to keep from crying out. My heart thudded in my chest and my breath drowned out the rustling of weeds as I passed by foliage still trying to recover. I made my way carefully towards the wishing rock, hoping to see her there.

She won't.

I turned in circles and tried to think where else she would go. I went towards the Tuckasegee, the sound still loud, even from here. In a few minutes I made out the foamy rapids, the usual gentle cascade whipped to a froth by what still run down off the hills. She won't there either. I hoped to God she hadn't fell in. I headed back to Stampers Creek when I spotted her. She was close to one of Momma's willow trees, floodwater lapping at her toes. I shivered with relief. The only thing moving was her hair, matching the swaying, long droopy fronds of the tree as they swirled in the water. Even with the wind, she didn't act cold, not like I was, shaking so hard my teeth was knocking together. I went towards her, aware of how lovely she looked, standing there shining in the moonbeam like an angel without wings.

I moved towards her slow, uncertain of her state. "Laci?"

Her eyes was closed, and it looked as if her lips moved. I leaned in close enough to feel the soft puffs of air from her breath. I repeated her name.

"Laci?"

She heard me that time, and her eyes flew open, big and wide, her gaze untethered from any show of fear. She come towards me as if we was out for a regular walk, took my hand and waited. She was making me nervous with all these odd doings lately.

"Did you get lost? Did you need to use the privy and couldn't find your way back? Maybe you was asleep? Was you sleepwalking?"

All these questions I had, questions I spoke out loud, knowing I'd never find out. I led her back to the fire, and it was clear to me she must have been freezing. Her lips was blue and so was her hands and feet. The area below her eyes was tinged a deep gray, like she was so tired. She sat down and reached behind herself as if to get her fiddle, and then she faced forward, hands collapsing into her lap. Such a simple movement. It was like a bird I once seen falling from out of a tree, dead from some kind of disease. Like her hands was dead. Useless without the fiddle. That was it. Maybe she was looking for her fiddle.

I said, "Come, get up. Let's go to sleep. I'll sing if you lie down."

I chose a song she liked to play, the Delmore Brothers, "Alabama Lullaby." I sang low, my voice barely above the crackle of the fire. I watched, worried she'd walk off again. Thankfully she didn't and it won't long before she lay back down too. I sang the verses over and over until I was sure she was asleep. I decided to stay awake so I could keep an eye on her. I won't about to tell Momma or Papa. They had enough to worry about. After Laci's eyes shut, I sat with my back to the fire and faced the woods. I stayed like that till first light. When the fire was down to embers, I threw on a log. I grabbed the bucket and went to the creek. I filled it, returned, and put the kettle on to boil for the coffee. I was already frying ham in the skillet and had mixed cornmeal and water for corn pone when everyone else stirred.

Papa's mood appeared a bit better when he said, "Why

shoot, Wally Girl, if I didn't know better, I'd say this outdoor living suits you."

I was so dog tired all I could do was reply with a yawn and a tiny smile.

Momma said, "You're a good girl, Wallis Ann."

I give her the same halfhearted smile. Laci sat up, flushed, eyes as clear as spring water. I finished cooking the corn pone and washed the jar out with some boiling water. I poured coffee in it, and then everything was ready.

I said, "Papa, will you bless the food so we can eat?"

He did, and we ate, and while we did, I watched Laci gobble hers down, apparently bearing no ill effects from her midnight wanderings. I nibbled at a corn cake and give my ham to Seph. His chubby cheeks looked less so this morning. I tickled his belly to get him to laugh, and he grinned, his tongue shooting out to lick the grease running off his chin. Hearing him giggle made me feel better.

Momma said, "You're not hungry, Wallis Ann?"

"No, ma'am, not really."

Papa glanced at me, and said, "Maybe you're working too hard."

Momma said, "I told her there was nothing wrong with hard work, except she ought to take care of herself too."

Their concern aggravated me, giving me an irritable feeling like an itch you can't scratch. I was perfectly fine, or would be if I won't slogging about the hillside at ungodly hours.

Papa said, "I'm not working you too hard, am I, Wally Girl?"

"Let's go." I stood to show them and myself, I was ready to work.

We set off for a different spot. We'd gathered all the downed trees we could in the other location, and still, Papa won't happy about the lack of finding those we could use.

He said, "Flood's done carried a lot of them off."

We began looking in an area beyond where Momma's stove rested and even further beyond. Every one we come across was either too big for us to handle or broken in half. Papa kicked at the ground clutter, shook his head and come to a standstill.

"This is near bout impossible. I need my saws. If I had my broad saw, we could take down the trees we needed, bigger ones at that."

I said, "But, if we had bigger trees, we might not be able to move them the way we are, and we might not be able to place them on the foundation, right?"

Papa scratched at his beard.

He said, like before. "Let's do what we can, while we can, fast as we can."

Papa's mood shifted over the course of the afternoon, and I found myself trying to find good trees faster to keep his spirits up. By the end of the day, we'd found only four more. Pete helped us get them to our camp area, where we'd decided Laci could peel instead of by herself in the woods, but it was a process even slower than finding them. Papa's frustration showed when he stopped working, his hands resting on his knees, his eyebrows drawn in that familiar line across his forehead. His mood hadn't improved come suppertime.

We gathered round our fire, and Momma pointed to the cornmeal sack, and said to Papa, "We have maybe another day or two. The ham, maybe three to four days, if that."

I noticed how stooped over he was, like the weight of his worries was breaking his very back. When I thought on it, I won't sure I remembered last time he'd laughed.

He growled at Momma. "When it's gone, then what. Is that what you mean?"

I'd been staring at the fire, but when he said that, I considered his words.

"Papa, you yourself said we had each other. And our name."

He said, "Neither one will feed us now, will it."

It was best not to talk. What we needed was some sort of miracle. Later on that night, I heard Momma praying softly for one. I listened on her words until she quit, right in the middle of one, as if she'd give out, or give up.

Chapter 10

Our deprivation has turned into a grinding hunger hard to ignore. My belly felt like a tight wad of hurt and more than once I had become so light-headed, I had to stop and stand a minute before I carried on doing whatever it was I had been doing. My thoughts had become fuzzy, and I'd gone to scratching lines in one of the trees nearby. As of today, we'd been four full days with no real food to speak of.

I got to humming once, so as to keep my mind from thinking on it, till Momma told me to be quiet. "There's nothing to sing about."

Our desire to sing and dance shrunk like my hollow gut, long gone like everything else. I've tried to think of ways to distract myself, except when your belly's controlling your head, it ain't easy to do. At night when lying on the scratchy pile a leaves, my hip bones press sharp into the dirt, and my ribs push out. I ain't never been delicate as Laci, that's a fact, but I feel like I'm wasting away. My frame, once composed of muscled legs, firm arms and strong back as sturdy as a man's, had gone weak, and I feared if somebody barely nudged me, I'd topple right on over.

Seph's nose was constantly running, and his cheeks weren't pink no more, while things was bad for Laci in particular. She stopped playing the make-believe fiddle altogether, and she also stopped going off on them wanderings a hers. No more unexpected disappearances down to the wishing rock, or elsewhere. She hadn't moved from the fire except to go and relieve herself in the woods, then she hurried back to it. She got so close the other day, her hair got singed. Had I not smelled it when I went by on yet another endless trip to the creek for water to boil, she could a burned herself bad. I pulled the burnt ends off, and she went to rocking herself and she ain't really stopped since. We smell perpetually of smoke, and our eyes stay red-rimmed. Last night I fell into this deep sleep, and the last sight I had was of Laci rocking and rocking. All of us was collapsing slowly, like the barn.

We started foraging for food. We found some blackberries, wild grapes, scallions, and dandelion greens a few times. We ate the blackberries and grapes immediately because we needed the sustenance. We moved forward together, Papa, Momma, Laci and I, lined up like World War I soldiers I seen pictures of in class, descending on the German ranks. We picked what we could, even the ones still sort a green, and we shared. The squirt of sweet juice in my mouth even from only three or four was so good, my mouth watered and watered for more. The deer, squirrels, raccoons and birds was getting to them though, and it was almost too much work for what we got out of it.

Papa and I continued to work on gathering trees for the cabin and I also searched for wild sumac berries to give to Momma. The few I found she soaked in boiled water and made us some sort of drink. It didn't taste none too terrible. It had a fruity, lemony flavor, though I think I wanted to taste something so bad, it could have been my imagination. Once, when I come upon some dandelion greens and scallions, I gathered them and Momma cooked it all together in the skillet, only it was so very little, it almost made me more hungry.

She said, "It's something to keep our stomachs from hurting so bad."

I didn't want to tell her she was wrong.

Come the morning after I found them greens, I went to get water for boiling, that endless chore I was beginning to despise. I took Seph with me, thinking to give him something to keep his mind off being hungry. I felt poorly, and he was looking right pitiful, otherwise I might have engaged him in playing. I took his hand and he come along with no fuss. I walked a little slower than usual, my legs trembling as I stepped over logs and the leftover rotting branches and limbs flattened from the flood.

I let go a him as we got close and said, "Don't you get near the creek and fall in now, you hear me?"

Seph looked at me, his nose running down his lip and he shook his head no. I took my forefinger and swiped the wetness from his upper lip.

"Okay then. You stay right here. Don't get into trouble."

"I firsty, Wally. I real firsty."

He worked his chapped, dry mouth, making little smacking noises as if to show me.

"I know. I'm getting us some water. You wait here, okay?"

I went down to the creek, taking care to dodge the softer areas where it had receded. I rinsed my hand of Seph's nose drippings, then stood a minute looking at how far it had dropped, a good two feet or so, though it was still high. Papa said it would take a long time because of the ever persistent drizzly days. We'd already been out here about two weeks, and because it kept raining every other day or so, the flow washing

down from higher points didn't help. I bent and dipped the
bucket in, filling it almost to the top. I wished I had two. It
would mean less trips. I thought about the crisp, cold water
from our well. Papa said he'd eventually figure how to get us
water, but it would have to come after he got the roof on the
cabin. Since we had a way to boil it, it won't urgent, though it
would sure taste better and save some work.

I set the refilled bucket down. Seph squatted by a rock with
a stick in his hand poking at the ground. Seeing he was preoccupied, I commenced to looking for chicory root from a plant
Momma showed me long time ago called Blue Sailor. I spotted
some near the embankment, and started gathering as much as
I could hold. After a few minutes, I checked to see what Seph
was doing, and couldn't believe my eyes. He was laid flat out
on his belly, slurping away like a dog at a small puddle of nasty-
looking water. In that brief second of shock, I pictured dead
animals, overrun privies, and no telling what all else the water
had come in contact with while creating these little contaminated cesspools. I envisioned poison filling his gut.

I threw the chicory root down and hollered, "Seph, no!"

He raised his head, muddy mouth quivering with uncer-
tainty and his already red-rimmed eyes filled. I run over to him
and yanked him up and shook him hard.

"No!" I yelled again.

I took my hand and frantically wiped at his mouth, like I
could remove the water he'd drank. I smacked him on the
back several times, like I would knock it out of him. He went
to crying and shaking, his hands flying up and down in distress,
like a little bird trying to take flight, wanting to get away from
me, away from my slapping hands. Shocked, I thought, *How
could I be so stupid? I should have kept him by my side!* He didn't
know no better, and I immediately felt bad for yelling at him,
and hitting him so hard. I picked him up and held him tight.

"I'm sorry, Seph. I'm sorry. It's okay, you was just thirsty, won't you? It's bad water, Seph! Bad water! Remember? I told you it's nasty and full of bugs and it could make you sick! Why didn't you do as I said?"

He was crying so hard he'd expelled every ounce of air in his lungs, his mouth wide, and he'd yet to take in a fresh gulp. In my panic I slapped him on his back again, thinking he was choking. His face turned purple as an eggplant.

I grabbed him by his arms and shook him, and yelled, "Seph! Seph! Breathe!"

He recovered from the shock of being hit, and took a good lungful of air and let out a wail loud enough to be heard in the next county. I felt horrible, certain he wouldn't understand why Wally had hit him. I never had. I rubbed his shoulders, smoothing my hand softly over the area. By now I was half crying too. I was surprised Momma or Papa hadn't come running after all the commotion.

"Oh, Seph. You scared me! Are you all right? Seph?"

"I-I-I was firsssssttttttyyyyy!"

"I know, it's okay. Look. Come on. Let's play a game. You want us to play a game?"

He wailed a bit more and I let him. I kept talking nonsense, telling him Wally won't mad, Wally was scared, and Wally didn't want him to be sick. Finally, he sniffed, relaxed in my arms and looked up at me. His eyes was so serious, so grown-up looking. I wanted to make it up to him. I needed to see Seph smiling at me again.

"Wally, you was scared?"

"I sure was. You give me a fright. Look a here. See these?"

I pointed at the chicory roots I'd dropped on the ground. "Can you find some more like this? We got to find where these little roots is hiding, see? You got to look for this," and I showed him the green leaves. "Then you got to pull real hard. And when you do? Out pops these little hiding roots. You're big and strong, you can do that, can't you?"

He hiccupped and nodded at the same time. I put him down. He bent over and did what I asked. I was overcome with mixed feelings as I watched his small hands work, looking at me for approval, and when I'd smile he'd go on back to his task. I kept a close watch and he kept licking his lips. He was still thirsty, yet I imagined a horrible pestilence weaving its way deep down into his body.

Every now and then he'd turn and say, "Like fis one, Wally? Like fis one?"

Worried sick, I reassured him. "Yes, like that, Seph. You're such a big boy!"

We gathered for only a little while, my heart not in it anymore, so I helped him. I took him back after a few more minutes and had him give Momma all the roots we'd dug for.

She smiled and said, "Oh now aren't you being such a helpful boy!"

She hugged him, and placed the roots out to dry, lining them up on the ground in a row, in an area out of the way. Seph seemed like he'd forgot all about my hollering and smacking the devil out of him. When he spotted Papa, he hurried over to where he was working with some small, flexible-looking vines. Papa was making homemade snares trying to catch a few wily squirrels who found it great fun to scamper up and down tree trunks right in front of us. Squirrel meat would be heaven. Even one tiny varmint would make a huge difference in my perception of our limited successes thus far.

I worried over having to tell Momma what I'd caught Seph doing, particularly when I noticed how strained she looked, so different from only days ago even. In the past her hair had always been perfectly combed. She always wore clean aprons and dresses, and smelled of the fresh mint she favored and chewed from out of her herb garden. Momma was sensible, no matter what had happened, she'd know what to do—if anything needed doing. It was for that very reason I finally got the nerve to approach her while she worked with the chicory roots.

I said, "Momma."

She stopped arranging the tubers and straightened up.

Some emotion tinted my voice, because she come towards me quick asking, "What is it?"

My stomach tightened. "I caught Seph drinking out of a puddle down to the creek."

She turned to look at him running in circles around Papa's legs.

She asked the first thing what had come to my mind. "He take in much?"

I didn't answer her question directly. I felt a need to explain myself. "I'd already got the water and decided I ought to look for the chicory. He was already drinking, so I don't really know."

The disappointed look she leveled at me was worse than if she'd yelled in anger.

I tried to reassure her, and myself, "I don't think he drunk much."

As it sank in, she become more bothered by it. "Why didn't you keep him with you? Even a little bit might could make him feel poorly."

"He won't far. I could see him. He was playing with a stick, and I looked away for a second."

Momma's disposition was testy these days, all of us on edge and feeling less tolerant for stupid mistakes. She glanced at Seph again, her lips clamped together.

Eventually she let out a sigh and said, "Let's hope he's all right. You know you got to watch him ever so close, Wallis Ann."

"Yes, ma'am." I already felt bad enough, and Momma's sharp tone, so unlike her, didn't help. Later on, while working near Papa, I wished I could rewind a clock and do the earlier part of the day all over. Seph got to crying as he followed Momma about, his hands pulling at her dress. Was he hungry? We was all hungry. That was expected. Was it something else? Momma stopped to pick him up, patting him.

Her voice sounded concerned when she asked him, "Are you tired? We're tired, aren't we?"

Seph only whined, then laid his head on her shoulder. He faced me and Papa, and it about killed me to see them blue eyes looking dull, and so . . . old. Come time to eat, we each had a handful a pecans Papa had found when he set the snares out, a bite or so of dandelion greens, and the horrible chicory root "coffee." Seph pushed against Momma's hand when she offered him a few nuts. He continued to act tired and cranky. There won't much conversation. There was a short prayer by Papa, and we each took our few bites, and swallows of the acrid chicory, and then we went to bed soon after the sun set. Laci and I huddled near as we could get to the blaze, our feet planted together as usual. I drifted off, wanting to return to dreamland where food was abundant and served inside a warm home filled with soft beds.

A distorted voice cut through my sleep.

"Seph?"

My eyes opened as Momma's voice pricked the edges of a murky, but satisfying, fulfilling dream. I sat up, my back as creaky as an old, worn-out chair. A light, first frost had come overnight, and I can't say how I was sleeping at all when it was so cold. My breath left milky little clouds suspended in the chilly air. Laci was balled up, hugging her knees to her chest, close to the dying fire. She shivered in her sleep. A wave of dizziness hit me, and it was like I viewed everything through a fogged window. My chest felt congested, and I coughed, then took a breath or two to quell my nausea.

Shivering violently, I poked at the fire, and when it sparked bright, I seen Momma with Seph in her arms. He won't moving. There was a foul smell drifting on the early morning air, reminiscent of a too full outhouse. I rose to my knees and seen something running down Momma's arm where his backside rested. His head rolled towards me, his mouth slack, eyes half closed. My own misery left, and alarm took its place.

I jumped up, asking stupid questions, as if I couldn't see for myself. "What's wrong? Is something the matter with Seph?"

Momma's face was fearful, and she said, "He's so hot. He's been sick a few times. I was hoping he'd get it all out and be fine, but now I can't rouse him."

Papa was beside Momma, staring at Seph like he wanted to do something and didn't know what.

He gestured at her and said, "Ann, he's done dirtied his self."

She laid him down on the ground by the fire and began taking his britches off.

"Momma, we don't have nothing else to put on him."

"I know, but he can't stay like this. It's the water, it's done made him sick."

I didn't know what to say or do. Papa began stacking wood in a different spot.

He said, "I'll build another fire over here. It'll help keep him warmer."

I went to Momma's side, picked up the clothes and said, "What do you want me to do? Should I try to clean them?"

Seph woke and whimpered.

Momma patted his arm when he abruptly sat up and cried out, "I gotta go!"

Momma didn't answer me, and barely had time to set him down when he took off running for the woods. As he went, a watery, brown discharge trailed down his legs. He stopped running, squatting right where he was. Momma made it to his side, and she bent down, her hands round his middle, talking to him. The foul sickness in him let go, and Momma's face lost what little color it had, going white as if all her blood had drained out like what was emptying out of Seph. She glanced at us, overcome with distress and alarm, until Seph cried out again. He struggled out of her hands, then crawled away from the spot only to give up what little was in his stomach. My heart broke seeing him being sick. Again. And again. When he was done, Momma held him, ignoring his soiled condition.

She said to Papa, "We got to do something! He's got to have medicine!"

I said, "I'll go. It's my fault. I'll go find Doc Stuart."

Laci appeared by my side, and I stepped away from her because I couldn't handle her clinging at the moment. Not when Seph was retching and dry heaving once again in the background, like his very insides was coming up.

Papa said, "You can't go off by yourself, Wallis Ann. I'll go."

"I was by myself for days when I couldn't find you and Momma. I took care of myself. I can ride Pete easier than you. I know where Doc Stuart lives."

Papa looked uncertain until Seph retched, then howled in pain.

He said, "Alright. See if you can find him. Tell him what's happened. It will take you at least a day and a night to get there and back. Hurry fast as you can. Remember, don't give Pete his head too much."

He went to get the mule where he'd him tied for the night. He helped me climb on him and handed me the reins of his harness.

Papa said, "Wait a minute."

He walked towards the fire. Momma was there with Seph in her lap, rocking and singing to him. She didn't look at me. Papa returned and handed me a pocketful of pecans.

He give me the jar of water, and said, "Drink as much as you can. Wished I could give you a pistol."

"I'll be all right, Papa."

I ate the handful of pecans and drank the water while looking at Papa's face. It was as worn as a piece of old rawhide, his eyes saggy with the newly formed bags underneath.

He patted my knee and said, "Be careful, Wallis Ann. Come back to us quick as you can."

"Yes, sir. I will."

He stepped away and give Pete a slap on the rump. I glanced over my shoulder only once, my eyes finding Momma by the fire, Seph's black hair against the white of her arms and Laci watching me leave. And when our eyes met, she started to come forward, and I turned abruptly. I couldn't worry about her right now.

Chapter 11

My legs curved round the warm, barreled rib cage of Pete as I headed northwest. The flooded area of the Tuckasegee required me to backtrack in spots impossible to pass, so it took a good hour before Cullowhee Mountain and Cherry Gap come into view, and for a second it was like staring at the faces of old, long lost friends. I would have lingered, only the image of Seph and him needing the attention of Doc urged me to hurry. I prodded at Pete's sides with my heels when he slowed as if to begin grazing. I tugged on the reins, refused to give him his head and he tossed it in protest, and finally did what I wanted. I hoped he wouldn't turn ornery on me and decide to get spunky and take off like he'd done in the past. I didn't think I'd have the strength to hang on.

A variety of trees, oak, ash, sugar maple and more what had withstood the flood rose all round me as I come to Mill Creek branch. Some had their roots exposed, like blackened arthritic fingers while the soaked spruce and fir give off a hint of their spicy odors. Cardinals dotted limbs here and there, an array of bright, scarlet spots, busy in their search for food. I passed the

Powells, kicking at Pete to get him moving faster because I couldn't stand such a desolate scene. I realized the worst must have happened since the place looked abandoned. The only time I stopped was to hop off Pete for my own needs every now and then. The pecans hadn't lasted long in my belly, and of course I was awful thirsty. Then I'd think of Seph's misery and any piddly discomfort I might be feeling seemed plain selfish.

I judged it to be dinnertime by the time I come to where I'd met the creepy Leland Tew and Joe Calhoun. The sun was at its highest, and if I was going to make it to Caney Fork by nightfall I needed to pick up the pace as much as possible. Off to the left was where I'd followed Joe Calhoun to help him out. Maybe one day I'd know what happened to him and his young'uns. I turned my attention to Pete, who picked his way around a tricky area littered with broken trees, an assortment of destroyed buildings and other garbage. I looked down, watching as he placed his hooves carefully around rocks and slippery muddy spots, concentrating so hard I didn't hear the creaking noise of the wagon coming behind me.

Someone said, "Hey now."

I turned to look over my shoulder at none other than who I'd just been thinking about. I pulled on the reins to stop Pete. Joe Calhoun, Lyle and Josie sat perched on the seat of a buckboard wagon. Joe leaned forward and give me a hard look.

He asked, "How're you, Wallis Ann Stamper?"

I said, "Mr. Calhoun, how you doing?"

He pushed his hat up on his head. "Call me Joe. Fine, thank you. We was on our way home. Where you heading?"

"Doc Stuart's place over to Caney Fork. My little brother drunk some tainted water and took sick from it."

He pulled his wagon beside me, and said, "I'll take you. We got room. Lyle, you and Josie git in the back."

"It ain't necessary. I've made good time."

Joe looked in the direction I was headed.

He said, "I reckon with things being as they are, you ain't heard. The town was hit hard. I doubt Doc's there. It's going to git dark in a few hours. You can't be riding round the countryside by yourself at night. Besides, I owe you for helping us out."

He was persuasive, sounding a lot like Papa.

He said, "I'll hitch your mule to the wagon, and take you and you can see for yourself."

He hopped out of his wagon as I started to refuse him. He come over to Pete, reached up and put his hands on me, helping me down. The idea of him being so close, smelling me, seeing how filthy I was, was enough to shut me up and do as he said. He helped me onto the seat of his wagon. I sat there, bunched in a knot, my arms folded over my waist, my bare, grimy feet tucked out of sight under the seat. I don't know why I felt so self-conscious, or worried how greasy my hair might be, or how I'd not been able to bathe in forever. Joe didn't act like he noticed. He'd likely be too polite if he did. He tied Pete to the rear of his wagon, climbed up and whistled at his own mule. The wagon lurched forward and when we was in the clear again, he chucked the reins and clicked and his mule went to trotting at a right good pace.

We didn't say much to each other for a while. He talked to his kids but they was quiet, shy about a stranger riding with them. Joe glanced at me, and I turned my head away to stare at the rushing ground going by much quicker than it would have with me riding Pete. I wanted to tuck my hair behind my ears, and instead, I let the lank, dingy strands fall over my cheeks hiding the anxiousness I was sure he would see in my expression.

After a while he said, "When did your folks get back?"

I thought of them huddled near the fire and worried about Seph. I could see my little brother and that sense of urgency made me impatient and not in the mood to talk.

My answer was a little short. "Couple weeks ago."

Joe said, "Aside from your little brother, everything else going along all right?"

"We're making do best as we can."

I clenched my jaw, and hoped he wouldn't ask no more questions. He didn't.

"Well, I'm real sorry to hear of your troubles." He didn't speak for a few minutes, then he said, "The Cullowhee dam broke and with the Tuckasegee flooding, not many escaped damage. Everyone, from Caney Fork to Little Canada, and beyond in the way of the dam or close to the river's had it bad."

"Yes."

I'd seen it for myself days ago and experienced it, and still won't sure how I was even alive. There was small talk here and there between Joe and his kids, and I only said what needed saying if asked. The day seemed awfully long. When we finally come into Caney Fork, it was bad like he'd said. Where houses should a been, there won't nothing except a few piled boards, or the ones still there looked like they was about to fall over. One house had a poplar tree driven through the very center of it, like driving a stake into the ground. There was a few folks around, and you could see where some had been getting a few of their things in order. I should a thought about what I'd do if I couldn't get a hold a Doc, but I hadn't. I'd been so focused on getting here, telling him how bad he was needed, that no outcome other than what I'd featured in my head was considered. I never thought about what if I'd come for nothing, or about Seph getting no help. This realization sent me into a terrible sinking spell once I seen how bad things was in this town.

Joe said, "Maybe I should ask someone if he's here or maybe close by. There. Let me go ask him."

He hopped down and trotted towards a man standing in the middle of what looked like a wasteland. The man stared at him as he approached. I watched carefully and when the man's head shook, I wanted to beat on the wagon seat. I could feel the sting of tears coming when, unexpectedly, I felt a soft touch on my arm.

"Miss?"

I swallowed hard, wiped at my eyes, and looked over my shoulder at Lyle.

His small face was grave. "You hungry?"

His question threw me for a moment. Joe was still talking to the man and looking grim. I'd rather wait for him to tell me, than assume, so I stared over my shoulder at Lyle again. In his hand was a long strip of jerky. He gestured for me to take it, moving the food closer. His eyes was steady, while little elfin Josie grinned at me from the spot beside her brother. My hand shook as I took his offering. I held the dried meat like I won't sure what to do with it.

"Don't you want to taste of it?"

"Sure. Yes. Thank you. That's really sweet of you to offer."

He turned red and sat down beside his sister. I stared at the jerky. It was the first real food I'd seen in days, and the smell made my mouth water. I bit down hard, pulling against the grainy toughness until I broke off a good-size chunk. I sat for a second with it in my mouth, feeling queasy, unsure I could eat without being sick. I closed my eyes, and began to chew while my stomach growled loudly as if telling me to hurry and swallow. Which I did.

Joe returned and got in the wagon as my stomach burbled with the unfamiliar sensation of actually having something in it.

He said, "I'm sorry. The man there said the doc come a day or so ago, for a few things, and that he's gonna be gone for a while. He's staying with some relatives of his over to Asheville."

I listened, while all sense of purpose and hope sank as fast as the sun lowering behind the ridge. There would be no doctor for Seph. What did this mean?

I said, "I can't believe it. I had to try though. We had no other choice."

Another wave of sickness swept over me and I broke out in a cold sweat.

Joe said, "You ain't looking like you feel too good yourself."

"I'm fine. I just got to get back quick as I can."

He said, "Don't worry. We'll stop at my place, give the mules some water and feed. It won't take long, and we'll be on our way."

It felt good to have someone make these decisions. I gripped the jerky, wanting to eat it, knowing I needed it, but my stomach wanted to act up. I waited, then took a smaller bite, chewed thoroughly and I didn't swallow that one so fast. After we'd been going along for a few minutes, Joe handed me a canteen he had under the seat. I couldn't decide what tasted better. The sharp, clean taste of his water, or the rich, meaty jerky. Between sips of water and small bites of meat, I recovered, and began to feel some better.

Joe made sure his mule kept a lively pace. We arrived to his cabin as the moon rose to the highest point in the sky, dressing the land in a creamy light. I was grateful, in hindsight, not to be stuck trying to make my way through the treacherous landscape by myself. I could make out how he'd repaired a good portion of where the tree fell on his cabin. Situated against the edge of darkened trees was the distinct shape of a cross what looked to have been painted white. Sally's grave. I shivered in the night air.

He said, "Wait here. Let me get some things and we'll keep going."

He hopped down and first thing he did was give his mule and Pete some water. Pete slurped and slurped like he'd empty the pail. He also give them some grain and then he went into the cabin. When he come out a few minutes later, he carried another canteen, a large bundle, and he'd brung coats for Lyle and Josie. Them coats only set it in my head how I wished I could bring Seph and Laci something to keep warmer. He helped Josie put hers on while Lyle shoved his arms into his, then hopped down to help fill the other canteen with fresh water. Joe placed the large bundle in the back. He come around to where I sat on the wagon seat and handed a quilt to me, and surprised by this gesture, I shook my head no. Sure, I wanted it, and yet I refused. It was likely Sally's own hard work and it was too beautiful, too nice a thing to take.

Joe lowered his arm, and said, "Don't be prideful. Ain't nothing wrong accepting this. Lots of folks is in a hard way. And, like I said, I owe it to you."

He held it out to me again, and this time I took it. I was tired of shivering, yet this simple act of kindness warmed me even more than the quilt would. I'd never thought I'd be in such circumstances, so needy. I wrapped it around my shoulders, burying my chin into the clean softness of it, more grateful than he could ever know. The quilt smelled faintly of wood smoke and fresh air, like him. He put the pails in his barn, checked Pete's harness, making sure he was secured, and last, he checked on his own mule and then he climbed onto his seat. Lyle clambered in and handed the canteen to Joe.

He took it, and while all this went on, it put an impression on me. Joe Calhoun was a methodical, thoughtful man. And his son was growing up just like him.

He turned towards me and said, "Alright then. Ready?"

"Yes."

He flicked the reins and we started towards my family. I wanted him to go faster, but it was dangerous going, and I couldn't ask him to do more than he already had.

After a while, he said, "You know, when I was a boy, I wore the same pair of coveralls near bout five years. Momma, she patched them over and over. I didn't wear no shoes till I was twelve, I think. We all got stories about going without. We've all been there, one time or another."

I said nothing though I understood what he was getting at. He appreciated what it was like to go hungry, to bear hardships, about not wanting to depend on no one. After a while I was fighting the urge to drift off to sleep with the sway of the wagon, no gnawing hunger, and the warmth of the quilt encouraging me to let go. I forced my eyes open and sighed. How could I sleep?

"You thinking of your little brother?"

It was peculiar, the way he had of knowing what all went on in my head.

"I should've watched him closer."

"Well, at three years old, he's likely got a mind a his own. Don't be too hard on yourself. We'll be there soon."

He snapped the reins, and the rest of the ride we talked on and off about Papa's plans for rebuilding and how he might go about it. I told him about the cabin, how we didn't have much of nothing to work with, how the flood had contaminated the well, and how we had to boil the water, and worst, how Seph had come to drink the bad. I didn't tell him about the lack of food, though, he might have guessed by the way I ate, the way I looked, and simply by my account of everything else.

When we got to the two poplars, I said, "Turn here."

We was almost there and I sat straighter, my thoughts going a little haywire with the possibilities of what we might find. We arrived in the predawn hours, and the dread I'd been able to keep under control took over. My mouth was dry and I was scared of how things might be, and what might have happened in the time I'd been gone. It was a bad feeling I couldn't shake. It had been a full day and night, and was near about morning again. Joe slowed down to circle round the big fallen oak, and after, we come to the cluster of pines and spruce bordering where our cabin once stood. The flickering light of the fire winked through the tree branches. It was quiet, but it was also

still early, and they could be asleep. Without thinking, I put my
hand on Joe's arm. He pulled on the reins and stopped.

"It might catch them by surprise for a wagon to come riding up out of nowhere. Let me go see."

"All right."

He started to help me, and I said, "No, I'm fine."

He settled back to wait. His kids had fell asleep, and I felt
bad about them being out all night, and not in their beds. My
body felt stiff, and I was dog-tired. I got down off the wagon
seat, keeping the quilt tight against me, as I began to make my
way through the gloom using the sputtering flame as a guide. I
didn't want to call out and wake anyone in case they was sleeping. Maybe the quiet was a good sign. Maybe Seph had got
better. I walked the well-worn path we'd made going in and
around the property. Momma faced the blaze, shoulders
hunched. Papa sat at her side. Laci won't sitting or sleeping.
She stood a little off to their right almost like she was afraid.
Laci seen me about the same time I seen her. I was shocked by
the look of her. Her hair was a mess, all tangled and wild looking, like she'd been grabbing at it. Momma and Papa looked
over their shoulders, their eyes landing on me. Papa helped
Momma stand, and I fully expected to see her holding Seph,
only her arms was empty. I searched beyond the fire, my eyes
flying to all the points illuminated, the trees we'd worked on, a
small stack of kindling and firewood, and . . . nothing else.

Where was Seph? The stillness was my answer, that and their
mannerisms, the quietness and the lack of questions about Doc
Stuart. The meat strip I'd eaten wanted to come up. I swallowed it down. All Momma did was shake her head, waving
her hand in a dismissive way until she put it over her mouth.
She leaned into Papa and he put his arm around her shoulder.
My inside voice cried, not Seph. *Not Seph.* He played in my
mind's eye. Running. Laughing. Throwing rocks in the creek
last summer. Trying to hold on to a slick, flopping trout Papa

had caught. Pink cheeks, robin's-egg eyes, brightest of smiles, innocence and ever-present unconditional love. My fingers wanted to feel the soft mop of dark curls. I wanted to hear his giggles and to feel his hugs.

That small voice called, echoed in my head like a ghost— "Wally?"—and faded.

Never again.

My brain snagged on my last moments with him when I'd wiped the muddy water from around his mouth, hitting him, my frantic fear overriding calm. I only wanted to rid him of what he'd took in. I thought about how I'd grabbed him tight, and hugged him after the hurt I'd caused. So fast. He was gone. His life had only been long as a whisper, yet his death delivered an impact like the strongest wind of the hurricane. *My fault. Mine.*

Momma realized there would be no Doc Stuart, and it didn't matter. Her crying, quiet as it was, broke me apart. I experienced a pain sharp as a driven nail through my chest. Papa couldn't figure out what to do with his self, and so he stared at his boots. Momma come towards me, grabbing at my hands as they hung useless by my side, pulled me into her, and then Papa did the same until they had me between them, like they'd done when they come home, only this time I was filled with a wretched sorrow and imagined a blackness come over me, what would never let go. I was certain this time I'd be sick. I went strangely hot and disoriented. I felt smothered, then cold. I couldn't hear a thing except the force of my own breath fighting back tears.

Momma said something, and certain words filtered through, something about what had happened. Something about the horror. Something about God stealing him away only hours ago. They was only words, yet they fell on me like giant boulders. Words I didn't want to take ahold of any more than I'd wanted to see Seph drinking the water. I needed time to sort all this out. I pulled away from them, not wanting to hurt them worse, but I felt pressured, my feelings of guilt a deep pond I wanted to sink into slowly until I was submerged over my head.

I whispered, "Where? Where is he?"

Momma didn't answer.

She begged, "Wallis Ann, you got to take care of him. Will you? Can you? I can't. I can't."

I glanced towards the barn, and Momma put her hands on my face, turning me away. She looked fragile as eggshells, like if I touched her too hard she might break. She shook her head, shaking off the thoughts she pictured. She stroked my hair, again and again. I stopped her, my hands around her wrists. There come the snap of a twig what made us all look toward the dim outline of trees, near the path I'd come up only moments ago. Joe Calhoun stood not twenty feet away watching us. He'd taken off his hat and held in front of him like people do at funerals. His gaze went from me to Momma, then to Papa, waiting patient until we could gather ourselves.

Momma finally acknowledged him. "Who might you be?"

I didn't sound like myself when I spoke to introduce him. My voice come out low, my emotions as breakable as glass. "This here's Joe Calhoun. I mentioned him when we got separated in the storm. He lives about twenty miles that a way. He helped me get to Caney Fork and here."

Papa stared at Joe hard. "Your papa was 'Whiskey Joe' Calhoun?" Startled, I glanced at Joe, then Papa.

Joe raised his chin. "That was him."

"Thought so. Thank you for helping our girl. It's best if you go on and leave now."

Joe's voice dropped a level and he said, "I ain't like him."

"Sure, sure. It would be easy enough to say that, only, you a Calhoun, ain't you?"

I spoke again. "Papa, he only helped me out."

"And I thanked him, and now he ought to be on his way."

Joe raised his hands, showing he meant no harm. "Sure. No problem."

Momma, her voice breaking, pleading, spoke Papa's name. "William."

Papa won't backing down, growing louder. "Whiskey Joe Calhoun was the devil reborn. I know at least two people who say he killed someone over a card game. A card game! I ain't having the likes of a Calhoun coming round here. A Calhoun's a Calhoun, through and through."

Papa's behavior mortified me, when Joe had only helped me out. "Don't talk to him like that, Papa. He's been nothing but kind."

Papa spun on his heels, his face as red as the head of a pileated woodpecker. "Don't you speak about things you know nothing about. I'll switch you right here and now to teach you better if'n I have to!"

My face went hot, like somebody shoved my head into the fire. I looked to Momma to talk sense to him. When Papa got riled, won't no stopping him. She turned away, and I couldn't believe it. They'd never been rude to nobody. Had never hit me. It was because of what happened. Seph's passing was causing them to be this way.

Joe gestured at me, and said, "Ain't no cause to be like that to her," and on another day, Joe's words would've caught Papa's attention, only Joe didn't bother to wait and see how that set with him as he kept right on. He said, "I'll say it once more. I ain't like him. Never was. Never will be."

He slapped his hat on his head, leaving the way he'd come, only to return seconds later with what he'd brung from his cabin. He ignored Papa's ranting about "A sorry Calhoun" and handed me the canteen of fresh water and the bundle he'd tossed into the wagon.

Papa said, "We don't need none of your kind of charity."

Joe didn't so much as give him a glance.

He kept his eyes on me and he said, "This here's for you, Wallis Ann. Yours to do with what you want."

He leaned in and spoke for my ears alone, "You ever want to come visit me and the kids, you'd be more than welcome. We'd be proud to have you."

He tipped his hat to Momma and took his leave. I gripped a hold of what he'd give me, one side of it still warm from his touch. I watched him go before I went close to the fire and set it on the ground. I sat down and Laci moved closer, leaning against me, shaking with cold. I untied the rope, and all the while Papa paced behind me. He continued insisting on making his point known.

He spit into the fire. "I ain't partaking of no charity. I'll provide for my family. I don't need no other man's help, especially a Calhoun's."

Momma, unable to deal with any more troubles, turned away from him and Papa quit stomping about, trying to tamp down his agitation a little when he seen how bothered she was by his behavior. She lowered herself beside me.

"Go on, Wallis Ann," she said.

I concentrated on unraveling the rope. There was two blankets. Next come two long-sleeved, heavy woolen dresses what had to have been his wife's, and inside them was a tin of coffee, a poke of grits, another of cornmeal, and some dried beans. A white square package held more of the jerky I'd eaten. There was some tin pans and tin cups. Spoons even. He'd put a pair of boy's pants in there too, intended for Seph, apparently a pair Lyle had outgrown. His generosity left me stunned. He'd given a quilt, two blankets, a dress each for me and Laci, and food. The vibrations of Laci against me prompted me to hurry and give her one of the blankets. If I hadn't felt so numb over Seph's passing and Papa's unexpected outburst at Joe, I might have dwelled more on the ever-so-tiny squeeze she give my hand as I set the thick blanket around her shoulders. Her fingers gathered it close around her body.

Momma took the food, and set it aside. I looked at the smaller of the two dresses, a navy blue one with a rusty red collar. Without a word, I left the fire and went behind the barn. I trembled as I pulled off what was essentially a rag now, then tugged on the clean, woolen dress, smelling of cedar, a scent of where the dress had been stored. It had been many, many days since I'd felt decent, since I'd felt like I had on proper clothing. My arms was mostly covered, and the hem of the dress come all the way to my shins. I felt warmer, and appreciated how well it was made, the tiny stitching of navy blue matching the blue material perfectly.

As I left the shadow of the barn, a long, pale-looking object leaned against a tree near the path. I went over to it. The initials JC was carved into the handle. I grabbed the shovel and marched towards Papa.

"He left this too."

Papa looked at it and then at me in the new dress. He didn't look none too happy, but he said not a word.

I motioned at Laci, holding out the other dress. "Come on, Laci."

We went behind the barn again, and once she'd put it on, she touched the soft material. Having all these good and necessary things would have seemed like a sign of better days ahead, but none of this really mattered, not after what happened to Seph.

Chapter 12

Burying Seph turned into a matter of urgency. Momma had asked me to take care of things, and once I was dressed, and Laci was dressed, she'd grabbed Lyle's pants and shoved them into my hands, repeating her earlier plea.

"Wallis Ann, please. Will you?"

"Sure, Momma. It's all right."

Papa took her along the path, as if a bit of distance might lessen her pain. They took Laci, too, and that left me alone. I crept towards the barn, and just inside the door lay Seph. Papa had put him on some boards he must have taken from the inside walls. I drew closer and looked down on his features. He was Seph and yet, he won't. Illness showed in his tight face, the distress evident by the way his lips had pulled away from his teeth. Like he'd died in pain. It hurt worse than anything I'd ever experienced to see he'd suffered on account of me.

His stillness was foreign and unfamiliar. He'd been nothing but energy, a delicate vessel filled with exuberant life, and his coloring was an unlikely gray when he should have been flushed and pink. Even in the chilly air, the slight odor of sick-

ness clung to him as did a hint of the odor of death. *Hurry up.*
I knelt and shoved a pant leg over each foot. I cringed when I
touched his cold skin, no longer soft and pliable. *My fault.* I
clenched my jaw and scraped the pants up over his small, bony
hips. I tugged his shirt down, wanting to cover him, to warm
him, even though I understood the ridiculousness of this
thought. My gut went sour, and I clamped my hand to my
mouth, rushing out of the barn, relieved nobody seen me gagging. After a few minutes, the feeling subsided and my breathing smoothed out. Weak-kneed, I retrieved one of the blankets
Joe give us. We would sacrifice it for Seph. I went inside the
barn, folded it over him, patted him one last time, and then I
went to get my family.

We went up the hill behind the barn to the Stamper family
graveyard. The storm made what would have been an easy
walk more difficult. Papa carried Seph, I carried the shovel,
and Laci and Momma followed directly behind me. I reached
to help Momma traverse fallen trees several times. In one area,
huge lichen-covered boulders sat, a mystery to the landscape
what told of ancient mountains from long ago. I could hear
her breathing heavy, her stamina waning from grief and the
way we'd been living. Her hand quivered as if she had the palsy.
As we went along, her face and lips growed ever more pale, her
vitality seeping out of her with each step.

We stopped near an exposed outcrop above the Tuckasegee,
where, in the spring and summer, rhododendron bloomed
heavy and thick. There was birds calling, and the whispery
voices of the trees as they moved agreeably with the cool
breeze. The sun played hide-and-seek with the clouds, and we
took a moment catching our breath while looking around at
the scattering of other gravestones inside the old wrought-iron
fencing. Some of the gravestones was knocked over. I helped
Papa straighten a few, and then left him to it, and went to huddle with Momma and Laci. It was like nobody was wanting to

get on with it, yet we had no choice. Papa found a spot near to Grandpa Stamper's stone and set about his work.

As time went on, the digging turned into him stabbing violently at the earth over and over, working out his demons. The ferocious way he mutilated the soil was in direct contrast to Momma. She sat on a small rock in the sun, Laci beside her. Her eyes was closed, and she was so still, if it hadn't been for Papa working like the devil was chasing him, I believe the birds would have landed on her thinking she was a statue. Papa had laid Seph down in the shade, and while Momma wouldn't look in his direction, all I could do was stare and stare at the small outline shaped under the blanket. After some time, Papa wiped his brow with his shirtsleeve and threw the shovel off to the side.

I wished I could tell myself his burying was beautiful, only there won't nothing beautiful about it. Nothing pleasing in the songs we whispered, our voices joined together for the first time in a long while. Standing in a small circle over the damp, cold hole, we sang, but there was nothing lovely about the idea of setting a child's body in the ground. It was plain ugly and I wished it to be over quick. Papa said a memorized verse or two after our quivering voices faded away on a final hymn. As we left, even the woods seemed hushed, with nary a birdcall. I wouldn't have admitted I was hurrying, only I was. It was too hard knowing the smallest amongst us, the one who'd held our hearts and souls together, was gone. On the hillside when Papa placed the small blanketed form into the earth, something got broke in our family, separating us so that we turned inside ourselves.

Back at the campfire, I sat close for the warmth while the coldest air of the year settled around me. Any sense of comfort I might have gained from its warmth was overshadowed by guilt, like I shouldn't enjoy warmth at all. Laci tried to stick her hand in mine and I pulled away, tucking it where she couldn't reach them. She put her head on my shoulder then. It felt like I'd been frozen from the inside out, and fought an urge to shrug my shoulder. I tolerated her touch, while my insides drew tight and unforgiving. Momma sat as still as she had up on the hill while Papa had to keep moving. He took his self on off to the woods, and after a while, noises what sounded like he was hammering on a tree echoed all around. Usually, I would've gone to go see if I could help. Today, it won't in me to work.

Days after, it was a repeat of the same. In some ways, I was waiting on Momma to break. Waiting on her to accuse me, tell me none of this would have happened if I'd not been so careless. I might would have felt better if she had. Got it out in the open. I felt sure it was like a slow-growing canker within her, or like nibbling on a rotten apple, every bite acidic and nasty.

One evening Papa drifted about with his hands in his pockets until he stopped in front of Momma and said, "Ann."

I could see her taking a deep breath, and without looking at him, she said, "What?"

She spoke in this new way, an off-kilter tone, a flat note to her voice.

"First snowfall's liable to come soon. I mean, even under the best of circumstances, with proper tools, this will take time. Way I see it, we only got one choice here. I need to fix the truck. We can't stay here, with no food, no way to get out of the weather. We're going to go to Hardy's till we get ourselves situated again."

Momma shielded her eyes from the lowering sun to look at Papa.

"What are you talking about, going to Hardy's?"

"Only for a while."

Her look said he'd took leave of his senses.

"You know you and that brother of yours can't be in the same room hardly at all."

"No, we don't see eye to eye, but we got to do something."

He raked his hand through his hair, giving him an even more disheveled look. "Only take a half day or so to drive. That's the best thing to do, for now."

Momma worried her thumbs, looping them one over the other while she moved her gaze from him to the setting sun. Papa, hands on his hips, waited. These past few weeks and the effort of simply making do showed. His face was grayish, hair and beard unkempt, coveralls filthy and shabby, the knees going threadbare. His shirt was in tatters. His boots was so worn at the front, I was sure his toes would soon poke through. What bothered me was his scraped knuckles, dirty nails, and thinning frame, all telling a story of effort and desperation. Papa had always been a hard worker, only there's a difference in the way backbreaking work treats a soul when there's a payout. When there's nothing to show for it, all it does is wear you down to a nub. Papa was slap worn down to something less even than that.

Momma shook her head. "I can't leave. We've just laid our boy in the ground and now you want me to leave him behind. I can't do it. Don't ask me. I won't go."

Papa held his hands out in a fashion what said he'd give in. "Okay, okay."

He sat down near her and nobody spoke for a long while. After a bit, I started making supper.

Momma made a move as if to help me, and I said, "I'll get it, Momma. Laci can help me."

Momma settled down by Papa, both of them silent, watching the fire sputter.

I said, "Here, Laci, stir the beans while I make us some corn pone."

She did as I asked, squatting by the skillet, spoon in hand, waiting for the beans to boil. The food given us by Joe Calhoun was running out. I won't about to make that announcement. A strange new level of monotony born of repeated steps with little gain and the lack of energy to affect any change slowly overtook us. Nobody talked about leaving again, and it was only a matter of time before something had to give. The jerky went first, while the grits, cornmeal, beans and coffee was carefully measured by me or Momma, a miserly tending, necessary for survival. The first hard frost come while a fingernail moon hung high in the night sky, like a cruel and crooked grin. I was awake, partly because I was freezing and partly for another reason. It was getting colder, and no matter how high the fire, we was entering into the season where it wouldn't do much good. I was up because of that, and also because I'd heard something. A rustling, scraping noise, though all was quiet now.

I searched the familiar bumps across the fire. Momma huddled under the blanket, but beside her there was no familiar shape of Papa. I left the warmth of the fire to see what he was about. Just beyond the glowing perimeter, the sparse light showed only cold woods. Soon the freezing temps drove me back to the hot, glowing embers. I pulled my knees under my dress and the material down over my toes. I waited to see if he'd come from the woods. And waited. And waited. The night sky give and a pale gold appeared at low edge of the sky, gradual in coming, as if the sun itself fought the idea of facing an icy morning. A heavy coat of rime covered everything, leaving a white crust on the grasses, weeds and trees so it all glistened and sparkled like the hillsides was strewn with glass. Papa was gone, off to see about the truck. I rose stiffly out of need, arched my back to stretch it out and then had to bend over to put my hands on my knees, waiting for the weak moment to pass.

I walked along the path, hugging myself while staring at a few sticks arranged in a half circle. Papa had made a large, awkward C. I took it to mean he was going towards Cullowhee, where he'd last seen the truck. I went back and set about stoking the fire, and getting water on for coffee and grits. After a while, Laci rose hugging on to the quilt for dear life. I handed her one of the tin mugs filled with hot coffee. Her hands tremored as she took hold of it, grasping it for warmth. The look of her worried me. I studied her thin face, the purplish tone to her skin, and to say we'd all lost weight was true, except Laci had grown as thin as a blade of grass. If I didn't know her, she might would have scared me as she'd taken on the look of something gone wild. I was by the fire with Laci, sipping hot coffee, the quilt shared over our shoulders when Momma stirred, and sat up. Her eyes met mine over the top of the blazing fire, and without me saying a word, she understood Papa was gone.

I got her a mug of coffee. "Here, Momma. Drink this."

She took it and sipped slow. When I got done with mine, I sure would have liked more. I considered making another pot, only that would be indulgent. Instead, I served Momma and Laci their portion of grits, and give myself what was left.

Momma scraped the white mush around on her tin plate, and she finally spoke. "He went off without a word. Stubborn as the day is long. I can't eat this. You girls want it?"

I said, "I guess. Are you sure, Momma? You ought to eat something."

She leaned over and handed me the pan. I watched as she went off towards the woods, to tend to her needs. I turned to Laci and give her most of the grits. She ate fast, putting the food in her mouth, barely taking the time to swallow between each spoonful. I took it as a good sign, her still eating. When Momma come back, she walked stiff, like all her old energy had been sucked out of her. Her hair hung down around her face, unkempt, and she didn't act like she much cared about anything.

I said, "Momma. How about when the sun gets up a little more, I wash your dress for you, and your hair. You can wrap the blanket around you while it dries."

Momma said in a flat voice, "I don't care. It don't matter."

I said, "Okay," and let it go.

When the sun rose over the top of the tree line, I filled the pail with water from the boiling kettle and let it cool some. I stripped off my dress and underthings, and dumped them into it. Laci's eyes growed big as I stood buck-naked out in broad daylight, while Momma only lay down as if to go to sleep. I had no soap, but I went to rubbing on my face good and hard, trying to remove the grime. Then I did the same for my arms and legs and everywhere in between. I dunked my head into the bucket and soaked my hair. I shivered and shook, but I was determined. I rubbed and scratched at my scalp, and didn't stop until my head went all tingly. I wet my hair again one final time to remove any grit I might have loosened.

I retrieved the quilt and wrapped it around myself while I got a stick and lifted my wet clothes out and hung them on a nearby branch. During this whole process, Laci silently watched me. I could feel her eyes on me and when I turned towards her again, I seen she'd shucked off her own clothes and was in the process of dumping clean, hot water into the pail. She went to washing her face, standing without regard, naked as I'd been. I studied on her, the shape of her breasts, her legs. She conveyed an air of mystery, because of her ways. Laci fascinated most everyone, even me. Momma always said coveting what someone else has was a sin, so I worked on never allowing my thoughts to go further than seeing, and noting our differences. I turned away as she began to wash her private parts.

I'd heard folks say a time or two, *God holds her tongue. She's been struck mute, but she's got God's hand on her.*

What intrigued me about her, and maybe them who made such observations, was the appearance at times that Laci knowed more than we figured. I could see her face change, a comprehension as subtle as the turning of leaves in the fall, yet I knowed her well enough to see it. I'd often thought, *What if she's as smart as any of us?* Plus, I'd always knowed Laci was right comely to folks. There had been a day, when I'd been about nine and I'd come to understand this without a doubt. We'd gone to a church to sing, and I'd seen how folks' eyes passed over me, nodding, polite an all, until they seen Laci. Their gaze never returned back to me unless I spoke. Even then, it was like they only spared me a quick glance afore their attention settled back on her. They was as interested in me as looking over a dried old ham.

Who could blame them? Laci looked like one a them porcelain dolls I'd once seen propped on a shelf down to Dewey's one Christmas, an expensive gift for some lucky little girl. I think mostly it was her eyes, what snapped with color similar to a young grasshopper, ensnaring them while shining with a cleverness such that folks expected her to break free of whatever it was held her quiet. They hung on to her expression as if at any moment she was going to break her years of silence and speak.

She never did.

I never spoke about how I felt passed over when such as that happened, how it was like being set aside for something what seemed more special, more interesting. It had always been like that, even with my own family. I was loved, of that I had no doubt, but I won't dumb enough not to see how Momma and Papa not only loved Laci, their sense of obligation to give her more in the way of attention required they do so, mostly because she'd come close to not being here. Any thoughts about how I felt disregarded would sound selfish, and would make no sense to anyone, when they'd only tell me how lucky I was to have my full faculties about me. If I had to say what it was about that what bothered me, it was most likely having to always hold them thoughts inside and how that sometimes made me feel I might as well be mute as my sister.

I sighed and called out to Momma, "You want me to wash your hair?" and that's when we heard a sound what sounded like a cough, coming from the direction of the barn. I turned in time to catch movement in the shadowy space of the doorway. Panicking, I run over to where I'd hung my wet dress, dropped the quilt and hauled it over my head. I grabbed the quilt again and threw it to Laci, so she could cover herself. Her eyes darted wildly between me and Momma.

Momma motioned at me, whispering, "Wallis Ann, don't you go over there."

I won't listening. Somebody was in the barn and I aimed to see who was, and what they thought they was doing. I didn't think about being in danger. I didn't think about what if they had a shotgun. I hurried over to the barn door and peered inside, letting my gaze adjust, separating shadows into shapes. A metal noise, like a can being dropped, made me jump.

Momma whispered loudly, "Wallis Ann!"

I yelled inside the barn, "Who's there? You come out here, right this instant!"

Someone come barreling towards me, catching me by surprise, and the vague shape of a man was all my brain made out right before I was knocked off my feet, the back of my head hitting the partially frozen ground so hard I seen stars. I heard Momma scream. My vision went hazy, and in that split second there was a distinct and oddly familiar odor. In spite of my aching head, I got up, glaring at Leland Tew as he gripped the shovel Papa had set against the side of the barn. The initials JC was partially covered by his grubby hands, but the soil from Seph's grave still rimming the edge of the steel is what made me angrier. He won't taking that shovel if I had to kill him to get it. His gaze shifted to Momma, who was heading our way, and back to me again. He waved it around in a threatening way.

He stated matter of fact like, "I'm taking this."

I said, "No you ain't. It ain't yours. Give it here."

Momma demanded, "Wallis Ann, don't talk to him! Who are you?"

He moved fast, and there was a whooshing noise as the shovel went by, barely missing my knees.

I jumped out of the way while Momma hollered at him, "You crazy fool! Leave her alone!"

He ignored her, and give me a coy grin and said, "Hooo boy! I seen you, you know. That purty skin like fresh milk squeezed from a cow's teats, all white and creamy. Your sister there too. She got herself a pair."

Leland Tew's hair hung in shaggy, long strands, and he had that one eye that tended to drift off. He give me the once-over with that rolling eyeball, stoking my anger, poking at me with his words the way he would a fire.

Momma, her voice low and trembling, said, "Wallis Ann. Go on and let him have it."

I was tired of being tired. I was tired of being hungry. More than anything, I was determined to be rid of Leland Tew, once and for all.

I paid no mind to her, and addressed him. "Give it here."

Tew leaned on the shovel, tilted his head and said, "What you got for me?"

"I ain't bargaining with you, not for what ain't yours to begin with."

He looked at the initials and spoke with an exaggerated tone. "Huh. JC? That Joe Calhoun. You know Joe Calhoun? Maybe you lettin' him stick his peckerwood in you. You lettin' him stick it in you?"

I heard Momma draw in a quick breath at his vulgarity. He made an obscene gesture with his tongue, and that's when I run straight at him, my hands held out and shoved him hard. Caught off guard, he stumbled backwards with a yelp and dropped the shovel. I grabbed it and swung it like a bat. It connected with his side and he yelped again. He spit at me and I whacked it against the side of his thigh. He squalled and hollered like he was dying. I swung it over my head. He seen I was about to whack him on top of his grimy head and with the look I must've had on my face, he turned tail and run towards the path, squealing like the pig he was. I went after him, shovel still over my head. I wanted to make sure he was good as gone and that he won't coming back.

Momma screamed at me. "Stop, Wallis Ann! Stop! He'll kill you!"

I didn't stop though. I chased Leland Tew like *I* planned to kill *him*. He turned around, and seen how close I was and caterwauled. He was more of a chicken than Momma realized, all bark and no bite, really.

He found his voice and screamed, "Git away, git away!" before he scurried around the bend.

I chased after him a few more seconds, then stopped and shouted a fair warning at his disappearing backside. "And don't let me see you come round here no more!"

I turned and went back towards Momma. I dropped the shovel to the ground with a clank and leaned over, my hands on my knees, still wheezing hard, and still hopping mad. When I caught my breath, I retrieved the shovel only to find Momma looking at me wide-eyed, her hand to her mouth. She stared like she didn't know what to make of me or at what happened. I won't sure I did either.

Chapter 13

The night after I'd chased Leland Tew off, a stiff wind blowed in out of the north, a sure sign winter would come soon. The gusts created a feeling of helplessness when a particularly strong one almost took our fire out, sending sparks over us just as we'd started eating supper. We had to beat on the blanket and quilt where some of the bigger ones burned tiny holes into the material. The beans I'd cooked looked like I'd added pepper to them. I tried not to think of the soot what settled over the top when I went to eat. We couldn't waste a pan of beans over a little ash.

The gusts got even stronger the next day, and I sniffed the air. There was a crispness to it, a sharp, intense cold. It smelled of snow. Then, the barn got to creaking and groaning like an old woman with the rheumatism. Smoke stayed in our eyes, and went down our throats and set us to coughing. I tried to do some more work on the logs, but most of the time I found myself wanting to sit, nose and eyes running, and wondering where we'd be in a week, a month or even a year from now. I couldn't imagine surviving a winter like this. Plain and simple, we wouldn't. The image of how it could go is what made me think Papa might be right, leaving might be our only choice.

The breeze blowed straight through my dress as I sat hunched over, contemplating how bad things could get, when an odd grinding noise from the barn made me lift my head. It come again, and with it, the building moved, sort a swaying like some live thing. The gusts increased, and with a loud screech the barn finally give up, falling in on itself in a matter of seconds, discharging a cloud of dust. The wind carried the airborne dirt straight over me, swirling like a dust devil before it lifted into the sky. Poor old Pete was only about twenty feet away when it happened, and the commotion startled him. He thundered off into the woods, tossing his head and braying. He come to a stop in between some trees, and showed his teeth in one of his ridiculous mulish grins.

Momma and Laci both jumped up from their spot by the fire, looking like they'd been touched by the cold hand of a haint. It was sure to have happened, and now it had, I was glad. I was glad because I still seen Seph lying in there in my mind. And it seemed like we'd all been waiting on it to fall in since we got here. I stood, brushed myself off and walked over to the pile left behind. There was good pieces in there. I was sure Papa would want to save them. Momma had her hands on her hips, eyeing what had become of the barn with a helpless look, like everything was spinning out of her control.

I said, "I'm going to see if I can loosen up some of them boards and maybe use them to fashion us some sort of shelter by laying them over there against that big pine near the fire."

Momma had already sat down. She waved her hand like she didn't care.

I said, "Laci, come on over here and help me."

Momma spoke sharp, unnatural like. "Wallis Ann, she's not strong as you, especially now."

Surprised, I said, "She won't have to do nothing heavy. Only help me get some of these boards loosened up, so I can stack the ones close by I want to use. She could put the broken ones aside for the fire."

"I don't want her to wear herself out."

Laci stood as if to come help, even with Momma saying she couldn't.

Momma pointed at the spot Laci vacated. "Laci, sit down."

Laci sat. Momma had only catered a little to one child over the other in the past, some towards Seph because he'd been the baby of the family, and a little towards Laci because of her issues, though I'd never felt too put out by none of it.

Maybe she was scared of Laci getting sick like Seph and still I persisted. "Maybe it would do her some good, get her moving about and warm her up. I tend to feel better when I'm doing something. She looked like she wanted to help. She still eats pretty good too."

Momma straightened up and fixed Laci with a look.

After a few seconds, she shook her head, and said, "No. She needs to stay here with me."

I shrugged like it won't no concern a mine, deciding now won't the time for me to start having any petty little jealousies over things what had always been part and parcel of our way with one another. I started towards the flattened barn and got to pulling on the boards, taking hold of the ends and yanking hard as I could to free them one by one. I took several of the longest ones first. The broken ones I added to the woodpile for the fire. I worked like I'd done when I first come, when I was by myself. Doing something give me a new energy and I kept my back turned to them while I worked and worked and worked because when I worked, I could almost believe I was warm. A while later, I heard Momma scraping at the skillet, fixing dinner. I ignored it and kept right on. I sensed it was well beyond the point of the midday when she come to get me.

She laid a hand gently on my bent back and asked in a quiet voice, "Aren't you hungry, Wallis Ann?"

I had plenty for a shelter, and what I was doing now was only work to be working, piling up wood for whatever Papa wanted to use it for. I *was* hungry though.

"Wallis Ann?"

I stopped and brushed my hand across my damp forehead. "Yes. I'm hungry. I'm always hungry. I'm tired of being hungry."

Momma twisted her hands. "I know. Come on and get you something to eat. Maybe you shouldn't do any more today."

It was as if Momma was feeling a bit guilty and trying to make up for her partiality earlier. It won't going to change nothing, so I spoke what come to mind first.

"If I don't do it, Momma, who will?"

"Maybe it don't matter at this point, Wallis Ann. Maybe it don't matter at all."

I won't sure what she meant by that. Hearing how she sounded scared me, as if she'd given up on things getting better. She'd been sitting and sitting, thinking too much maybe.

"Sure it matters, Momma. We can't give up, can we?"

Momma's gaze circled around the property, from the line of trees what give a bit of seclusion to where the cabin had stood, then on to the fallen barn, the wasted garden, right over to the flattened fodder in the field beyond the tree line, and then back to me.

"I don't know. I don't know anything anymore. I'm only trying to get through each day. Come and eat. I don't need you falling sick neither."

I tossed the board I held onto the others and followed her to the fire, where she'd saved some of the food she'd cooked. I ate with a faked enthusiasm, only to appease her while Laci eyed the extra corn pone Momma give me to munch on as she ladled out the watery beans in a pan.

When I was done I said, "I think I'll go check the traps Papa set out. Maybe something's in them now."

Laci shivered like a newborn calf, looking weak as one too, and she'd make the going slower, but I felt sorry for her right then. I seen how she needed me.

I hesitated, then said, "Momma, can Laci come?"

Momma had picked up the bucket and the skillet, about to go down to the creek to clean the pan and to retrieve the evening's water. Once more she looked Laci over. What was curious was how Laci tucked her trembling hands behind her as Momma studied her. Laci stared back, peaceful, almost like she was wanting to persuade her.

Momma sighed, then said, "Well. I reckon it might be all right. Go on with Wallis Ann, and the both of you don't take too long."

"No, ma'am. I'm only going to check them traps and we'll be right back."

I hurried, and soon the brush, and pines swallowed us up. We located the two traps Papa set not too far off. He'd put a few pecans down as bait, never going back to check on them after Seph got sick. I figured nothing would be in them. I was wrong. The small, tan, brain-shaped nuts he'd laid in the center, after cracking the shells between his palms, had enticed two victims. Big old gray squirrels, each hung by the neck. Excited at having squirrel meat, I hurried over to the dangling bodies, and quickly got them down.

I released Papa's snares from their necks, and encouraged, I told Laci, "Let's look for something else to use to bait and reset these traps."

Holding on to the squirrels by their tails, I began walking deeper into the woods, looking for an acorn tree while Laci followed. We went further and further, until I finally found one. I laid the squirrels down, and pushed the leaves aside at the base of the trunk to uncover the small, round nuts. I scooped them into my hand, and showed her. She reached out and I put them in her hand to hold. Next I scraped about for a rock to crush them open, thinking if I did half the work, a squirrel might be more inclined to investigate. I found a good-sized one to use, and squatted to dig it out of the dirt.

When it was free, I reached up and said to Laci, "Here, let me have them acorns."

I held my hand midair, only no acorns was dropped. I looked back at her, seen the direction of her gaze. Something about her expression, wide-eyed, caused me to freeze. The acorns she held fell out of her hand right then, scattering around her feet. She was staring at something, and the hairs on my neck pricked straight up. I twisted so I could confront whatever it was, afraid it might get to us before I had the chance to do something. A large red wolf sat not more than thirty feet away. My fingers gripped the rock tight. It didn't move and neither did we. A few seconds later, two sets of eyes, identical to the momma wolf, peered out from behind her. Pups. She licked her mouth and blinked.

One of the youngsters poked its nose forward, catching our scent, and the adult let out a low rumble, growling a warning at her pups—or us. The young ones faded into the scrub behind her. I heard Laci breathing fast above my own hammering heart. I began to formulate a plan to run at the wolf screaming and waving my arms if she come at us. Only she didn't move. I shifted my weight slow and careful, letting my fingers creep along leaf-covered ground to brush one of the squirrel's tails. I kept my eyes on her as I dragged it towards me so I could grip it in my hands. I rose to my feet slow, deliberate, my gaze locked with hers.

Bending forward, I tossed one of the squirrels and it landed halfway to her. She curled her lips back to show her teeth. Dear God, don't let her take it as a threat. I stayed still as she bowed her head low, catching the scent of it. She come for-

ward a step, and raised her head to snarl a warning at us. Even
with her aggressive nature, I was certain by now she won't
going to attack. She come forward another step, and another,
and when she unexpectedly rushed forward, I stumbled backwards into Laci. The wolf grabbed squirrel and took off the
way her pups had gone, her big brushy tail the last I seen of
her. Laci's hands was on my shoulders as I let my breath out.

I said, "Come on, Laci. Hurry!"

I didn't drop the rock. It was all I had if the wolf decided to
follow us. I didn't hear or see no signs of her after that, but re-
setting the traps won't going to happen, least not right now. We
hurried to the campfire, and I didn't mention what happened,
or else Momma wouldn't allow me to set foot nowhere.

I held up the squirrel, triumphant. "Momma, look!"

It was the first smile I'd seen on her face since Seph passed
over.

Momma said, "Praise God, we're going to eat good tonight!
I'll stew it if you'll clean it."

I hurried down to the creek with the squirrel, where I
skinned and gutted it and carried it back to Momma. She
placed it in the skillet and added water before dragging the pan
over a section of our fire. That afternoon it was all I could
think about. I only wished it was the time of year for ramps,
they would've added just the right touch of seasoning and
would've made stewed squirrel perfect, but I won't one to
complain over not having that little extra.

Occasionally I'd catch a whiff of it as I went about gathering
up wood to keep ourselves stocked. My belly would rumble
loud, but it didn't bother me like before because soon I'd have
something to put in it. The breezes died down later in the afternoon, and I was able to get working on the shelter. Momma
watched me for a while, and to my surprise she got up and
helped.

As we worked, I said, "It still smells like snow."

She glanced up at the gray clouds what looked heavy, like big, bulging sacks ready to burst. When dusk was upon us we finished arranging the boards to suit our needs. I took the quilt, and draped it carefully over the wood. Laci and I gathered up pine branches, and tucked them underneath. Next, I lay the blanket over top of them inside the shelter, and it looked a bit like a snug little cave. I went over to the fire to watch Momma stir the squirrel, and the meat started to fall off the bones. She took the bigger ones out and we sucked on them hard.

When it come time to eat, we didn't gulp it down. We ate slow as we could. We savored each bite, and the rich taste nearly brung me to tears. After we cleaned up, we crawled underneath the shelter, and soon the snow went to falling as the light went out of the sky. Heavy, wet flakes come hard, and I worried it would spoil all our hard work. It took no time to coat everything white. I was closest to the opening, and I went out at one point to add more wood to the fire. I took a pine tree branch and tried to knock snow off the top of the shelter, off the quilt, which when wet would weigh too much to hold up. The shelter was good but it won't going to stand a lot of wet snow, or if the wind come up again.

I stayed awake, unable to sleep, watching as the white flakes fell. It might have been around midnight when it finally stopped. I went out again, added wood to the fire once more, knocked more snow off, then I scurried inside, my feet so numb with cold, I had to put them towards the blaze until some of the feeling come back. If Papa showed up with the truck right then, I wouldn't have hesitated climbing in and telling him, "Let's get out of here." This was only a dusting, barely two inches, and winter won't really here yet. It would be impossible living this way for too much longer. I could see that now.

I finally fell asleep. Morning come and when I opened my

eyes, I had to squint against the dazzling bright white of sun on snow. I smelled coffee. It couldn't be Momma, she would have had to crawl right over me and Laci to get out. I poked my head out. Papa squatted by the fire cooking something in the skillet what smelled like side meat. From the look of him, he'd been through some bad times, his clothes like ours, filthy dirty, yet when he seen me, he smiled. I crawled out, went to him so he could hug me tight.

He pointed to the shelter. "I knowed I could count on you."

It won't only the glow of the fire what warmed me.

I nodded my head towards the barn. "It fell in. I used some of the wood, and put the rest aside."

"I see that."

"It got right airish, blowing hard and down it went."

"It won't too far from coming down when I left. It was bound to happen."

He poked at the side meat, turned and pulled *eggs* from a burlap sack he'd set nearby. I almost fainted when I thought of how good a runny egg would taste. I hadn't had one in so long, they almost didn't look real. I stared at them, my mouth watering. At the edge of the woods a half-licked salt block was keeping Pete busy. His long tongue petted the sides of it, and then swirled over the top. He'd even thought about good ole Pete.

He cracked an egg on the edge of the skillet.

I asked him, "Did you get the truck running?"

"I did. It's on down the path, not too far from here."

"Papa, how'd you get this food, and the salt block?"

"Well, that's what took some time. After I worked on the truck, I helped a guy haul some wood and supplies to his place up on Cherry Gap. He give me the food as payment. I got the salt from another guy who lost his milk cow in the flood. And see? This is what I'm talking about. There's always ways to make do."

He cooked the eggs and I stared at the food like that wolf eyeing them squirrels. My stomach rumbled and wouldn't stop.

"What's other folks doing? Are there lots of other ones who lost their homes?"

"Right many. Some's left. Others are trying to rebuild. It's not easy getting materials in."

"Are we going to leave here?"

"I reckon so."

"What about Pete? How can we leave Pete?"

"He'll be fine. Wild mustangs out west survive the winter. Don't you worry none about Pete, he can take care a his self."

Momma heard us, and come out from under the shelter. She and Papa hugged in silence, any disapproval she might have held gone now he was here again.

He let her go and said, "Soon as we eat, we're gathering up anything worth taking, and we're leaving."

I half expected Momma to insist she won't going nowhere, but she didn't. She appeared worn down, as if her convictions had collapsed right along with the barn. Like she'd said, maybe none of what we'd tried to do mattered at this point. I crawled into the shelter and pushed on Laci. She was facing the other way, and I couldn't see her face. When she didn't move, I leaned over and put my hand on her side. I could feel her breathing, slow, like she was still asleep.

I pushed on her again, "Laci, get up."

She flopped over onto her back and wiped at her face. When she looked over at me, Lord, her bloodless, white skin under the wild tangle of hair gripped me in the middle, made me want to hurry quick before we lost her too. Laci was hurting and couldn't tell nobody, and it pained me to see her looking so poorly. Any smidgen of resentment I might have had towards her yesterday left me quick.

I rubbed her arm softly and said, "Papa's here. He's got something to eat what will make you feel better. Come on."

She rolled over on to her side and crawled out of the shelter, and I followed. We gathered round the fire, and as we ate, the only sound was the scraping of our spoons through the tin pans, and the sound of the fire crackling. I give Laci part of my egg, side meat, and half of my piece of corn pone. I thought about winter coming and if I'd had any doubt about leaving, or whether or not we might could make it, my answer was Laci, because staying here would be a death sentence for her. Her hands shook as she held her pan, the spoon trembling all the way to her mouth. It was fine to leave for a little while. I wanted to ask Papa when we'd come back, only I was too nervous, and too aware how hard it was.

After we finished, I said, "Momma, I'll clean this up."

She nodded and I gathered up the dirty pans. I dreaded sticking my hands in the freezing water, only I wanted one last look at Stampers Creek. I wanted to see the weeping willows, the wishing rock, the bend of the creek, and all I was familiar with because who could say when I'd see it again? I hurried to get there, and when I finished cleaning everything, I found I couldn't linger. Actually, I couldn't hardly bear looking at what I'd come to see. Instead of taking the time as I'd wanted, I hurried away from the place I loved most.

Chapter 14

The inside of the truck smelled dank, the same way our root cellar had smelled. After putting our few household belongings in the back, Momma climbed in the middle, and Laci slid in beside her. I didn't think Laci's thin legs could've stood my weight, so I squeezed into the narrow space left on the seat and shut the door. I rested against it, shivering more from nervousness than cold. Papa got in and looked over at us sitting all scrunched up. Everyone was church service quiet, our breath suspended in front of our faces. He cranked the truck, and the engine sputtered, then cut off. Momma shifted on the seat, her fingers started worrying her knuckles. If the truck didn't start on the next try, I was prepared for her to tell me to open the door, to tell me to get out. In my mind, I seen her marching straight back to the campsite.

He tried again and with a belching backfire, the engine caught. Momma relaxed and closed her eyes as if to send up a little prayer. Papa let the engine have another minute to smooth out before he put it in gear, and turned us around. Being so close together, I noted this almost immediately; we smelled right bad, and because we was no longer out in the open, it was strikingly noticeable. I breathed through my mouth, and thought how this leaving certainly felt reminiscent of that night weeks ago. Like we was repeating the past. I didn't bother to look back this time either. I refused to think in detail about what it meant.

Momma finally asked Papa what had likely been setting heavy on her mind. "Where are we going, William? Do you have a plan, or are we leaving with no idea what we're doing?"

Papa said, "We'll head down to Hardy's, see how it goes."

Momma made some sound, blowing air out of her nose. That was the extent of the planning discussion. We come to the two big poplars and made the turn onto the dirt road, and soon come to the split between the trees where Cullowhee and Cherry Gap mountains showed off a smattering of left-over oranges and reds from fall. Seeing the trees on the cusp of entering into their dormant state for winter, their beauty was still something, and I wished Papa would stop the truck for a minute. Instead he drove fast down the road, like he was in a hurry to get to where we was going before Momma could change her mind.

Momma sighed, giving me and Laci a quick once-over. "Look at us. What a sorry-looking smelly bunch we are. Even your brother's going to have a hard time putting up with us."

Papa said, "You don't remember much about Hardy."

Momma said nothing.

Papa insisted everything would be all right. "He'll be glad to see us. It's been years. Maybe he's changed. You remember Uncle Hardy, don't you Wally Girl?"

I said, "Yes, sir."

Momma grunted, then she said, "If that stingy brother of yours has changed his no-good ways, I'll be shocked. And you know the two of you being together for too long's like mixing gas and a match."

Papa said, "Hardy won't turn away kin. He's always been

contrary, but he ain't going to deny his own a place at his table."

We got to Highway 107, and Papa turned south. We passed by abandoned cars, a few of them covered with parts of busted-up trees and stumps. We seen buildings partially washed away, and people still working to organize the cleanup process. At one point in Cashiers he pulled over. He got out, and so did I to look at one of the bridges heading north that was washed out, along with several buildings, because it really *was* something to see what the water done. When we got back into the truck, Momma was sitting up stiff and straight.

She said, "We've already been driving over an hour and there's not one area untouched by them storms and you're out there sightseeing."

Papa put the truck in gear and Momma quit talking again. Just past Cashiers we entered the state of South Carolina and then he turned off the 107 shortly thereafter. We only stayed on that road a little way, and before long, Papa turned onto a narrow dirt path not much different looking than ours. We went up and up the twisting trail, lined with huge pines, maple, and oak, until we come to a small cabin set back against a thicker stand of trees. The cabin had ivy creeping up half a one side, and a rusty tin roof. The front porch sagged in the center, and an old wooden rocking chair moved with the wind. Two-toned jugs, the lower half a dark russet and the upper a lighter color, sat around the yard. A hound dog come crawling out from underneath a back section of the cabin and shook off. Papa parked beside a truck sitting next to the cabin, its body as rusty as the tin roof. He stared at the cabin as he turned the engine off.

Nobody come to the door. There won't even a flicker of movement at any window.

Papa hesitated, then he got out and said, "Wait here."

He went up the two steps, onto the porch and tapped on

the door. He turned to look at us, and when he did, the door swung open. A man I took to be Uncle Hardy held a shotgun at the ready. When he seen Papa, he lowered it. I could see no resemblance at all between the two of them. Uncle Hardy had a big belly, whereas Papa was rail thin. Uncle Hardy wore a pair of long johns, stained down the front and on the knees and elbows, and from his cheeks and chin hung a long grayish beard. He had on boots over the long john bottoms like this was how he went out and did chores. He frowned at Papa and then at us in the truck, and when Papa held his hand out to shake, the gesture won't returned. Papa dropped his hand and shoved both into his coverall pockets. I could see him talking. Uncle Hardy didn't bother to look at him at all. He kept his eyes on us, head tilted like he was studying on what was being said. Papa gestured towards us once, and eventually he quit talking.

Momma mumbled, "I said this was a bad idea. Hardy's not married, never been married, and there's reasons for it."

I didn't want to stay here neither. It was looking better and better to face winter at Stampers Creek or take our chances anywhere else other than the likes of this place. Papa motioned towards the truck again and Uncle Hardy turned and went inside, leaving Papa standing on the porch. Papa followed, and a minute later he come out, his head down so I couldn't see his expression.

He come up the driver's side of the truck and said, "We're gonna stay here for a few days. Come on in."

Papa opened the door for Momma and then he got the few eggs and side meat what had been left over from this morning. I opened my door, and got out, then Laci. We waited in the yard and Papa started for the front door, yet none of us moved. He climbed the steps, and looked over his shoulder.

He repeated his self. "We're staying here a few days."

Slowly we followed him inside Uncle Hardy's house. I noticed three things immediately. It was very messy and the room was filled with more of them jugs, while stacks of newspapers was everywhere. Another set of stained long johns hung just inside the door, and the kitchen held nothing but heaps of dirty dishes. There won't hardly a place to sit or stand. It was very warm, and very small. And I think we might have smelled better than the inside of the cabin. There was an old wood table, a total of three chairs. Uncle Hardy was already sitting in one, an old cane back near the fireplace. Papa pointed Momma to one of the other ones and he sat in the last one. I took Laci over to stand by the fireplace.

It was the first time in days I thought we might could quit shivering, until Uncle Hardy spoke gruffly, "Don't block all the heat. Stand yourselves over there."

He pointed to a spot by a tiny window facing the front yard. I went to it and Laci followed. It seemed like it had to be the chilliest spot in the room. There was a draft coming through the cracks, and Laci stood sort a hunched up, while I tried to make myself shrink into the background.

Uncle Hardy turned his attention to Papa, and said, "Ain't got much. Can't be eatin' three times a day."

Momma's face flushed and she shot a mortified look at Papa.

Papa raised his hands up, and said, "We don't want to put you out none. We got a bit of food here to help out. We only need a few days, then we'll be on our way."

Uncle Hardy spoke in a raspy manner that produced a harsh cough. He hacked and hacked, and didn't seem well. His mood won't much better.

After he'd recovered from the coughing fit, he said, "Them young'uns can go on and get some wood in. They's grits up over the stove, some beans and they's a few turnips and taters in the cellar. If'n we gonna eat, it's got to be cooked. I ain't cooked nothing today, been too tired."

Momma rose from the chair, and went to the cook stove in the corner of the room and stoked up the fire.

She said, "Wallis Ann, go on outside and get more wood and go on into the root cellar and get them taters and turnips."

Uncle Hardy said, "Get three of each. That's all can be spared day to day. Got to make it last. Ain't had a good crop in a while."

Momma's mouth went flat and she shot Papa a hard look before she turned to the stove.

I said, "Yes, sir."

Soon as I went out the door, the hound come up on the porch, and sniffed at the hem of my dress, then my legs, and finally my hands as I held them out to him. I patted his bony head, and for a man who seemed to not have much food, the dog sure won't starving. He was nicely filled out, more meat on his bones than on mine. He ducked under the house, but his condition made me think a little better of Uncle Hardy. Wood was stacked in the front yard, and I picked up several pieces and set them by the door. By the side of the house a worn, crooked wood door sat at a slant near the bottom of the house. I lifted one side up and went down the tiny steps into the small, dank little room.

I could see the taters sitting in a wood box and another with some turnips. I also seen he had a few jars of shucky beans, maters, and peaches. I couldn't see Uncle Hardy canning and thought maybe a neighbor might have shared. I wanted to get a jar of peaches even though he'd not mentioned them. I wanted to open one up and eat the entire thing by myself only I bet he knowed the exact number he had, so I left them, went up the steps and closed the door. Back inside felt good compared to the outdoors, though I was almost claustrophobic inside the confined space.

I took what I'd brought up to Momma and she shook her head as she worked. She somehow managed to find what she needed in all the clutter. She sent me out for water, and boiled a big pot of it, washed out the skillet and a few pots, then started cooking. When it was ready she give Uncle Hardy and Papa their plates first. I waited politely for Momma to dole out our share.

She motioned at me. "Wallis Ann. Come on and get yours and Laci's."

I took the plates she offered and sat on the floor near the wall where I'd been standing. Laci seemed like she was too frightened to move, or to even eat. She'd stayed in the one spot since Uncle Hardy spoke to us. After Papa said a short blessing, including Uncle Hardy in it for his generosity, I looked down at my plate and almost cried. I was so hungry, and there was about as much food as what would fill up a bird. Two small sections of potato, a few small pieces of turnip, a spoonful a beans, and half a piece a corn pone. Laci's was the same. I looked over at Momma, and it looked like she had even less. And there was Uncle Hardy, watching every morsel we put in our mouths. When Papa dragged a piece of corn pone through his beans, Uncle Hardy frowned at him, like maybe Papa was enjoying it a little too much. I was glad when we finished because it was only then Uncle Hardy quit watching everyone and finished eating, taking his time and smacking his lips loudly.

Soon as the sun went down, Laci and I settled in to sleep beside the fireplace, next to Momma and Papa. There was no extra blankets, only what we'd brung with us, and still too wet to use. Uncle Hardy slept behind a curtain strung up in a corner of the room. His bed was built out from the wall, and loaded down with dirty quilts. I don't think I would have wanted to use one if he'd offered it. Of course, he didn't. The pillow had a dirty spot directly in the middle where his head lay. He snored something terrible. There won't much sleep for none of us that night.

* * *

The next day, Uncle Hardy told me and Laci to go outside. "Y'all might could do some work round here, earn your keep if'n you're gonna eat my food."

I won't about to question his authority in telling us what to do. I started for the door with Laci in tow.

Papa stopped us. "Wallis Ann, stop. What do you want done, Hardy? These girls have had a hard time of it already."

Uncle Hardy spit into the fire. "Wood's got to be chopped. Won't hurt them none to do a little round here."

Papa said, "I'll chop the wood if it needs chopping, but you already got a stack big enough to last weeks."

Uncle Hardy fixed Papa with a hard stare. "You always was too big for yer britches."

I said, "I can do it. Laci can sit in the sun and watch me."

Uncle Hardy said, "See?"

Papa said, "Wallis Ann, don't move."

I froze again. Uncle Hardy reached down by his chair and raised a jug to his mouth. He sort of snickered as he took a swig, and Momma, who was cleaning a pot, looked fit to be tied.

Uncle Hardy said, "If'n she wants to, let her earn her keep."

Papa's jaw tightened. "I'll say what she can or can't do."

Papa motioned at me, and we went outside, Laci following, and then Momma too. Nobody wanted to stay in the house with Uncle Hardy.

Papa said, "You're a good girl, Wallis Ann. I appreciate you trying to smooth things over, but your uncle Hardy would have you chopping wood, then he'd think of other things, and it would never end. Don't think I don't know how he is."

"He ain't like you, Papa. He's meaner'n a snake bite."

Papa looked down the path, and said, "He's always been that a way."

He went to the wood pile, and I went with him. For an

hour or so, it was like old times with me and Papa working together, Momma sitting on the porch in the rocking chair and
Laci perched on the steps watching us or flicking her fingers
over an imaginary instrument. When the sun was straight over
our heads, we paused for a spell to get some water. Admittedly,
I craved it almost more than the scanty food. It was the sweet-
est, best tasting I'd had in a long time. It was the one thing I
could have as much of as I wanted, and I drank and drank to
fill the hole in my belly. That night after we'd eat another pal-
try meal, we bunked down in front of the fireplace again. I was
dog-tired. I could hear Momma and Papa murmuring to each
other, and I went to sleep to the hum of their voices, too tired
to care what they whispered about.

Day in and day out, it was the same thing. Early one Sunday
morning after we'd been there two weeks, Papa woke me. He
put his finger to his lips, and motioned for me to get Laci up.
Momma stood by the door. It was clear we was leaving and it
give me such a good feeling, I forgot about feeling so hollow
inside. Papa went to Uncle Hardy's table and laid down a fifty-
cent piece. My jaw dropped because I thought we ought to
keep it. Uncle Hardy was a stingy, mean old man.

Papa motioned for Momma to open the door carefully and
Uncle Hardy kept snoring, even as a draft of cold air moved his
curtain about. We stepped outside into crisp fresh air. The hound
dog, whose name I never asked, crawled out from under the
porch and shook. He let his tail wag, give us the once-over, and
come over to press his nose into my hand as if to ask, *Where y'all
goin'?* I give him a good, long rubbing over his head and body
while Papa, Momma and Laci piled into the truck. I almost
wished I could take the dog with us. I headed for the truck,
looking back, and he wagged his tail at me before he scooched
back under the porch, and hard for me to admit, I realized he
was better off than us.

After I got in, Papa said, "I sure hope it starts."

I held my breath as once again, our fate was placed on this poor old truck. It did. Papa put it in gear, and we rolled down the hill. I shot a look over my shoulder and Uncle Hardy was rubbing his belly as he stood on the porch. There was a small, curly puff of smoke rising in the air from his chimney, and I thought about being cold all over again, but I didn't care. No matter what we had to do, anything else had to be better than staying with him. I turned away to face forward, not understanding how somebody could be so hateful. Momma sat with a little smile on her face, almost cheery looking as we headed down the bumpy trail.

The sun crested the hills, and by midmorning our optimism was a little less bright because we'd had no food, having eaten what we'd brought with us. I thought of what Uncle Hardy had in his root cellar and wished we'd took some of it. I considered if that would have been like stealing. I thought of that fifty-cent piece.

We come to what looked like a harvested sweet tater field and Papa stopped the truck on the side of the road.

"Let's see what's out here."

Momma was flabbergasted. "William, are you serious? You want us to go digging around in someone else's field?"

"Can't nobody see. There's not a soul or cabin nearby. Could be a tater or two been left out there, maybe more. We got to have something to eat."

Momma said, "We should have stayed put on Stampers Creek."

Papa left the truck, slamming the door. I sat for a moment watching as he bent over and began digging and felt bad he was out there on his own.

I said, "I'm going to go help him, okay?"

Momma shrugged and when I got out, Laci wanted to come too. There was times when I wished she'd understand it won't right. Momma needed somebody too at the moment. I put my hand up to stop her.

"Stay here with Momma, Laci."

She settled down onto the seat, and commenced on rocking. I was beginning to perceive it as a sign of distress. I followed Papa out to the field, and we dug around for an hour, neither one of us talking, and neither one of us finding not one measly little tater.

He finally give up and said, "There's nothing here, let's go on back."

I straightened my aching back, feeling dizzy and faint, and a bit mad at finding nothing. I walked to the truck with Papa, the thick silence as tangible as our hunger.

Chapter 15

We kept going south like dandelion pods, floating with the wind and with no sense of where we might land. After a while we come to a sign saying we was entering Oconee County, South Carolina. The land was full of rolling hills and as we rode along we didn't see much, a house here or there, and after a while Papa pulled the truck off to the side of the road when he spotted a little white church and a couple men standing outside smoking.

Papa said, "Maybe we ought to try a little singing. Maybe these folks is feeling generous since they just got out of church."

Momma shook her head. "William, for shame. Nobody has a blunt nickel to their name for that sort of thing, and even if they did, they've given it in church this morning."

I was disturbed by the idea altogether.

I said, "We gonna ask for a handout?"

Papa grunted and we drove on past the church. It got on into the late afternoon, and we come to a small crossroads, in the center of a tiny town called Pearl Springs. A small cluster of folks stood outside of a country store, and Papa quickly jammed on the brakes.

He said, "Girls, get ready, this is it. I got a good feeling. Let's entertain these good folks."

Momma whispered, "Dear God, this is crazy."

We was about to do what I'd feared, and here we had these strangers looking at us with suspicion as Papa parked the truck. Surely we looked something awful to these clean folks, what with our filthy, smoky clothes, our greasy, uncombed hair and thin faces. Momma looked gaunt and pale, and Laci the same. I put my grubby hands up and felt along my cheekbones. I closed my eyes, feeling nothing except shame, even though we couldn't help ourselves. Still. What might these people think? We couldn't get out and sing—no, beg. I sure couldn't.

"Papa . . ."

He was already halfway out, waving his arms to get their attention. "Hey now, folks! Listen up! Me and my family here . . ." He turned around and motioned for us to *get out of the truck.* "Me and my family here, we're known as The Stampers, a singing group the likes you've never heard."

Papa seemed to think recognition of our name would have traveled all the way down here, like saying "The Stampers!" give us star quality, made us official, like the Monroe Brothers, or the Coon Creek Girls. I guess it did make us sound like we'd been somewhere, experienced worldly things. I slid out, dragging Laci with me. She was trying to tuck in behind me, which was like trying to hide a horse behind a goat. It was like we was on display, because everyone turned to stare. This one girl about my own age talked with another girl, pointing and laughing behind their hands. I dropped my head. I stared down at the now snagged and linty dress I wore, at my scratched-up, dusty legs and feet. My breath hitched in my chest as I fought wave after wave of embarrassment as Papa's voice droned on building us up. I felt like my very soul was eat up with shame as people went quiet, a few of them looking like they felt sorry for us.

Papa set his hat down in front of his feet. If I thought I'd felt shame at his introduction, I was now absolutely mortified. He started singing "Black Jack Davey," stomping his boots in a rhythmic clog, while waving at Momma and urging her to join in. Weakly, she began singing, though she didn't dance with him like usual. I come in on the second stanza because I couldn't let Momma carry it all on her own. Poor Laci had no fiddle, so all she could do was keep to herself, and the singing really lacked something without her fiddling to back us up. We done the best we could. Two ladies about Momma's age clapped politely in time, until we finished the first song, but then Papa went on to "The Little Old Cabin in the Lane," and as if he couldn't stop, he started on "Short Life of Trouble," which seemed right fitting at the moment. Folks started drifting off by then as if to spare us any more humiliation, and when there won't but three left, our voices faded. The ones left was the two women who'd clapped and a man who smiled encouragement at each new song, and whistled a few times when Papa started stomping his boots and pounding out intricate footwork. Papa noticed folks leaving and finished with a flourish.

The man come forward and said, "Y'all sound good though it seems like you've run into a spell of hard luck."

Papa spoke in a quiet voice. "That we have."

"What all happened?"

"We lost our home, food crops, livestock, everything, in them storms what come through North Carolina just over a month ago. None of that don't matter much as the fact we lost our little chap when he took sick after drinking some tainted water. What's left of our lives is what you see."

Momma kept her face turned away, and the two women who'd stayed back a little went over to her side.

One took her by the hand, and said, "They's nothing worse than losin' your own child. I knowed it for myself."

Momma's voice trembled when she spoke. "It happened so fast."

The woman nodded. "Hard as it seems, if it had to happen, the Lord seen fit to take him. All what matters is where he is now."

Momma remained passive, unable to break down and cry in front of strangers.

The man said, "Well, look a here. Y'all sure are some mighty fine singers, and I imagine even better under other circumstances. See now, I run this here store. I'd be proud for you to come on in and let me get you some things to help you on your way."

Papa said, "We don't want to put no one to no trouble."

The man said, "No, no trouble at all. Name's Ammon Johnson. This here's my wife, Harriet, and her sister, Hazel Moore."

The women nodded at Momma.

Papa shook Mr. Johnson's hand and said, "I'm William Stamper, this is my wife Ann, and these are my daughters, Laci, and Wallis Ann."

"We're pleased to meet y'all."

Mr. Johnson led us inside, where he pointed to a wood display with candy in it.

He said, "You girls get you a lollipop, and some a them Mary Janes, if'n you want."

I hadn't had any candy since last Christmas, when I'd found a peppermint stick, caramels, and a pack of Wrigley's gum in my stocking. I chose two lollipops and several pieces of Mary Janes. I handed half to Laci. It was real hard not to cram all of it into my mouth at once. I ate the Mary Janes slow as I could and watched what Mr. Johnson give Papa. He gathered up some loaf bread, cheese, coffee, a few cans of pork and beans, can peaches, a long link of hot dogs and some oranges.

He put the items in a box, and said, "What else?" as if Papa was shopping with money.

Papa shook his head, overcome by the generosity.

He said, "It's a gracious plenty. I can't pay. When I get on my feet, I promise you, I will come and pay you for all a this. Tally it up, and I'll write you an I.O.U."

Mr. Johnson made a gesture, and said, "It ain't necessary. We've all had our share of hard times. We know what it's like."

Papa gathered up the box, and shook Mr. Johnson's hand again. "I won't forget this kindness."

"It's nothing."

Mrs. Johnson and her sister come forward to hug Momma, then me. When they went to do the same to Laci, she backed away from them, hands gripped tight behind her, looking at the floor, her jaw bulging on one side with a Mary Jane.

I felt a tinge of embarrassment while Momma explained her odd behavior. "Our Laci's not one to talk, or even sing, but she's got musical abilities you didn't get to see because she lost her fiddle in the flood. She's not used to strange folks. Please accept our gratefulness on her behalf."

Mrs. Johnson said, "She plays fiddle? Well, it just so happens we have two, don't we, Sister?"

Hazel Moore said, "Sure do. Only I can't play mine like I used to since I got the arthritis. Let me fetch it. She's welcome to it. It's only sitting up in my room, gathering dust."

She opened a door and we could hear her slowly climbing the steps, a dull hollow sound. She eventually returned, fiddle and bow in her hands, wiping it off with a cloth. She approached Laci, who held her head down, arms folded looking like she wanted badly to disappear. She'd finished the Mary Janes, and likely wanted to unwrap the lollipop, but not while she thought she was being stared at. Hazel Moore went up to her, leaned down and put the instrument where Laci could see it, almost under her nose. Laci's face flushed, the color rising under her skin like watching pink color deepen as the sun sets. She raised her head to stare at Hazel Moore, her mouth slightly parted, and then she looked at Momma.

Momma spoke, encouraging her. "Go on, Laci, take it."

Laci handed me the lollipop, and took the fiddle the way you'd capture a butterfly, gentle and easy. As she was rejoined with the one thing on this earth what could show us her spirit, a change come over her instantly, like shoving open the door on an old room what had been closed a long, long time, or pulling open the drapes at a window and letting the sun shine in after days of rain. She didn't need coaxing to play. She placed it under her chin, and drew the bow across the strings. She made a few adjustments, tuning it. How she knowed to do this, none of us could explain. She tilted her head and listened to the tone and then her fingers danced up and down the neck, nimble as soft, wiggly earthworms. She commenced on to playing "Amazing Grace," and the sound filled the room, resonating with purity as fresh as new snow on the ground, or the first sweet scent of jonquils after a long, cold winter.

Laci shut her eyes tight and swayed, lost to everything but the song. When she finished, she left the fiddle under her chin for a few seconds, her throat moving as she swallowed over and over. She lowered it and cradled it in her arms like a baby, and she couldn't stop staring down at it while the Johnsons and Hazel Moore couldn't stop staring at her, their expressions a mixture of astonishment and wonder.

Finally Mr. Johnson said, "I think that's the most beautiful rendition of 'Amazing Grace' I ever heard. She's got a gift all right."

Papa and Momma looked real proud, and happier than I'd seen them in a long time. They thanked the Johnsons, and Hazel Moore again.

Finally, Papa said, "We ought to be heading on."

Mr. Johnson said, "Where y'all going?"

Papa said, "Further south, I suppose."

"We wish you luck. Stop by if you come this way again. We'd be pleased to hear Miss Laci any time."

Papa went to the truck with the box of food, and Laci scrambled in with what mattered most to her. As we turned around and left, waving through the back window at that nice group of folks, Papa considered this first attempt a grand success. He got fired up, talking about stopping whenever, wherever, saying our musical abilities would have everyone begging for more, while I thought his choice of words interesting. He talked with the self-assurance he used to have at Stampers Creek, and he made big promises to Momma.

"It's going to get better now, and soon as we get some money saved, first thing we'll do is buy them girls some shoes. We'll take our money and go back to Stampers Creek, and build us a new place all over again."

What could Momma say? She wanted to give us what we needed, only her heart won't into this plan entirely. We felt alike, her and me. Looking a handout is what we'd be doing. Her heart and mind stayed behind with Seph, while I wanted us to not go on wishing on the stars, so to speak. Afterwards, each time we stopped and Papa announced we was going to perform, Momma's voice, what used to sound so strong and wonderful, come out less and less powerful, a paler version of before, like her very soul was fading away like the food always did. We traveled up and down the same stretch of highway and Papa was always able, somehow, to come up with gas money from a song here and there. We went to places like Big Creek, Merry Mountain and Tucker's Branch. Then Stoney Creek, Bonny's Peak and Little Top.

Once we set up camp near to what like an abandoned tobacco barn, until this old man come out of it with a shotgun and yelled at us. "Git off'n my property ya bunch a no-good bums!"

He fired a shot into the air, and we heard the pellets scatter, some hitting trees nearby. When Papa tried to talk to him, he fired another one, and we left quick. That was the night Momma cried herself to sleep. It seemed to me we was always barely hanging on, and I'd had the notion we'd never have enough to buy anything, not shoes, or decent clothes, much less food. I had paid attention. There was only this ongoing cycle of singing, earning a bit of money, and Papa turning right around and spending it on gas and a little for food. He maintained this was our best choice. He couldn't seem to see how people wouldn't look at us directly sometimes. He didn't seem to notice how Momma had lost her spark, or how Laci had come to be clingy as ivy growing along the side of a tree, barely letting me go tend to my privy needs.

One day after we come to a crossroads we'd passed a few times, Papa took a turn and drove a ways before pulling off to the side of the road for the night. Without a word, I rolled out of the stuffy truck. It was cold, but it felt better outside, fresher, and easier to breathe. Papa got out and stretched while Momma stood looking around as if trying to figure out how to settle herself somewhere, only her look said, *Where?* Laci got out and sat on the footboard of the truck, and began playing, as if she was trying to make up for lost time. Papa had parked close to the woods, and I took off to go collect firewood and water. Too often it had occurred to me living like this won't much different than being at Stampers Creek.

After I got the wood and water, I said to Momma, "Can I go explore a little?" I wanted some time alone, if I could get it.

"Don't wander off too far. It's getting on towards dark."

It didn't take long to lose sight of them, or the truck. I stayed close to the creek, as good a guide as anything. The deeper I went, the quieter it got, until a noise come, faint at first, then a bit louder as I continued. I kept stopping to listen, certain I was hearing a waterfall, and I began to wonder if I would find it

before Momma would get to worrying about how long I'd
been gone. I hurried, appreciating there was no snow, the
ground a bed of fallen leaves, which made it softer to walk on.
The noise got louder, turning into the familiar roaring I was
used to back home. Soon, I made out the ridges of a rocky area
through the trees. Within seconds I come to a clearing where a
calm pool lay, and above it, a waterfall of about forty feet.

What I couldn't quite comprehend was the person standing
right at the edge of the rocky outcrop. He held his arms above
his head, like he was stretching, only it was what he did next
that took my breath straight out of my lungs. He dove off the
edge, falling with the water, straight down. I screamed, and
clapped my hands over my eyes, certain he'd set out to kill his
self. He landed with a loud splash. I didn't want to take my
hands from my eyes, only he might need help. I dropped them
and looked, expecting a body floating in the water. He popped
up and shook the water from his head, before turning his head
this way and that, like he was listening. Somehow, above the
roar of the fall, he'd heard me. I scurried backwards, ducking
behind a large boulder, my heart skipping along like I was
jumping up and down. He crawled out of the pool, and stood,
casting his eyes about. I didn't dare move.

He called out, "Hey? Somebody there? Hey!"

I eased my head around the edge of the boulder and got a
glimpse of him coming in my direction, wet and shivering. I
shrank from view. The rustling sound of him searching got
louder as he got closer. I had to see how close. I dared peek out
again only to find him facing the rock, and I shriveled up tight
against it. I quit breathing. I shut my eyes. I heard the crunch of
sticks and dried leaves. Suddenly, there was a damp odor like
creek water with a hint of fish.

I flushed hot when he said, "I'm looking right at you."

I let out my breath and opened my eyes. He was smiling at

me, hands on his hips, head cocked with curiosity. He was tall, lean, with sandy hair, long on top and short on the sides.

I gestured weakly at the falls. "I seen you jump. That fall's got to be thirty, or forty feet! I thought you was trying to kill yourself."

His head went back and he laughed. I felt like a fool.

My face went hot and I crossed my arms. "Well? What person in their right mind jumps off a waterfall when it's near bout winter?"

He stopped laughing, yet didn't lose his smile.

He swept one arm in front, bowed slightly, and said, "Clayton Jones, High Diving Act for Cooper's Family Fun and Shows. Count this your lucky day! You got to see me perfecting my act for free! Actually, I use this waterfall whenever we're in Oconee County to practice, see."

"Cooper's Family Fun and Shows? What's that?"

"A traveling carnival. Ain't you ever seen one?"

"No."

"What's your name?"

"I got to get back to my folks."

"Sure, okay, but can't you tell me your name?"

I hesitated, unsure. Momma would tell me to mind my manners. Papa would say I ought not be talking to strange boys. I decided he won't a stranger, not anymore. He'd told me his name, and a bit about his self. And he looked friendly enough.

"Name's Wallis Ann Stamper."

"Wallis Ann? I sure do like that. It's different."

I didn't know what to say, other than thank you. "Thank you."

"You're welcome. Where you from?"

"A place called Stampers Creek. North Carolina."

"Stampers Creek? Never heard of it. I'm from here, well, not here exactly, but South Carolina. I caught on with Johnny

Cooper and his crowd about four years ago when Mom died of the cancer, and Pops, he got to carrying on with someone he decided to bring home. Her name's Doreen, and he tried to say she was only gonna keep house for him, but it was more than that, and I decided I had to go. I jumped a train and got off in Greenville. Seen the show there, and started working for them, doing odds and ends. They had this high dive act, and when the guy broke his leg falling off the ladder before he even got to the platform, I said I'd do it. I been doing it ever since. I've always been a bit of a daredevil, guess you could say. I like this way a living. It ain't like real work. It's fun."

I listened, wishing I could think of something interesting to talk about. As he told me his story, I watched his face, the way he moved his hands in big gestures, how he shifted from foot to foot. Up close, he had eyes like that old hound back at Uncle Hardy's, soft brown. Gentle. Next thing, I was comparing him to Joe Calhoun. Tall, blond-haired Joe. Clayton was a little bit taller, and whereas Joe was solid built, thick through his body and limbs like a sturdy tree, Clayton had a stealthy like movement what reminded me of an old barn cat we used to have. Clayton talked like he'd known me a long time, and Joe, although polite, was quiet, not talking near as much.

Clayton turned a smile on me, his expression quizzical.

I said, "It was nice talking to you. I really got to go. I told Momma I'd only be gone thirty minutes or so."

"You ain't told me nothing much about yourself."

I could see him trying not to stare at my dirty clothes, and shoeless feet. I tucked my limp hair behind my ears, all too aware of my state.

I motioned slightly, a weak flip of my hand in the direction of our camp. "Not much to tell. I'm with my momma, papa, and my sister, Laci. We're sort a traveling around, I guess you could say. We do some singing."

"Singing? You mean like an act?"

"It's not what we usually do, I mean yes, we sing, just not the traveling part. We had us a place and there was this bad storm and then come a flood. We lost everything. Papa decided this was what we needed to do for the time being. What we had to do really, with winter coming and all."

"What do you all sing?"

"Folk music. Gospel. I really got to go. Nice to meet you, Clayton."

I turned and started going along the path the way I'd come, hurrying away from him while trying not to appear too anxious to put distance between us. My entire body felt awkward and uncomfortable, aware he was likely staring after me, and maybe judging for himself the nature of our situation.

He called out, "Hey! Wait!"

I hesitated before I stopped and turned to look at him.

He come running and stood beside me, still wearing the same smile, and it suited him, and his ways. He seemed like a sunny kind, a lighthearted, fun-loving person, and it was nice to be around somebody who was happy. I found myself wanting to smile at him.

He said, "I practice here most every day. The show's set up near Tucker's Branch, and it'll be there long as the money's coming in. Come watch me here anytime, if you want. I don't own the waterfall."

His invitation eased my mind, and I grinned at him, and it seemed a long time since I'd done that. My face felt all tight and hot, and he kept staring at me, which was fine, although I couldn't imagine what he was seeing, until he made another comment.

He said, "Shoot, Wallis Ann, them dimples a yours remind me of my old sweetheart, Janie Mae."

Him saying such a thing so quick had me going all wobbly legged like a newborn foal.

He began walking the other way, jumping up to swat at a tree branch before yelling, "Say you'll come back!"

I hesitated, and before I could think, "Okay, I will!" flew out of my mouth.

I run fast as my bare feet would allow, following the creek, noting the deep shadows cast before me, the sun having dropped below the ridgeline and making the horizon flare like a red-hot stove. Momma would be having herself a spell, and Papa was liable to make good on his threat once and for all, and actually switch me. I'd been gone at least an hour. Soon enough I seen smoke from the campfire, and heard the thin reedy tune of Laci playing a song. I swooped into camp and found Momma and Papa in a heated argument, not even worried about me and where I'd been after all. Laci put her fiddle down and scurried over, back to dogging my every footstep. Finding Momma and Papa in a spat made me want to slink back into the woods where it was quiet, and peaceful. Nothing had been cooked, and I tuned into what the argument was this time, not surprised when Momma repeated the usual.

"We have nothing over our heads, and little more to eat than before."

Papa said, "We'll be fine, Ann. We'll go back to Hardy's before I let you or the girls go hungry."

"Huh. I'd *rather* go hungry than stay with him. My point is, we're no better off."

That's where the argument ended. Quietly I began putting together a little bit of supper. Some beans. Some corn pone. That night around the campfire there was no prayers, no asking the Lord to bless us and keep us safe.

Chapter 16

Papa insisted on going a bit further south each day, driving through little smatterings of towns here and there. Those who even bothered to listen to a bunch of scrappy-looking folks sing till their throats was raw must've believed we was off our rockers. At the end those long days, I urged Papa to return to where I'd met Clayton, telling him water was convenient and besides, no one had chased us off like before. Momma was withdrawn most of the time, and when she did speak up, she'd comment on money spent driving hither and yon. Papa turned her off like a radio most days.

Clayton was always at the waterfall, and always entertaining. His confidence sat well with his good humor. I'd never had a friend like him before. Not even in school. These times with him was special, and the more I spent alone with him, the more I wanted to escape from our worries.

"Watch this!" he'd yell, and then do some ridiculous dive as if entertaining me was the most important thing he had on his mind. Afterwards, he'd get serious, and would practice till his mouth, fingertips and toes was blue. Clayton had more energy than anyone I'd ever seen. He couldn't sit still a minute. Some-how, at some point, our time together would end with him chasing me around the woods, ducking behind trees only to spring out, grab me and swing me around. It was like a game, only I realized he was doing this so he could put his hands on me. I was more than happy to follow suit, and would run from him shrieking, until one day I got dizzy, and had to stop. I stooped over, my hands on my knees, I broke out in a cold sweat and feared I might throw up right at his feet.

"Wallis Ann? What's wrong, you all right?"

"I'm fine."

"You sick? Should I go get your folks?"

"No! I'm fine. I didn't eat much today."

"What do you mean? Why not?"

I shrugged. "It's nothing. I'm all right."

"You don't look all right. You're white as the inside of a bis-cuit."

I flipped my hand, dismissing his concern, wishing I had the biscuit he talked about.

He said, "You sure?"

I figured out a little lie. "Momma says I have iron poor blood."

"Oh. Maybe you should eat more."

Would, if I could.

Eager to move on, I asked him, "What do you want to do now?"

Clayton was still giving me the once-over.

"Sit. Tell me more about your family. You ain't ever said much about them. You said you had a sister? What was her name, Laci?"

"Yes."

"She older?"

Hesitant, I rubbed my hands across the tree trunk we sat on. "Yes, she's older and she's . . . different."

"What do you mean?"

I don't want to talk about Laci.

Clayton only looked curious, and I relaxed.

"She don't talk. Never has. She can play any instrument you give her though. Piano, fiddle, banjo, dulcimer . . . no telling what else."

"Really!" Clayton sounded impressed. "And you sing?"

"Yes."

"Sing something."

"Now? It would sound better with Laci and her fiddle."

"So, bring her next time."

I wished I hadn't said that. I didn't want to share Clayton. I didn't want to admit it, but that was the truth of it. Had it been anybody else, I wouldn't have minded bringing Laci. I liked having Clayton looking only at me, trying to get to know only me. There won't no chance of him comparing the two of us if he didn't never see her. No chance of me fading and disappearing into the background like usual. I was sure this is what would happen. He'd get to thinking about how pretty she was. He'd get to thinking, *Well gee, Wallis Ann here, she's kind of a plain old gal—if I liken her to her sister.* Them thoughts was doing me no good, yet I couldn't help but feel possessive about Clayton; he was *my* friend. His suggestion to bring her along, although innocent on his part when he had no idea of my inner turmoil, sort of riled me up and my voice was dismissive, hard when it come out.

"I don't know about all that."

Clayton leaned back a little studying my face, which was *not* helpful. "Okay, well sing then."

I began singing parts of a song I liked, called "Careless Love" by Bessie Clayton. I'd heard it on the radio down at Dewey's store a few times. When I finished Clayton sat quiet, staring down at his hands, and I couldn't tell what he'd thought of it, good or bad.

"I reckon you didn't like it none."

"I did like it. A lot. Anyone say you ought to be singing on stage?"

"No."

"Well, you should."

"Shoot, I ain't that good."

Clayton snorted. "You ain't good? You are too. I'm telling you. Don't you believe me?"

"I don't know. I guess so."

We sat quiet for a few minutes. In truth his words made me happy, and though I'd been told before I had a good voice, coming from him was different.

Clayton broke the quiet spell when he said, "Look, I got to get back. If the show goes like last night, there'll be a big crowd, and I got to help feed the miniature ponies, and all."

"Miniature ponies?"

"Miniature ponies, a two-headed sheep, and a pretty big snake, to name a few of the animals the show's got."

Clayton's world certainly won't like mine.

I said, "It sounds like an odd place."

"Sure, it's a bit odd, but odd is ordinary at a carnival. Hey, tomorrow I'll bring you some spun sugar."

"What's that?"

"You never had spun sugar?"

"No."

"You wait. You'll be begging me to bring you some every day. Will you be here?"

"I'll try."

"Hey, Wallis Ann?"

"What?"

"You remember what I said the other day."

I shook my head, unsure of what he was getting at.

Clayton smiled. "You don't?"

"Well, I don't know. You say lots of things."

"I said your smile reminds me of Janie Mae. You remember me mentioning her?"

The water rushed over the edge of rock, crashing onto the jagged ones below before settling into the cove. My blood pumped through me the same way, as if it was rushing through my veins only to collect into the center of my chest where my heart beat. Clayton looked at me with expectation, and I in turn considered him. I won't quite sure what he wanted. We sat side by side on a fallen tree trunk and he unexpectedly leaned over and planted a kiss on my cheek. It caught me unawares, and I placed my fingers on the spot that tingled like a thousand butterflies had landed there. My eyes flicked in his direction. He was grinning, and I quickly looked away. For October, the air felt heated, not cool as it had been before.

Clayton cleared his throat. "Didn't you like that?"

"I don't know."

Clayton spoke with his ever-present confidence. "You did. I can tell."

I shook my head, denying it.

He won't bothered at all. "Well then, I'll have to do better next time."

"If there's a next time."

Clayton didn't look so sure anymore. It did me some good to know I could control this situation more than I'd realized, until he dipped his head down again and kissed me directly on my mouth, his arms going around me tight like he thought I might run. And I might would have, it scared me so bad. And then, something happened. I started kissing him back. I let him press his lips to mine, let him open my mouth with his, and do what I'd only read about in the romance magazine I'd kept secreted away from Momma's eyes, forever lost now to the river water. I got dizzy for reasons altogether different than hunger. I pulled away, and covered my mouth with both hands.

Joe Calhoun. He unexpectedly invaded my thoughts the way

Clayton invaded my mouth. I shouldn't think about Joe. Especially since Papa couldn't stand a Calhoun, no matter how nice he'd been. I forced the memory of him away. Clayton kissed me again, and it was like the first time had been to see if he liked it, and the second time to show me he did. After a minute or so, he pulled away.

He brushed a hand through his hair and said, "That was really something else, Wallis Ann. Maybe I should've done that earlier. You got some high color to them cheekbones now."

All sorts of strangeness and wonder flooded my middle, crept along my legs and into other places I'd be embarrassed for him to know about.

Clayton stood to go. "I wished I could stay longer. Especially now."

He reached down and grabbed my hands, pulling me up. I was unable to untangle my thoughts enough to speak.

I located my voice and managed a reasonable sentence. "I need to get back too."

Clayton said, "I'll see you tomorrow, right?"

I nodded dumbly.

"You sure you're all right?"

I nodded once more before I turned towards our camp.

He yelled like he done before. "Promise?"

I stopped long enough to raise my hand and yell, "I promise!"

The entire way to camp, I kept my fingers placed over my mouth, the scene rolling around in my head again and again. I hurried, and as I drew closer, I smelled the wood smoke, and worried about what kind of mood Momma would be in. Lately it changed like the weather. I didn't hear Laci on her fiddle, or anyone talking. The campsite seemed too quiet. I broke through the cover of trees and spied Momma sitting in the truck while Papa sat by the fire. Laci stood off by herself, holding her fiddle tight, not playing, not even plunking on the strings.

I slowed to a walk and made my way over to sit with Papa while glancing over my shoulder at Momma. "Papa?"

He didn't lift his head or answer.

"Papa."

Nothing. I went to Momma. When she seen me at the window of the truck, she shook her head. I left them alone, went to the fire and lay down. My belly growled, and funny little black pinpoints floated in front of my eyes. Laci come over and set herself opposite of me, feet tucked against mine. She held on to her fiddle, and seemed to drift off quick. I remained awake, my gaze shifting between my parents. Something must have happened while I was gone and there was a feeling of guilt for not having been here, as if I could have done anything about it. Momma stayed in the truck overnight, and Papa did nothing about it. It had to be cold not being near the fire. They each took their positions and nobody was giving in.

The next morning, Momma was by the fire and she had her say. "I'm tired of this endless charade. We need to find real work. If you won't, then I will."

Papa refused to look at Momma. After a minute, he stomped over to the truck and left. I trusted he'd return with something, if only to prove he could look after us. I spent the morning doing what I always do, gathering wood and boiling water. Afterwards, I sat by the fire, warming myself, trying not to think about how hungry I was. Papa's absence give me expectations and I hoped he wouldn't disappoint us. There won't much talking between me and Momma. Laci sat snugged against me, head on my shoulder, or hand holding mine, or leaning on me in some way. Her clinging sent an odd feeling through me like I'd been crammed into a tight space. It made me want to get away. I stood, and Laci jumped to her feet too.

I said, "Stay here with Momma."

Momma spoke, her tone sharp. "What are you about, Wallis Ann?"

"I'm going to the waterfall."

"You've been every day we've been here. There can only be so much exploring. What all is so interesting in them woods?"

I'd never lied to Momma, or kept anything from her before. I said, "Nothing. It's just nice there."

Momma said, "There's plenty of them at home. You never cared much about going off to see one."

Her questioning set off a feeling of guilt, and I was afraid my face would betray my words. I come up with a different sort of reason.

"I like to be alone sometimes."

"Alone? In the woods? It's not a good idea. Take Laci with you."

"Momma, there's nothing for her to do."

"Wallis Ann, soon as you moved, she jumped up. I was going to tell you the other day to take her along only you took off before I realized it. Take her with you. This gallivanting off alone isn't a good idea."

Fearful Momma would stop me going altogether, I nodded, and said to Laci, "Well, come on then."

Soon as we was out of sight of Momma, I started fussing at her, saying mean, hateful things.

"I wish I didn't have to always have you hanging on. It's not fair. Do you think it's fair? You're the oldest but I'm the one who always has to do more, or give in, and do things with you because you can't—or won't—do them on your own. Maybe you just don't do them on purpose!"

I frowned at her, waiting to see how these words registered, if at all. Laci slowed down. I mean she moved so slow, I wanted to get behind her and shove her down the path. I stomped ahead, acting like I didn't care if she followed or not. A minute later, I regretted what I'd said. I'd never spoken a sharp word to Laci. What was wrong with me? I stopped and turned around.

"I'm sorry, Laci. I didn't mean it! I'm hungry. I'm always hungry! Ain't you hungry too?"

The words I'd said sat heavy as rocks, and when I'd spoken them, I might as well have actually hurled a few at her. Laci seemed to ignore me and studied the new surroundings. With a big sigh, I grabbed her hand again, and after a few minutes, we come to the log where Clayton and I sat the day before.

I said, "Sit here with me, Laci, I'll tell you a secret."

I kept hold of her hand, and sat while she made up her mind. Soon her body, warm and sweaty, lay against me. I felt a thickening in my throat, and I cleared it.

"You know what happened yesterday, Laci? This is a big secret. I'm going to tell you about it like it's a story. You like stories, right?"

I proceeded to detail how I met Clayton. Who he was, what he looked like, and what he did with the traveling show. I pointed at the waterfall, and described how he leapt from the falls. I told her he was going to bring some spun sugar today. I didn't tell her he'd kissed me. That was too much of a secret thing, and besides, what did Laci think about most of the stuff I babbled on about anyway? I wanted to hold on to it, a secret I could keep tucked away like how you might hide money, or something else you consider valuable.

I talked more about the spun sugar. "He said it tastes like candy. We like candy, right, Laci?"

Right then I heard a hoot, like an owl calling. It was Clayton's signal. I hooted back, and Laci grabbed at my shoulder, her fingers digging in.

"It's okay. It's Clayton, the person I was telling you about, my new friend."

Clayton walked around the bend, and when he seen Laci, he stopped like he won't sure if he should approach us or not.

I motioned at him and called out, "This is Laci!"

He come forward, the look on his face was one of interest, although he stood some ways from me, polite, more quiet than usual.

He scratched his head, and shoved his hands in his pockets. "Pleased to meet you, Laci."

She shifted away from him, even though he won't anywhere near her.

Clayton held out a paper sack to me. "I got you some a that spun sugar. It's flattened a bit, but it'll still taste good."

He stepped closer, and handed me the sack. I opened the bag and looked inside. It smelled like cake, and it looked a lot like the cotton we'd seen in the fields, only pale pink. I was puzzled by the look of it.

He said, "Here, pinch off a piece like this."

He reached in and pulled some off. He popped it into his mouth, and opened it to show me it was gone, in seconds.

"It melts fast in your mouth, like snow melts in your hand."

I pulled off a small piece, and put it in my mouth. My eyes flew open in surprise at the fuzziness that lasted only seconds and left a lingering sweetness. I got another piece, even bigger. My stomach rolled in appreciation.

"This is so good! Laci, here, try some!"

I plucked another wad and put my hand to Laci's mouth, intending to place it on her tongue. Clayton watched this with interest.

"Can't she eat on her own?"

Laci grabbed my wrist, and snatched the spun sugar from my fingers and popped it between her lips. Her mouth moved a little, and she dug into the sack for another piece.

Clayton smiled and spoke to her directly. "You liked it, eh? It was good, won't it?"

He sat on the log beside me, and Laci hopped up. She stepped over it, and faced away from us, towards our camp.

Clayton said, "She don't like me much, I don't think."

"It's okay. It takes her getting used to a stranger. Thank you for the spun sugar. It's really good."

I held the sack out to him.

"No, you keep it, it's for you."

"Thank you."

I held on to it, and there was an awkward silence, something we'd not suffered from before.

I said, "If you want, you can go on and practice. I told her what you do. It'll be fine."

Clayton looked at the fall. "So. She understands, she just don't talk?"

"We think so."

He seemed subdued. I got off the log to follow him.

I turned to my sister. "Laci, I'm going to stand there so I can see. You want to watch too?"

She didn't move. I shrugged my shoulders, a little bit of that earlier aggravation seeping in again. I moved to the spot where I could watch, looking over my shoulder now and then to see what she was doing. She'd gone to rocking. I focused on Clayton, who was practicing doing his dive, which always scared me something fierce.

I said, "Laci, come watch Clayton practice."

She moved her head the other direction like she was listening for something and ignored me. I sighed and let her be. Clayton dove time and again. I applauded and cheered him on, and soon my worry over Laci eased. I sort a forgot she was with me. My heart beat fast as I tried to imagine how it would feel to stand where he did and jump. I wondered how he'd ever had the nerve to do it the first time.

Clayton held up one finger, meaning last one. That was when I remembered Laci, wishing she would come watch, and when I looked back to coax her over, the log was empty.

I run towards it, stopped and spun in circles, yelling, "Laci! Laci!"

A crow cawed, the hoarse sound eerie, and it echoed until it was swallowed up in the silence of the woods around me. I rushed back to see Clayton looking up at the spot where I usually stood. I motioned frantically with my hands. I waited until he climbed out of the water, and then I went back to the edge of the woods, calling her name. He was by my side in seconds.

I cried out, "She's gone! She's done this before, not in a long time though."

"Where would she go?"

"I got no idea! Our camp is a good ten minutes away."

I twisted my hands, frantically looking about.

Clayton said, "You go that way, and I'll go in this other direction. Come back to this spot every few minutes until we find her."

"Okay."

I took off and he did too. I kept calling her name, hoping she'd appear. I regretted what I'd said to her on the way here even more. Laci probably seen this little adventure like a betrayal. I spoke hateful to her, and then put her in direct contact with a stranger. Maybe it had been my yelling and carrying on while Clayton dove, behavior she'd never seen out a me.

In the middle of a thicket, I turned in a circle. "Oh, where are you?"

I could hear the panic in my own voice, and after a few minutes, all I could do was return, hoping maybe Clayton had found her. Except would she even let him get near her? Would she run from him and make things worse by getting hurt? I come to the log we'd sat on and there was no one there.

I yelled, "Clayton!"

No answer. I didn't wait. I went back into the woods again, going a little further. I come to another waterfall, revealing the land was uneven, and this water fell onto a group of jagged rocks. There was so many dangers, and it made me hurry back to the other fall, all the while looking for a flash of bright hair. I got to imagining all sorts a bad things. I mashed my hand against my mouth and pictured telling Momma and Papa that Laci was lost in the woods. That's when I heard footsteps along the forest floor, creating a crackling sound like breaking bones. Clayton led the way with Laci on his heels. I was dumbfounded. She followed behind him, meek as a lamb. I sank onto the log, my relief causing my legs to feel like jelly. I stared at my sister.

Now she was back, and not hurt, I got aggravated. "Laci? Why'd you do that? Why'd you run off?"

Laci, head down, scurried behind me and put her hands on my shoulders. I twisted out of her grasp, and she dropped her hands in front of her, clasping them. Her fingers was reddish in color. She'd been eating some sort of berries, and Clayton held them in his hand.

"She was eating these, raking them off the branches and cramming them into her mouth. They's silverberries, and all right to eat."

Clayton's gaze was quizzical. Embarrassed, my words come out full a sarcasm. "I know what they are."

He said, "Things are pretty bad for y'all, ain't they?"

I shrugged. "We've seen better days, that's for sure."

"Listen. I mentioned your family and the singing to Johnny Cooper. He said he'd be willing to listen. Might sign y'all up to join. Now's the time as he's looking new acts."

"Papa ain't ever going to consider doing such as that."

Clayton stared. "You make it sound like a traveling show is something bad."

Uncomfortable, I said, "It ain't that."

"What then?"

"I can't see him agreeing, is all."

"It ain't a bad deal. Johnny would pay some of the take, and you'd get meals, and a place to sleep. The show provides tents for performers and workers to stay in."

"I don't know."

"Ask him. All you got to do is ask."

"I'll think about it. Papa's got his way of doing things."

Clayton said, "Johnny's looking a new act is what I'm saying, so now's the time."

It did seem like the answer, only it won't our way of living. A traveling show? It seemed foreign, too outlandish. After me and Laci left, I thought about Clayton's suggestion on the walk back. Papa might would consider the idea. How could working in a traveling show be any worse than what we was doing now?

Chapter 17

Back at camp I sat beside Momma so she couldn't look me in the eyes. I wished I could set her backbone and shoulders straight, or even see a bit of the old gumption in her again. The weeks of struggle had pressed a weight on her spirit, seeming to bend her frame. We sat in the quiet. Papa had yet to come back, and the silence was like something was about to happen. When the sound of the truck come, my heart shivered inside my chest along with the rest of me. I got to thinking about how to explain the possibility of coming to know Clayton, and about this idea of his that now seemed as far-fetched as Uncle Hardy having a change of heart.

The truck come into view, covered with mud and pieces of cornstalks stuck to the lower half like Papa had drove it straight through a cornfield. He got out and I peeked to see if he'd take out some cornmeal, or maybe some beans, anything to show his leaving had been worthwhile. He did none of that, coming towards us as empty-handed as when he'd left. Nary a thing to show for a daylong absence. For only the second time since Seph passed away, Momma put her face into her hands and her body folded over as if she wanted to sink right into the ground. Papa come over to the fire slow. It tore him out of the frame to see her get this a way.

He shoved his hands in his coveralls and said, "I'm sorry. I tried."

His face, so bleak and despairing, his failure setting a deeper divide between them. This was the moment I needed. I rose from my place beside Momma, my hands twisting one over the other as I cleared my throat.

I said, "Papa."

He only stared at Momma and her disappointment.

I persisted. "Papa."

He give me an impatient look. "What, Wallis Ann?"

I took a deep breath, and as I'd featured how I might do this in my head, I tripped over words, the tone of my voice shrill and odd to my ears.

"I got something to tell you. You know how I been going to the waterfall?"

Momma lifted her head and my eyes fastened on the sleek, wet channels running down her cheeks.

"Well, see? There was someone there named Clayton."

Momma's jaw tightened.

I talked faster. "He works for a traveling show. Cooper's Family Fun and Shows. He's a high diving act."

Papa spoke sharply. "Wallis Ann, what's this all about? What's this got to do with anything?"

I won't good at persuasion, I was good at working, doing as I was told, and singing. This was all brand-new, and Papa's impatience didn't help. Then there was Momma giving me an offended look. Laci picked that moment to start playing a tune on her fiddle. Frustrated, I marched over and snatched it from her hands.

Shocked, Momma said, "Wallis Ann! What has got into you?"

Holding Laci's fiddle tight in my arms against my belly, I shoved the rest of my words out before everything come apart.

"I'm trying to tell y'all about a job. It's about us getting a job. Clayton said a man named Johnny Cooper, who owns the traveling show, might want to hear us sing. Said if he liked us, he'd pay some of the take, and we'd have meals and a tent. That's all. It's about us maybe having a steady job singing."

I held my breath, waiting for the words to sink in, squeezing Laci's fiddle so hard I heard the wood creak. Papa's reaction stunned me. He didn't dismiss it immediately, he only rubbed his hand across his face and pulled on his beard.

He said, "Huh."

Momma said, "It's not practical."

Papa said, "What?"

Momma said, "Oh, dear God. I know you're not seriously thinking on this. You'd have us go work in some sideshow?"

Papa raised both arms in the air. "For Christ's sake, Ann! What else we gonna do?" And then Papa said something what surprised me most. "What if Laci or Wallis Ann gets sick like Seph? What will you think then about deciding so quick against the best idea that's come our way so far?"

Momma reacted like he'd slapped her. She jerked back and then her chin come forward, and her eyes tightened. "Let's not forget who was in an all-fired hurry to bring Seph home."

Papa dropped his head. "We ain't got no other choice here. What would be wrong in seeing about it? It ain't a permanent thing. It's only temporary."

Momma worried her hair. "I don't know. It don't seem fitting."

Papa said, "Way I see it, we got three choices."

Momma frowned at me like she couldn't understand why I'd mentioned such a thing.

Papa kept on. "Go to Hardy's."

Momma cringed.

"Keep going around on our own like we been doing."

She heaved a heavy sigh, and her shoulders slumped.

"Or, join them carnies for a little while, and make some money."

Momma flipped her hand in a dismissive way that said, *Do what you want.* I imagined she give in because of what he'd said about Seph. It had put a fear in her.

I said, "He said that Cooper feller's looking for new acts right now, but we got to be quick about it."

Papa said, "Let's go see about it then. If it don't work out, we're going to Hardy's. And that's that."

Momma looked disgusted, but she got busy gathering together our few things and Papa kicked dirt on the fire to put it out. I went to hand Laci her fiddle, and she jerked it from me. Surprised, I studied her, but she only rubbed at the wood with the end of her sleeve. I shrugged and went to help Momma tote our cookware to the truck. It took us only a few minutes to finish, the only sign we'd been there the blackened pit from the campfire.

Inside the truck, I said, "He said it ain't far from here, they's set up near to Tucker's Branch."

Papa said, "I know where they're at. I seen 'em earlier."

Momma didn't ask what he'd been doing or how his truck got so dirty, disinterested since he'd come away empty-handed. The hills seemed to watch in silence as we made our way down Highway 28. The prospect of meeting Johnny Cooper and knowing his opinion could mean a return to Uncle Hardy's had me wishing we didn't look as scruffy as we did. We come to a curve in the road where foothills rose over a big, flat open field filled with tents and rides, and more vehicles than I'd ever seen at once in my life. Papa had the windows cracked, and I smelled a strange mixture of odors, from pungent animals, to something like exhaust from Papa's truck, and most powerful of all, food. My mouth watered and after catching a whiff of that, I sure hoped he liked us enough to hire us out.

Papa turned into an area where several others had already driven. People milled about, and as we rolled and bumped through the flattened grass field, I heard a loud voice crying out, "Step right up, come on, let me guess your birthday, a penny to guess your birthday!" There was pigs being led to a small racetrack, a merry-go-round with kids screaming as they went round and round. I took in the signs telling about all sorts of sideshows, with Jungle Monkeys, a Snake Enchantress, and a bigger sign declared FREAKS! SEE THEM, ONE AND ALL! It looked like a very odd and bizarre world, and some part of me was scared of it, while the other part of me was excited. Momma gazed at some of the show folks standing near a section where off-white tents was lined up in neat rows.

The area looked to be private, and she turned her head and said to Papa, "What do we do, walk up and announce ourselves?"

Papa parked the truck, and said, "I reckon. I guess I'll go ask for Mr. Cooper."

He approached the group of workers, and spoke to one of them, a rough-looking man who reminded me a little of Leland Tew. The man spit on the ground and pointed to a tent. Papa tipped his hat, looked over his shoulder at us, then walked to the tent. The workers turned to stare at the truck, smoking their cigarettes and studying us like we was too boringly normal for the likes of this place.

Momma said, "This is a bad idea."

"Momma, we don't know for sure yet. It might work out."

"Hm."

She reached out a hand and brushed down Laci's hair, licking her fingers and making an attempt to flatten down the stray hairs around her forehead, but her hair was so wild, and dirty, it didn't do much good. I didn't touch mine. It felt pure tee gummed to my head, and it was useless to worry with it now. Papa come out of the tent with a man who had silvery hair and a mustache what drooped down past his chin. He'd been eating right good as his belly led the way.

When Momma seen them, she said, "Wallis Ann, get out!"

I obliged and we spilled out of the truck in all our dirty glory, rank, starving and desperate for a chance.

Papa spoke quick and eager. "This here's my wife, Ann Wallis Stamper, my oldest daughter I told you about, Laci, and our young Wallis Ann, voice like a songbird."

Mr. Cooper, sounding bored, said, "Uh-huh, uh-huh, uh-huh. Show me what you got."

We shifted around into our usual positions, Laci to Papa's left, and me to Momma's right. It never got easier for me, and my insides curdled like a glass of milk gone bad. I tried to settle my nerves down. Without prompting, and likely because of the habitual way we stood, Laci tucked her fiddle under her chin and drew the bow over the strings, sending out a high, sweet note. The ones who'd been standing around, nudging each other when they seen our raggedy clothes, stopped talking and give us their attention. Laci started with a real familiar song, "Shall We Gather at the River," and Papa began with the opening verse, then Momma and me joined. Our voices soared out and into the trees, and it seemed like our singing could touch the clouds above our heads.

I closed my eyes and I didn't think about how we looked, or anything. I simply opened my mouth and sang knowing this moment needed to shine. We had to be our best. We had to eat. Suddenly, it was like I wanted to be doing this. I wanted to sing because of what we'd been through, I wanted to sing for losing Seph, and there went an unlikely tear streaking down my filthy cheek, though I didn't care how it looked to anybody right then. Papa, Momma and I harmonized, belting out tune after tune between gospel and the old folk tunes I was most familiar with. I eventually opened my eyes and stared out at a gathering crowd. I'd never seen so many folks in my life. They stood, mesmerized it seemed, and I thought, *Maybe we sound okay. We sound okay, or we sound real bad.*

Mr. Cooper grinned from ear to ear, nodding at everyone like he'd discovered us, and I noticed at some point Clayton appeared and stood front and center of the gathering crowd. He was smiling, looking proud. Another man who looked like he was a ringmaster because of his coat with long tails and shiny shoes tilted his head, like he could picture himself announcing us. Mr. Cooper finally waved his hand indicating he'd heard enough. We'd sung four songs and ended the final one with a long, stretched-out note.

He led the crowd in a round of applause, and said, "How about that, folks? This here's my newest act, and if you want more of them, be here at seven sharp tonight! The Stampers, folks, that's their name, get used to it because you're gonna be hearing from them!"

The crowd applauded again, and I felt it might be all right, we might do fine.

Mr. Cooper come over and shook Papa's hand hard, and said, "You all is gonna do fine, fine. Come on, let's get them details worked out. Bring the missus along too."

He led Papa and Momma towards the cluster of tents, and I watched as they ducked inside the one he'd come out of. I shifted foot to foot, feeling uncomfortable and conspicuous, grateful when Clayton hurried over to us. The crowd dispersed on its own, and I was glad to not have them keep standing around looking at me and Laci.

Clayton seemed pretty excited. "Hey, I see what you mean

about your sister on that git fiddle there. And you sounded great too, even better than yesterday. How'd y'all end up here so soon?"

I motioned towards the tent. "We was at a point, so to speak, and Papa decided."

"Well, now, see? I was sure Johnny would go for the idea."

The words I'd typically find to keep the conversation going didn't come. Trying to talk to him here was different than at the falls. I couldn't think of a thing to say, not with Laci pressing up against me, not with the effects of so little food, and the effort to sing. All of it together had sapped the very last bit of strength out of me.

"Can we sit down somewhere?"

Clayton said, "Sure, come this way."

"I can't go far from Papa and Momma."

"We're going right over here. See them benches? They got all kinds of snacks. You want something?"

He led me and Laci towards an area that said CONCESSIONS.

"Like what?"

"Name it."

"I ain't never had a store-bought snack. We always made ours."

"You and Laci sit right there. I'll bring you all something, it'll be a surprise."

We sat and Clayton walked to the man behind a makeshift counter. When he come back he held colorful bags.

"Look a here. I brung you Lay's tater chips, some Twinkies, and a couple Snickers bars."

I'd seen these things, just never had them. He opened the two bags that said Lay's and handed them to me. They smelled like nothing I'd ever imagined. I give one to Laci and she took it and peered down into the depths. The bags crinkled loudly as we dug our hands in. The chips looked like the fried taters we used to fix sometimes for Saturday night suppers, only much thinner. I'd been hungry for so long, when I started, I started slow, placing a chip in and chewing carefully. They was so good that, without thinking, I picked up speed and went to shoving in handful after handful. Laci did the same thing. We crammed salty chips into our mouths like starving dogs gnawing to get the most out of a bone.

I finished the bag in seconds, and then grabbed for the Twinkies. I tore the wrapper off one and shoved half in, closing my eyes, and savoring the yellow fluffy cake and creamy center. I didn't look to see what Laci did, because I'd finished that and was now on to a Snickers bar. I took a bite and half got gone. I heard a noise and raised my eyes to see Clayton staring at us, stunned, his eyes wide, and sad. Was that pity I seen in them? I dropped what was left of the candy bar on the table. I chewed and swallowed and it felt like it was sticking somewhere between my throat and my belly. My stomach knotted, sending distress signals by way of little shooting pains as I fought not to be sick. I was worried I'd lose all of it on the ground since it was the first food I'd had in I don't know when.

Clayton rubbed a hand through his hair. "Damn, Wallis Ann. Why didn't you tell me? Why didn't you say y'all was in such need?"

Laci was still eating her candy bar, chocolate traces on her fingers, eyes searching the tabletop for more as she took the last bite of her Snickers, eyeing what was left of mine. I shoved it towards her and she crammed the rest in her mouth. I breathed slow and easy to calm my stomach.

I mumbled, "We ain't ones to talk of our troubles. We make do for ourselves."

Clayton give me a look as if I was the strangest creature he'd ever met. Meanwhile, we sat here in the center of a carnival, with its oddities advertised, and I was the one he thought peculiar? This struck me as hilarious. I started laughing, bending over and gripping my tightened waist, gasping. I couldn't seem to stop until Laci, who'd been sitting quite still, put a hand over her stomach, and looked distressed. I stopped my crazy laughing.

I said, "It's all right, Laci. You ate too fast, and too much. Like me."

Clayton offered us more food. "You want I should get her another bag of chips?"

"No, no, that'll make it worse."

"Maybe you both ought to have you a cold drink? I can get y'all one right there."

He pointed to a line of people standing patiently, coming away with drinks, peanuts and popcorn.

I squashed my pride and said, "Okay."

Clayton hurried off and returned juggling three bottles and some popcorn. The popcorn reminded me of last Christmas and using one a Momma's needles and some thread to create strings of it to go round the tree. I took a swallow, and the sting of carbonation down my throat was another reminder. I'd go with Papa to Dewey's for cornmeal, flour, sugar, and coffee. He'd always buy us a "dope" as he called it, which was bottles of Pepsi, plus some peanuts for the ride home. We'd dump the peanuts into the bottles and ride along, swilling and crunching the nuts and talking about whether or not we should catch us a mess of fish. Our world sure had changed, and it had me wishing for home, despite the excitement surrounding me.

"Thank you. I've not had one in a while." As I said it, Momma and Papa come out of the tent. Papa shook Mr. Cooper's hand, and I took that as a good sign. They started towards us, and Clayton stood as my parents got closer, his hand out.

"Sir, Clayton Jones."

Papa eyed Clayton down the length of his nose. "And I suppose you're the big time, that high dive act."

"Not so big, no, sir."

"Well, son. You're either the craziest or bravest person we ever heard of."

"Thank you, sir."

Clayton spoke so formal like. Papa's cheek twitched, and he give Clayton the once-over, like he couldn't decide if he liked him or not.

He eventually said, "Maybe I'm the one who ought to thank you for suggesting to Mr. Cooper here his show might need a singing act."

Mr. Cooper spoke enthusiastically. "That's right, that's right. Y'all are gonna fit right in." He paused to look at us. "Looks like you could stand a meal. Ain't no harm in going a little hungry, but ain't no need if there's work to be had."

He rubbed his hands together, and said, "I'll let you folks settle in. Clayton can show you around to your tents, where to eat, and all."

Papa nodded, and shoved his hands in his pockets, while Momma's expression remained flat as she stared dully at the commotion of the carnival swirling around us.

Chapter 18

Clayton said, "Come on, I'll take you to the yard, and you can see where you're gonna sleep."

We followed him to this "yard," which was nothing more than a collection of tents behind a giant Ferris wheel. I'd only ever seen a picture of one, and it was impressive in real life. A few workers sat outside of their individual tents, playing card games, doing their wash, shaving in front of tiny mirrors hung on a post, or simply smoking cigarettes and talking. Some had painted faces on but were in regular clothes. They sat wearing the big, wide smiles of a clown, or sad face, and it was a right bizarre thing to see. Laci bumped into me, so intent was she at looking at them. A girl who looked about my age, maybe a little older, passed us leading a zebra by a halter, and she had on a pink satin outfit, with tights and these funny-looking flat shoes.

Clayton pointed to her and said, "That there's Trixie and her zebra, Zippity Doo. Her family performs dressage and as part of the horse show, she works with Zippity Doo and this little bitty monkey called Mr. M. If you can believe it, he wears a red riding coat and rides on a dog."

I shook my head cause I'd never heard the likes of such things. He waved at Trixie, and she waved back while staring at us intently.

Someone hollered out, "Hey! Is them the Forty Milers we heard about?"

Clayton didn't stop.

I said, "Forty Milers?"

Clayton said, "Yeah, it means someone who's new, and someone who might not last long enough to travel forty miles with the show."

Papa said, "We already been at least that and then some traipsing around these back roads."

I felt conspicuous, no different than the first time I sung all them years ago, imagining every single eye on us as we traversed the sawdust path around the tents. News sure did travel fast of newcomers. I noted how some studied on Laci, their gaze lingering and curious. Maybe it was her red hair, or her pale green eyes. Whatever it was, there was murmurings not expected for our ears, yet I heard them. "Wild as the mountains she comes from" and "Sumpin's different in that one there."

Momma walked quick, looking neither right nor left, while Papa nodded here and there if someone gestured. We stopped in front of two tents at the edge of the tent city.

Clayton pointed and said, "These was used by a couple jugglers who got into a fight, beat each other half to death and Johnny Cooper kicked them out. He don't tolerate such foolishness."

Papa glanced at Momma and said, "Ain't that good to know."

Momma said nothing.

Clayton said, "They got a food tent that a way. You'll smell it 'fore you see it. It's for us workers so we don't eat what's intended for paying guests."

Papa nodded quick and said, "Right."

"And a water truck will come by and fill your buckets for drinking and washing. Twice a day."

"Great," said Papa, as he rubbed his eyes like he was too tired to think of it all.

Clayton shuffled his feet awkwardly, not daring to look my way. Neither of us was as comfortable and easygoing as we'd been when alone at the waterfall.

He said, "Okay, then. See y'all at the show later tonight. I'll be doing my thing at eight sharp. I hope you can stick around to see it."

Without waiting to hear if we would or wouldn't, he loped off, and I made a point to pay no mind to his leaving, turning away before he was even out of sight because Momma was giving him a hard look as he left.

One tent was a little larger than the other, and Momma pulled the flap aside on it and inside was two cot-like beds. There was also a washstand and on top of it was a porcelain bowl and pitcher, and two small camp-type stools at the foot of each cot. There was a stack of old sheets and towels someone had folded and set inside on the cots. All these things seemed luxurious to have after what we'd been through. Momma spotted something on the ground and bent over to get a better look, then motioned to Papa.

"What's that?"

Papa ducked inside and peered at the two small whitish objects lying in the sawdust. He moved them with the toe of his boot.

"Looks like . . . teeth."

Momma backed away and said, "Good Lord."

Papa bent down and raked them into his hand. He went out

and threw them near the line of trees while Momma put her hands on her hips, silent again. I went into the smaller tent beside Momma and Papa's and Laci followed. Once my eyes got used to the dim interior, I could see two cots, like Momma and Papa's, and also like theirs, a small wooden table with a bowl and pitcher. Laci plopped herself down onto one of the beds and a puff of dust rose and made her sneeze. I exited the tent. Momma was whispering to Papa, and she stopped when I come out. It was a lot to get used to, and some of my earlier excitement was overshadowed by little things I'd noticed; the lack of sounds I was used to like rushing water from a mountain stream, and the wind rustling through the trees. Birdsong was only faint and sporadic from some distant limb, and there was a strong odor of dung from the animal waste. Horses, mules, a few goats, along with a couple elephants and a camel ambled about in an area where they'd been staked out or grouped together in corrals.

Even more than the carnival's chaotic look and smell was the idea of working with the likes of a tattooed man I'd seen called Edmond, and another man who'd been performing a fire-eating trick, with a sign stating he was La Diablo! There was a bearded woman, with a sign saying she was called Lucille, a magician called Morty, and I'd seen a tent for the two-headed sheep Clayton spoke of. Everyone and everything was so unusual, and I couldn't see how we'd fit in.

"Papa, what you reckon folks at home will think when they hear we done took up with a carnival?"

He shrugged and said, "Don't matter long as we're earning our keep."

"Yes, sir."

"We're lucky. That Cooper fella said long as they draw in good crowds, they'll stay put. I'd just as soon not end up in Florida."

This was the furthest I'd ever been, and though I wondered

what Florida looked like, I won't inclined to go either. I went and looked inside the buckets sitting beside the tents. Both was full of clear, clean water, and had been set on the side that got the most sun. I went inside mine and Laci's tent and got our pitcher and filled it from one of the buckets. I moved the other bucket into the shade for drinking.

"Momma, you want me to put some of this water in your pitcher for washing?"

Momma spoke with a gloomy tone. "I suppose."

A large woman with black hair, lots of eye makeup and clothes colorful as a rainbow swayed by near our tents and stopped when she seen us. "You the new singers?"

Momma shot a look at Papa what said *We don't belong here,* before she answered the lady. "Yes."

The fat lady wiggled ringed fingers in a greeting. "How do. Name's Nancy Cole, but you know, for show purposes (she said it like *poi-puses*) they call me Big Bertha."

Momma cleared her throat, and said, "Which do you prefer?"

Nancy Cole or Big Bertha laughed, and everything about her moved the way water moves, with a lot of ripples and waves.

She said, "Big Bertha's what most everyone calls me, so you can too."

Momma was cordial, yet distant. "Nice to meet you, Big Bertha."

Big Bertha cocked her head, and said, "Ya know, I got just the thing for ya. Wait here."

She sure could move good and fast for a woman her size. She weaved through the tents, and Momma stared after her with a worried frown. "I can't imagine what she's got we could use."

I couldn't either but I was still curious. When Big Bertha returned a minute later, she pressed two bars of soap into Momma's hands.

"It's French milled. A sort of welcome to the show gift from me to you."

Momma's mouth curved up as she took the soap. "Why, thank you so much. How generous!"

Big Bertha said, "My husband, Walter, had it made for me in a little shop down in Georgia. I got more than I'll ever use. It's all he ever give me, back when he was alive, God love 'im."

Momma said, "I'm so sorry for your loss."

Big Bertha flipped a nonchalant pudgy hand. "It's all right. He's been dead a few months. Keeled over one day and that was that."

"What a terrible thing."

Big Bertha sighed. "I think it was the stew I made, but who knows? God rest his soul."

Momma's eyes widened. "The stew?"

Big Bertha put a hand to her mouth and giggled. "Could've been that. I look like I like to cook, but I really don't know how."

Papa made an agitated sound in his throat, maybe wishing she'd move on, only Momma took it as a hint to make introductions.

She gestured towards us and said, "This is my family. William, my husband, Laci, our eldest, and Wallis Ann. We had us another chap, a boy . . ."

A horn sounded and Big Bertha cut her off. "Pleased and all, but I got to skedaddle to my perch. Break's over. See ya around."

We watched Big Bertha moving as quick and agile as someone half her size.

Once she was out of sight, Momma spoke with a thoughtful tone. "She didn't seem too put out at her husband's passing."

Papa said, "She didn't."

I was most interested in the soap she'd brought. "Can I have a bar of soap?"

Distracted, Momma handed me one and said, "I wonder why she mentioned stew?"

Papa shook his head, and I took the soap and went inside the smaller of the two tents. I stood with my head over the basin, pouring water from the pitcher and letting it run through my hair. I rubbed the soap through it and washed my face, inhaling the scent of roses. I picked up the pitcher again, and this time I poured slower, letting the clean water stream through my hair, and watching as the water in the basin turned murky from my soiled head. I thought about Clayton, and what he might think if he seen me in a set of decent clothes, with my hair and face clean. At least I could do this, and when I finished, I dumped the filthy water out, and then Laci took her turn, washing hers clean as mine. I picked up our camp stools, we exited the tent, our heads still wet. We sat by the fire Papa built, finger-combing our slick, wet strands. Him and Momma had went and washed up too, and with everyone's faces and hair clean, the improvement was amazing.

After a while, Papa said, "Well, let's go find us something to eat."

The chips and other things we'd eaten earlier was long gone. We walked until we come to a long tent where the smell of food lingered in the air like smoke. I didn't know what was cooking, and it didn't matter. We went inside and stood a minute, getting our bearings. Tables and chairs sat in the center with a few scattered off to the side. Towards the back was a covered wagon of sorts, and a short, skinny little man who stood over several steaming pots, stirring something in one of them. A few workers sat at tables, but they seemed too tired or too intent on eating to pay us much mind.

We approached the small cook, who wore a dirty apron with a strap hanging off his shoulder. He saw us coming and began pulling tin pans out from under his counter and piling food into the plates. He loaded them with beans, these funny-looking long sausages, biscuits and corn on the cob. He handed us each a steaming plate. I tried to hold my hand steady when I reached out to take mine.

He winked at me and Laci, and said, "Hey, girlies, when you git done with your grub, I'll fetch you a peach fritter."

I said, "Yes, sir!"

Never in my life was I as happy as I was right then. Even Momma shifted from looking so grim to a more kindly expression. We sat down at one of the tables, and Papa said the quickest blessing I'd ever heard. I fell into eating, trying to fill the bottomless void in the middle of my body while Laci hunched over her plate like someone might take it from her. I understood the feeling. It seemed too good to be true sitting here with these full plates, and more where it come from. None of us could quite finish what we'd been given. I took the almost empty pans back to the man at the counter. He stood off to the side of his cooking area, with a cigar poking out of his mouth. He seen me and come to the counter, reaching out to take the dirty plates from me.

He said, "Hey, girly, you get enough?"

"Yes, sir. Thank you."

"Hard times, huh?"

"Yes, sir. Right hard."

He puffed on the cigar. "Food's plenty here. You'll have enough."

We must have looked like we needed it. "Yes, sir. Thank you."

He nodded, and said, "Name's Paulie. Call me Paulie."

"Nice to meet you, Paulie. I'm Wallis Ann Stamper."

I gestured over my shoulder to Laci, Momma and Papa, who was standing by the tent opening waiting on me. "That's my older sister, Laci, and my momma, Ann Wallis Stamper, and my papa, William Stamper."

"You're part of the new singing group."

I was sort of surprised he already knowed about us, but I would eventually find out this was how it was working within such a group. They heard everything about everyone.

"Yes. That's us, The Stampers."

Paulie nodded. "Good to know you all."

"Likewise. Well, thank you for supper, Mr. Paulie. It was real good."

"Just Paulie."

"All right. Paulie. See you later."

"Here, kid."

He handed me several bundles of wax paper, each with a wrapped peach fritter, still warm and soft from frying with a dusting of powdered sugar over the top.

"Thank you!"

My mouth watered. I hurried to Momma and Papa, and passed them around. There was a bit of moaning from me as I bit into it. It tasted good as the ones Momma used to make with peaches off our peach tree. As we made our way back to get Laci's fiddle, the feeling of being full and fed showed in the way we strolled along the sawdust path between the tents, relaxed and easy. I spotted Trixie again, heading the other direction from before.

She waved and hollered, "Good luck at your show tonight. I'll come watch if I can!"

I waved back but kept quiet as I recollected Momma saying before, ladies don't yell. We got Laci's fiddle and made our way into the main midway area filled with shouts of ride goers, exhibits and games. Right next to the arena tent where we'd sing, I spotted a really tall, narrow structure with a tiny platform at the very top, and a huge wooden tub at the base. It reminded me of an old washtub only much bigger. This had to be where Clayton would dive. There was a lot more water to land in at the fall, and I couldn't imagine how he'd do his dive into that little bit of water. We entered the arena tent and inside was a small wooden stage not quite centered with a half circle of bench-like wooden seats in front. Laci eyes darted here and there, like she couldn't take it all in at once.

I leaned over and said, "Laci, it's just like when we go to a church and other gatherings. Ain't no different, only a few more people is all."

It didn't help matters none when more and more visitors started filling the tight space, laughing loudly, and shouting out to one another. This place held the noise, and she went to trembling, and breathing sort a rapid. She ducked behind me, but my shorter stature didn't allow much protection from all them staring eyes. All I could do was let her be, and hope she'd manage until we went onto the stage. I won't sure how she was going to make it, though. She sounded like a locomotive.

I whispered to Momma, "Laci's getting herself worked up."

"I hear her. Can't do nothing about it."

"But, what if she won't play?"

"Wallis Ann, can't do nothing about it, now can we?"

Momma plastered a smile to her face while folks sitting close to where we stood stared and pointed at us like we was a sideshow of freaks instead of regular people. I felt edgy and worried because despite our clean faces and hair and our full bellies, we still had the look of the destitute with our raggedy clothes, and me and Laci barefoot as newborn babies when all them, kids included, wore shoes. I hoped we'd get started soon so we could show these people we only looked the way we did cause we'd hit us a bit of a rough spot. I looked for the man who'd worn the fancy coat.

A worker called out, "Mr. Massey!" putting a name to him as he come into the arena area. Laci's breath hit the back of my neck in dramatic puffs. I pressed against her, thinking maybe she'd feel more secure. I tried to ignore the shaking of her against my shoulders. Mr. Massey looked for Mr. Cooper, and as the crowd clapped their hands, the noise rising, he swooped in. It was like everything was timed. He nodded at Mr. Massey, who approached the center of the arena. *Please say something, announce something, and quiet them down.* Without warning, Laci shoved me from behind, and with a loud and unexpected squawk I stumbled forward, landing in the line of sight of Johnny Cooper and Mr. Massey.

Mortified, I exclaimed, "Laci!"

Momma grabbed my arm, yanked me back into place and hissed, "Wallis Ann, what in tarnation are you doing?"

The crowd murmured and pointed. I reckoned I looked like a beet as I glanced at the mass of people, settling on Trixie in her bright pink performing outfit glaring amongst all the dull browns, grays and blues. Her appearance struck me the same as I felt, like I was just as obvious, until I noticed nobody was even looking at me. They was looking behind me, at Laci. I turned to see what held their attention, to find Laci looking crazy as they come. Her brilliant hair, although clean and shiny again, all of it was pulled forward and hung in front of her face like she was trying to hide behind it, using it like a curtain. You could see a few strands moving as she breathed in and out, yet you couldn't see her face at all.

I leaned towards Momma, meaning to whisper to her when Laci must have had all she could take, and broke from whatever set her off. She flipped her hair away from her face, raised the fiddle to her chin. She drew the bow harshly across the strings, creating a loud and awkward shrieking tone, like a wildcat screaming at night. The crowd buzzed louder with questioning tones.

I heard somebody say, "I sure hope I didn't pay my hard-earned money to hear that. Godawful, is what that was."

The ones close to him seemed to agree.

"Oh boy, my head's gonna be hurtin' she keeps it up."

"I thought the sign said 'talent beyond belief.' I sure can't believe they call that talent."

"Let's hope she was only warmin' up."

I'd never heard a bad note out of Laci until then, and it left my own ears ringing. It reminded me of the time Seph got hold of her fiddle and sat on the ground sawing the bow across the strings and making it wail like he was killing it. Mr. Massey shot a look at Mr. Cooper.

Somebody hollered, "I might need to get my money back!"

Papa took a step towards Mr. Cooper, like he was going to have a word with him, when Laci drew the bow again. This time, the fiddle sang out a series of quick and sure notes to a song she didn't play often, called "Bonaparte's Retreat." It was a fast song and required her fingers to fly. She played it the way she'd been breathing, a frenzied outpouring, her hair swinging in time with her arm movements. The crowd settled down, everyone mesmerized, and Mr. Massey and Mr. Cooper stepped away and let her go. She went on to "Brushy Fork of John's Creek" and to "Li'l Liza Jane." Before she got done, Johnny Cooper motioned at Mr. Massey to get on the stage.

He darted up there with Laci still playing like she was trying to lose something inside herself.

He shouted to the crowd, "How's about a round of applause for that special treat. Come on, folks! This here's The Stampers, and like we promised, you're gonna love 'em!"

Momma and Papa started for the stage, and I was left with Laci, who continued playing.

I whispered, "Laci, come on with me."

Laci pumped out the last of the notes to "Li'l Liza Jane," and I grabbed her arm and hauled her up the two small steps and onto the stage. The crowd let out a little uncomfortable laugh

as we found our usual places, me settling Laci on Papa's left before I hurried over to Momma's right. Once we was in place,
the crowd burst into polite applause, and I prayed it wouldn't
set Laci off again. Mr. Cooper and Mr. Massey beamed at
everyone and bowed to the audience like it had been planned
this way. Laci clutched the fiddle to her chest, her hair covering her face again. I wished Papa would brush it out of the
way, only I was afraid she'd get a good look at all these strange
faces and no telling what might happen.

He leaned down to her and I could barely make out what
he said. "Wildwood Flower."

Laci wanted to play so bad, she tossed her hair out of the
way again, brung the fiddle up and began. Finally, we was able
to relax into our routine. We harmonized, and soon I was
wishing I had shoes. Laci would usually play a set of songs we
clogged to, and it had been so long since I'd been able to
dance, I was itching to let go. I had an energy I'd not had in a
long time, and the stage was perfect for it, giving a hollow
wood ring as Papa stomped his boots in time to the tunes we
sang. The crowd got into our singing, and some folks even did
a little flatfoot or buck dancing in the sawdust scattered on the
floor in front of the stage. Everyone was having a good old
time, and I felt good and warm all over, almost like when we'd
pull back the rug on Saturday nights back home and clog till
we was too tired to move.

After we'd been singing a while I seen Clayton near Trixie. I
went hot all over instead of warm. He waved, and even though
I didn't wave back, I smiled big and bold at him, and sang
proud. I felt good hearing the way we sounded, our voices
echoing and ringing out over the heads of the people there.
When I looked again, I was sort a disappointed he was gone.

We sung until Mr. Massey stepped onto the stage several
songs later. "What do you think? Ain't they special? Ain't they
grand? Do you want them to do you one more?"

The crowd stomped their feet on the floor and cried out, "One more! One more!"

It had been such a long time since we'd felt so good, and felt so happy, I could a sung all night. It seemed like things was turning around for us after all our hardships, and I sure felt we was due better times.

Chapter 19

We stood a few minutes soaking in the applause and feeling right proud of ourselves. Even Laci had calmed down enough to peek out from behind her hair.

Mr. Massey said, "Folks, I sure hope you enjoyed The Stampers as much as we did! If you'll please exit out the front there, that's right, move right along for our next thrilling show, the high dive act!"

The crowd began filing out, and Momma and Papa smiled at each other, something they'd not done in weeks, luxuriating in the moment of how well it had gone after our bumpy little start. Mr. Cooper come over and handed Papa some paper bills and coins. It was a good feeling, earning our keep, but now I was anxious to see Clayton jump from the tall platform. All them times watching him practice at the waterfall didn't compare to the anxiousness I felt after seeing the height of that skinny pole and the little platform.

"Papa, can't we go watch Clayton?"

Papa, with a pocket full of money and riding high on our success, was agreeable. "Sure, I suppose we could go see what all the fuss is about," only Momma said, "I'm rather tired. I'd like to go on to the tent."

I was disappointed because I figured I'd have to go with them. Papa hesitated, looking from Momma to me.

I said, "Please, can I watch?"

He studied the crowd, and then he said, "You know what?"

"Sir?"

"I think you're owed some free time for all you done back home and since we left. Here you go, Wally Girl. Buy you and Laci something to eat and drink, and watch the show, see some sights."

Papa handed me a whole quarter. I'd never had so much money in my life.

"Yes, sir!"

Momma said, "William, you sure it's a good idea for them to be alone?"

"They'll be all right, Ann. This here's a family crowd, and besides, it's high time they had a bit of fun."

Papa took Laci's fiddle, and got ahold of Momma's arm with his other hand. "Come on, Ann, let's you and me take us a little evening stroll. Look a there at them stars overhead!"

Momma allowed another little smile at him, and said, "Talking about stars. We did all right tonight, didn't we?"

They drifted off in between the tents, talking soft to each other, arm in arm, looking almost like old times on Stampers Creek.

After they was out of sight, I turned to Laci. "Come on, let's hurry! I don't want to miss it!"

I weaved around the crowd, keeping Laci separate from the jostling elbows and crush of bodies. A big gathering clustered together near the front of the platform, held back by ropes near the big tub of water. It seemed to me, those nearest the ropes might get splashed. I took us to the concession stand and got two Pepsis and two bags of peanuts. I give Laci hers and then moved us to the left-hand side of the platform out of the way of everyone. I kept turning this way and that, looking for Clayton. There was a small tent set off to the side, and a minute later he come out of it and the crowd clapped and whistled. I hoped Laci would be less bothered by the noise outside, though it was hard to pay her any mind when he approached the ladder to climb.

Clayton was serious about this diving business. He wore a swimsuit with a strange style top with thin straps over his shoulders like some of them undershirts some men wear. His body, although lean, was muscled, and toned. He didn't see me at first, and I wanted to get his attention, let him know I was there, only his intense expression kept me quiet. I felt Laci against me, and she was looking over my shoulders, staring intently at Clayton. He raised his arm to the crowd and when he began a long, slow climb, he spotted us. He threw us a quick smile and a wink. His attention sent a glow through me, like the sensation of warm sun on my skin. Every twenty or so steps, he'd stop and lean out to wave at the crowd and at us.

The higher he went, the louder the oohs and aahs. I slurped on my drink and chewed furiously on the peanuts. I couldn't stop watching as he went up and up and up, and I began to think, *It's too high. That's way too high.* The crowd become quiet when he got close to the top. He leaned against the structure, his arms behind him, hands gripping the metal poles. After a minute, he shook out his arms, and his legs, one at a time. Finally, he let go of the metal, and with nothing between him and the ground, he stepped out onto the tiny platform. I stopped drinking and eating. He looked so small.

Mr. Massey spoke in a low, dramatic voice. "Folks, that's fifty feet up. Young Clayton here's been doing this for two years. He's fearless, but still! Something could happen! Watch carefully! This death-defying leap happens in seconds!"

I wished Mr. Massey hadn't said something could happen. I

tilted my head back, and so did Laci. My hand went to my neck and I thought on the day I first seen him jump at the waterfall, and how I'd screamed. My throat swelled with the need to do the same thing now, and I pressed my lips together, holding it in. He placed his toes right on the edge and looked straight ahead, not down. There won't a whisper in the crowd. Everyone had their faces turned to the night sky, where a spotlight shone directly behind him and another shone on the wooden tub filled with water. He held his arms out, not moving for several seconds. And then, he did look down, and when he did, it was like he simply fell, holding his body straight, his arms still straight out forming a perfect human cross.

It was a beautiful thing to watch as he hurtled down, slow and then faster. The gasps of the crowd was like a collective hiss, yet he remained as silent as an owl swooping after prey in the dark of night. Somebody squealed, but thankfully, everyone else only gaped in awe and fear. Laci's fingers almost squeezed the blood from my hand and then, he hit the water. A loud, cracking noise echoed over the tents. The splash was enormous, and sure enough, the people closest to the part of the roped off area to the front got soaking wet. After the noise from the crowd died down, another hush fell over us all. There was no sound from the water.

The crowd began to buzz with anxious questions. "Where's he? Reckon he's flattened out in the bottom? Why don't he swim to the edge and show us he's all right?"

Mr. Massey cleared his throat.

He whispered into his mic, "A death-defying leap, folks. What a show, what a show."

Someone called out, "He ain't showed his self yet."

Someone else said, "Yeah, might not a been so death defying. Could be dead."

I wanted to tell them "hush!" A few in the crowd tittered and I got madder and more uneasy as seconds went by. Then I heard a gurgling sound, followed by a squelching noise, and up popped Clayton, wearing a big old grin, his arms raised beside his head in a victorious manner. He swiped a hand across the top of the water and sent a spray into the air at the crowd, who yelled their approval. The applause went on and on.

Mr. Massey said, "Well now, there you have it, folks, another spectacular show by this young daredevil of ours! Give him another big round of applause!"

Clayton had partially climbed back up the ladder and hung off it waving to the crowd. He kept turning towards me and Laci, keeping his eye on us while he celebrated with the audience, his chest and the front of his legs visibly red. When he climbed down, the crowd began to scatter, some going towards the rides while others headed for some of the other attractions. He stepped over the rope and come to stand beside me grinning and wiping his hair with a towel.

"Well? What did you think?"

"It was scary, and unbelievable!"

"You liked it, huh?"

"Oh yes, most definitely!"

"What did you think, Laci?"

Laci paid him no mind, as she studied a few clowns walking by. I spoke for her, as usual. "Well, I guess she might have liked it, but if she did, she won't tell. Like I said, Laci don't talk."

"I know. I figured since she's never seen anything like that, she might have had some sort of reaction."

I suppose it won't surprising Clayton was curious about Laci. She was mysterious since nobody understood what went on in that head of hers, and then she'd turn right around and play this beautiful music. People couldn't help but find her intriguing.

I said, "I was too busy watching myself, so I didn't notice what she might a done."

Clayton changed the subject and said, "Hey, you want to go

see Trixie's show, and after, we can go look at the two-headed sheep. Whaddya say?"

I glanced at Laci, wishing I could have Clayton to myself.

Hesitant, I said, "Sure."

"Okay, wait here."

He disappeared into the tent and come out a few minutes later dressed in dry clothes, his hair slicked back.

"Come on, I know all the shortcuts."

We stayed to the rear section of the main midway, and everyone who worked for the carnival called out to Clayton.

Some said, "I see you survived—again—you crazy nut!" Others said, "So, you and the devil still got a deal?"

Others only whistled or hooted. He waved at the carnival barkers who managed the games, and called out to the money collectors for the sideshows.

Some shouted, "Who you got there with you?"

He introduced me and Laci as we went along. "This here's Wallis Ann, and her sister Laci, they's the new singing act. Y'all be nice to them or you'll have to deal with me!"

Everyone seemed to know and like Clayton. We went into another tent, a little bigger even than the one we'd performed in. It held a corral, and outside of the corral, circling all the way around, was rows of wooden bench seats. It held a familiar smell of horses, and hay, and manure, and I breathed it in deep. Clayton pointed out Trixie's momma, who wore a fancy-looking riding habit, as did her papa. They walked two beautiful black horses, big as I'd ever seen, around the square shaped ring in a warm-up. One horse looked to be seventeen hands, while the one Trixie's momma rode was a little smaller.

Clayton said, "You ever seen horses like this?"

"No. They're beautiful."

"Friesians is what they are."

They put the horses through various steps without seeming to move, while the horse performed. Afterwards, Trixie's routine was like watching the reverse of her parents', with her bright clothes and the zebra, the monkey and the dog. It was a lighthearted performance, yet very daring. Trixie stood on the zebra's back, dropped down to ride along its side, and did other acts of balance. The monkey mimicked her every move while riding the dog as they went around the ring. When the show was over, Trixie come over to us, and Clayton properly introduced us.

"This here's Wallis Ann, and her sister, Laci. This here's Trixie."

"Nice to meet you," we said at the same time, which made us laugh. Trixie looked at Laci and the first time ever, I didn't have to explain Laci's silence. It was like Trixie understood somehow she won't like other people.

She said, "This one's special."

Without reaching out to touch her, she said, "Good to meet you, Laci."

And then she said, "What are y'all gonna do? Clayton, you taking them to see the giant snake? Don't let him take you to see that thing. It's hideous."

I said, "He didn't say nothing about no giant snake."

Clayton acted offended. "Aw, come on, Trixie, don't spoil it!"

She said, "I got to go change for the next show, but maybe I'll see y'all around later on!"

We left the arena and the odor I'd noticed before got stronger as we approached a line of tents with signs strung across the front advertising GIANT ANACONDA SNAKE! and TWO-HEADED SHEEP! So, this was the giant snake they'd talked about. Could it really be as big as twenty feet? The very idea of something I'd only seen grow to maybe three feet sounded impossible. Elephants chained to pegs pounded into the ground was being washed down with buckets of water. They swayed and flipped long gray snouts up and down or searched the pockets of the workers washing them. I could've watched them forever, but Clayton was talking.

"This here's the tent for Sheba and Shiloh."

He led us around the back and lifted a flap. Inside stood a small wooden corral with a sheep's rear end pointed at us and the two heads nowhere in sight because the animal was eating. Clayton whistled and the sheep turned around to face us. I was captivated. Both heads moved independent of each other, with one looking like it wanted to keep eating and the other wanting to keep looking at us.

"Can I pet them?"

Clayton said, "Yeah, go on, Sheba and Shiloh don't mind, do you, girls?"

The two heads bobbed in different directions. I carefully reached over the little corral and patted each bony head. They was awful cute, even with the deformity. They had floppy sort of ears, and soft mouths nibbling my fingers. I wondered what Laci might do.

"Laci, you want to pet them?"

Laci kept her hands behind her back, which more or less told me what she thought of the idea.

Clayton held his hand out to her and said, "Here, give me your hand."

I said, "She ain't gonna take hold of your hand, Clayton."

Then, Laci made a liar out of me when she did that very thing.

Stunned, I said, "Laci?"

Clayton give me a little smile and led Laci forward. Stupefied, I watched as she allowed him to keep hold of her hand as he placed it over Sheba and Shiloh's two heads, lowering it slowly and carefully. He moved her hand along their knobby skulls in a stroking motion, smiling down at her. She wouldn't look at him, but the fact she let him do this was so unusual, I could only watch with incredulity.

After a minute, and feeling a bit bewildered, I said, "I sure seen a lot of things, but ain't that something."

Clayton said, "Oh shoot, wait till y'all see the snake in the next tent over."

Except I won't talking about that. His hand over hers, they petted the sheep together while I tried to decide what was happening to Laci. Studying her features, I seen no fear or anything other than she looked perfectly content. Clayton smiled at me over her head as he continued to hold her hand and move it along the sheep's head. He looked pleased with himself. Clayton eased his hand off of hers, and she kept on rubbing the sheep's two heads.

While she was preoccupied, he come over to me and said, "Y'all sure put on a mighty fine show."

"So did you."

"Did it scare you?"

"Well, yes, I couldn't never do something like that. Fifty feet in the air!"

"No, silly, did singing in front of all them people scare you?"

"I don't know. I was a bit nervous. It didn't help none when Laci pushed me out in front of everyone before we even got started. Everyone looked at her, but she showed them when she got to playing on her fiddle."

"Why'd she do that?"

"I think the crowd was getting to her, the noise and all. She ain't used to it. None of us is."

He nodded, then went over and placed his hand on top of hers again, following along as she continued to pet the animal. He leaned down to whisper something in her ear, and a little sour mood come over me. I felt a tinge of relief when her expression stayed as smooth and blank as a glass window. Some small part of me wished she'd start rocking, or grab at her hair, ruining its sleek, burnished look. Laci glanced at him and despite the flatness of her mouth, and lackluster eyes, something tensed in her face, reminding me of the day by the Tuckasegee, when I'd seen a similar expression I couldn't put my finger on.

An awareness, or a hint of understanding. Like then, quick as it was there, it was gone.

Clayton looked back at me and said, "Y'all wanna go see the snake?"

"Okay, but after, we probably need to go on back to our tents."

He led us out and like before, we didn't go through the front of the snake tent like anyone else. We slipped through another secret flap, where a slit had been made to allow workers access without going by the paying customers. Clayton explained how handy it was when cleaning out the animal areas, or for feeding and watering them. The smell inside the snake tent was musty and stale. The lighting dim, it felt warmer than the other places we'd been. Clayton pointed to heated stones placed around the perimeter. In the center of the tent sat a large wooden box erected on a table. The table had heavy black material draped around the lower half of it, and when Clayton took my arm to lead me closer, my nervousness at seeing something so unfamiliar and strange took hold of my senses.

I pulled back a little, and he teased me. "You scared? Ain't nothing but a snake."

Laci went to the box and looked down at it.

Clayton said "Snake!" directly in my ear, causing me to jump. He giggled like a kid, like he thought scaring me was right funny, but I didn't.

I frowned and said, "Ha-ha."

I heard a rustling noise coming from the box, and I crept over to stand beside Laci. The snake was stretched from one end to the other, and sort of folded in half. It had to be about fifteen foot long, and when I considered all the other ones I'd ever encountered out in the woods, it was like comparing a field mouse to a possum.

"What kind is it?"

"A python."

"What does it eat?"

"Mostly mice, or rats, like any old snake in the woods."

A man come into the tent area through the secret opening, and Clayton said, "Hey, Darren." He said, "This here's the snake handler, Darren."

Darren didn't have much to say at first. He was short and stocky, with heavy black whiskers and long black hair. He come towards the box and we moved aside. He reached down to stroke the snake, and it rippled, and moved slightly. The rustling noise I'd heard earlier come again. Despite Darren's gruff look, I could see he cared about it. Darren stared at me, a question forming on his face.

Before he could ask, I backed away and said, "No."

Darren said, "Aw, come on. It only feels like leather. Go on, Hercules don't bite. He's a squeezer."

Clayton said, "He's right."

I hesitated, and then eased my hand down into the box, and Darren said, "Like this, go in this direction, not the other way. The other way you'll only feel the scales."

I did as he said. He was right, the snake's skin did feel like a lot like leather, a little rougher maybe, and the movement under my fingers as his body swelled and flowed made me think of a cat stretching with enjoyment. I pressed along the snake's back, feeling bones too. After a minute or so, I withdrew my hand and Darren gestured at Laci.

I said, "I don't think she'll want to touch him. It's a lot different than the sheep. Do you want to, Laci? She kept her hands behind her. "See? I didn't think so."

Like everyone else, Darren considered Laci, like he won't sure why she didn't speak, or why she couldn't make up her own mind.

I explained, "My sister don't talk. She's musically gifted, but she's never spoken a word."

Darren said, "That right? Can't blame her. Not many around here I want to talk to myself."

Clayton stood by Laci and held his hand out to her again, like he'd done with the sheep. A feeling of satisfaction come over me again when she kept her hands tucked away. Clayton dropped his hand and shrugged. I motioned at him we was ready to go.

"Thank you," I said to Darren.

He flipped a hand at us and went to get a small box, and Clayton said, "Uh-oh, yeah, good time to go. Feeding time."

We exited the tent, and it hit me how tired I was.

I said to Clayton, "Thank you for showing us around. We got to go."

Clayton tilted his head and said, "Maybe tomorrow we can ride the Ferris wheel?"

"Sure, okay then."

He shoved his hands into his pockets and hunched his shoulders a bit.

"Clayton?"

"Yeah?"

"I ought to thank you proper for suggesting we come here. Thank you. Papa said as much. I imagine he'll mention it when he sees you next time."

Clayton won't looking at me. His eyes was in a spot somewhere over my head, on Laci. "It won't nothing. It only made sense. Johnny's always looking a good show."

I nodded, and began walking away, picking at the little fuzz balls the dress kept gathering each and every day. Laci fell in step beside me. Something kept me from turning around to see if Clayton watched us. I didn't want to see what I might see. A short distance later, I squinted at Laci's profile as she walked beside me, at her small upturned nose, the wide set of her mouth, and how, even in the nighttime, her strands of her hair shone under the moonlight with hints of light. I'd never thought so much about our differences ever before, believing I had my own appealing qualities and Laci, well, Laci was Laci. Until now. In this moment when Clayton's eyes won't on me but on her, it was just like I'd feared. It stuck in my mind he likely considered me like an Apple Pan Dowdy and her as a beautiful, layered cake topped with elegant icing. She was a flower, I was a weed. Her presence was like a light-scented breeze in spring, whereas I was more like an unexpected gust coming up the side of a mountain.

Buried memories rushed forward, and I thought of other times this sort of thing had happened, little incidents what had likely bothered me, but I'd kept tamped down out of guilt. Like the time we'd gone to a fall apple festival to sing about a year ago, and there'd been a boy there. I'd spied him coming up in a truck with a man I figured for his papa. He'd not come in time to see us sing, and I remembered having a vague feeling of relief Laci had gone off with Momma to get a cup of cider. He and I made eye contact like young folks do, and he'd come over to hand me a polished apple out of the basket he carried. He'd said they'd come from his family's orchard.

His name was Brice, and I'd bit into the apple, tasting the sweetness of it, sweet as the smile he offered me. I looked over his shoulder at Momma waving, motioning me to rejoin them. I ignored her, acted like I hadn't seen her while I smiled at Brice, his eyes on me, and mine on him. When her waving got more emphatic, I told him I'd be right back and hurried away. He'd followed me though, him and his basket of shiny apples, and that sweet attentive smile. All Laci done was plant one a them looks a hers on him, a piercing right through your gaze you couldn't look away from, and that was it, I faded away from his view, and gone was any interest in me. The apple turned sour in my mouth. I spit it out in my hand, hid it till I could throw it away, along with any hope I'd ever measure up in anyone's eyes for being just me.

And there was a more recent time, when we'd been down to Dewey's store, me, Laci and Papa. The usual group of old men was sitting in back by the coal stove, corncob pipes stuck between creased lips, smoke hovering like mist over their heads.

They was talking quiet, but I'd overheard one a them say, *Shame a purty gal like Laci is how she is, and downright shame that younger one, what's her name? Oh yeah, Wallis Ann. Too bad she ain't got none a that purty Laci got. When Laci comes around ole Wallis Ann don't stand a chance.*

I'd heard it, and felt something cold rush through my body like I'd jumped into the Tuckasegee in dead of winter followed by the heat of anger. I considered stomping over to them old coots and letting them know I'd heard what all they'd said. Only Papa asked me did I want a peppermint stick, and I'd let it go. Partiality towards Laci was something I'd got used to, even from Momma and Papa. Nobody meant nothing by it, it was simply on account of folks' belief Laci was suffering in some way and not able to live life to her full potential. I reckon we was all expected to make up for that.

Chapter 20

Clayton come to our performances regularly. Each night, after they ended, Papa give me money and allowed me and Laci to walk around with him for a little while. This was a freedom I'd never had before, and though I wanted to spend time with Clayton by myself, I figured Papa won't never going to allow it. Two girls walking around with a boy won't the same as only a boy and a girl walking around.

The very first night we rode the Ferris wheel, Clayton said, "Let Laci ride in the middle."

It kind a hurt my feelings when he suggested the seating arrangements.

My face must have showed disappointment, because he quickly said, "In case she gets scared, she'll be between us." When we stopped at the top, he said, "This is about as high up as the pole I climb to do my dive."

Off to my right, the twinkling lights of the carnival below reminded me of a night sky in reverse, almost like how the stars shone over the ridges of Cherry Gap and Cullowhee.

I pushed the thought away and turned to Clayton. "What did you think first time you stood there and looked down?"

"I was more afraid of not having a job. Considering all, I'm lucky to have had a way to work all this time. If I'd not joined the show, I was picturing myself in a soup line."

"Least you'd a had the soup line."

Our turn of hardship was still fresh in my mind, and I didn't ever want to be that hungry again, if I could help it. The smell of funnel cakes, hot dogs and all sorts of other smells followed us everywhere we went. It was odd, but even with all this food available, I always seemed hungry. After the Ferris wheel we usually rode the swings, and only once did we climb onto some contraption what spun us in circles and plumb turned my stomach inside out. When I was finally able to get off, my ever-present appetite sank somewhere down into the bottoms of my legs. I tried to laugh it off like nothing was wrong, only I ended up sitting on a bench nearby. It took me several minutes before I felt better while Laci won't phased at all. Clayton hurried off to buy me a Pepsi. I sipped on it, and eventually my stomach quit flip-flopping like a fish on the ground. We avoided that ride from then on.

That night a wave of homesickness bore down on me heavy as a sack full a grain, and for the first time in a while, I thought of Joe Calhoun and wondered what he was doing. How his boy, Lyle, and little Josie was getting along without their momma. Had he fixed his little cabin up, and what they might do for Thanksgiving and Christmas without a momma there to cook for them, to make their presents, to decorate a tree? My homesickness usually cropped up during quiet times, when we won't busy, and so I tried to get real tired such that I wouldn't have time to think sad thoughts of home.

Most nights we watched the crowd play games, or we'd go see the strong man lift the bar said to weigh two hundred pounds straight over his head, and ended most evenings by getting some spun sugar. I loved watching the man take a paper cone and swirl it around and around inside a barrel of sugary fluff being heated by some sort of special blower—as Clayton explained. You could see remnants of cottony-looking pieces floating inside it, while the smell of sugar wafted around us like the scent of honeysuckles, reminding me of spring in the mountains. Clayton would hand me the cone with a huge amount spun around it big as a beehive. We shared it by plucking pieces off and popping them into our mouths, savoring the sweetness.

Those was the good times.

Then there was confusing times when Clayton would get to asking questions about Laci. I tried to ignore that twisty sort a gut feeling I had, an idea he was starting to like her, maybe even better than me. It tried to eat its way into me like a worm into an apple. I argued with myself as to why, while simultaneously holding on to the fact he'd kissed me, after all, and most likely only wanted to know about the one person I spent the most time with.

Clayton's questions was mostly about her musical ability. "How'd she learn to play all of them songs?"

I told him about being in the church years ago, and how she'd watched a lady playing piano, then played the song from memory.

"Somehow she does it. She hears it played once or twice, and she can play it."

Clayton was intrigued, and he stared at Laci with a hint of awe. On a different night he tackled another topic.

He said, "Laci's never talked? At all?"

"No."

"Since she was born?"

"That's right."

"What you reckon is wrong with her? She's got to be real smart, playing music, and all."

"She is smart. Smarter than most. You know, Clayton. She's sitting right here. Ain't like she can't hear us."

"Oh, right." He leaned over and whispered in my ear. "What you reckon caused it?"

I sighed. "The granny woman said she was the color of a blueberry when she come out."

"And it caused her to be like that?"

"I guess so."

Another night, he suggested asking her questions.

"What for?"

"Just to see."

"To see . . . what?"

"I don't know. Maybe she'll say something."

These conversations frustrated me. "Why would she all the sudden talk? I've talked to her every day since I can remember and she ain't never spoke a word to me. Besides, she ain't some experiment. She ain't one a them sideshow freaks."

His mouth dropped open, and then he shut it, and his face turned red.

"I didn't mean nothing by it."

I was conflicted, wanting to spend time with him as long as I could while at the same time I wanted him to stop asking questions about Laci, especially with her sitting right there. What did we know about what she might think or feel? And why didn't he ever ask anything about me, about what I liked to do, and about what I wanted?

One night, after he'd started the questions about Laci again, I jumped up and said, "We got to go."

Clayton said, "Tomorrow?"

I acted like I didn't hear him and walked away, Laci's cool, dry hand stuffed inside my sweaty one.

He called out, "Wallis Ann? Wallis Ann!" and I kept right on going.

That night I wrestled the sheet on my cot into a ball of worry over how rude I'd been.

I wanted to go find him the next morning, let him know I was sorry, except right after we had breakfast, Papa said, "We're going into town to get a few things."

I tried to look for him as we walked to the other side of the carnival to get the truck. We passed by his small tent near his diving pole, and the flap was pushed aside, but he was nowhere in sight.

Papa drove to Tucker's Branch, a typical little town with a few houses set on the hillside looking over the railroad track that followed along a road barely big enough for two cars to pass on either side. There was a small store similar to Dewey's, the sort of store what had everything. Farm supplies, food, tools, whatever they could get by train, I suppose. Papa pulled out some money and counted a few bills.

He said, "Time you girls had you some shoes and new dresses."

This was another experience we'd never had, store-bought dresses, so this was a new and exciting thing what lifted my mood some.

Momma, worry making her words sharp, said, "We ought not spend our money so soon. We ought to save it and get ourselves back home where we belong." Then she glanced at mine and Laci's bare feet, and sighed, softening. "I reckon these girls need shoes, though."

Papa said, "It's all right, Momma, everything's gonna be fine. We'll make the money back."

Not only did we get new shoes, we got two new dresses each. I tried mine on, the first one a navy blue and green plaid, and the other a bright red with a black collar. I felt like a brand-new person, like I'd shed my old skin the way a snake does. I couldn't deny I hoped the dresses would catch Clayton's eye. After I'd finished trying mine on, Laci tried on hers. One was a deep green with a white collar, a color what brung out her eyes and hair. Laci looked right pretty in it, but it was the other dress what made me go still. It was lavender, a fetching color for Laci, only it was the way it fit her frame and it give me the thought I would never look like *that* in a dress. My dresses lost some of their appeal.

Even Papa said, "Hooey! I don't know if I ought to buy that one or not. Might get them young bucks too riled up."

Momma looked hesitant, then she said, "Our Laci's turned into a young lady, and it's high time she looked it."

Momma picked out two for herself, both flowered. Papa got two shirts and a pair of coveralls. She picked out a pair of shoes, and Papa looked at a shotgun, hefting it to his shoulder and peering down the barrel. His decision made, he took all the items to the front to pay while we went outside to wait for him in the truck. It was a pretty day, hard to believe it was almost Thanksgiving since it felt warm, with the previous cold we'd experienced on Stampers Creek a long-ago memory. Papa come out of the store with the packages all wrapped in paper, and tied with string.

Momma said, "I can't remember last time we had boughten clothes from a store," as if she was sad about having to do so.

Papa said, "I think it's been since the first year we got married. Before I bought you the sewing machine for Christmas."

Momma nodded. "I think you're right." She sighed. "Hard to believe we lost so much in that awful flood."

Papa said, "Now, Momma."

When we parked in the dusty lot beside the row of tents, I thought on Stampers Creek, the taller peaks and valleys, and the early morning mist settling in the hollers, created a feeling similar to the sensation I got riding on the downward turn of the Ferris wheel. We got out of the truck, and all of us stood a moment as if to prepare ourselves. I could hear workers shouting, the clanging of somebody hammering and the screams of people riding rides. We walked slow, like we was dreading the chaos. It was hard getting used to the traveling show when we was mostly familiar with the soft rush of a creek, birdsong, and the lowing of cattle in pastures.

Before the show that evening, all of us took care bathing. Momma had found an old cast-off galvanized tub what used to be used for the elephants, and asked if she could have it. She set it in her and Papa's tent and filled it with warm water. We took turns washing like we used to do at home on Saturday nights. We put on our new clothes and our new shoes, turning out fresh as if we was off to church. We stood admiring each other before we went to the tent cookhouse. I was feeling proud of my appearance, even more so when old Paulie noticed and smiled at me.

As I reached for a plate of food he'd fixed, he said, "Well, hey now, look at you, girlie! Ain't you all gussied up?"

I inspected my dress and shiny shoes.

"I guess I am. Thank you," I said.

After we got our food, we sat at our usual table and although no one else said anything about our crisp-looking clothes, a few of the working men cast looks our way, mostly on the sly at Laci, who ate intently, entirely unaware of the attention she was attracting in her lavender dress. It was hard not to notice how quiet it got when we stood to leave. I looked behind me as we walked out and every single man had set their eyes on her exiting the tent. Some leaned in, whispering to one another and pointing at her. Papa noticed too.

He muttered to Momma, "They better keep their eyes in their heads, or else. Not one of them is good enough for either of my girls."

Momma said, "Maybe you should think twice about them rambling around this place, then, hm?"

I hoped Papa wouldn't pay the comment no mind. At the arena a crowd was already starting to gather for the seven o'clock show. Soon the benches was full, as they had been since the first night. We didn't waste time and got started, Papa queueing Laci to play something we hadn't done before, one we could clog to. There was plenty of room on the stage to move about, so while Laci fiddled, and Momma sang, me and Papa showed the crowd how it was done where we come from. Our feet in our new shoes beat out a steady rhythm on the wooden platform, in perfect time to the tune.

We started with a basic step, the double toe shuffle, and then did a chug, and then added in other steps like wring the chicken's neck, broken wing, and rabbit dance. Soon it turned into a variation of our own intricate steps, with some improvisation, a competition between me and Papa. We always had us good time, one trying to outdo the other, and the crowd began to clap in time. Some was familiar with our type a clogging and joined in at the front of the stage. Eventually we had to stop because we was getting out of breath and wouldn't be able to sing a lick if we kept at it. After an hour, we come to the end of the show and Mr. Cooper who'd heard all the hooting and hollering from inside the arena tent come over and took Papa aside.

Mr. Cooper pointed my way and said, "Girl's got some fast feet, but, I tell you what"—and he pointed at Laci—"that one there? She could be a real showstopper. I've seen the crowd watching her. There's something special about her. She draws the eye."

I was glad Clayton won't around to hear his praise of Laci. I got to looking for him, and didn't see him in the usual spot he watched our performance. And Mr. Massey said nothing to the crowd about "step outside and see our next exciting act." Clayton had always performed every night, right after us, yet Mr. Massey had made no announcement.

I interrupted and asked Mr. Cooper, "Ain't there any high dive show tonight?"

He said, "Young Clayton seems to think we'll get bigger crowds if he only performs a few nights a week, instead of every night. We'll have to see."

I wanted to ask where he was, only I didn't dare in front of Momma and Papa.

Mr. Cooper looked at his watch and said, "I got to go see about some of the exhibits."

He handed some money to Papa and left. Papa jingled the coins in his hand, and as if remembering what Momma said earlier, he pocketed the money without offering me any. I told myself I really didn't want to walk around the carnival anyway, yet the change of plans spoiled my mood. I was feeling the pinch of regret even more about the way I'd acted toward Clayton, now that I couldn't fix it. I went into mine and Laci's tent and flopped facedown on the cot. Laci followed me and sat on the edge of hers, holding her fiddle and plucking at the strings. I turned on my side, facing away from Laci, wondering where he was and what he was doing.

I hadn't realized how tired I was until I jerked awake feeling like I'd been asleep for a while. Everything outside was quiet. The shows usually shut down around ten o'clock, and the stillness told me it was well past that. Also, there was no glow against the pale canvas sides reflecting lights from the rides. From some distance away, I heard laughing, and the high strains of an instrument. I slowed my breathing and concentrated. It sounded like a fiddle, yet different. Could somebody else play? I reached over to Laci's cot. My fingers felt her sheet, a blanket, and nothing else. I leaned over even further, my hand moving along, up and down, expecting to touch her warmth. The bedding was cold to the touch.

Laci won't here. She was gone, yet I lay there as if needing to persuade myself because she'd not done this in such a long time. Seconds later I drew the flap aside and looked towards Momma and Papa's tent. Their own flap was down and tied tight. I could hear Papa snoring. I ducked back inside and pulled on my shoes. Luckily, I still had on my dress from earlier, so I didn't have to light the lantern to see to put on my clothes. After I slipped on my shoes, I left the tent again, and stood outside for a moment, listening. The music sounded like it was coming from the other end of the tent area, closer to where Trixie and her family stayed, as well as Darren, and La Diablo. I hurried through the maze of tents, my ears tuned in and following the odd tune.

The first thing I seen was a campfire. And around the campfire was a circle of workers, men and women alike. I drew closer, unable to see who played this sort of music I'd never heard played before. It was different from the usual folk or gospel tunes we was used to and I began to feel scared. This couldn't be Laci, and if it won't her, where was she? I stopped and stood listening to the haunting, slow, pure quality of the music, so unusual and intriguing. One of the workers seen me standing a few feet from them, and he stepped back and I caught a partial glimpse of Laci, still in the lavender dress, and barefoot. The soles of her feet was dirty black, like she'd spent some time walking around. She was half hid by the others entranced by her playing and hadn't noticed me there. She even moved different as she played this strange song, sort a swaying back and forth, her hair flowing like the music, as her fingers went up and down the neck of the fiddle. I come closer, and a few more people turned, poking at the person next to them, whispering and gesturing at me and moving off to the side to let me through.

Then I seen who was sitting right beside her. Clayton. He smiled at her as she played, watching her every move, occasionally looking at the faces around them, like he was so proud. Clayton's gaze circled the crowd and come to the spot filled in by me. It did my soul some good to see him almost jump, and then look guilty and embarrassed. I didn't acknowledge him, smile or make any move. I let Laci finish the song, and when she put the fiddle down, everyone clapped except me and Clayton.

Abruptly he stood and pointed at Laci with excitement. "Wallis Ann! I know. I know. I'm sorry! I'm sure you're wondering how Laci come to be out here. It was by accident."

I frowned. "An accident."

He pointed to the fire eater, Diablo. "He found her. She was standing outside his tent. He has a phonograph and plays classical records all the time. He was playing Bach's chaconne. She must have heard it and it drew her to his tent. When I seen her, she was standing with her fiddle to her chin, and sort of following along soft like. Then Diablo took the record off and she sat down where you see her sitting now, and she started playing it, over and over. We're all out here listening because, I'm telling you, Wallis Ann, it's unbelievable what she done!"

Mr. Cooper come from out of nowhere and said, "He's right. Like I told your pa earlier, she's got something extraordinary. I'd like to make her a solo act. Been thinking about it some days anyway, and now? After what I seen here tonight? It would be crazy not to do it."

I couldn't see Papa agreeing to this, and I said as much. "He won't agree, Mr. Cooper. Laci . . . needs people who understand her, how she is. She's used to performing with us, she's never done it any other way. She's particular about who she's with, who touches her. He won't allow it."

"Seems like she's doing all right, look at her."

I glanced at Laci, who remained seated, the fiddle resting in her lap. She looked like she was quietly listening. Clayton sat back down beside her, grinning while a slow anger heated my chest, and flashed over me quick as a lightning striking in the summertime.

"Papa ain't gonna agree to it."

Mr. Cooper continued, "You leave everything to me, young lady. You're not in the position to make decisions, you don't know what I got worked out with your pa."

"No, but I know my sister."

Mr. Cooper's eyebrows rose and his tone turned persuasive. "New experiences might be good for her. She's been sheltered in them mountains all these years."

What he said won't true. Laci hadn't been sheltered any more than me. I held my hand out to her. She looked at me, and I felt an unfamiliar sense of panic, remembering her unexpected moments of stubbornness. My hand, suspended in the space, shook slightly. Everyone looked from her to me.

Mr. Cooper said, "See, she's . . ."

Laci stood and tucked her hand into mine, and I was so relieved my legs felt as weak as when I'd first climbed out of the Tuckasegee. Likely I'd only imagined the hesitation, but I was grateful any doubt on my face was hidden by the fact there was only a campfire for light. I led her away, saying not one word to Clayton, or anyone else.

As we walked to the tent, I was in a state of disbelief. Back at our tent, Laci laid down, and I crawled onto my own cot and turned on my side facing her. I reached out, touching her shoulder, waiting to see if she would brush her fingers down my arm. She didn't. I listened as her breathing slowed down, becoming an easy in and out of a deep sleep. It was only then I closed my eyes, except sleep was nigh on impossible. My thoughts swarmed like gnats driven crazy by summer sweat, and I come to a peculiar conclusion. Lots of folks had paid Laci attention in the past, and it had never mattered to me much—not until Clayton showed up.

I'd thought of him as mine, and mine alone. I hadn't wanted to share his attention from the beginning because his interest towards me at the waterfall showed he was truly liking me for me. He'd made me think maybe I *was* pretty, and maybe he'd like me in *that* way, the way I'd started to think after he'd told me I reminded him of that girl, Janie Mae, and how he'd pressed his mouth to mine. My thoughts had stayed on him, and the possibilities of our friendship more than anyone be-fore—ever. I'd liked a boy here and there in my class at school, but not like Clayton. It dawned on me then, the reality of my situation. How was anyone ever going to notice me when Laci was always beside me?

Chapter 21

I slept late the next morning, and when I opened my eyes it was unusually bright inside the tent. Remembering the previous night, I crawled out from under my covers, and hurried to put on the dress given to me by Joe Calhoun, saving my new ones for the singing. I shivered in a cold air, knocking a thin layer of ice off the top of the water in the washbowl. Winter was finally making its way here. I splashed my face and barely took the time to dry it before I ducked out of the tent to see Laci sitting beside Momma in front of a fire. Papa sat with them, hands between his knees, looking grumpy.

Hesitant, I sat down and said, "What's wrong?"

Momma said, "Mr. Cooper come by this morning."

Mr. Cooper had already come. Papa glared over the campfire at me, and Laci got to rocking, and it took me no more than seconds to understand they knowed what happened.

I chose my words with care, as Papa continued to scowl in my direction. "Diablo, the fire eater? He plays different music than what we listen to, on a phonograph. She heard the music."

Papa honed in on the parts I left out, as I should've known he would.

He said, "You mean you girls went off last night. After we went to sleep."

I proceeded with even more caution. "We was only gone a few minutes."

Papa shifted his gaze to Momma, his expression conveying disbelief.

Momma shrugged at him and said, "You're the one taught her to be so independent, William."

I tried to explain further. "Laci heard the song being played, and learned it like she learns all the songs she knows."

Papa considered what I'd said, and turned to Laci, "Laci?"

Laci kept on rocking.

Papa said, "Laci, play the new song you learned last night."

She turned her head away from him, hair falling over her face as if to hide.

I went into the tent and come out with her fiddle and handed it to her. She laid it in her lap.

"Laci, won't you play the new song for Momma and Papa?"

She bent forward like she seen something on the ground.

Momma said, "Leave her be. I reckon we'll hear it when she's ready."

Papa said, "Might as well go on to the cookhouse and get breakfast, it's gettin' late."

Laci tucked the fiddle under her chin and began playing the song, sounding like somebody we didn't know. It lasted several minutes, and when it was over she went and put the fiddle back in the tent.

Papa stared after her. "Ain't that something, Ann?"

Momma appeared just as surprised.

She managed to say, "It sure is."

Papa said, "I'm gonna have another chat with Cooper. If he insists on her playing longer, he's gonna have to pay more."

I said, "She won't want to play on stage by herself."

"Mr. Cooper says that's what he wants. If I tell him no, he could tell us to pack our stuff and get on down the road."

"What if she won't do it, though? You wanted her to play and she didn't want to. She only did it when she wanted to. Laci knows more than we think she knows."

Momma raised an eyebrow. "What do you mean, Wallis Ann?"

"She waited and when Papa said we should go eat, then she played the song."

"Your sister's done things like that all her life."

I wanted to tell Momma what I'd seen long before we come here. I didn't get the chance because when Laci come out of the tent, I didn't say anything more. There was something un-common, something altered, and it made her seem a bit like a stranger.

Papa said, "Let's get on to the cookhouse."

When Paulie seen us enter, he said, "I was about to give up and start on dinner. Got a few sausages. A few biscuits. Some corn mush, that's about it."

Papa said, "Don't matter, whatever you got is fine."

He filled plates and handed Momma and Papa theirs. They went to our usual table and Paulie served me and Laci. As usual we ended up with an extra helping of corn mush.

"Here, let me put you some extra sorghum on it for you and your sister. That'll help you last till dinnertime."

Ever since I'd met Paulie, I'd thought if he'd been about twenty years younger, he might have taken a shine to me the way he was always winking and giving me extras. That changed in the next instant when he looked at Laci. He mo-tioned at me, secret like. I leaned towards him, hoping he won't about to make me feel uncomfortable by admitting he had taken a fancy towards me. I had no reason to worry.

He reached into his apron pocket to pull out a slender, silver harmonica, and nodded towards Laci, and said, "I got this here for you to give to your pretty sister. I've been coming to hear her play every night, and I thought maybe she'd like to learn this."

I felt myself draw up. Even Paulie was knocked silly by Laci. I took the harmonica from him, and without a word, I spun on my heels, mumbling my thanks. We went to the table, and I slid the harmonica across the table to Laci. I could sense Paulie's eyes on us. Laci took it and turned it over in her hands, then set it on the table and started eating.

Momma said, "Who gave you that?"

I mumbled, "Paulie."

"Is something wrong, Wallis Ann?"

"No, Momma. I'm hungry, that's all."

"Well, eat your breakfast."

I glanced around as I ate, looking for Clayton. Most everyone was already gone, off to start preparing rides, shows and games for anyone who would come. Visits to the shows was light during the weekdays while folks worked their farms, or worked in town. After suppertime, things picked up, and you could hear the screams of folks on the rides, and the clanging noises of games, and bells when there was a winner. We hurried to finish, and as we got ready to leave, Laci left the harmonica behind on the table. I got it, and followed everyone out. When we got to the path leading to our tents, Papa hurried off to talk to Mr. Cooper about Laci.

Momma said, "Let's wash some things."

"Sure, Momma."

I give Laci the harmonica once more, and she turned it over and over, then laid it down again. Shrugging, I went to haul water, running after the water truck at one point to get extra. That was how we spent the rest of our morning and on into the afternoon, washing what we slept on, underthings, and about anything else we could get our hands on. It felt good to work. I missed the physical labor at Stampers Creek where every day began and ended with more than we could get done in a day. Work always made you feel like you'd accomplished something. After we finished, I fussed around inside the tent, moving mine and Laci's cots from one spot to another, and then back again. I felt restless, still troubled about Clayton and wishing I could catch sight of him somehow. Later in the afternoon, I heard a familiar voice outside the tent.

I looked out of the flap to see who it was, and spotted Big Bertha, dropped in for another unexpected visit. Momma, ever the politest of hostesses, dug out the coffeepot we'd used at Stampers Creek, and made some coffee. I decided to stay in the tent and leave Momma to handle things. I picked up the new harmonica and puffed into it. It made a honking sound, like a goose. Whatever in the world had Paulie been thinking? Big Bertha, whose voice matched her size, got to talking about nothing really. She seemed kind a lonely. Momma listened to her go on about this and that, and then she started on her husband again. Momma made appropriate comments and noises until, finally, Big Bertha heaved herself to her feet, preparing to leave.

She said, "I'm thinking about quittin' this place."

Momma said, "Really? Why?"

Big Bertha snorted.

I peeked out and her blond curls bobbed with indignation. "Why? How would you like it if people come simply to stare at you, while laughing and poking their fingers into you, like you won't a person? What if you heard them say ugly things, even when they know you can hear? Things like, my God, she looks bigger'n the biggest hog I own. What you reckon she eats, an entire cow?"

Momma shook her head and said, "I reckon I wouldn't like it one bit. How long have you been doing this?"

Big Bertha's shoulders drooped and she said, "I don't know. Seems like all my life, but probably ten years. Thing is, when

Walter was alive, I didn't care so much what people thought. Now he's gone, I got nobody cares about me, my feelings nor nothing."

Momma patted Big Bertha's arm. "Try to only think about the good times you had with him. As far as leaving, maybe you ought to. If you're not happy?"

Big Bertha pulled a handkerchief from somewhere within the folds of her clothing, and swiped at her eyes.

She flipped a hand and said, "Where would I go? Somebody like me? Ain't got no family left. I reckon folks here is about as good a family as I'm able to have at this point. I won't ever have nobody love me again like Walter. You know I was only foolin' about the stew, right? I'd never hurt Walter. I loved him."

Momma said, "Of course you wouldn't. And sure, this seems like a nice-enough place, you have friends here. I mean, folks seem nice enough and all."

Big Bertha said, "Stick around, you'll see."

Which could a meant anything. Big Bertha was puzzling, her moods swinging like a sickle. Momma nodded and smiled at her, but I could read her look and it said, *You're crazy as a Bessie bug.*

Big Bertha said, "It's getting on late. Thank you for listening to me complain and whine. I probably shouldn't have dumped on you. I barely know you."

Momma smiled again. "Don't you worry none. It's fine."

Big Bertha waddled off, and we could hear her sort a mumbling, arguing with herself as she made her way to the other side of the yard.

I stepped out of the tent and said to Momma, "Big Bertha sure is something else."

"Losing the one person who loves you is hard because love is healing, it can take away hurts like that. It can make you see things differently."

Momma's words got me thinking hard about Clayton. He'd

caused feelings I'd never had, and a considerable amount of anxiety seeing him so close to Laci. But, was that love? I won't sure. Papa would've said I was too young to be thinking on such things, though some girls my age who'd come to school didn't never show back up again because they'd gone off and got hitched. Or worse. I looked up and seen Papa hurrying back from seeing Mr. Cooper, his face all knotted up like he had a headache. He plopped down on the stool Big Bertha had vacated.

Momma said, "What did he say?"

Papa shook his head. "He's the boss man. I tried to tell him it'd be good to have a bit more money seeing as Laci was going to be working extra, and what you reckon he said? No. Said if I want to earn more money, I could help clean up after the show animals. Said she won't going to have to play long enough to justify it. Yet, he wants her learning more songs."

Momma's tone was incredulous. "That sure don't seem fair. How's she supposed to do that? She can't be going off to some stranger's by herself."

"That young buck Clayton was there and said he'd take care of it. Got a way to hook up that contraption near his tent. He said, Laci could learn that a way. Boss man said have Wallis Ann go too. Said he's seen all three of them roaming about together, so it ought to not be a problem. We can't afford to lose this job. Anyway, he'll be here shortly."

I looked at Papa, my heart slipping a beat. "Who?"

Papa said, "Who else?"

I could only guess. A moment later we heard whistling and Clayton strode towards us with a smile. The sight of him caused a tiny lurch in my chest. Love for someone outside of my family was unknown, like all the other new experiences I'd had around him. The taste of cotton candy. The Ferris wheel. The sideshows with strange people inhabiting tiny tents, their particular oddities on display. Clayton stopped whistling when he seen the look on Papa's face, while Momma ignored him, going inside their tent and closing the flap.

Without a word, I went and got Laci, who still sat on her cot like she was tired. "Come on with me, Laci."

We left out of the tent to see Clayton waiting awkwardly, looking everywhere but at Papa.

Papa more or less growled at him. "Have them back in an hour."

Clayton hesitated, and dared to ask, "What if she ain't learned a new song by then? Mr. Cooper . . ."

Papa said, "*One hour.*"

"Yes, sir."

We started for his tent without a word between us. It won't like it had been, with the previous easygoing way we'd enjoyed one another's company. A mood hovered, stifling and bitter. I walked fast, hurrying, and Clayton kept pace with me easy enough, saying nothing about my silence.

When we come close to his tent, he cleared his throat. "Is something the matter, Wallis Ann? You seem . . . mad."

"I'm not mad."

"You sure?"

"Yes."

"Okay. I got the phonograph and a different record. Let's see what Laci can do."

"If you say so."

I heard some noise from Clayton. I didn't bother to look at him. The phonograph sat on a similar wooden table as the night before. Laci went and sat beside it like she was aware of the purpose of being there.

I was about to tell her anyhow when Clayton spoke up. "Laci, listen to this new song. See if you can play it."

He started the record. I sat on a nearby stool and pretended to be looking elsewhere while secretly watching him watching her, looking for what I don't know. A special look? Laci rarely ever looked anyone in the eyes, except me, Momma, Papa and Seph when he was here. She listened to the song playing, her head tilted to the side.

Clayton told me about the record he'd selected. "It's another Bach song. It's called Sonata Number Two in A Minor. It's a pretty long one."

I nodded, then sat festering, wishing I could simply fade away, yet the music and watching Laci learn kept my attention. It was, in a word, exquisite. Clayton seemed to forget I was even there, spellbound as Laci worked through the music, and in that way, I guess I got my wish.

I'd disappeared.

Chapter 22

It come as no surprise Laci learned the song quick as she did. Clayton played it twice and then she played bit by bit, all the way through, like she'd heard it a hundred times already. Wonder filled his face as he chose a small section of the record to play, stopped it, then waited as she placed her fiddle under her chin and coaxed out an identical rendition. She lowered her fiddle and waited for him to move the needle to some other spot. In random snippets here and there, Laci proved she could play the song, having only heard it fully two times. Clayton gaped at me while pointing at her.

He said, "I ain't never seen the likes of nothing like it."

I said, "I reckon not. Laci's remarkable."

"She sure is, she's something else."

It won't what he said, but how he said it, and it made my heart feel like it had been exposed to a deep freeze, creating a deep ache in response. The walk back was just as quiet, the three of us side by side yet seeming very far apart. Clayton glanced at me a time or two. I refused to look his way, as I won't in the mood for prying questions. Although we hurried, the hour was gone. Closer to our tents, he slowed down like he wanted to talk, only I kept going.

He said, "Wallis Ann."

With a sigh, I stopped and turned around. "What?"

"You sure there ain't something wrong? You seem different."

I stared into his serious brown eyes for what I thought I'd seen there before, only now they hid his thoughts, like Laci hid hers.

I said, "So do you, Clayton."

"How am I different?"

I won't sure how to answer him. I couldn't say, *You're being too nice to my sister.* I'd thought at first his attentiveness to Laci was all because of me, only now as things went along, it didn't seem like that at all. I recollected the kiss, and then, after meeting her, he changed, transferring his attentions.

Without thinking, I blurted out, "Why'd you ever kiss me, Clayton?"

A fiddle string plunked, an interruption distracting enough to make him look at Laci. Papa had joined Momma, and they glared in our direction. I could feel Papa's disapproval from where I stood.

Clayton looked at them nervously too and said, "Maybe we could talk tonight. After the show?"

"I guess."

I walked away without waiting to see if Clayton had anything else to say.

Laci didn't follow me until I turned and said, "Laci!"

When we got close enough, Papa said, "She better have learned it."

"She knows it, Papa."

Momma watched Clayton leaving and turned to me. "You look upset, Wallis Ann."

"I'm not upset!"

Momma shook her head like she couldn't fathom what had got into me.

At the cookhouse tent, I spent most of the time shoving my food around instead of eating, glad when we left so I could give up the pretense. We went to the arena as scheduled and immediately my eyes was drawn to a new sign sitting at the entrance. SPECIAL SHOW TONIGHT! CLASSICAL MUSIC PERFORMED BY THE MOUNTAIN MUTE! *The mountain mute.* Whatever aggravation and confusion I'd been feeling about Laci went out of me as I gaped in shock. I pointed without a word, and Papa stopped dead cold in his tracks.

Momma yanked his shirtsleeve. "No! Oh no!"

Papa jerked his arm from Momma's grip and marched over to the sign, grabbing it off the stand as Chili Mac stopped taking money from the long line of folks.

Chili Mac yelled "Hey! What're you doing? You ain't supposed to tetch that!"

"Damned if I ain't! Where's Johnny Cooper?"

Chili Mac pointed inside the tent while all the people who'd been waiting in line pointed at us.

We could hear the people muttering, "There she is, the mountain mute! That's her, right there! I seen her the other night! What all you reckon's wrong with her?"

Papa said, "Come on!" as he stomped inside the tent, yelling, "Cooper!"

Momma said, "Oh dear God," as we followed. Papa and Mr. Cooper got into an animated discussion, arms waving about, with Papa's face going red as a tomato while he waved the sign in front of Mr. Cooper's face. I ain't ever heard Papa sound the way he did right then.

His voice held a quiet warning. "This here's my daughter you're talking about."

"I ain't said nothing what ain't true. She don't talk and she's from the mountains. It's all true!"

"You're trying to make her seem like a sideshow, like a freak, and she ain't no freak. I won't have you putting her on display. We don't need your money this bad."

I'd never seen Papa in such a state. He lifted his arms and slammed the sign against a raised knee. It busted in two and he tossed the pieces to the ground. Mr. Cooper tried to smile at the flow of people still coming in, filling the arena to standing room only. He smoothed his hand over his hair, nodding at them like nothing won't wrong, everything's fine here.

Arms held out, Mr. Cooper made a gesture what said *Calm down,* and in a tight but calm voice, he said, "Okay. Okay. Please, Mr. Stamper, ain't no need of getting all riled up!"

Everyone was watching. They could tell something was going on.

He sounded a bit whiny when he said, "I assure you, the sign, seeing as how you broke it, will not be replaced."

Papa leaned down to Mr. Cooper. "And I want ten percent of the cut, not seven."

Mr. Cooper puckered his mouth, and his face twisted like his feet hurt. "Fine, fine then. That too."

Papa said, "Deal?"

"Deal."

They shook, while I'd gone red hot as a poker at Papa over his dickering like she *was* a freak.

I pulled on Momma's sleeve. "How can he haggle over her? It don't seem right, that ain't no different than Mr. Cooper."

Momma's expression was hard, like the day the doctor said, "idiot savant," yet she didn't make a move to stop him.

She shook her head. "Your papa's feeling a bit desperate, Wallis Ann. We need this money. Don't worry. He won't allow Laci to be humiliated."

I thought he already had, though I reckon he was as upset as me. When he come over to us, I could have sworn I felt heat coming off him.

He said, "I can't believe he thought he could pull that stunt."

Momma said, "It's all over now."

Clayton seen us standing together near the platform, and ventured over to stand at my elbow.

I snapped at him, "Did you know anything about that sign out front?"

He looked surprised and said, "What sign?" and the innocent look he wore seemed genuine.

I looked away. "Never mind."

Mr. Massey hurried in, and without consulting with Mr. Cooper, he began talking about the show for the night. "Ladies and gentlemen! Do we have a special treat for you!"

Mr. Massey motioned at Clayton, and Clayton put his hand under Laci's elbow escorting her away from us and onto the platform. He held her fiddle while she sat down on a chair placed in the center of the platform, and much like her petting that two-headed sheep, it seemed curious how she went along with things where Clayton was involved.

Mr. Massey went on, "See this girl here, she's a mount . . ."

Mr. Cooper yelled, "Hold up, wait!" and hurried over.

The crowd buzzed and whispered. Mr. Cooper held a private conversation with Mr. Massey, gesturing at Papa. Mr. Massey stared our way, his expression as flat as a fallow field. Mr. Cooper backed away giving Papa an apologetic look. Clayton bent over Laci, talking in her ear.

Mr. Massey yelled, "Ladies and gentlemen, let's hear it for our mountain miss! Laci Stamper!"

Clayton stepped off to the side of the platform, staying where she could see him. She sat motionless, the lavender dress spread out over her knees, gripping her fiddle tight. She peeked through a strand of hair to her left, and then to her right. She'd become aware we won't there with her, and suddenly I was scared for her and wanted her to do good. I wanted her to make us proud, to prove to everyone here she *was* special. I held my breath until she bent her head to the left, and placed the fiddle under her chin. Everyone hushed, and it was as if they all leaned forward at once in anticipation.

With her right hand holding the bow to the strings, she pulled out a long, sweet note. She played the songs she learned, the sound saturating the arena like a warm rain falling and drenching a drought-stricken land. I would like to say she played flawlessly, only the songs won't familiar enough for me to know. It seemed in my mind, she played pretty as a lark singing. When she finished, it was clear the crowd loved her. She lowered the fiddle and then her head as if to avoid seeing the people before her. Everyone jumped to their feet, pounding out approval with their boots on the seats and their hands. She remained seated, her face bleached of color, like she'd just woke up from some sort of stupor.

We hurried towards the stage, and Papa give her his hand. She rose from the chair to stand beside him, and I quickly moved the chair off the platform to make room. Papa didn't bother to wait for Mr. Massey. He began singing "Black-Eyed Susie" a cappella, and at the start of that familiar song, Laci went to playing with a fervor I'd not seen before, her arm cranking furiously to the mountain tune. We sang a few songs. When Papa and I started clogging, I put all I had into it, beating my shoes against the boards in a steady rhythm, working out my anger through clogging. I sang loud, and clogged hard, trying to expel all them new feelings about what was happening, all of it bubbling inside of me like a hot spring. I glanced out across the crowd once to see if Clayton was watching. He won't nowhere I could see, and my mood plummeted the same way I'd seen him fall from that tall platform.

Finally, it was over, and the crowd left, going on about the show they'd seen. The inside of the tent felt hot and stuffy, and all I wanted was to get out into the night air. I wanted to go to the tent, lie down, close my eyes, go to sleep and forget. About everything. I didn't care about what Clayton wanted to tell me. As the crowd was leaving, Mr. Cooper come, handed Papa some money, and left without a word.

Papa pocketed the money, and Momma said, "Ain't you going to count it?"

"I don't want to know."

"What do you mean you don't want to know? The place was full. He told us it would hold a hundred people. He gets twenty-five cent a person, so we ought to get two dollars and fifty cent."

"I can cipher on my own, Ann. I know what we ought to get, but I'm tired of arguing for the night."

"But if you don't tell him now, you can't prove it."

"I ain't messing with it tonight, I said."

Momma heaved a frustrated sigh. We left the arena tent, skirting around the crowd by Clayton's platform. I hoped he'd look for me where we usually stood. I hoped he'd notice I won't there, and worry about it. As we made our way through the yard, Momma and Papa spoke politely to some of the other workers here and there.

They shouted, "Heard that oldest gal was something else!" and "What kind a music was that?"

Papa said, "Just music."

I breathed in deep, noticing the smells hung thick and strong, even in the cold. One had to get outside the boundaries of the traveling show to get to fresh air. I raised my arm to sniff my sleeve, and even my clothes smelled like this place. Once inside our tent, I took off the blue and green plaid dress and hung it over the line in the corner Papa had strung up for this purpose. Laci took off her lavender dress. I lay on my cot, closed my eyes, tried to empty my head as Laci laid her fingers on my bare arm, tracing the tips back and forth until we both fell asleep.

The next morning when I woke up, my thoughts about Laci's performance and the attention she got went to festering like a sore. Even though all of us performed, we might as well have got off the stage and left her to it alone. It won't no matter to Momma and Papa because they was proud of us both, but it got stuck in my craw, this idea my singing and dancing won't appreciated. I got to remembering how I went with a few of my classmates to a clogging contest held down to Cullowhee a couple years ago. Momma, Papa, Laci and Seph, who was only a baby at the time, had come to see me dance, and I was proud I could show them what I'd been working on in secret. We did all kinds of dancing and included steps like Kentucky Drag, Shave and a Haircut, and the Cowboy. We won the trophy too, and that was probably the only time I felt I won't being likened to Laci, the one time I done something where nobody else noticed her over me. It had felt real good, and I had wanted that day to last forever.

I went out of the tent, ignoring Laci as she reached for my hand, wondering how it would be if the only person I had to worry about was me. I went about my business like she won't there, trying to whitewash my thoughts towards this fresh idea of an existence as an individual person. She come towards me time and again and I turned away, refused to look at her when her eyes sought mine. It felt odd. Mean-spirited. Unnatural, in fact. I found I couldn't keep up denying her. We'd always been so close, I couldn't see things no other way. By dinnertime, I relented and Laci hurried over to press against me hard like she was trying to make up for the lack of contact.

Laci being on her own in some capacity was unlikely, and I doubted there'd ever come a time we'd go our separate ways. I thought of five years from now, ten years from now, my whole life laid out before me with Laci attached in some way, a constant companion, no matter what I chose to do. I would never be just me, Wallis Ann, uniquely set apart from her, or her wants. That was when, maybe for the first time ever, I understood, my own wishes for what I wanted to do with my life might not matter. I'd never thought of it before, and I pushed that fact away, knowing if I spent too much time dwelling on it, this tinge of resentment I was starting to carry round was only going to grow.

The next two nights the arena tent was packed. Word had traveled to other areas and we heard folks was traveling in from Walhalla, Seneca, and Long Creek, and other places to hear Laci play. I didn't see much of Clayton, and considering how Papa had been about her learning songs and the way I'd acted, I won't surprised. I didn't stick around to watch his high dive either. I'd hoped he'd search me out, and when he didn't, I went back to our tents, expecting he'd come the next day. I pictured him taking my hand, telling me he'd missed me.

The third night, and still Clayton didn't show up to watch us although he had his own show. Again, I made myself go back to our tents with Momma and Papa, only to collapse on the cot, filled with despair. Laci lay down without getting undressed, and I started to poke her, tell her to get out of her good clothes, and thought, *If she wants to sleep in her clothes, who cares?* It was the last thought I had before I fell into a deep sleep.

The crunch of footsteps outside the tent woke me and I immediately sensed something off. Gritting my teeth, I turned over. Laci won't in her cot. Angry and frustrated all at once, I yanked on a dress not caring which one it was. I put my shoes on and slapped the tent flap she'd left untied out of my way, and walked into the cold night air, my breath creating small vaporous clouds before me. I looked to Momma and Papa's tent, knowing they slept. Footsteps a short distance away caught my ear and under the bright moonlight, I seen two figures walking together. I recognized them as sure as I'd recognized my own self in the mirror.

My heart went wild, beating like it was trying to escape my body. I hurried to follow, tucked away in the shadows. They walked slow, like they had all the time in the world. Clayton looked over his shoulder now and then, like he was nervous about getting caught. I was unsure of what to do. The idea Laci went willingly give me an uneasy feeling. They went by other tents carefully, then by the cookhouse. I ducked behind what I could here and there, while trying not to lose sight of them. They passed Diablo's, and Trixie's family's tents. They went by the diving platform, and his small tent.

Where was he taking her?

Finally, they come to a section roped off, a grassy area where the horses and mules was kept. I scooted behind a large tree, my throat dry as the sawdust I'd just walked over. Clayton whistled low and a horse come to the fence. He reached into his pocket and pulled out an apple.

He give it to Laci, and I could hear him say, "This here's my horse, Nugget. See? He likes you, I can tell by the way he's wanting you to give him that apple."

He placed a hand under Laci's arm and urged her to hold the fruit resting on the flat part of her palm, the same way Papa had showed us a long time ago. The horse lipped the fruit, carefully taking it from her. I could hear munching noises as it ate. Then Clayton did something so unexpected, so startling, I almost cried out. He leaned in, and dipped his head toward Laci. He hesitated, then he kissed her exactly like he'd done with me. She pulled away from him, pushed against his chest like she was scared. I wanted to go to her, but I was frozen, my feet unable to receive what my brain told them.

What happened next was as shocking as seeing Seph drink the tainted water.

She stepped close to him, this girl who'd only ever wanted certain people to touch her, pressing against him so her breasts touched his chest. He put his arms around her the way he'd done me, and it was like I was standing at the edge of the waterfall and he was pushing me over the ledge. I leaned against the tree, the bark digging into my wrists and hands. I began to back away, only I couldn't stop watching as he kissed her, again and again. It seemed Laci was kissing *him* too when she put her arms around his shoulders, and he drew her closer still, his hands gripping her waist. I felt sick to my stomach the way I had after eating too fast when we first come.

I began inching along backwards, keeping close to the tree line, hiding myself in the shadows. How stupid I'd been to think Clayton would like me. My legs felt like boards, unbendable, my thoughts as sharp and hard as the wires of a barbed-wire fence. I thought I might would cry, only I couldn't. My eyes stayed dry as a used-up well. I don't remember much about leaving, only that I stumbled a few times, like a drunk man I'd seen once. Somehow I found myself at the tents and somehow I went through the motions of undressing again.

I laid down, hearing my own heart inside me, an erratic pounding I couldn't escape. Before long, there come the stealthy movements of someone trying to be sneaky. Then a male voice whispering. What kept me still was the shock of what I might see again. A few minutes went by, and then Laci come into the tent, slowly feeling her way over to her cot. Even in the dimness, her features stood out, the dark circles of her eyes, the line of her mouth, yet it was the curve of it, clearly seen in the predawn light what sent an icy chill over me. Bewildered, and amazed, it showed something I'd never seen, in all my born days. Something Laci never ever done, not to our knowledge.

She smiled.

Chapter 23

True winter bore down the next day bringing a biting wind and a hard freeze. It was Saturday before Thanksgiving, and typically the show got lots of the locals selling collards, sweet taters, or molasses. I doubted anyone was going to feel like being outside on a day like this. I was suffering another affliction, miserable, my strange inner hurt so different than when Seph died. It was a hurt unlike anything I'd ever known. I kept seeing Clayton's head bend down to Laci and each repeat of it, made me feel like I'd stepped out into an icy wind without a stitch of clothes on. It made me want to huddle under my cot covers and never come out. I didn't care nothing about eating, seeing to my chores, talking to Trixie or anybody else I might run into. Especially not Clayton.

I watched in secret as Laci rose from her cot. It had been a long time since I'd paid attention to her body, and now as I stared at her, I resented every difference we had, a sort of intolerable awareness of everything. Her shimmering hair, creamy skin, liquid soft eyes, long legs, slender arms. Her breasts. Every part of her I seen through Clayton's eyes. It caused a commotion inside me, everything exploding into an internal uproar what made me grit my teeth. She tugged on her old dress, pulling her hair free before sitting down on her cot, patiently waiting for me to do up her dress. I twisted onto my other side and pretended I was asleep. I wished she could understand. I wanted her to know how I felt. I could see for myself in the clear light of day, she won't any different, and I wondered if any of what I'd seen happened. I questioned whether the smile had been real. Maybe I'd only imagined it.

After a few minutes, I heard rustling, felt a cold draft, and heard Momma speaking. "Wallis Ann didn't button your dress? Come here, I'll do it."

I raised up, peeked through the opening in the flap at Laci's fixed expression. There won't anything there to hint at what happened. I lay down again, resuming my study of the canvas wall. My eyes traced the pattern of a water stain in the shape of a lopsided heart. I was still in the cot looking at that crooked heart when Momma come in, a mass of cold air following her. The flap to the tent dropped with a popping sound.

She said, "Are you sick?"

Yes.

"No, ma'am."

"Get up then, get dressed, and be quick about it, if you want to eat with us."

"I ain't hungry, Momma. Not really."

"Then you must be sick." She laid a warm hand to my forehead, "Well, you're not hot. Does your stomach hurt? Are you having your . . . ?"

I shook my head hard, grabbed at her hand, and pressed it to my face.

Surprised, she said, "Wallis Ann? What is it? What's wrong?"

I almost cried then.

I whispered, "My stomach's not got a thing to do with it, Momma."

"Well then, what is it? It's not like you to be lazing about. Is it your head?"

My heart.

"Yes, ma'am. It's my head, it hurts bad."

"I'll see if I can go find some aspirin. You're not going to come eat then?"

"No, ma'am."

"Should I bring you something?"

"No, ma'am."

"All right then, we'll be back soon."

After I was sure they was gone, I got dressed, put on my shoes, and sat down on the cot. It was like being lost in the woods. I didn't know what to do. If you're lost, it's best to stay put and not move, it'll only make things worse. The longer I sat there, the more fidgety I got. It won't in my nature to do nothing but twiddle my fingers. I stood, deciding I wouldn't sit around. I left the tent, and went to the water buckets. I filled all the pitchers in the basins with clean water. I went and got our bedclothes again, even though we'd just washed them, dragged it all out the washtub near the fire, heated the water and boiled them. I scoured everything good, dumped the water, heated some more and did the rinse. I hung the bedclothes over branches to dry. Then I snatched Papa's undershirt, his dirty coveralls, our underthings, and did the same to them. After that, I looked for something else to do. I found a big pine branch with a broad end and set about sweeping the campsite.

By the time I got all that done, I *was* sort of hungry, so I put on a pot of fresh coffee. I sipped on it, figuring I'd get on to chopping some more wood, when everyone returned from eating. Momma handed me a ham biscuit from Paulie, wrapped in wax paper and some aspirin too. I took the aspirin and refused the food.

"Wallis Ann, you need to eat or you'll get sick."

She pushed the biscuit in my hand, and got to looking

around. "My word, I thought you had a headache? You done all this while we went to eat?"

"Yes, ma'am."

Usually Momma's acknowledgment was uplifting. Not today. I choked down half the ham biscuit, and took the aspirin.

Papa said, "She's always been our hard little worker, ain't that right, Wally Girl?"

I blurted out, "Papa, would you please stop calling me that?"

Surprised, Momma looked to Papa as his chin dropped against his chest.

He looked a bit hurt as he asked, "You don't like me calling you that? It's only a little ole name."

"I'm not five, I'm fourteen. It sounds like the name of a little girl."

"I see."

My request had come from out of nowhere. Even I was surprised by it.

I continued, "You call Laci only her given name."

"Well. That's true."

I went into the tent, and lay on the cot again, and much to my annoyance, Laci followed me. The flap was left open and I glanced at Momma and Papa, sipping on the remaining coffee I'd left in the pot, and talking between themselves with a lot of frowning and head shaking, and I overheard Momma saying something about "young woman, like Laci."

Laci got her fiddle and sat on her cot, facing me, the instrument in her lap. She made no move to play it, she only took the edge of her dress and began to polish the wood.

"Laci."

Laci's eyes remained fixed on her task, rubbing the same area of wood.

"Laci, did you go somewhere last night?"

On and on went the rubbing, round and round, over and

over. I pictured grabbing it and throwing it across the tent. My jaw clenched at the thought, and my fingers curled into my palms.

My voice sounded strange, more insistent. "Where did you go? Did you see someone? Laci?"

I could have screamed as she tipped her head the other way and made no move to stop polishing her stupid fiddle. I thought about confronting Clayton, only it would be too embarrassing to admit I'd followed them. Maybe it wouldn't happen again. Maybe Clayton only kissed her out of curiosity. What was done was done, as Momma said, and there won't nothing I could do about it. I should try to forget, act like nothing was wrong, let bygones be bygones. The decision made me feel better, like I had a choice about how I handled things. I got up and Laci hurried to slip her hand into mine like always. Some part of me inside relaxed, like when you hold something heavy, set it down, and you get to take a deep breath as your muscles go loose and quit burning with the effort.

Same as asking Papa to not call me Wally Girl no more, as if I couldn't help myself, words spewed from me like water from a spigot. "Laci, you didn't know what you was doing, right?"

Laci waited, patient and serene.

"Last night, Laci? You and Clayton, you didn't know, right?"

I moved closer, gazing into her eyes. Pools of green, moist, clear, as a mountain stream. Innocent, blameless, Laci. It won't doing no good to keep pushing for what won't there.

When we come out of the tent, Momma said, "Come sit by the fire."

"I thought me and Laci might walk around some, find some fresh air."

"It's awful cold."

"We'll be fine, Momma. Walking will keep us warm."

We headed towards Trixie's tent, and the cold air surrounded us like a fog. Despite the less-than-pleasant temperatures, a few locals had come, some brung jams, jellies, pies or cakes to sell. I spotted Trixie with Zippity Doo in a small ring, putting him and Mr. M through one of their routines. Mr. M was dressed in a thick little jacket, and he bared his teeth at me in a grin as he climbed off the zebra to sit on Trixie's shoulder. I dug into the pocket of my dress, and found a peanut to give it to him. He snatched it with his little man hands and crammed it in his mouth, chewing fast, tiny button chocolate eyes blinking quick, before coming over to my shoulder. He turned himself upside down, feet still clinging to my shoulder as he reached into my pocket to poke around looking for more. He sure was the cutest thing I'd ever seen.

He give up and went from my shoulder to Laci's. She tolerated Mr. M sitting there. He seemed fixated on her hair, and he began a grooming routine, picking out strands and searching them before letting a few drop. Laci sat real still, like she was barely breathing.

Trixie said, "Wallis Ann? You look like something's eatin' you up."

"I do?"

"Yep. You got this little pinched area between your eyebrows."

"I got a headache."

"Must be a good'un."

I cleared my throat. "Trixie?"

"Yeah?"

I leaned in and lowered my voice. "Trixie, how well you know Clayton?"

Trixie let out a little laugh and stage-whispered, "Well enough, I reckon. Why the whispering?"

Maintaining a lower tone, I said, "I wonder what sort of girls he likes?"

Trixie give me a measuring sort of look.

She asked, "Is that why you look like a dog been kicked?"

"Do I look that a way?"

"Kind of. I can't say what sort a girl he likes. I ain't ever seen him with one."

"You ain't?"

"Nope. Only y'all, ever since you showed up. Why? You likin' him?"

I didn't know Trixie well enough to know if I could trust her.

"Me? Not me."

"Then Laci here?"

"No, no. I was only curious. I mean, he seems nice enough and all."

Trixie maintained a dubious expression, like she'd figured things out despite my denials. I watched Mr. M work his way around Laci's head, threading through her hair, piece by piece.

I changed the subject. "How did y'all come by Mr. M?"

Trixie watched him working on Laci too, and said, "We got this little rascal from another show. They was right mean to him. Actually, I sort a took him. Snuck him outta his cage one night, kept him quiet with bananas and oranges. Poor thing, he was about half starved."

"I can't believe anyone could do such meanness to that little critter."

She said, "Me neither, but they can, and they do. Wanna help me with those big guys there?"

"Sure."

I helped her brush down the Friesians, which I loved doing. Laci followed us, Mr. M still riding her shoulder. I offered her a brush to work on the horses, but she didn't seem to want to be near them. She stood about fifteen feet away. I didn't understand how she'd do something for Clayton and not me. I kept trying to get her to pet one a them big black horses and she never would. After an hour or so, I told Trixie we had to go.

She said, "Thanks for your help," and she leaned in close and said, "Hey, want me to talk to Clayton?"

"What? No!"

Trixie snickered. "Whew! Calm down. I won't."

"Okay, please don't. I was only curious."

I coaxed Mr. M back to Trixie's shoulder, and as we went to leave, I turned to wave. Trixie was still watching us, that slight knowing smile making me wish I'd not asked about Clayton. I led us through the tents in a roundabout way so we was less likely to bump into him, although it was hard when it seemed there was always folks popping out of nowhere. Diablo grinned at us from afar, and turned back to the two people waiting for him to shoot a ten-foot flame from his mouth, an astonishing stunt. He had scars on his ears and cheeks from past accidents.

When we got back, Papa was telling Momma we won't going to perform that night. Nobody was. Mr. Cooper had come by and said the crowds was too small and it won't worth it.

Papa said, "I can't see how making a little money over no money is a good decision. I also heard some of the show folks is wanting to head down to Florida."

Momma said, "I won't go any further than this, William. I mean it."

Papa repeated his old argument. "I know, Ann, but it's the dead of winter. If we don't go with them, we'd have no other choice than what we had before. Traveling show, Hardy's, or home."

She fell silent. What little bit of happiness she might have had after we got here, even with the peculiarities and all, was getting harder and harder to maintain. We went to get supper, and Paulie wanted to know if my headache was better and I said it was. I kept my eyes averted so he wouldn't ask me nothing else. Clayton sat eating with some workers and other performers. He raised both arms like he was asking, *Where y'all been?* I shrugged at him and went to get my plate. It was hard keeping my eyes from tracking back to him. I allowed myself a little peek when we left, and to my disappointment, the spot where he'd been eating had been filled by some other worker.

Having no performance sent all us to bed early. With the show shut down, it was unusually quiet. This should have helped me get to sleep, but instead, I lay on the cot, wide-eyed and alert. I thought about our warm, snug little room at Stampers Creek, our garden, Momma tending her flowers, Papa working at the sawmill, and Seph running about laughing and chasing dandelion seed pods. Joe Calhoun come to mind out of nowhere, and it seemed I couldn't feature him clearly anymore, like he was fading in my mind the way an old photograph does. I glanced at Laci. She'd changed positions, and now faced me. Best as I could tell, she slept and I huffed, wishing I could.

I heard a scuffling sound, and then the crack of a stick breaking. Laci sat up, startling me. I watched how she turned her head this way and that, listening. Something kept me from letting her know I was awake. She grabbed the blanket off her cot, wrapped it around herself, and went to the tent flap. She pulled on the tie, and peeked out, looking the way the noise come from, and then she slipped from my view, leaving the tent flap untied. I thought, it's happening all over again. I heard a whisper, and then a shuffling sound. I slipped off my cot and eased the flap aside ever so little, allowing an opening enough to see without being seen.

Laci sat by the dying campfire and Clayton was hunkered on his knee beside her. I was torn, part of me wanting to ask him what he was doing here, and the other part of me wanting to see what happened. I couldn't make out anything except the low rumbling of his voice. He stood and held out his hand, and she put hers in it. He bent down and picked up a lantern and a blanket, and that bothered me. Why did he have those things? I grabbed my blanket and wrapped it around me, and when I looked out, he was leading her away.

They went a different direction from the other night, towards the woods along the path used by the bigger wagons. I slipped out of the tent. I had on no shoes, and only my shift underneath the blanket. I let them get some distance, and the further we went, the worse I felt, a feeling of guilt growing in me, knowing I should protect Laci. After a few minutes, there was a small clearing and he stopped there. He set the lantern down and lit it. He adjusted the flame before he turned to her, held out his arms. Laci didn't move. He went towards her and carefully hugged her the way Papa would hug us sometimes, letting her lie her head on his shoulder. I took all this in, while that new icy spot inside me swelled big and solid until I was sure the very core of me had turned white and hard.

He released her, took the blanket, unrolled it and put it on the ground. I felt like a bizarre intruder in the shadows, like I was the one doing wrong. He pulled Laci down beside him. Everything he did, he'd wait a few minutes before he moved on. And he talked the entire time. I'd have given anything to be able to know what he said to her. They laid side by side. Maybe they was only going to look at stars. I hung onto that while another, more cynical part of me knowed better. A minute later, he leaned over and kissed her, and he kept on until her arms went around him. The scene before me got wavy and distorted. I swiped at my eyes and my hand pressed against my mouth when he moved her shift from her shoulders. Her breasts was exposed, and he touched them. It was too much and yet I couldn't stop myself from staring. I watched as if I was somewhere else, like it won't me. I had the thought I couldn't let him do what he was doing. She didn't know no better.

Except Laci slipped the straps of her shift further down, and wiggled her hips, removing the clothing until she was naked.

She lay down again, and while I was trying to figure out how she knowed to do this, he removed his own clothes, and I stared at the thatch of dark hair at the top of his legs and nestled within it, his manhood. He kissed her again and began touching her everywhere, moving his hands from her breasts to between her legs. I seen how she let him get on top of her. He raised up, shifted, and stopped. He did the same thing again, while Laci turned her head left and right. Her face scrunched like he was hurting her. I lowered my head, fighting the urge to yell at them, to shout, scream, to confront them. Demand the answers I thought I deserved.

I heard Clayton grunt. I looked up, seen him shift again. Laci's face relaxed, and he began a rhythmic movement of his lower half. Her legs come off the blanket to wrap around him as he moved, and moved, and moved. All this was done in complete silence, except for Clayton who spoke an occasional word. I was certain I heard what he said at one point, as clearly as I seen what they was doing, this act between a man and a woman. His *I love you* floated on the breeze to my ears. I tried to tell myself it won't *love*. I told myself this was the most horrible thing I'd ever seen, no better than two animals in rut. My throat went rigid and fixed as my eyes. How could he do this? I felt misled, duped, and mostly stupid, while pure, raw jealousy squeezed my chest, and become as all-consuming as the blood sickness.

Chapter 24

Clayton seemed to find excuses for being around. He showed up regular and I always held on to a slim hope he'd look at me again, *see me,* and somehow Laci would fade away in his mind the way a shadow does on a cloudy day. He'd first spend time with Papa, who got to talking about crops, our land back home, working for the show, you name it. Papa turned friendly, adding even more hurt and anger to how I already felt.

A few days after *that night,* Clayton dropped by and had the nerve to ask, "Hey, Wallis Ann, where you been?"

"Right here."

"Aw, come on. You know what I mean. You ain't been coming to watch me dive anymore. You don't talk to me much anymore."

I told him the same thing I'd told Momma lately. "I been too tired."

Clayton looked disappointed in that answer, but I was put out enough such that I didn't really care. Of course I was tired, skulking around after them on their midnight rambles, yet I couldn't seem to stop myself. It sure was something watching how Laci changed when she was with him, how she seemed like another person altogether. It was the intimacy between them, this tremendous secret they held, which only served to make me feel even more of a trespasser. Observing those nightly encounters give way to a bad feeling. Like at some of them churches where we'd seen snake handlers. Watching them I was certain someone was going to get bit—sooner or later, and my muscles had got all tense, knowing it was only a matter of time till something went wrong. I was told my faith was weak, and needed strengthening, but I never did hold on to no snake.

Clayton said, "You been acting different. Did I do something wrong?"

"I'd say."

"So I have. What is it? It ain't fair you won't even tell me."

"It ain't fair you don't know your own self."

He give me a funny look, and before he got suspicious, I made the excuse I had to go help Momma. I suspected he seen I won't good company right then. A gloomy summer storm cloud looked more cheery than me. Laci sat on a camp stool with her fiddle, sending out random notes of songs now and then. He got involved talking to Papa, and I got the chance to study on him and Laci. There won't a hint of what they was doing at night. Only evidence was Clayton give this little secret look towards her when he took his leave. It was so subtle, I wouldn't a thought a thing about it—if I hadn't already witnessed the inexplicable. I felt myself getting into a slow boil over that little glance what lasted the rest of the evening.

It's what propelled me to sneak behind them. It was getting harder to watch, especially when I went to imagining it was me, and not Laci, Clayton was loving on. Me he held and kissed. Me whose dress he pushed aside, his hand touching the damp, secret place between my legs. Me who give him what Laci was giving him—knowingly, or unknowingly. I wondered what Papa would do if he found out? What he'd do if he found her sneaking off into the woods, letting a man take her clothes off, sometimes even helping him herself? It come to me, Laci was thinking real different about things, more so than we'd ever considered. She was feeling things like any other normal person. And she'd somehow grasped the dealings between a man and a woman as natural as anyone.

I couldn't stop thinking of what I'd seen. How did Laci know about that, anyway? Maybe it had come natural to her, like her playing music. Maybe it won't nothing but instinct, like how critters know what to do from the moment they come into this world. Maybe she'd simply followed his lead, like she'd always done with me if I done something she'd not ever seen. All this thinking about them and what they done was like picking up a hammer and whacking my thumb over and over again, creating so much pain, the entire middle part of me felt torn and tender. If I tried to ask her about it, or tell her how I felt, would she know or even understand what she'd done? That's what made it worse. As upset and mad as I was, any effort I made to get her to respond would be like a moth beating against a window in a futile attempt to get at the light. It would be senseless because she'd never be able to tell me how, much less why.

Thanksgiving Day come and my mood had descended into something resembling a huge black hole, so deep I couldn't find my way out. Holidays, usually a happy time at home, had me wanting to leave, even if it meant going back to Uncle Hardy's. I would rather suffer his stingy ways than have to try so hard at pretending everything was fine. I worked silently around our tents, chopping wood, doing anything. Doing everything.

Soon I run out of even the made-up things to do, so I meandered over to Trixie's to help her tend to the animals and Mr. M. As I walked up, she was using a body brush on one of the Friesians.

She glanced at me over the horse's back and said, "Boy. You don't look no better than you did last time you come by."

I put my hand on the horse's shoulder and watched the muscle twitch.

"What's the matter?"

I shrugged and grabbed a currycomb from the pile of grooming tools on the ground nearby and went to work on the other horse.

"It ain't got something to do with Clayton, does it?" Trixie offered. She stopped what she was doing long enough to study my reaction to her question. "It does! What's going on?"

"Nothing!"

"Oh come on, Wallis Ann. Your look says it all."

I was too embarrassed to tell her everything, so I said, "It's nothing. I think he likes Laci."

"Really?"

I regretted saying it soon as I did. I didn't like how she latched on so quick, or the way her voice rose at the hint of gossip. It was too late now.

"Yeah. I mean, he's been coming by to see Papa, and I've seen him looking at her. I'm probably wrong."

"Oh." She sounded disappointed. "Do you like him or something?"

"Not really."

"Well, you don't look none too happy."

"I worry about Laci is all."

Ever skeptical when it come to the topic of Clayton, Trixie said, "Uh-huh."

For somebody I hadn't known long, she sure had me figured out. I got busy with the currycomb and changed the subject. I talked a blue streak about Thanksgiving at Stampers Creek, and asked Trixie all sorts of questions about her family. I stayed until I was done with the horse, only so Trixie would see I truly won't bothered at all. When I returned to our tent, it was time to wash, put on clean clothes and go eat the special Thanksgiving supper Paulie fixed.

The cookhouse tent was already filling with workers and performers alike, everyone gathering together for a change instead of eating in shifts, and the packed tent was steamy and warm. Paulie had found a bunch a creasy greens near to one of the creeks, and he'd mixed those in with some collards he'd got from one of the local farms, and that pungent scent mixed in with other odors, human and animal alike. Some of the workers had shot wild turkeys. Paulie had dressed them out, and he even made a corn pone dressing. The food looked almost as good as Momma's. Paulie served heaping piles of mashed taters, dressing, gravy, greens seasoned with fatback and biscuits. I only picked at the food, while occasionally shooting moody looks at Clayton as he sat at his usual table with Diablo, Mr. Massey, and other workers. Laci ate like her legs was plumb hollow and she couldn't fill them up. I caught Clayton looking at her so many times I almost threw my plate across the tent at him.

Momma kept on commenting over my lack of appetite until I sort of growled at her, "I said, I ain't hungry."

She drew back like I'd slapped her, while Papa stopped eating altogether and didn't look none too happy with my tone.

"I'm sorry. It's . . ."

Momma said, "I know. You're tired. That's all you been saying over a week now. You've been in this pitiful state long enough. Wallis Ann, what is it, is something else wrong?"

"No."

Momma shared a glance with Papa before she resumed eating while Laci stared at my plate. I give a sidelong glance at her empty one, and figured she was wanting me to give her the food I'd not touched. I did something spiteful then. I understood it was, and still, I did it. I heard Papa say, "Wallis Ann?" but I didn't stop. I took my mostly full plate up to Paulie and handed it to him.

He looked from it to me, to it again. "You done? Seems like a waste a good food. You ain't hardly tetched it. Don't you want to give it to Laci?"

"No. I don't."

I spun on my heels and left the cookhouse tent. I didn't look at Momma, Papa or nobody. I drifted around the mostly silent carnival, feeling sorry for myself. The only noises come from the occasional huffing sort of noise from some of the animals who'd been watered and fed earlier. I considered the possibility of telling Momma and Papa, for no other reason than I couldn't hardly stand the thought of Clayton and Laci being together anymore. I wanted to stop it. I wanted someone else to hurt like I was, and though I had no idea how I'd even begin, it got stuck in my head to *tell, tell, tell*. What mouthful of food or two I'd taken churned in my stomach as I thought about what I was about to do.

At our tents I sat by the fire waiting for everyone. The sound of footsteps come soon enough. My hands got cold and sweaty, and I swallowed over and over. I nervously brushed a hand over my hair, thinking I couldn't do it. I was losing my nerve. Two figures come into view. Momma and Papa was alone. They made their way by the fire and went to warming their fingers.

"Where's Laci?"

Momma sighed, leaned down to poke at a log, as Papa tossed another one on. My heart fluttered like it might falter or quit altogether. I was sure they was put out with me for leaving the cookhouse tent like I'd done. The flare of the fire lit everything around us with a deep orange glow, while their shadows stretched into black, skinny giants behind them. My insides tightened. There was only one person Laci could be with, and knowing this solidified my decision.

My tone too sharp, I said, "Is she with Clayton?"

Momma sounded exasperated. "What in God's name has got into you, Wallis Ann? Yes, she is. If you hadn't left so quick, you'd have been there when he stopped by the table and said he'd wanted to take you both for a walk."

When them floodwaters tossed us out of our truck, we'd had no control of where we'd end up or how we'd get there. That was how I felt right then. Like I had no control, only this time over my words.

My voice dropped low, and when they come out of me, it sounded hateful, forced. "He'd rather be alone with her anyway."

Momma stared at me with an odd look. "What do you mean by that, Wallis Ann?"

Now that I'd started it, the words wouldn't stop.

I choked on them like I was being forced to take a vile dose of medicine. "You don't know what all's been going on. You and Papa got no idea, and if either of you did, you wouldn't have never let Laci go with him."

Momma shot a look at Papa, who was in the process of lifting a log off the woodpile nearby.

He dropped it onto the embers, the force of the log landing caused a heap of tiny devil snow to shoot up into the air and fall in a shimmering rain around us. *How fitting,* I thought, *it's like being in hell.*

He put his hands on his hips. "Wallis Ann? What are you talking about?"

"Clayton and Laci. They been sneaking out at night. They been . . . doing things."

Papa took a step backwards like I'd hit him. He stared at me for a split second, then he looked to Momma, who'd put one hand over her mouth in shock. Papa's mouth thinned out, his

lips set in a severe line, and his eyes turned so dark, like a blackness or something evil took a hold of him and stared out at us.

His voice was low and terrible. "What do you mean doing
things? What sorts a *things?*"

My knees trembled first and from there, that shaking took
over my entire self. Papa's big fists clenched, then unclenched,
and he looked like he might tear someone apart, limb by limb
and wouldn't think twice about it. I went to panting, my
breath coming in panicked little gusts like I'd been running,
and I could feel tears starting to come. I hated crying. I de-
spised how my voice sounded as I tried to explain, and I
couldn't seem to form sentences.

"I. They. Clayton and Laci. They was. Together. Naked."

Momma said, "What? Laci? Wallis Ann! Are you telling us a
story?"

I spun around to face her. "Momma! Why would I make
that sort a thing up?"

Papa said, "I'm gonna kill him."

Momma tried to grab him, and he yanked his arm out of
her hands. This was not what I'd expected. I hadn't thought of
how they would react or what might happen. Papa's anger was
big, bigger than my hurt maybe, because his face went slack so
that he looked even less like himself than he had a few seconds
ago. It was like the person inside of him, the person we
knowed, was gone. He run inside their tent and when he come
out with his shotgun, Momma's hands templed in prayer, and
she bowed her forehead to her fingertips. I grabbed at his
shirtsleeve tight and he jerked his arm up hard, almost tearing
off my fingernails.

I yelled, "Papa, please, don't! Don't hurt nobody!"

He wouldn't even look at me when he said, "What did you
think, Wallis Ann? Did you think I'd hear that and do nothing?" To Momma he said, "Go on and pray, but praying ain't
gonna help him now. That son of a bitch been coming around

here and all he was doing was sniffing after her like a dog after a bone."

Papa leaned down so his face was close to mine, the heat of rage coming off him like I was standing right inside an enormous blazing fire. I wanted to run, to get away from him.

"And what about you, Wallis Ann? Has he touched you too? Goddamn it, has he?"

"What? No, Papa! No!"

"Don't you lie to me! You tell me *now* what he's done!"

I shrank from him, thinking about the kissing, and desperately looked to Momma for help. She stared at me in horror, stunned.

I cried out, "He's not done nothing to me!"

"How long you known about this?"

I dropped my gaze. I couldn't look at him.

"Goddamn it, Wallis Ann. What the hell?"

I stumbled to Momma, and she held out a hand as if to ward me off, turning her head like the sight of me sickened her.

"Momma, I'm sorry!"

Her face was white, and she shook her head as if denying my apology. Angry words spilled from her mouth.

"I thought we'd raised you right. Weren't you supposed to be looking after her? Dear sweet Jesus, I can't believe you let this happen."

She didn't have to say, *The way you was supposed to have looked after Seph.* Without warning, everything I'd been holding in the past few months come out of me like Seph's sickness had come out of his mouth.

"I'm always having to look after Laci! I'm always having to explain Laci! I can't hardly have a minute to myself without having Laci stuck to me like a burr!"

Momma face went hard as the wall of granite rock over to Salt Gap. She kept staring at me, like she didn't know me, her expression reminding me of the day she'd almost touched the body of a long, slick hellbender salamander while working near Stampers Creek. Disgusted. Shocked. Dismayed. I wished I'd never said nothing. I wished I'd confronted Clayton instead. I'd only been thinking out of spite.

Papa grabbed my arm and said, "Come on!"

I yanked away from him, and hollered, "NO!"

Papa said, "Wallis Ann. You get yourself on down that path, and now."

"Momma!"

She turned away as Papa snatched my arm again, his grip so tight, later on I'd have a bruise. He hauled me towards Mr. Cooper's tent. As Papa yanked me along, there stood Laci and Clayton only twenty feet in front of us, near the Ferris wheel, and I went ice cold.

Papa seen'em too, and he dropped my arm, and yelled, "Hey! Get the hell away from her!"

At the sight of Papa running straight for him, shotgun aimed, Clayton's features shifted from smiling to openmouthed alarm. He took off, pulling Laci along behind him. She tripped, almost falling, and he caught her and resumed running. Papa barreled after them, and I was scared for what he might do.

I followed shouting, "Laci!"

It looked like she tried to twist around at the sound of my voice, except Clayton darted around the corner of a tent and they both vanished by the time we got to it. People scattered at the sight of Papa with his shotgun, charging like a black bear.

He yelled, "Stop him!" only everyone looked at him, confounded because they didn't know who he meant or what he was doing.

Papa finally stopped running, and seconds later I caught up to him.

He said, "Come on!" and led me back the way we'd come. Soon we was in an area where nobody had seen the commotion, although everyone still shied away from him, looking like he was. He stampeded Mr. Cooper's tent and proceeded to chew on him about the caliber of some of people he was hiring.

Mr. Cooper held up his hands, and said, "Whoa, whoa, whoa, now, Mr. Stamper. What's the problem?"

"That goddamn young buck you hired has disgraced my daughter! She was an innocent till he put his filthy hands on her! She don't know any better!"

I shifted uncomfortably, refusing to look at Mr. Cooper.

Mr. Cooper said, "Well, hang on now. I seen them walk by here not more than five minutes ago, hand in hand. That seems pretty normal between two young people. It ain't disgraceful to hold hands now, is it?"

"That ain't what I'm talking about. Them walking around. I'm talking about something *else*."

Papa spat on the ground while Mr. Cooper eyed his shotgun. He said, "What you aiming to do with that?"

"I'm gonna shoot his ass, that's what I'm gonna do. He's gone and forced himself on her! He'll pay for what he's done! She's not to blame for this!"

I remembered how Laci took off her clothes, and the thought made me shake my head.

Mr. Cooper said, "You disagree with your papa?"

Papa twisted around and said in a voice so different, if I'd closed my eyes I wouldn't have known who was talking.

"Is there something else you need to tell me, Wallis Ann?"

His question flustered me, and I shook my head hard, as if emphasis would cover deceit. Papa's anger was already burning out of control and I won't about to stoke it. I sure didn't want to get burned any more than I already had. Papa didn't take his eyes off me, even when Mr. Cooper started talking again.

"He's a big part of my show. I can't be having my main folks getting shot up. Maybe this is all just a misunderstanding."

Papa jerked his thumb at me and said, "It ain't. She'll tell you."

A swarm of jagged, disconnected thoughts swirled in my head, like looking at oneself in a broken mirror and seeing fragments instead of as a whole.

Papa said, "Wallis Ann?"

I mashed my lips together.

"Wallis Ann."

I swallowed and without looking at either of them, I whispered, "They been doing . . . things."

Mr. Cooper said, "*They*. Sounds mutual, Mr. Stamper."

Papa aimed the gun at Mr. Cooper. "Get that goddamn disgusting thought out of your head. Laci's never been off on her own. She's naïve, and she sure as hell ain't here for his entertainment."

Mr. Cooper sounded skeptical. "Uh-huh. Fine, then. Let's go on see if we can't find 'em."

He led the way from his tent, hollering out to some of the workers nearby. Papa breathed heavy, his fury seeming to build again at Mr. Cooper's lack of alarm.

"Hey, boys! Come on! Got to get us a little search going on."

Soon a small group had gathered up, and Mr. Cooper, without giving out any particulars, said they were to all go and look for Laci. He made no mention of Clayton at all.

"Find the girl. Y'all know what she looks like."

He turned to Papa, and said, "So, we'll find your girl and how about you leave young Clayton be?"

Papa shot a look at him. Mr. Cooper shifted his shoulders and turned away to direct the workers. They spread out, and people went to calling out "Laci!" Some went and got lanterns.

I said to Papa, "She likes the Friesians. She fed them apples."

He looked at me, like he won't sure if he should trust my word, but he motioned at me to follow him and we checked that area. Towards the woods, I noticed how the tiny flicker of lights from search lanterns dotted the blackness like fireflies, and I hoped Laci might see the lights and come towards them. We went back to where Mr. Cooper was giving directions to anyone new who joined. There was a few groups of two or three skirting around one area of woods.

Finally, in a low voice, I said to Papa, "I can show you where else they went. Maybe she's there."

He was some calmer by now, and he stared at the ground for a few seconds, and then nodded.

I said, "We got to go back towards our tents."

He said, "Lead."

There won't nothing but the sound of our breathing, and hurried footsteps. When we got to our own tents, we stopped, and Papa told Momma what happened. She sank down onto the camp stool, like her legs couldn't hold her up. I couldn't speak at all. I couldn't offer her a thing. We left her behind, and I led Papa along the path, then into the other section of woods different from where the others was looking. We ducked out of the way of tree branches, some of them scraping across my cheeks before I could grab them. I tripped a few times over some of the bigger stones I couldn't see. I didn't recollect having so much trouble when I'd followed Laci and Clayton, and Papa's silence over my clumsiness made me uncomfortable, his usual concern overshadowed by his anger. We finally come to the edge of the tree line and stood facing the clearing.

"Here," was all I said.

Papa started across the small meadow, looking around, and then searched the other side of the clearing. Laci won't here. If she'd been here, we'd have spotted her easy enough.

Even so, I called out "Laci! It's me, and Papa. Laci! Are you here . . . ?"

Papa walked around in a circle, looking at the flattened grass, kicking aside a stick or two.

I offered a suggestion. "I could wait. Maybe she'll turn up."

He stared towards the dusky woods and we could faintly hear the other men calling out from all the way across the carnival, "Hey, girlie, yoo-hoo!"

He handed me his shotgun and turned away. I thought he would leave without speaking. He hesitated, and faced me again, shoving his hands into the pockets of his coveralls.

He said, "You should a come to us. You should a known better. I'm right disappointed in you, Wallis Ann."

He walked away without looking back. Them words was the worst thing he'd ever said, even worse than him questioning me. I'd rather he'd a whupped me. I waited until I couldn't hear him no more. When I was sure he was gone, I could feel a few tears gathering in the corners of my eyes, threatening to roll down my cheeks, but it wouldn't feel right, it would only feel like self-pity. I tilted my head back and studied the stars glittering in the night sky and tried to empty all thoughts, so my mind was a vacant vessel. I refused to ruminate on where Laci might be, or what might have happened. All of my earlier anger and jealousy had dissolved. I eventually left the clearing to wait along the rim line of trees. I leaned against one, and set the shotgun beside me. It got even chillier and I worried Laci might be as cold as I was. I settled down to wait the rest of the night, with plenty of time to think about what I'd done—or not done.

At dawn, I rose to my feet, took the time to look around once more, called to Laci, hoping against hope. The sound of birds starting their morning song was all I got in return, that and the scraping of squirrels looking for nuts. I picked up the shotgun, and made my way back, my feet crunching sticks, the sound seeming loud in the early morning air. Momma sat by the fire but Papa was still off with the others searching. When she seen me, she said nothing, her face as chilly as the morning.

She handed me a cup of hot coffee, eyes gone dark as the liquid. I sat near the fire to thaw out. I swallowed hard, determined to be strong. A minute later, she reached out for my
hand, and held on to it, and I gripped hers in return. I couldn't
be strong anymore, and tears of gratefulness slid down my face,
and dripped into the hot coffee she'd handed me. I tilted the
cup, and drank deep, as if I could swallow our sorrow.

Chapter 25

The second day passed. Desperate, Papa took off to Tucker's Branch to report Laci missing to a sheriff with the last name of Baker. Sheriff Baker started coming every day, poked around, made notes, then left and, in Papa's opinion, was about as helpful as a cat on a squirrel hunt. After a week passed with no sign at all, the search slowed. It was like everyone got discouraged. If we'd found a scrap of material, a shoe, anything, it would have been something to keep folks going. There won't a single solitary thing found. Like Morty the Magician's rabbit, they'd vanished. If it hadn't been for her clothes, her beloved fiddle, the rumpled cover on her bed, I'd have wondered if she'd ever been here at all. Yet, when I closed my eyes, she was everywhere. I felt her hand in mine, heard her music in my head, caught the red gold of her hair in the setting winter sun.

I missed her more than I could explain.

I regretted everything.

Workers trickled back to work again, and performers drifted off to practice routines.

Bright and early one morning, a little over a week after their disappearance, Mr. Cooper come by looking uncomfortable.

"It's high time for us to move on. Crowds thinned out considerably, what with the cold weather and the holiday season here."

Papa offered no comment.

Mr. Cooper said, "We're going down south to Florida, a place called Gibsonton, and winter there."

Papa was stony faced, and Mr. Cooper, hands in his pockets, didn't have much else to say.

He walked off, then turned back, and said, "No hard feelings, I hope, on how things was here?"

Papa watched a bird fly over.

Mr. Cooper cleared his throat. "Hey, look, keep them tents here. They're yours to do with what you want."

Papa conceded that one gesture. "Thank you."

Mr. Cooper said, "Well."

He glanced around, then took his leave. The noise of the tents, rides, and sideshows being dismantled, the shouts of men and clanging of tools echoed around the woods and beyond filling the air for the rest of the day. I watched from a distance for a little while, but when they went to take down the high dive platform, I hurried back to our tents. Papa was gone, off to Sheriff Baker's yet again, and in the meantime Big Bertha was there and handing Momma more soap as a parting gift.

"It ain't much, but everything else is packed, and I seem to recall you liked it."

Momma said, "You don't need to do this, but thank you. We do appreciate your thoughtfulness."

Big Bertha said, "I sure hope your girl turns up. Can't imagine what it's like for all of you."

Momma's face was pale and set. She held the soap, appearing to not know how to respond. Meanwhile, Big Bertha won't in any hurry. She settled in, chattering on like we didn't have nothing to do but sit around and answer silly questions.

"Reckon your husband will have the sheriff look in Walhalla? Or one a them other towns? Reckon she might a gone that far? No tellin' with them long legs a hers how far she could have got."

Momma studied Big Bertha with an expression like she was talking in a foreign language. I stepped forward to spare her any more well-intentioned comments.

I said, "Thank you again, Miss Bertha. Momma and I was getting ready to . . ."

Big Bertha lumbered to her feet. "Yes, yes, shoot, look at the time, I got to finish getting my own stuff together."

That worked to get Big Bertha on her way, only here come Trixie with Mr. M, barely missing Big Bertha's exit by about five minutes.

Trixie said, "Hey, Mrs. Stamper."

Momma said, "Hello, Trixie. You girls talk. I'm going to go lie down."

Mr. M rode Trixie's shoulder, and I stood next to her so he would crawl onto mine. I give him pieces of biscuit from breakfast, which he ate in delicate small bites, chewing in his human like manner. Mr. M was more skittish than usual, and he went from my shoulder to hers, to mine again.

Trixie said, "He knows we're getting ready to leave. He sees all the commotion, hears things banging, and I think it makes him feel unsettled, confused."

"I know the feeling."

Trixie said, "She'll be fine. Laci is liable to turn up any day now, hungry perhaps, but fine."

I appreciated Trixie's words, but Laci had never been on her own before, without me, or someone in our family to watch out for her. She was likely afraid. She could be hurt. I couldn't bring myself to think of anything worse.

She said, "Will you stay and keep looking?"

"That's what Papa wants to do."

She reached out to hug me, and Mr. M let out a screech of protest.

Trixie said, "I hope we all meet again someday, Wallis Ann."

"Me too."

Trixie give me a little hopeful smile, but I think we both had the sense once they left, we'd never see each other again. Towards evening, after Papa come from the trip to Sheriff Baker's looking like he always did, Paulie appeared with a box of food. He'd brought the things what could be stored without spoiling. Salted pork, dried beans, rice, cornmeal, grits and taters. Coffee, flour, salt, sugar. Matches. He set the box down with a thump.

Momma peered into the box and said, "Thank you so much, Paulie."

Paulie's face was red, and he was a bit out of breath having carted the box all the way from across the other side of the carnival.

He managed to say, "Hope this'll do for a while."

Papa said, "This is too much. You've got a lot of folks to feed, and we don't want to take from your supplies."

He stood with his big hands folded in front, still wearing the dirty apron he always had on. "I ain't worried about them buzzards. They get a plenty. All I hope is you find your girl."

"We hope so too."

"How long will y'all stay?"

"I can't say. Till we find her."

"I'll keep hoping."

"Thank you."

As Paulie went to leave, he give me a final wink and nod, the kindest thing anyone had done towards me in over a week. I would miss Paulie, I thought. Soon as he was out of sight, Papa sat down, looking beat and dispirited. Momma waited for him to tell her any news. She wouldn't ask, she was too afraid, and I was too.

He sighed heavy after a minute, and said, "Sheriff Baker said longer it goes without them finding something, less likely our chances are."

Momma blanched, and when she spoke, her voice shook. "I don't know why you told us that. You could a gone all day, all week, all month, and not said it."

Frustrated, Papa said, "If I hadn't a told you, you'd have asked!"

"And you could a said, he's working on it. You could a spared me."

Nobody spoke after that. We moved about the campsite like we was strangers, like we'd each gone up a different mountain and stationed ourselves far apart.

It got on towards suppertime, and though I won't really hungry, I asked, "Is anybody hungry? Should we go on to the cookhouse?"

Papa snorted like a bull, irritated by my question. "I ain't in the mood to see all them people again. Fix something from what Paulie brung. Might was well get used to doing the cooking again."

I dug out the skillet, and set about fixing a meal, using the campfire like in the old days. Momma come over to help, and we worked side by side, not talking. She made biscuits, while I put on the side meat to fry. She boiled some beans. We didn't cook much, thinking ahead to how long it might have to last. It was going to be like Momma always said, back where we started, only worse. After we ate, we went to bed. It was hard with Laci's empty cot beside mine. I sat on it, then lay down and turned my head on her pillow, hoping to catch her scent there. That was how I fell asleep.

* * *

Morning come with a deep quiet all about and none of the usual noises I'd growed accustomed to. I sat up, sensing something different. I slipped outside in the early dawn and was met with the sight of bare, flattened grass all around us. Sometime in the middle of the night, while we slept, the traveling show had moved on. I'd heard none of the big wagons moving, none of the animals, not even a whisper. Muddy, trampled areas, where hundreds of visitors had walked over the past weeks, could now be seen. It was very odd looking in that I could also now see mountains clearly as well as the farmland what had been hidden behind rides, and tents and wagons.

It was like being abandoned.

The barren fields left me gloomier than ever. I wandered over to where the arena tent had been, looking at the impressions left in the ground, like ghost prints. The high dive platform area had icy patches where the water had been dumped onto the ground. Where the cookhouse tent stood, scraps of leftover food was left in the dirt, and a flock of crows flew into a tall pine nearby, cawing in protest at my intrusion of their meal. I moved on to where the sideshows used to be, and then on to where the Ferris wheel had stood. I drifted through all these spots like I was lost and looking for something I couldn't find. I looked across the acreage to where our lone tents stood. They looked so tiny, so deserted against the vacant surroundings, like they didn't belong.

I walked close to the area where the Friesians had been staked out. There was bare spots on the ground where the animals had grazed. I gazed about, my eyes passing over a patch of bushes near the woods, an unassuming gray and brown cluster of branches, and it was there I seen a spot of color what looked out of place. My breath caught in my throat. I hurried over and as I drew closer, a scrap of lavender material fluttered on the lower branch of a thick bush. I bent down, snatched it up, and looked closely at it. It was torn from Laci's dress, I was certain, but what caused me to run back to our tents fast as I could was what was on the material.

I hurried into their tent, and said, "Look. Look at this," while flapping the piece under their noses.

Papa narrowed his eyes and took it saying, "Where'd you find this?"

"In the pasture near the woods where they put the horses, and the zebra."

He showed Momma, and said, "I'm going to get Sheriff Baker."

Momma gaped at the material, at the dark brownish stain smeared on it.

I felt I ought to say something. "It could be just dirt."

Momma shook her head. "I know what dried blood looks like."

I went back out and stoked the fire, putting a pot of coffee on while I waited for Papa to get back. It was the quickest Sheriff Baker ever come. Papa come bumping along across the emptied carnival spot with the sheriff directly right behind him. He got out of the truck and motioned for me and Momma to come. Then we all got into Sheriff Baker's car and I showed them where I'd found the cloth.

I pointed. "There. It was hanging on that lower branch right there."

Sheriff Baker looked at the branch first, then he carefully went along, staring at the ground, moving some of the debris aside every now and then. He went around the bushes and come out again.

"I don't see nothing more. Let me go have a better look this a way."

We stayed by the car as he walked into the woods, poking along here and there, until he was out of sight.

Papa said, "He ought to see if he can't get someone to get

one of them hounds back over here. Let'em see if they can scent her from it."

Momma stared at the woods with a mixture of fear and hope on her face.

He come out after about half an hour. He had more of the material in his hands, another piece smaller than the one I'd found, but it also had the same color stain on it.

He said, "How well did you know these here carnies?"

Momma and Papa looked at each other.

Papa said, "You insinuating they had something to do with it?"

Sheriff Baker said, "Well, it's kind of odd how quick they left after she went missing, don't you think?"

Papa said, "They helped us search for her. It don't seem like they'd do that if they had her."

Sheriff Baker said, "Pure speculation, but I got to consider everything. This don't mean she's come to harm. If they took her for the show, I doubt they'd want to hurt her. There won't any more blood found on the ground. Look, I'll see if I can't reach out to some of my contacts down in Florida. How's that sound?"

Such a tiny thing, yet we had hope now. Sheriff Baker drove us back to our tents, and took off. And then we waited. And waited. Days later he come back, his expression grim. He parked his car, propped a foot on the bumper and pulled out a cigarette. He lit it and let a plume of smoke blow from his mouth to hover over his head before he began.

He said, "I called down to Florida. That traveling show arrived and the sheriff's office down there conducted a, what'll I call it? A secret search. Turned all them wagons they use upside down, inside out. No sign of her. I'm sorry."

He might as well have said Laci had passed. An emptiness come with his words, and my stomach felt like a giant fist dug into it and wouldn't let up. It was strange how someone so quiet could be so loud in my head, how someone who'd taken up no more space than any other human could seem as large as the entire universe. Momma and Papa didn't speak. They accepted what he said, like they'd come to some conclusion. Sheriff Baker kept coming every few days, only to say there was still no sign of Laci. Momma got more despondent. I'd never seen her so torn apart. Having no answers, no finality, I began to see, was much harder than a finite end like with Seph.

We couldn't leave, not when we was stuck, expecting something, while receiving nothing. Papa got to where he didn't want to see Sheriff Baker coming no more, unless he had news, and he told him so. We didn't see the sheriff none after that. We hovered around the tents, wordless, and lost. I heard distant church bells chiming "Silent Night" and other songs for about a week, and then "Auld Lang Syne" and that told me Christmas season had come, and was gone.

One morning in early January, when hoar frost turned everything white as snowfall, and our breath sat heavy in the air, Papa said, as if to himself, "We done what we could. We've looked, and we've looked. Sheriff has looked and ain't been back. We lost her, and we ain't getting her back."

Momma cried out as if in pain. "Don't say it! We will get her back. We will!"

Papa didn't argue. He let what she'd said go.

An hour later when it seemed Momma had got ahold of herself, he said, "We're going home. I don't know what else to do, Ann."

Momma pressed her hands together as if praying, and shook her head.

Papa said, "Sheriff Baker will get word to us there. It ain't like we'd not keep in touch."

Momma started doing what Laci used to do, rocking. I couldn't offer any comfort, because what would I say? I'm sorry all over again? Papa set about taking down the tents and I helped him. Like in the old days of working side by side, we went along fast and efficient. Now he'd made a decision, it seemed he wanted to get on with it. Momma quit rocking, and sat frozen, she didn't even look like she breathed. I worked around her, gathering the camp stools and carrying them to the truck. I folded mine and Laci's clothes, got her fiddle, and wrapped it in her blanket. I set all those things aside and helped Papa take our tent down. By dinnertime, the sun was as high as it would get, and we was packed, ready to go.

Papa didn't even have to tell Momma. She got up and stumbled towards the truck. There was a heaviness to mine and Papa's steps as we carried the last remaining items. Momma got in the middle like she always did, and then me. It struck me how, as we'd gone through these last few months, it was like all we'd been doing was traveling down a road towards this bittersweet ending. Nothing could change what we'd been through. As we rolled across the pasture slow, I looked out the window, remembering every moment what led us to this point. The night of the hurricane, my time alone in the tree and at Stampers Creek. My joy at seeing my family safe, our despair and misery at losing Seph, the desolate days of hunger, meeting Clayton at the waterfall, the carnival as it had looked when we'd first come to it, Laci playing fiddle, Laci in her new dress, Laci and Clayton. The memories repeated, flickering like heat lightning in the summer, until I wished I had a key like what got used with the truck so I could switch them off.

Momma said, "Are we stopping at your brother's?"

Papa said, "No."

Momma made no noise, but her eyes closed in relief. It would only take us half a day to get to Stampers Creek. The idea we would be home before nightfall didn't seem real. We stopped once for fuel, and Papa bought me and Momma a drink and some peanuts. Under any other circumstances I'd have enjoyed that, but we only ate to keep from going hungry, not for enjoyment. Off Highway 28, he stopped again at a general merchandise store.

"I'm getting some tools to replace what was lost. Won't take but a minute."

He went in and come out with a chiseling tool, a bow saw, a draw blade, and some nails. Eventually, we turned onto Highway 107 and studied the still flattened trees what hadn't been cleaned up. We was lucky the northbound lane and the bridge to cross over to the road home hadn't been washed out like some others further north. Despite the storm damage that still lay about, familiar territory spread before us, and soon we come to the two poplars. Papa slowed down at the clearing between the trees so we could look for a moment on Cherry Gap, and Cullowhee Mountain, and beyond to distant familiar valleys. I felt a big lump coming into my throat, and it was as if I'd been gone for years instead of a few months.

Papa lowered the gear on the truck, and we climbed the winding hilly path. I leaned forward, looking this way and that. Everything was gray, barren, and with not a hint of color, but it was beautiful in my eyes. It was an unlikely time to come home during the coldest time of year, but I no longer cared. It was home. We rounded the last bend, and there was the yard. The collapsed barn. The leftover stone foundation. I seen movement near the foundation, and I could hardly believe my eyes, old Pete, looking a little thin, was hanging around, his coat full and thick with winter hair. He turned his head, and when the truck stopped, he lifted it and drew his lips back from his teeth. I got out of the truck and hurried over to him. He sort of shied away, until I held my hand out, and he got a whiff, and then he brayed long and loud.

It seemed to me he might have been telling us, *Welcome home.*

Chapter 26

We only bothered putting up one tent, and I placed my cot in with Momma and Papa's, a way to combine our body heat. It didn't count for the perpetual chill in the air what had nothing to do with weather. Aside from the sadness, which thickened every day like ice on the pond, there was the disagreement on the decision to be here. One avoided it, and the other couldn't stop talking about it.

Tearful, Momma said, "We should never have left. It would have been easier to get news if we'd stayed."

Papa said, "The river level is back to normal. I can catch fish."

She said, "We don't have Laci. Nothing else ought to matter."

He said, "Now I got me this here shotgun, I can hunt too. Wallis Ann can set traps. We'll get to working on them logs and it'll go fast now we got the tools. Right where we left off. We'll have us a new cabin in no time."

I said, "I'll help you, Papa."

He didn't even spare me a glance, so intent was he on Momma letting go of her idea.

Momma said, "We ought to take ourselves right back down there. We could be there in no time."

He shook his head, not wanting to hear it, while I wished someone would simply acknowledge me in some way, even if it was to remind me all over again how I should have told them. This went on, and at one point Momma even threatened to take Papa's truck in the middle of the night. Papa informed her she'd strip the gears and then we'd have no truck. I tried to make myself as small as possible. I did my chores, and did them quick. I didn't complain if I was tired, cold or sad. Laci's fiddle sat in the corner of the tent, and I would hold it every now and then, as if I could soak some of her spirit into me, but all it did was emphasize her absence. Whatever I'd felt about Clayton was consumed and replaced by the grief and guilt I felt over her.

Regret was something I carried around, and held so tight inside me, I could barely breathe. I pulled my shame on like I did my clothes, wearing it all day, unable to look Momma or Papa directly in the eyes. At night, I wallowed in a soul-pulling guilt so complete, the darkness of night matched what had settled deep inside me. All them things what controlled me, the way I'd let my jealousy and anger take over, sat within my heart so heavy, my chest held a permanent ache, and it seemed no amount of time could ever take it away.

It come to me the solid love I felt for her, deep as our deepest hollers, and what wore on me most was how that love hadn't been strong enough to alter the way I'd behaved, hadn't changed the dark jealousy what had rose up and come from out of me as unexpected as her disappearance. *How could that be?* Momma had warned me about this very thing, the coveting of what someone else has. She was right. My envy was to blame, only my learning it was too late. I should've listened to her, should've knowed she was right.

I imagined one scene over and over. How Laci's face would

look. How she would put her hand in mine again, and how it would feel. At night was when I asked God to give me another chance, to bring her home so I could show her, even if she didn't care, or it didn't matter to no one but me. I just wanted a chance to make it right, to make this pain go away. I pressed my right hand into my left, closed my eyes, and prayed softly, only it was like talking when it's cold outside and the steamy mist from your breath disappears in seconds. I pictured them prayers as weak and erratic as the fluttering a baby bird's wings, unable to make it where they needed to be. They would never reach God's ear. I still asked Him though, and promised I wouldn't never put Laci in danger again. Never, ever be mad at her again. I would only show her the love and care she deserved.

Every day Papa went into the woods and would shoot a couple squirrels to eat. Momma, would take them silently, and stew them. She'd make biscuits, and while Paulie's food had been good, this food tasted of what I was most familiar with, though my stomach wanted to reject it. I noticed the air, how it held a cold winter crispness, the scent only of trees, the land around us, and a hint of wood smoke. I breathed in deep, several times a day. I couldn't seem to get enough. One thing was certain, I had plenty of time to put what happened into perspective as I fetched water for boiling, cut wood for the fire, and went to stripping bark off the logs Papa brought and dumped in a pile. He worked like Old Scratch was after him, the old devil from my childhood Momma and Papa used to say was gonna get me if I didn't do as told.

I, too, worked hard like usual, and while I did, I come to the conclusion I'd been more curious about Clayton than anything. All he'd said or done, I'd honed in on because he'd stirred up new feelings. Being away from him give me plenty of time to recognize our differences. It was likely he'd never built a cabin by hand. I doubted he'd ever gone hungry, had to start a fire using rock and punk wood, or heard a screech owl. I couldn't picture him wringing a chicken's neck or bleeding out a hog during hog-killing time.

Mainly, I worried about him having something to do with Laci's disappearance, and because of that, any feelings I'd had was squashed, like a trap snapping shut at the first hint of pressure. Even though there was still this little niggling impression he won't as bad as we thought, the ways of my thinking give me a setback of sorts and I felt almost like I did when I'd discovered him with Laci, filled with disappointment and sadness.

After we'd been home about a week, I heard a "Hoo ha! Hoo ha!" coming across the holler as I sat beside a stripped pile of logs.

Me and Papa was hard at it, and he pulled on Pete's harness to make him stop.

He shaded his eyes against the glare of a bright winter sun, and then slapped his hand against his knees and said, "I'll be a son of a gun!"

It was the Powells. The Powells we thought was long gone and likely dead, coming towards us, big smiles on their faces.

I said, "It's the Powells!"

Momma stood by the tent, washing one of Papa's shirts and some of our underthings, and hanging everything out to dry. She heard the shouting and turned to look. When she seen them, she dropped what she held and hurried across the yard.

She cried out, "Lordamighty, I can't believe it!"

Everyone started talking at the same time.

Mr. Powell said, "My word, it sure is good to see y'all!"

There was hugging between Mama, Mrs. Powell, and me, and back slapping between Papa and Mr. Powell.

When things settled down a little, Mr. Powell said, "We'd noticed smoke over this way."

Papa said, "We been here just over a week."

Mr. Powell said, "We hadn't seen nothing in so long, we figured we ought to come check it out."

Papa replied, "We was here some weeks after the flood. Wallis Ann said she'd checked on your place, said it was gone. Honestly, we didn't know what might had become of you."

Mr. Powell said, "Seen where she'd scraped her initials and a date on the post. It was real smart, considering how things was so tore up. We'd caught word y'all was all in one piece from Joe Calhoun over to the next holler. He come by few weeks ago to see if he could help us out. He wanted to know if we had any idea as to where y'all might have gone to. I said I didn't know, but I was sure glad to find out y'all was all right. I suspected you'd come back sooner or later."

Momma said, "We got some coffee, won't you sit a spell and have some?"

Mrs. Powell nodded and said, "That would be mighty fine. We've been having to be right careful since stores is having trouble getting stock in."

Momma said, "Yes, we've had to do the same," and then fell silent as she made the coffee.

It was only midmorning, but it was nice to sit around the campfire and catch up. As the Powells sipped and shared a bit of what happened to them, we found out they'd been in Charlotte visiting Mrs. Powell's sister and had missed the flood altogether. They couldn't come home for a while due to the roads, and by the time they did, we was gone. Mrs. Powell looked around our yard with some hesitation.

She leaned closer to Momma and whispered, "I'm afraid to ask . . . but, where's your little chap, and Laci?"

Momma's head dipped down, and she couldn't speak. Mrs. Powell took her hand, and for a long few moments nobody said a word.

Papa cleared his throat and then told our story in the

briefest way possible. "Seph took sick a few days after the flood. He drunk some water, and we sent Wallis Ann to get the doc, but it had got hold a him so bad he didn't make it. He's buried on yonder hill. We went on trying to put things right, working to rebuild, but for everything we did, it seemed there was a setback. Finally, we decided maybe we ought to use our God-given talents and make some money singing. It won't easy. Then we had a chance to join this traveling show for a while. Been down in South Carolina some weeks, and it was going along all right until—" and Papa stopped.

I held myself real still. I didn't look to see if his eyes was on me. The fire crackled and popped, and the Powells waited.

The silence went on until Mrs. Powell, in a hesitant manner, asked, "Did . . . she take sick too?"

Papa said, "No. You might say, we think she got took."

Mr. Powell's tone was incredulous. "Took? What do you mean?"

"Sheriff there seemed to think them show folks snatched her. They was real keen on her music and all. We'd done all right down there. Got nice crowds in to hear us. But it was when Laci learned some new music, the likes we'd never heard of, the owner must a got dollar signs in his eyes. They got her, stole her away we believe."

Papa stopped again.

Momma heaved a big sigh and finished the explanation. "There was this young man. He could have something to do with it. We don't know."

The Powells' expressions conveyed their astonishment at this news, both of them sitting and staring at Momma and Papa in disbelief. Mrs. Powell made a clucking sound and shook her head.

She said, "I declare, that has got to be one of the saddest out-comes from all I've heard happening in this area. Losing two of your young'uns is horrible, but not knowing exactly what's happened to one? Why, it's unimaginable."

Momma and Papa made a point not to mention me at all, and their avoidance showed how much they blamed me. If they'd a said, "Wallis Ann did this, or did that," even if they'd a told a part truth, it would meant they didn't hold me to account so much. Humiliation come over me and I could hardly breathe for it, like they was hiding what I done out of pure shame themselves.

Papa changed the subject. "Is there any word on anyone else in the area, how's things towards Cullowhee, East Laporte and all?"

Mr. Powell seemed glad to change the topic. "Things is slowly coming around. It's gonna be awhile 'fore roads and bridges is fixed. Trains ain't running yet. Be careful with what you have. Eat sparingly. We been having to hunt regular to keep food on the table."

These were things we was accustomed to, and while the adults went on and talked on the work yet to do, the mention of Joe Calhoun brought him to mind. It had been a while since I'd thought of him, and the idea of him asking after us seemed like something he'd do. I was reminded again of how he'd been so helpful to us. Giving me and Laci dresses. Blankets and food. How he'd helped me to get the doc. Papa had let it be known how he felt about the Calhouns, yet the Powells didn't seem to have any bad judgment of him, and I'd formed my own opinion given how he'd helped me.

The Powells went to leave, and Mr. Powell said, "I can come give you a hand over here, help you get things started."

Papa said, "Much obliged. Wallis Ann works bout like a growed man, but puttin' up the roof sure would go quicker with another set of hands."

Mr. Powell nodded, and said, "Let me know, and I'll come."

"Sure do appreciate that."

After they was gone, we worked some more, taking advantage of the hours left. We'd already fell into a ritual of sunup to sundown, and while the weather was always our biggest challenge, we had tried not to let it interfere much. We'd lose sleep now and again when snow come, because like before, we had to keep it from piling on top of the tent, and would have to get up at all hours to knock it off, plus keep the fire going.

We spent many days climbing the hillsides looking for good timber till my leg muscles burned like I was standing near a hot stove. There won't any chore Papa asked of me I didn't do. Handling Pete, scraping and peeling logs, notching them out, or holding one end so he could place the other. I worked with him to fashion a front and back door. On days we couldn't work because of the weather, and had to sit in the tent, I won't sure who was most despondent, me or him. I was happiest outside, keeping busy. I was grateful Momma didn't chide me on working so hard. Maybe she'd come to realize I needed it, like she needed solitude.

Despite the fact we won't as comfortable as we could a been, and food was getting on scarce end once more, time went by faster than I'd have thought. One morning I awoke feeling the ache of the previous day's work, and heard a robin singing outside the tent. I listened, and the song come again.

Momma's eyes was open, and watching me. "There'll be a spring thaw afore we know it."

"Yes, ma'am. It's coming on early March."

I preferred not to think of time so specifically. Keeping track of days to my way of thinking meant knowing too much. I only paid attention to sunrises and sunsets.

I sat up and said, "I'll get the coffee going."

After I was done, I looked at the progress of the cabin. We had the walls set midway, and it was getting hard for me to be of any use to Papa. The wall height was getting such that I couldn't hold one end of the logs for him. They had to go at least another two feet higher before we got to the roof.

Papa come out of the tent, and made an offhanded comment. "Should've had us some linseed oil."

I studied his profile. His face was thinner, harder looking.

"Yes, sir."

"Reckon them bottom logs will last all right without it."

"Yes, sir."

There won't the same ease to our conversations anymore, and he fell silent as I leaned over to pour the coffee. That day he went across the holler to Mr. Powell's place, and afterwards Mr. Powell joined in to help Papa with spots I couldn't reach. They agreed Papa would help him finish with his own roof in exchange.

Mr. Powell said, "Ought to go with a gambrel, like we'll be doing. It's best with that steep pitch for water runoff. Just thinking ahead and all."

Papa said, "Yep, and it'll make shingles last longer."

Mr. Powell said, "You going with hand-rived?"

"Them's the best looking, in my opinion, though it might take a while longer."

Mr. Powell agreed, and then said something what got my attention. "I could get us another pair a hands, the Calhoun feller over here. I'm sure he'd be happy to help."

Papa looked uncomfortable and he spoke carefully. "You know him pretty good, eh?"

"Sure do. Can't say much about his pappy. He was a son of a buck, but young Joe Calhoun? Now there's a fine, upstanding young man as I ever did meet."

Papa still won't sure. "How'd you come to know him?"

Mr. Powell tamped some tobacco into his pipe like he was thinking on another time. He placed the stem in his mouth, and struck a match against the bottom of his work boot. He held the flame over the small bowl and sucked in his cheeks a few times. The tiny flame flared above the bowl. I watched as it dissipated, while Papa waited for the answer to his question.

Mr. Powell puffed a few seconds, and then he said, "We practically raised him. We used to live close to his pappy's place over to Cherry Gap 'fore we come here, and let me tell you what. That young man went through hell, him and his momma. She died when he was young. I wouldn't doubt if Joe's pappy didn't kill her."

Papa said, "That right?"

Mr. Powell went on. "Some nights we could hear him yelling at her, or the boy. The missus, she couldn't hardly abide by it. It got so bad one night, next day, she told me she had to go over there, used the excuse of taking some blackberry jam. She come back, her face white as a lily. Said young Joe was sitting on the steps. Said she asked to see his pappy. Said young Joe got himself up, moving backwards up the steps while facing her, like he was hiding something. His pappy come out, half drunk, and didn't see the missus. He pushed the boy back down the steps. That's when she seen how his back was all striped where he'd been whupped. Joe's pappy turned all sweet and charming once he noticed her standing there. She give him the jam, but seeing what all was going on like to tore her out of the frame. She started going over, taking things for them to eat, although she'd of preferred his pappy not get a drop. She eventually got a chance to ask if she could "borrow" Joe for some chores. He come ever morning before school to milk the cows, feed the chickens, and whatnot. Missus, she'd send him off with a good breakfast and some dinner to eat at school. It went on a while until he was doing chores in the evening, and eating supper with us most nights. When school ended, she went to his pappy and it was 'Can I borrow Joe for the summer?' And his pappy couldn't a cared less. Joe, he got to staying the night, and when he was about fifteen or so, he moved in with us. He's a good man."

As Mr. Powell talked, Papa's expression had gone from uncomfortable to something like shame.

He said, "Good thing your wife found out what was going on. I'd never heard nothing good about the old man, and you know they say an apple don't fall far from the tree."

Mr. Powell said, "It can be like that. In his case, it's like he ain't even of the same tree. He must a been like his momma. Heard she was kindly and gentle."

Papa looked thoughtful. "I got nothing against him coming if you vouch for him."

Mr. Powell said, "That I do."

A few days later, Joe Calhoun returned to Stampers Creek. It was a bitter cold morning, but sunny. Patches of snow still lay on the ground, and I was busy trying to clear the area where we'd work. It was an unnecessary chore, but I needed something to do. It had been six months or longer since the last time I'd seen him, and I was having a hard time remembering exactly what he looked like. I heard the clopping of horse's hooves and when he come around the curve of the path with Lyle riding behind him, and little Josie in the front, I stopped swishing the end of the pine branch around in useless circles. This strange, overwhelming sense of the familiar rushed over me like standing in a downpour, a peculiar sense like seeing someone from my own family coming home.

Joe didn't see me at first. He lifted a hand in greeting to Mr. Powell, and Papa, who stood by the cabin talking about what they might could do in a day with another pair of hands. Joe waited till Lyle had dropped to the ground before he handed Josie down to him, and then he got off the horse. Mr. Powell shook Joe's hand, and then he scooped Josie up. He swung her around and her laughter rang out, as pure as the early birdsong I'd heard this morning. Momma was already on her way over to greet everyone, and she shook Joe's hand, then bent down to say something to Lyle, whose face flamed red as a strawberry. She squatted down to Josie's level, and the little girl gazed at her, half shy, half curious.

Josie, so close to Seph's age, conducted herself with the simplicity of all children that young, a lack of awareness or opinions, other than what they see right before them. I could see Momma wanting to hold her, or at least touch her in some way. She missed Seph intensely and seeing another child his age likely filled her full of the melancholia. I moved to go towards her, thinking she might get upset. When I did, Joe, who'd been watching his children, saw me. He studied me the same way his daughter studied Momma. My hair was below my shoulders now, and I'd not had time to put it up, but I had washed it, and had put on one of the new dresses, and my new shoes. I hoped I looked some better than what he'd seen me in last time.

Momma spoke, "How old is she?" and he turned to her.

She brushed a hand over Josie's hair.

Joe said, "Three going on four."

Papa was still slow to warm up. Awkward, he thrust his hand out to Joe for a handshake.

By way of explanation for the sudden change, Papa said, "Jim here tells me you stayed over to their place for some time and worked for them."

Joe said, "Yes, sir. Mr. and Mrs. Powell, they's family to me."

"I don't think I ever properly thanked you for what you did right after the storm. What all you brought. Thank you."

Joe raised a hand. "No need. We all was having tough times then."

And with those simple words, Joe Calhoun took Papa's guilty conscience and pushed it away.

Joe turned to me and said, "Good to see you too. Lyle? Remember Miss Wallis Ann? Josie, go say hi."

Both children approached me, and I smiled down at them. Josie immediately grabbed my hand, and held on, swinging my arm playfully. Lyle remained reserved, staring at the ground, but when I looked away from him, I felt his eyes on me. His gaze won't the only one I sensed. Joe appeared to study me as well, only I refused to look directly at him. I was filled with too much sadness and guilt, and thinking the world could surely see what I done. It clouded everything before me, like trying to swim in a muddy pool of water. And it didn't matter much, for I was certain he could only see me the way I seen myself, a scrappy girl who could work like a man, who didn't favor fancy things, a little bit of nothing all that extraordinary. Plain and simple as they come.

Chapter 27

What took the longest was forming the shingles. Mr. Powell and Joe did that job, which required patience and several red oak tree logs. Joe estimated we needed a couple thousand shingles. Four hundred shingles for every one hundred square foot while Momma beamed over the size of the new cabin in general, bigger than the old one by a good eighty square foot. The number of shingles was a mind-boggling number, but once the men got to working, they stacked up quick. Soon as they was made, Papa put them on. Before long, the roof was done and Mr. Powell brought Mrs. Powell over and everyone drank some of his homemade wine to celebrate the roof raising. We was all flushed with the wine. This would have normally been a time when Papa would have suggested some singing and dancing, only nobody did because it didn't seem appropriate for any sort of celebrating really, not without Laci.

It was the first of April, when Papa, Mr. Powell and Joe moved inside to work on the floors. They sawed logs in half, laid the boards side by side until the knotty pine floors was done, and the rooms now glowed like melted butter. The smell of fresh-cut wood was heaven, and I think Momma allowed herself to feel a little bit happy knowing we'd soon move inside. At least she looked a bit like she used to. And she was over the moon with admiration for Joe Calhoun. She was certain if it hadn't been for him, we'd still be looking at only the foundation. It was possible. He had a knack for organizing and finishing the work of three men.

She would say, "That Joe Calhoun is one hardworking young man." Or, "That Joe Calhoun is so smart, look how he figured out the sigoggling problem with the one side of the cabin."

That had been something. It seemed the foundation had settled because of water underground, and the crookedness, or sigoggling as Momma called it, was solved by shimming a couple rows of logs to a point where the crookedness went straight. I'd never seen Momma hug nobody but us, or one of the church ladies maybe, but she give Joe a big hug when he finished.

My mind stayed consumed by Laci, even though I tried best as I could to turn my thoughts in a different direction. Momma and Papa understood I was struggling mighty hard and they was too, only they didn't bear the burden of guilt like I did. Not only for Laci, but for Seph. As time went on, guilt soaked into my skin, muscles and deep into my bones. It tugged on my soul the way the Tuckasegee had tried to drag me under, and my apparent melancholy got Momma into the habit of asking me what I was thinking at least once a day when I got too quiet.

"Nothing, Momma, I ain't thinking about nothing in particular," is what I said.

If only she knowed what went on inside a me and how my heart felt like somebody stuck it in a thresher and put it back, shredded all to pieces. How I seen everything through the murky haze of what I done, while the sharp and pure knowledge of my own ignorance followed me about the way Laci had. I weighed how careless I'd acted. What set me back even more was recollecting all them times I'd seen that strangeness in her expression, coupled along with them odd wanderings a hers. All them little signs what showed me I should a knowed better. Laci had been changing, I'd seen it and ignored it. I'd refused to recognize anything except my own hardheaded self-ishness, thinking on nothing but what I'd wanted, even when I should a known Laci was needing me more than ever.

Because of all that, won't nothing agreeable or pleasing to me no more, not food, not company, not seeing the progress made on our new cabin, or even knowing all our efforts was finally paying off. *What did it matter,* like Momma had said all them months ago.

Papa made a weekly trek over to Dewey's store where he'd call down to Sheriff Baker to check in. He never had no news, and I was certain there never would be any. By middle of April, the cabin was ready for windows to be cut. Momma got right aggravated when Papa and Mr. Powell went to get some sup-plies and Papa done the unthinkable. Like with the ham, he bought glass windows out of the rapidly dwindling stash of money made from our singing.

She fussed at him, but then he showed her seeds he bought for a garden, and he said, "Spring has sprung, and so has our cabin, and now, so will our new garden."

He staked off an area where the old one had been, and Momma soon got to whacking at the soil, hoeing and weed-ing, and setting the tiny seeds into the banked rows of dark, rich dirt. One late afternoon, when the men was finishing the windows, Momma invited Joe, Lyle and Josie and the Powells to eat to finally celebrate moving into the cabin. After we ate, I gathered the dirty pans to carry them down to the creek to wash and surprisingly, Joe fell into step beside me.

"Wallis Ann?"

"Yes?"

He took some of the pans from me and knelt down by my side to help.

I said, "You don't need to help. I don't mind."

Joe smiled and said, "I know, but I got to figure out a way to talk to you somehow."

I didn't know what to say, so I got busy dumping creek sand into Momma's skillet. Then I got busy scraping at the pieces of food stuck to it and Joe got to talking. He filled my head with ideas of what he wanted to do to help out others, as well as plans he had at his own place.

"You know, I been thinking I might start doing like what I done here, going around to other folks who ain't been able to fix their places, help them rebuild. It's something I been thinking about. What do you think?"

"It sounds like a good idea. Very generous."

"You think so?"

"Sure. It's going to take a long time for folks to rebuild, but with help like you give us, it would go a little quicker."

"I could work out something with them. Barter things. I was thinking maybe your papa and I could work together, and Jim Powell too. You reckon your papa would be interested? You think you all might go back to singing?"

Surprised at his idea of working with Papa, I said, "I don't know about the singing. We don't much feel like it lately. You'd have to ask him about all this."

"What about you? What do you want to do?"

"What do you mean?"

"You know, a year from now, five years?"

I sank back on my heels. I was shortsighted because I couldn't picture moving on. Not yet. I could only picture the long summer ahead, and all the things me and Laci would have done together. Swimming in Stampers Creek, picking huckleberries, tending the garden, putting up vegetables with Momma, planting new fruit trees, fishing the Tuckasegee. Whenever I went down to the river, I seen her in my mind's eye, sitting on the wishing rock, fiddle crooked naturally into the bend of her arm, head bent to hear the music that mingled with the water's flow. I pictured us swinging on our old porch swing, the sun on our arms and legs, bare feet dirty from our ramblings, as carefree as if we was only young'uns again. I had to start thinking different. Maybe I would go to school when it opened again. That was all I could think of, my future as stunted as a garden without sun.

Joe said, "Wallis Ann?"

I went to scrubbing the pan, hard and quick. "Ain't much to think about, really. Just try to get on with life best as I can, I reckon."

Joe was quiet for a while. I glanced over at his hands, well worn, and strong, hands of a man who won't afraid of work neither.

He said, "I ain't gonna tell you they'll find your sister, even though it might be the right thing to say. All I'll say to you is you got to have a little hope, and you got to think about yourself sometimes too. You see the cabin there?"

I looked to where he pointed. "Yes."

"If you walked inside it right now, and closed the door, what would you see?"

I quit worrying over the skillet for a second, unsure what he was getting at. Eventually I said. "The walls, a roof, the floor."

"But, what if you wanted to see out, beyond the walls? What if you wanted to see the woods, the river, the mountains and the sky? What if you wanted to see as far as you could?"

"It needs windows."

"Right. Windows give you a view, otherwise, you can't see nothing, no matter how hard you try. It ain't much different in how we look at our world from inside ourselves."

He stood, and as he went to walk away, he briefly touched

my shoulder. It took me a long time to finish the pans and rinse them. I thought about what Joe said, and what he was trying to tell me. He was saying I ought to see what's around me, that I was looking only inward, not outward. Again, I was taken aback by his ability to know so much. I'd forgot about that. The sun was gone, and only a streak of raspberry-tinted light was left peeking through the trees. I made my way to the cabin where Momma and Papa was already inside and getting ready for bed, and Joe was long gone.

The smell inside was comforting, a cleansing odor of cut wood and along with the night air growing warmer, and all the hard work of the day, it should have made it easy to fall asleep. Momma and Papa wished me a good night and went to their room. They settled down quick while I lay awake, my eyes staring at the closed-off walls, and all I could think of was Joe's words, his wisdom. He was right, but I couldn't help how I felt. I turned on my side, and stared at the empty spaces where I imagined Laci and Seph would have slept.

The weather got warmer day by day. April give way to May, and by then Papa and Joe moved from working on the cabin to working on a toolshed, and then a shelter for Pete. Meanwhile, me and Momma inspected the pie safe and the stove at the edge of the woods. Sadly, the pie safe was beyond repair after so long in the weather, but Momma's Glenwood C stove looked pretty good. The outer cast iron area had rusted in many areas, but after I chased a family of mice out of the inside, we worked ourselves into a sweat cleaning it best as we could. When we got done, Momma then built a fire in it and that took care of things better than soap and water. Later on in the day when it was cool enough to touch, Papa and Joe moved it inside.

We clustered together in the kitchen looking around at how the inside of the cabin was starting to really look like a home.

With the kitchen and sitting area together, and two small doors, one off to the right for Momma and Papa's room, and a new one to the left, which was mine, it was close to the way the old cabin had been except for one thing. No attic room, and secretly I was glad, it wouldn't have seemed right to climb the set of steps alone. Momma built another fire in the stove, then got to rolling out biscuits on the worktable Joe had built her one day out of leftover wood. She put them into the oven to bake, and of course she'd asked Joe, Lyle and Josie to eat before they went home.

"We only got some beans, biscuits and ham, but you're welcome to it."

"Thank you, but I best be getting them home before dark."

Momma seemed disappointed while I was relieved. I felt irritable and tired.

Joe turned to Papa and said, "We ought to start thinking about seeing to a water source."

Papa said, "It's like you're reading my mind. Instead of digging another well, maybe we ought to run us a wooden trough to the side of the cabin here, fit it with a rope to lift and lower as needed. We could build another spring house over it while we're at it."

Joe said, "We got a trough like that and it's real handy."

Momma said, "It'd sure be easier to get water."

Joe was good as his word. Within a few days, we had water from the creek at our fingertips. It was right nice, easier on me for sure since I'd been the one hauling from the creek, but my mood still didn't improve much.

One day Momma said, "Wallis Ann, have you been struck blind? Can't you see how he looks to you every time he's finished doing something around here? It's like a puppy following after you, begging for a crumb. At this rate, he'll be on to a barn, fence, wood shed, corn crib, and anything else he can do, looking to you for some sign of appreciation."

For the first time in a long while, a hint of the old Papa showed up. "In that case, don't give him the time of day, Wallis Ann."

I said, "Don't worry bout that. Half the time I can't tell if it's day or night anyway."

Momma and Papa looked at each other, and I said, "How can all this really matter?" I gestured around the cabin, and pointed at the surrounding yard. "Without Laci? Or Seph?"

Momma said, "We're not forgetting them, Wallis Ann. You, out of all of us, you've always done what needs doing, even when it didn't seem to make sense. You've always been the one to see the bright side, been practical. That's all we're doing. You know it's not been any easier for your papa or me. We're going to keep on having hope until there's no possibility of having it anymore. That's all we can do."

I listened to what Momma said, and if I could have taken her words, shoved them deep inside me and held them close until I was sure they'd do me some good, I'd have done it. Instead it was like my mind, my spirit, had formed some sort of hardened callus nothing could penetrate.

I waited to see if she was going to say anything else, and when she fell silent, I said, "Yes, ma'am. I'm going to the river. I'll be back in a little while."

Momma sighed with frustration, but I went on with my gaze straight ahead, still blind, unable to get beyond my pain. At the river, I took my time, doing what I'd come to spend a lot of time doing since we'd returned, which was to watch the sun set. I'd walked along the edges for a while, poking at young dandelion shoots emerging, and spotted a few rainbow trout as they caught a current and rode it waiting on food to pass them by. They all pointed in the same direction, a hierarchy based on size, the larger in the front. You had to know where to look, how to train your eyes so you could separate them from the rocky bottom, or the deep green, quiet pools. I must have watched them a good hour or more.

At one point I thought I heard a shout, coming from the direction of the cabin. Pete was notorious for getting into the
feed when he shouldn't, and I pictured Papa yelling at him. I
cocked my head listening. It got quiet again, so I stepped onto
the wishing rock, and knelt down, leaning over a quiet pool of
water, my hand holding my hair so it didn't get wet. I stared
into it, not looking at my reflection, instead I looked at the
world behind me. I gazed at a mirrored sky, watching how the
tiny ripples and undercurrent distorted the view, like my vision had gone all wobbly. I hummed a little tune under my
breath that faded, and turned into a gasp when the water
echoed back a figure over my shoulder. I froze, unable to determine if I'd finally seen a haint even though I seen exactly
who it was. I twisted on my heels to face her, proving my eyes
won't lying. She was real. I won't imagining things.

"Laci?"

I took in her appearance.

I repeated her name, still trying to understand. "Laci?"

Her hair was clean and fixed in a long braid. She wore a new
dress. She had on the shoes Papa had bought. As if she'd only
been gone for a few minutes, and not months, she reached out
to slip her hand in mine. Then she done something what made
me go weak in my legs and sent a shiver through me like it was
the dead of winter again.

She opened her mouth, licked her lips, and then, with a bit
of effort, she said, "Wall-is. Ann."

Chapter 28

She said my name again, with less of a hiccup and clearer. My smile stretched wide as my elation at hearing her voice for the very first time overwhelmed and mesmerized me. She clung to my hand while I searched for what was different in her expression, because something was. Like I'd seen before, there was a deepening of understanding, an awareness what didn't fade away this time. I had the impression there was yet even more, like something had broke loose inside her, bubbling up for us to see, and that it would continue to do so.

I said, "How did you get here? Did you come alone?"

Laci turned to go to the cabin, leading me instead of the other way around. She held my hand so tight, my fingers was numb by the time we reached it. Momma and Papa stood outside with Sheriff Baker, and Clayton too, looking nervous while Papa glared at him. Strangely for me, seeing Clayton held about as much excitement as watching Papa whittle on a stick for hours. The way I'd felt before had run its course, the way some fevers consume you one minute and are gone the next. I was glad. I felt released, relieved, lighter, and my heart didn't ache at the sight of him. Laci let go a my hand and hurried to Momma, who softly placed a palm alongside her cheek, shaking her head like she couldn't quite believe she was actually here.

"Lord, child, I never thought I'd set eyes on you again."

Papa stood on the other side, his own hand running down her arm, like they both needed to touch her, to assure themselves of her presence.

Sheriff Baker said, "There's a bit of a story about all this, whenever you're ready."

Momma waved a hand towards the cabin, "Come in, please. We don't have much in the way of furniture yet, but we got some coffee."

We filed in, and stood by the fireplace. It was cooler inside, and the sheriff's boots made a solid sound against the strong wood floor.

He looked around, and said, "Looks like you've made good progress getting things situated." He paused and pointed at Clayton. "Far as your girl here, you got this young man to thank, believe it or not. Son, you want to tell them what happened?"

Clayton looked like all his blood had drained out of him, his features had gone pale, even his lips. He swallowed, and glanced at Papa, who stood with his legs firmly planted, arms folded over his chest, putting off the air of a man who would need a lot of convincing.

Clayton said, "Yes, sir." And he turned to Papa, and spoke directly to him, glancing occasionally at Momma as if she might offer him a bit more support, or at least be less intimidating. Her expression was not unlike Papa's. Suspicious and doubtful. He looked away, and shifted uncomfortably as he began.

"First, I want to apologize. I shouldn't have done . . . certain things. I hope you'll hear me out, let me explain because I know all this wouldn't have happened if I hadn't been with Laci to begin with. Sure, you can blame me because she run off, but I didn't have nothing to do with what happened after. When you come looking for me with that shotgun, I got scared, I admit it. That's why I hid, and Laci was with me. All I could think was stay out of sight, let things cool down. We went into the Giant Snake tent, but she must have got scared because of the way I'd acted. Me running, pulling her along like I was. In her mind, I won't acting right and she didn't know why. I let go of her hand only a second, and she took off. I lost sight of her quick, so I went to Johnny Cooper and told him what happened and he told me to stay out of sight, and he would help with the search. Of course, later, when everyone got to looking for her, I wanted to help, only I couldn't."

Clayton glanced at Papa, and said, "He didn't tell me what he intended to do. I swear it."

Papa's tone was sharp. "What he intended to do?"

Sheriff Baker interrupted Clayton. "I found out where the show had gone as far as other states. Turns out this particular outfit has been accused of keeping someone against their will before. A woman . . . without legs from Virginia. He knew because of your Laci being mute, she couldn't give anything away."

Papa said to Clayton, "You want to work for people like that?"

"I didn't know! I don't work for them anymore. No, sir. I quit."

Skeptical, Papa said, "And so, how does this make you not mixed up in this somehow?"

Sheriff Baker spoke up for Clayton. "Well for one, I've never known someone guilty to come to the law for help. Usually they run the other way. Go on, son, finish your story."

Clayton nodded. "The show always goes to Florida in the winter, but it was strange to leave in the middle of the night.

That told me something was fishy, plus the fact I kept coming up on the notion Laci would go home if she could. And when the search went on and on, and she didn't turn up, that seemed strange. Then, after we'd been on the road for a week or so, I noticed one of the workers taking food into a particular wagon they store the tents in. He'd come out without the plate. I went over to the wagon and listened. I heard something, a scuffling sort of noise. I kept watch until I figured out where he was putting the key. I got in one night and she was in there, hidden behind a stack of old tents, locked away. Like a dog. I was as mad as I've ever been because"—and now he looked at me, like he wanted me to understand what he was about to say—"I love her."

I showed no emotion because I didn't feel much of anything other than wanting him to get on with his account so we could understand what Laci had been through.

He turned back to Papa. "I got her out of there, only now we'd traveled hundreds of miles. I didn't know how to explain it when it come to telling Sheriff Baker here, without sounding like I had something to do with it. That's where Laci comes in."

Papa leaned in towards Clayton. "What do you mean, that's where Laci comes in?"

"I talked to Laci the entire way, told her I was bringing her home. It took us a long time. I had no idea if anyone was even looking for us, but I hitched rides for us as often as I could get one. I bought us food often as I could. When we got to South Carolina, I went straight to Sheriff Baker. I told him everything. He didn't believe me neither. He was getting ready to throw me in jail, only Laci said, 'No.'"

Momma laughed outright at that, and Papa snorted. "Huh. This is where your story gets off course. That ain't possible. Boy, you best not be lying about such."

I interrupted. "Papa, Laci said my name, down by the river a little while ago."

Momma put her hands on the table, and leaned over, like she needed help to remain on her feet.

She raised her head. "I can't hardly imagine it. Is it possible?"

Clayton said, "Yes, ma'am. It is."

Papa rubbed his beard and glanced at Momma, who shook her head, still unable to believe.

Clayton said, "There's one more thing I want to mention, if I could?"

Papa nodded.

"I'd like to marry Laci."

Papa's mouth dropped open and Momma shook her head, more in disbelief than saying no. I didn't know if she was sad, or happy at Clayton's request. I was still trying to grasp Laci having spoken.

Papa said, "Son, that's all fine and good, but . . ."

All of the sudden he stopped and turned to Laci, gazing into her eyes. Laci returned his stare, her features calm and steady. She sure didn't look like she'd suffered. She looked almost happy.

He asked her, "Laci, is this what you want?"

After all we'd heard, everyone was spellbound, waiting to see what she'd do. With a small smile and barely a nod she gave her answer, yet both gestures in our eyes was as big as all the mountains and valleys around us. As big a miracle as we was likely to ever see in our lifetime. Papa nodded, satisfied, but he needed more assurances and he got down to brass tacks, facing Clayton again.

"How do you intend to support her? How are you planning to make money since you're no longer employed?"

Clayton tilted his head towards Sheriff Baker. "I'm considering becoming a deputy for Jackson County, if the sheriff here will put in a good word for me."

Papa turned to Momma like he had no idea where to go from there.

Momma said, "Well. I think we need to see how things work out. Won't be a wedding for some time."

Clayton said, "That's good enough to me. I ain't going nowhere."

After that, the sheriff had to go, but Clayton stayed. Momma set about fixing him a bed of sorts so he could sleep in the kitchen. Considering this new, altered relationship, I was grateful I no longer thought of him the same way. It had been a day filled with wonderment at what took place, and later on, as we lay in our cots, Laci beside me like in the old days, it occurred to me she'd changed more than the rest of us from all that happened. I seen how she'd picked up her fiddle, set in the corner of the room, and played a bit of a song here and there, but it didn't appear to have quite the same allure as before. It was as if her attention had expanded and now included a bigger view of her world, an opening of her mind, a clarity what enabled her to reach beyond the confines of the instrument. Like the windows Joe talked about when he'd tried to encourage me to see things in a different way, this had happened for her.

The next day, the startled look on Joe's face seeing Laci sitting in the kitchen captured my own feelings all over again. Each time I went out and come in and seen her by the fire with Momma struck me anew. Joe stayed aloof around Clayton, sizing him up at a distance, while Lyle was intrigued by what Clayton used to do. Lyle followed him around peppering him with questions about jumping from waterfalls, and the high dive platform. Joe and Papa was set to begin work on a new corn crib, and Clayton was put to work fashioning a new clothesline for Momma to hang the wash. Laci sat in the sun watching Josie, while I went to help the men. When I stopped to look around for a second, I was almost dizzy with gratitude at all we'd been given.

After I'd worked for an hour or so stripping bark with the draw blade, Joe come to where I sat on the ground.

He watched me for a minute, then said, "I was thinking maybe later on, when we get done, you might want to go down to the creek and do some fishing? I brought a couple bamboo poles. Lyle's about to have a fit to fish there."

I glanced at Joe a little longer than usual, and didn't give him an immediate answer. His face flushed red.

He said, "If you want. I mean, maybe you'll be too tired by then. I just thought . . ."

I stopped him when I said, "No. I'd like to. I'd like to very much."

One thing was becoming very clear to me and that was how alike we was, and I wondered how, after all this time, it took me so long to notice. When the day was over, all of us gathered inside the cabin, around the table Joe had somehow managed to build on the sly. I looked around at the faces, happy, and a little melancholy remembering the little one missing.

Papa said, "Let's bless this food," and I gratefully bowed my head, believing with all my heart we'd been put through hardships for a reason, and come away from them stronger than ever.

After we ate, as promised, Joe grabbed the poles, and with Lyle and Josie following close behind, we made our way to Stampers Creek. We sat on the embankment and I laughed at Lyle, who was coming out of his shell around me while little Josie pressed against my side. Every now and then her tiny hand would sneak into mine, a miniature version of Laci's. It was when Joe took hold of my other hand on the way back up to the cabin in the twilight of the evening, I experienced another moment of lucidity, and I thought of that time in the truck, in the middle of the flood when Papa had held Momma's face, and stared at her with such love.

Joe's hand in mine felt perfect, and the vision I held in my mind was as transparent as a pane of glass wiped clean as I pictured all I could have. I understood what was set before me, this bright future, mine and Joe's, if I wanted it. I gazed about in wonder as if seeing everything anew, and when my eyes eventually rested on him again, all the hard times fell away, like the sun clearing a morning mist. We walked along, hands held tight, taking our time as the familiar and peaceful trickle of water slid over the nearby rocks of Stampers Creek and the call of a distant nightingale serenaded us home.

Acknowledgments

I wish to thank the following people for their remarkable dedication, support and encouragement. I can't imagine taking this wonderful journey without any one of them.

To my editor, John Scognamiglio, I'm grateful for your enthusiasm, vision and, most of all, your unwavering belief in my writing. Working with you is truly a pleasure.

To my agent, John Talbot, of Talbot Fortune Agency, thank you so much for your steadfast support and commitment through the years. You are a staunch advocate for my work, and your excitement and passion for my writing keeps me motivated and inspired.

To Vida Engstrand, Lulu Martinez, Kimberly Richardson, Lauren Jernigan, Paula Reedy and so many others at Kensington, what unique and individual talents you each have, and I greatly appreciate all that you do. I'm truly indebted to each of you!

To the loyal readers and book cheerleaders I've met online, Susan Walters Peterson, Kristy Barrett (Kristy Bee!), Deborah Massey Haynes, Susan Roberts, Nita Joy Haddad and so, so many others, your enthusiasm and praise mean the world to me.

To the independent book stores I visited, a tremendous thank you for supporting me.

To Jamie Adkins, owner of The Broad Street Deli and Market, you went above and beyond! No words are enough to express my gratitude.

To all of the book clubs, and in particular my very own, The Thursday Afternoon Book Club, thank you doesn't begin to express my appreciation for your support and interest in my writing!

To my tribe over at The Reef, and to The One we call QOTKU, a.k.a. Janet Reid, thank you all so much for your support, your special messages, but most of all, your friendship.

To my loving family . . . thank you again and again for your love and support. Along with your joy for the shared successes, your encouragement sustains me and keeps me going.

To Blaine, my generous and loving husband, thank you for all you've done, and continue to do. I truly would be lost without you.

THE ROAD TO BITTERSWEET

Donna Everhart

ABOUT THIS GUIDE

The suggested questions are included to enhance
your group's reading of Donna Everhart's
The Road to Bittersweet.

DISCUSSION QUESTIONS

1. Wallis Ann is pragmatic and determined, and she handles even the most difficult of challenges as if she's much older than her fourteen years. Do you think this came naturally to her, or do you believe she conformed given what was required and expected of her?

2. Laci, Wallis Ann's older sister, is a mute, but very gifted girl. Wallis Ann observes random moments when Laci seems to be undergoing possible developmental changes, like when she notices a change in her expression, as well as the odd midnight wanderings. What do you think was happening to Laci?

3. Do you think it was fair for Momma to depend on Wallis Ann so much for Laci's care, considering Wallis Ann always put Laci first, before her own needs even?

4. When do you believe the relationship with Wallis Ann and Laci started to change? What did you notice?

5. With regard to Momma, do you find Wallis Ann the stronger of the two? What was your impression of Momma?

6. Wallis Ann bears tremendous guilt for some of the events in the story, from her little brother, Seph, drinking "tainted" water, to Laci's disappearance. Is there anything you think she could have done differently to avoid these tragedies?

7. What is your opinion of Clayton? Do you think he was wrong to befriend Wallis Ann, only to turn and focus on Laci, given her challenges?

8. Do you think he exploited Laci's disabilities, or do you believe it was young love—which is sometimes irrational?

9. Papa's desire to provide for his family was evident in all he tried to do. From leaving Stampers Creek and taking them to his brother, Hardy, in South Carolina, to declaring they perform for money. His efforts, while commendable, weren't successful for the most part. How do you think this made him feel, as the head of the family, the provider? Do you think he made bad decisions, or do you think he did what he could, given the circumstances?

10. Wallis Ann feels invisible at times, as if she's being "passed over" in favor of her sister. She feels she can't speak her mind because of Laci's disability, and thinks she might as well be as mute as her sister. She assumes what people will say or think if she were to do so, perhaps viewing her as ungrateful. Do you think if she'd spoken up about her feelings early on, Laci's disappearance might have been avoided?

11. From their initial meeting, it's apparent there was some sort of connection between Wallis Ann and Joe Calhoun. In the end, Joe tells her she has to think about herself, see the world around her. He recognizes her sole focus has always been Laci, yet Wallis Ann still can't let herself do this. If Laci had not returned, do you think she and Joe would have had the chance for a future? Do you believe she would have given up on having something for herself out of this guilt?

12. Laci speaks her sister's name for the first time after she's reunited with her. Do you believe this occurred because

Laci's desire to be back with her sister was so strong, her mind overcame this particular obstacle because of their extended separation?

13. Little Josie, Joe Calhoun's daughter, likes to tuck her hand into Wallis Ann's, much like Laci has always done. What does this signify to you?

14. Water is a major theme running throughout the book. From the Tuckasegee River, which took and gave life, to the waterfalls, a natural part of Wallis Ann's environment, yet symbolic in the way she meets Clayton, a risky free fall in of itself. What was the significance of the water to you?

Connect with U(s)

Visit us online at
KensingtonBooks.com
to read more from your favorite authors, see books
by series, view reading group guides, and more.

Join us on social media

for sneak peeks, chances to win books and prize packs,
and to share your thoughts with other readers.

facebook.com/kensingtonpublishing
twitter.com/kensingtonbooks

Tell us what you think!

To share your thoughts, submit a review,
or sign up for our eNewsletters, please visit:
KensingtonBooks.com/TellUs.